Also by R

The Hunter &

Danger ISBN 978-1-913567-33-0

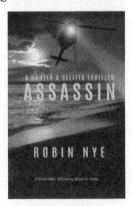

Assassin ISBN 978-1-914913-43-3

Available from Amazon and all good bookshops

RETRIBUTION

Retribution

Published by The Conrad Press Ltd. in the United Kingdom 2023

Tel: +44(0)1227 472 874
www.theconradpress.com
info@theconradpress.com

ISBN 978-1-915494-53-5

Typesetting and Cover Design by:
Charlotte Mouncey, www.bookstyle.co.uk

The Conrad Press logo was designed by Maria Priestley.

Printed and bound in Great Britain by Clays Ltd, Elcograf S.p.A.

To Sue

With all best wishes

Robin Nye

June 2023

RETRIBUTION

A Hunter & Selitto Thriller

Robin Nye

For my dearest Barbara
and all the gang at Tonbridge
Helen, Emily, Lee, Jack, James and Mia
Love you all

1
Sunday 26 April

The pilot watched, fascinated, as the low morning sun threw up the monster shadow of a Cessna Citation onto the grass verges surrounding the aircraft as it came to a halt at the end of the taxiway, awaiting permission to proceed to the runway and take off. He had manoeuvred his own aircraft along the same taxiway leading from the airport terminal, and was now heading towards runway zero-three-right at London's Biggin Hill Airport. He would be the next to take-off behind the Cessna.

It was a bright and crisp late April morning, a gentle westerly breeze just doing enough to disturb the distant orange windsock, not a cloud in the azure blue sky. Ideal flying conditions. In fact, ideal conditions for the flight he had planned for today.

As he inched up the taxiway, the pilot was making his last-minute checks, flicking switches and scanning the dials in front of him. Satisfied that all flaps were correctly set, that he had enough fuel for the journey, and that all the aircraft's sensors were working, he radioed the tower to get clearance for take-off behind the Cessna.

'Biggin, this is Golf Papa Mike Kilo November ready for take-off.' The pilot spoke in measured tones into a small microphone protruding from his headset and positioned adjacent to his mouth.

The voice from the control tower crackled into his headset.

'Roger, Kilo November. Cleared for take-off after the Cessna. Runway zero-three-right. Wind two-one-zero at zero seven knots. After take-off, heading one-two-zero and climb flight level three zero. Call Biggin on one-two-eight decimal four. Over.'

'Kilo November. One-two-zero, level three zero. Thank you, and have a good day!' The pilot flicked a switch on the instrument panel and peered out of the cockpit windows as he watched the Cessna finally leave the ground and climb into the clear air. He scanned the area to his left and right, checking that there were no other aircraft in his field of vision. He then turned onto runway zero-three-right and stared down the mile and a half of black tarmac. His fingers gripped the throttle levers and gradually pushed them forward at the same time as he eased off the brake. The aircraft started to roll forward and quickly picked up speed.

The pilot kept his eyes on the flight information display, watching as the aircraft's speed raced up to the take-off safety speed, always referred to as V2. By this time, he had already started to pull back on the control stick as the aircraft launched itself into the skies. He quickly gained sufficient height to make his first manoeuvre, banking the aircraft to the right on heading one-two-zero. He was soon up to flight level three-zero so he called Biggin Control to get permission to change heading to one-three-five and climb to level four-zero.

'Roger, Kilo November,' the voice again crackling in his ears. 'One-three-five and four-zero. Continue contact Biggin on one-two-eight decimal four.' The pilot made a minor course correction and then had a look out of his side window. *Excellent*, he thought. He was just where he wanted to be as the aircraft skirted around the north east of Sevenoaks. He made a further minor course correction and reduced his speed a fraction.

The aircraft flew on.

The pilot continued to watch the landscape slip by underneath him until he eventually espied the landmark which told him that it was time to put the rest of his plan into action.

He quickly made one final course correction which he knew would attract the attention of the Biggin Hill Controller. He was not wrong.

'Kilo November, this is Biggin TC. You appear to have veered onto course one-seven-two. Return to one-three-five immediately and maintain four-zero. Confirm that you understand this instruction.'

Disregarding the message from the Controller, he removed a small electronic device from one of the pockets in his denim jacket and clipped it onto the control panel in front of him. He flicked a tiny switch on the side of the device before removing his communications headset and laying it on the vacant co-pilot's seat.

'Kilo November, this is Biggin TC!' The tinny voice of the Controller leaked out of the headset, his irritation with the situation evident. 'Your course of one-seven-two is not approved. Return immediately to one-three-five and four-zero.'

The pilot now made a further course correction whereupon a small red light started to glow from the transmitter. He immediately felt the aircraft start to descend and watched intently as the hands on the altimeter in the panel in front of him spun round as they recorded the diminishing height in feet, down through the three thousands and into the two thousands.

The headset on the co-pilot's seat continued to broadcast the increasingly exasperated tones of the air traffic controller as the aircraft made its own final adjustment to its new co-ordinates and progressed on its way, still gradually losing height but not speed.

'Kilo November. This is Biggin TC. Urgently report your position. Repeat – urgently report your position.' There was a pause. 'Kilo November. This is Biggin TC. Do you read me?' Another pause.

'Kilo November. Do you have a mayday situation?'

The pilot leaned across to the control panel and flicked a switch to disconnect the radio.

The aircraft flew on.

2
Sunday 26 April

It started as a low hum.

The occupants of Tideswell Manor didn't hear it. They wouldn't have heard anything. The excesses of the previous night were clear to see. Empty bottles littered the vast open space on the ground floor of the mansion house where mock Grecian pillars reached to the cavernous ceiling to prevent the whole edifice from collapsing. Half-eaten plates of food lay around on tables, on expensive chintz settees, or simply on the floor. Some of the food had been trodden into priceless Persian rugs which were spread throughout the mansion.

Needles and syringes liberally adorned most of the flat surfaces along with burnt out candles and blackened spoons. A dusting of white powder was clearly visible on some of the furniture. Small squares of tinfoil and razor blades were scattered over the floor and glinted in the sunshine.

Two naked bodies clung to each other on a French baroque chaise longue, a trail of discarded clothes leading back to the patio doors. An empty bottle of Bollinger lay forlornly on its side on the floor having given up its contents many hours ago. All around there was further evidence of the excesses of the night before.

Shards of broken glass and the remnants of glass crack pipes created another surreal carpet of light as the sun streamed in through the acres of floor-to-ceiling windows. Outside, a long swathe of green grass stretched away into the distance. The sunshine also gently reflected off the tiny ripples of water as they danced across the surface of the swimming pool.

And, as the hum increased to the level of a deafening roar, the avian fraternity took to the skies, their squawking completely drowned out by the whining of turbo engines.

In the mansion, time stood still as four and a half tons of aviation engineering hurtled into the building at around 150 mph.

The resulting explosion could be heard for miles around, disturbing a lazy Sunday morning for many of the local residents.

The occupants of Tideswell Manor were, however, not disturbed – and were never likely to be disturbed again.

3

Sunday 26 April

Detective Inspector Sarah Hunter of Kent Police pulled up the collar of her police-issue emergency response jacket as she leant against a Vauxhall Astra patrol car in the fluorescent yellow and blue livery of police forces throughout the UK.

In the distance, she could see the smouldering remains of Tideswell Manor, once the country seat of earls and lords and others of the landed gentry, but more recently owned by a successful eighties rock megastar.

It had started life as a Tudor manor house but had been significantly redesigned in the Palladian style sometime during the 18th century. Subsequent owners had added huge columns across the front of the house as well as connecting the house to its outbuildings by means of elaborate colonnades. Although it was generally considered that Tideswell was a bit of a mishmash of architectural styles, it was sufficiently cut off from the outside world to not really attract criticism from the purists.

There were, however, some who would no doubt be rejoicing at its demise, particularly if they had been able to survey a landscape on which one or two of the columns remained defiantly upright amongst the rubble of the others. Several fires were still burning fiercely amongst the fallen masonry and, every so often, there was the muffled sound of an exploding gas cylinder.

The ground surrounding the mansion was awash with the blue strobing lights of the emergency vehicles – fire appliances from stations throughout Kent, ambulances from the South East Coast Service, a few police patrol cars, Crime Scenes &

Forensics vans and other vehicles which displayed no identification but normally attended events such as this. A Kent Air Ambulance helicopter had recently landed close to the mansion but so far their services had not been required. Which was an indicator that there would be few survivors – if any.

In the air above the mansion, a couple of helicopters hovered like a pair of vultures waiting to pick over the carcass of the stricken building. No doubt they had been hired by TV news channels who were vying for the best view of the devastation on the ground, Sarah thought as she shoved her hands deeper into the pockets of her jacket.

There was also a drone with a camera mounted on it which was providing up-to-the-minute information for those on the ground who were in charge of the efforts to contain the blaze. Thankfully, the only point of access for the public was at the end of the one mile private driveway which led from the main road to the mansion. One police car across its entrance was a sufficient deterrent for the ghouls who habitually turned up at these events.

Hunter was on the periphery of a discussion between her boss, Detective Chief Inspector Alan Iversen, and his boss Superintendent Hannah Eaves. A long time ago, Sarah had noticed that events of this magnitude always brought out those who normally only drove desks around offices at Kent Police HQ in Maidstone. In fact, Eaves was known disrespectfully as the 'Queen of Desk Jockeys' by some of the jokers in the lower ranks of the force.

About all they could do at the moment was stand and watch as the Kent Fire & Rescue Teams scurried around with hoses and ladders, and the medics continued the relentless task of stretchering body-bags to the fleet of waiting vehicles for transportation to the morgue.

In the distance, Hunter had espied the two pathologists from Tunbridge Wells, Norman Partington and Toby Swartzman. They had the grim task of certifying death and then helping to record the exact position in which the body had been found. Lastly, they would tag each of the bodies for identification purposes when they arrived at the morgue.

An ever-increasing number of white-suited Crime Scene Investigators were standing ready to enter the site when it was safe to do so. They would be combing the site for clues, planting their little flags and placing their small plastic cones on the ground as more evidence was unearthed. Photo flashes were frequently lighting up various parts of the site unaffected by the fire as evidence was starting to be collected for closer inspection back at the forensics laboratory.

Later – indeed, much later – all this information would be converted into hard evidence to show exactly what had happened here.

A lone figure, also wearing an emergency response jacket, was making its way across the field to where Hunter was standing. Despite the face mask, she easily recognised acting Detective Sergeant Elaine Jennings who had been standing in for DS Ted Selitto since he was attacked and left for dead in a horrific helicopter crash the previous year.

Sarah rated Jennings highly and had pushed for her elevation from the rank of detective constable even if it was only on a temporary basis to start with. She liked the pragmatic approach which seemed second nature to Jennings, and she was always impressed by her attention to detail. The two women had worked well together over the last few months, and Sarah was keen that Elaine should maintain her DS status after serving a short probationary period.

'God! What a mess!' Jennings exclaimed, pulling her face mask down so that it hung just under her chin. 'Looks like a bomb's gone off in there.'

Hunter had detached herself from Iversen and Eaves and beckoned Jennings to follow her so that she could get an update without interruption from her superiors. The two women now walked slowly to a new position where they could get a better view of the scene of devastation.

They watched as a turntable ladder inched its way into the sky from the back of a huge transporter which had arrived in the grounds. A small platform was attached to the top of the ladder, and it looked as if two Kent Fire & Rescue officers were aboard. As the ladder became fully extended, the platform was manoeuvred so that it was now directly over the ruins of the building. This allowed the two officers to direct jets of water directly into the heart of each blaze.

Hunter watched as the jets of water criss-crossed the area in which the fire had been contained, ever-grateful that it was not her standing at the top of the ladder.

In the meantime, Jennings was bringing her up to date with what she had learned.

'I got in on one of the KFR briefings and the idea is to assess the safety of what's left of the building before they go much further. The one problem they have is that there are far more bodies than they had initially estimated. Looks like there was some sort of all-nighter last night with an unknown number of people attending. They've discovered lots of expensive motors parked in the field behind the house.'

'Shit! What are they estimating?'

'No estimations at the moment because there's too much fallen masonry. The roof collapsed onto the first floor and much of that floor collapsed onto the ground floor. They'll need specialist lifting equipment.'

Hunter thought about this, trying hard to picture the scene in her mind.

'What about the plane?' she eventually asked.

'Almost unrecognisable. There's no way they can get to the pilot at the moment, and it may take some days before they are able to do so. A guy I was talking to said that removing the plane would be not only very difficult but also very dangerous. They're also going to have to get hold of specialist equipment, some of which may have to come from Europe.'

'Registration of the aeroplane?'

'Yep, got that and phoned it through to Grace.'

'Good!' Hunter was pleased that at least things were moving on that front. DS Grace Kendall was an important part of the Tonbridge CID team with indexing and referencing skills of the highest order. If anyone could track down the history of the plane, it would be Grace.

'There's one other thing that you should be aware of,' Jennings said, fiddling with the mask which was still tucked under her chin. 'One of the ambulance crew I spoke to mentioned that there might be children amongst the dead.'

'*Children*?' Hunter exclaimed. She looked at Jennings who simply nodded. 'For fuck's sake!' she muttered under her breath before turning back to the smouldering ruins of Tideswell Manor.

All police officers had a particular aversion to investigating the deaths of children, and conveying the death message to anxious parents was one of the most harrowing and gut-wrenching experiences known to man or woman. Sarah Hunter had had plenty of experience of this on the streets of London when she was with the Met, but she knew that it never got any easier to deal with child-related incidents.

'Looks like some of the party guests might have brought their families,' Jennings continued. 'Make a weekend of it in the country. There's plenty for kids to do here – bouncy castle, swimming pool, small funfair. Lots of nature trail walks as well.'

Hunter just nodded, staring intently at the scene of devastation in the distance. There was precious little they could do by staying here, she thought, so she turned and made her way back to where Iversen and Eaves were in conversation.

'I'm going to get back to base so that I can brief the team and get our investigation underway,' she declared, trying to avoid eye contact with Superintendent Eaves.

'Okay, Sarah,' Iversen replied. 'Doubtful there will be anything to get our teeth into for a few days so using the interim period for planning seems sensible.'

'I also want you to work with SCD on this,' Eaves butted in. 'This is a major incident. It'll be all over the nationals and the TV news.' She looked skyward as the two helicopters continued to jostle for position in the frantic drive to be the first with pictures of the destruction on the ground. 'In fact, it could be international news so I want to make sure that the Kent Force is seen in the best possible light.'

Hunter's shoulders dropped. She had worked with the Serious Crime Directorate before but found that they often wanted to look at a much bigger picture than was the reality of the crime she was investigating on the ground. They tried to see things that actually weren't there. But she knew that she couldn't rail against their involvement. This was certainly a major incident, and the top brass would be keen to be seen to be involved. Just because it had happened on her patch counted for nothing.

'I also want you to liaise closely with Margot Westwood at Maidstone,' Eaves continued. 'She's a civilian PR expert and will be coordinating all the press relations work so she'll need to call on you for interviews with journalists, although most of the TV stuff will be done by us at Maidstone.'

Iversen looked across at Hunter. He knew how much she hated dealing with the press. But she remained calm under his scrutiny, not giving him the satisfaction of seeing that she was seething inside.

'Yes, fully understood, ma'am,' she responded. 'Okay, we'll be off now to get our investigation set up and I'll wait to hear from the SCD gang. DCI Pennington I presume?'

Eaves nodded.

'I'll also make contact with Ms Westwood as you have suggested.'

Eaves nodded again.

With that, Hunter turned and set off towards her car, hotly pursued by Jennings who clearly did not wish to get stuck with Iversen and Eaves on her own.

'Bloody woman!' she hissed under her breath as Jennings caught up.

4
Monday 27 April

The sun looked like a magnificent red orb spinning in the sky as it was gently squeezed between the distant horizon and the trough of low cloud which was creeping ever closer to the shoreline. A lone offshore wind turbine stood, sentry-like, in the middle distance and a few small fishing boats bobbed about on the incoming tide, their occupants no doubt pulling in nets, setting pots, gutting the day's catch.

The sound of rubber squelching over the wet brick-laid lower promenade signalled the arrival of one of an army of early morning joggers who descended on this part of the seafront on a daily basis. There were some dedicated runners like the man in black lycra and expensive trainers who was now heading off into the distance. And there were some who were just out for a bit of exercise like the woman who jogged past clutching her mobile phone, earbud wires disappearing into an unkempt clump of black curly hair, colourful bandana pulled down on her brow. She didn't appear to be making any serious effort to get fit but seemed to be enjoying herself nevertheless.

Detective Sergeant Ted Selitto painted a lonely figure as he sat on a low brick wall a few metres away from the old Victorian Bandstand which had been a focal point of Eastbourne's seafront for over eighty years. He appeared mesmerised by the sound of the gentle lapping of waves on the shingle beach in front of him. He occasionally turned his gaze towards the Wish Tower, one of a string of Martello towers built along the south coast to defend England against Napoleon Bonaparte,

Emperor of the French, in the early 1800s. Today, it was a site of historical interest and a tourist attraction.

As another jogger went past, this one carrying a barbell in each hand, Selitto's thoughts strayed to that fateful night the previous year when he very nearly lost his grip on life. Even now, he only had very hazy recollections about what had happened, and it had taken weeks of corrective surgery and recuperation to get him fit enough to be transferred to a newly-opened centre in Eastbourne which provided care for those who had suffered major trauma.

He watched as a dog and its owner splashed their way through the surf as waves tumbled onto the stony beach. He was so wrapped up in observing their playful antics that he barely noticed another person approaching from his left.

'Thought I'd find you here,' the woman said as she sat down on the wall along from Selitto.

'Boss! Is that you?' he asked, turning his head slowly to focus on her.

DI Sarah Hunter watched as Selitto reached an arm out to her. Shuffling up so that she could be closer to him, she took hold of his hand in both of hers, giving him a tight squeeze.

Her first thought had been to thank God that he seemed to be getting over his ordeal. Every day was an improvement. The last six months had been hell for her without Ted Selitto by her side, and she was so relieved that the doctors were now saying that he was making some real progress.

The previous year, he had come as close to death as he was ever likely to during his lifetime when he ingested a deadly combination of toxins. A team of doctors and consultants from the London Hospital for Tropical Diseases had worked tirelessly to keep Selitto alive. It was touch and go for many weeks until his body suddenly responded to a new antidote which had been specifically developed to treat his condition but had not yet received a licence from the MHRA, the regulatory body for the licensing of new medicines in much of the UK. Despite this, his medical team had decided to administer the antidote under the auspices of a clinical trial, and had been amazed at the positive reaction the new drug had on Selitto's condition.

After that, he had spent a long period in rehab whilst regaining his mental and physical strength, and he had now checked into a new trauma recovery clinic in Eastbourne. Those in authority at the clinic also thought that he was making good progress and, by all accounts, he was probably going to be fit enough to return to light duties in two or three weeks' time.

Sarah Hunter had followed his progress every step of the way, often spending all night sitting by his hospital bed when he was so ill that the honest opinion of the medical staff was that he might not make it to the morning. Although she didn't really have any religious conviction, Sarah had found herself praying during those dark days and nights – it had just seemed right to ask for help from a higher authority in the circumstances. And, much to her amazement, it had helped her get everything into perspective to the extent that she felt better able to cope with the dread fear that she may lose him.

She now looked across at Selitto. Dark glasses covered his eyes which had been damaged when the toxin had been sprayed into his face. The glasses helped to restrict the amount of light which the eyes had to filter, and gave his eyesight more chance of making a full recovery.

Much of the rest of his face was covered in a surgical mask

which was aiding the healing of extensive damage caused by a combination of acids which had been mixed in with the toxins. Nearly all of the skin on the lower part of his face and neck had been burnt off in the attack, and it had been a long process getting skin grafts during visits to the Queen Victoria Hospital in East Grinstead.

Having followed his long journey back from the brink, today she was in Eastbourne just to check on his progress at the trauma clinic. She instinctively knew that she would find him at the beach so she had walked along Grand Parade, looking down onto the lower promenade where she had quickly spotted him.

The sun was now attempting to break through the cloud throwing sharp shafts of bright light on to the sea at the furthest extremity of the horizon. A small sailing boat was caught in one of these pools of light like an actor might be caught in a spotlight on stage.

'Thanks for coming,' he whispered, turning back to face the sea.

'Well, I had to see how you were settling in to life at the seaside,' she replied, trying to inject some humour into her voice. 'Anyway, how's the accommodation at the clinic?'

'Very comfortable but, if I'm honest, the clinic itself is a bit too institutionalised for me,' he said earnestly. 'Everything has to be done on time all the time. We follow the same schedule every day from the time the centralised wake-up alarm rings in the morning to the time we are encouraged to go to bed in the evening. There's not much time for socialising and, in fact, some of the others have been very seriously traumatised and seem to want to be on their own all the time.'

Hunter could imagine that this sort of environment would not suit Selitto who was a naturally outgoing person. Now focussing her attention on a man and woman who were gingerly testing the temperature of the sea before wading out to deeper water for their morning swim, she started to wonder whether this was really the best place for him at this stage in his rehab programme. She also wondered how he might react to news of the plane crash.

'Do you get to see or hear the news at all?' she asked.

'No TV or radio,' he replied, 'in case it sets one of them off. I can get access to a newspaper if I want to but I can't really be bothered. Why do you ask?'

'Well, we've got a big one on our hands right now which is all over the news – TV, radio and newspapers.'

Hunter then told him about the destruction of Tideswell Manor and gave him a heads-up on the limited information they had so far gathered.

'Blimey!' Selitto exclaimed when she had finished. 'Will you still have time to get down here?' Although she couldn't see his mouth, she knew that his eyes were smiling at her and that his comment was more in jest – but she decided to play along.

'Everything's changing almost by the minute but I'll still get down here to see you as much as I can,' she said, feigning a concerned and saddened expression.

'Glad to hear it!' he exclaimed, staring out to sea. The swimmers had finished swimming, the tide was starting to recede and, for the moment, the joggers had stopped jogging. He suddenly felt weary.

'Can you walk me back?' he asked, getting up stiffly and

swinging his arms across his chest to get the circulation going. Hunter handed him the single hospital crutch which had been lying on the ground behind his feet. 'I don't really need this for walking. It's more of a comfort thing because the ankle's still not quite right.'

They crossed Grand Parade in front of the imposing statue of William Cavendish, the Seventh Duke of Devonshire, who had been sitting on top of his plinth since 1901. The wide tree-lined pavements of Devonshire Place were bathed in the morning sunshine which also accentuated the brilliant colours of the late spring flowers which still surrounded the many trees lining the route.

They walked slowly as Selitto asked a couple of questions about the Tideswell Manor incident. Hunter answered as best she could after which they walked in silence, both deep in thought. Once they had arrived at the War Memorial roundabout, Selitto indicated that they should bear right along Trinity Trees. They continued to walk in silence until they came to the imposing gates of the clinic.

'You say all this is drug-related?' he asked, turning to face Hunter.

'Early indications are that there was a lot of material lying round the place and it's doubtful that anyone was *compos mentis* when the plane struck.'

'Any connection to our case last year?'

'How do you mean?'

'Well, getting rid of people involved in drugs. A suicide mission to kill a group of people who, for all we know, are suppliers, dealers – or even drug lords and ladies. The results of a plane crash aren't that different from an assassin using snake venom as a deadly weapon. Just gets rid of a few more people all at one sitting.'

This hypothesis had also flitted across Hunter's mind so it was interesting to hear that Selitto was thinking along similar lines.

'Just a thought,' he said as he turned to walk up the drive to the doors of the clinic, waving the crutch in the air as a sign of farewell.

But the seed of an idea was already beginning to grow, and it would soon worm its way into Sarah Hunter's thought process.

5

Monday 27 April

Through the curtains of exhaustion and sleep, she is vaguely aware that all around her has become quiet. Is she dreaming? She doesn't think so because she hasn't been able to dream while she has been in this room.

Every time she closes her eyes, the same ghastly images invade her consciousness and force her to open them again. She only rests when her little body can no longer stand the pain of its existence and her heart feels like it is giving up its fight for survival.

She looks across to the dim lighting that filters into the tiny room through a circular window which has been cut into the steel door. She thinks it looks like a porthole on a boat.

How long has she been here?

The light is flickering.

Please! Please don't go out! Please don't leave me in the dark!

She is terrified of the dark and always sleeps with her bedside light on at home. But this isn't home, and there is no bedside light. Or bedside table. Or any other furniture apart from the bed she is lying on surrounded by its filthy and soiled sheets.

For what seems like days now, she has heard voices in the corridor. Faces would suddenly appear at the porthole but just as quickly disappear. The voices have got quieter as the time has passed by. She senses that something has gone wrong. When she first came into this room, faces would appear at the window for a long lingering look at her naked body lying on the bed.

But that all suddenly changed.

Was it an explosion? Had the building above her collapsed?

Whatever had happened, it had panicked the other people around her.

She had wanted to get up and see what was going on, but she was in so much pain that even the thought of standing up made her feel nauseous.

She remembers that, soon after hearing the explosion, the door had burst open and she could feel rough hands scooping her frail body off the bed. She was carried unceremoniously into the corridor, her head crashing into the door as her assailant almost lost his footing.

She dared to open her eyes but all she could see were people crowding around a doorway at the end of the dimly lit corridor.

There was an urgency in their voices. Two men were trying to push a big shiny steel door. As they stood back to see what progress they had made, she noticed that the door had no handle. The men started pushing again. Women behind them started pushing the men.

The man who had her in his arms had suddenly dropped her onto the cold stone floor and ran to help the others who were trying to open the door. She had struggled to her feet but then simply collapsed – the effects of exhaustion overwhelming her. Another man had grabbed her and taken her to a room further down the corridor where she was thrown onto a bed.

She was quickly aware that there was another body lying on the bed beside her, curled into the foetal position. She could hear soft sobbing. Words which she could not understand were being whispered with an increasing sense of urgency.

Suddenly her whole body convulsed. In the pale light filtering in from the passageway, she could make out the frizzy hair and the dark skin of a young girl's body. She started to cry as she reached out a trembling hand to touch the girl. She instinctively knew that this was her best friend and soulmate. She moved closer so that their bodies were touching, and she gently wrapped an arm around the girl. She knew she had to look after her. She knew she had to keep her safe. She dared not move.

6
Monday 27 April

Sarah Hunter made her way out of Eastbourne along Kings Drive, past Eastbourne General Hospital and onto the Polegate Bypass. As she was approaching the Boship Roundabout at Lower Dicker, she saw a road sign for Tunbridge Wells and, on a whim, she took the exit for the A267. An afternoon at the morgue at Pembury would be a good use of her time.

During the journey, she reviewed her discussions with Ted Selitto and tried to analyse the extent of his recovery. He was clearly going a bit stir-crazy following over six months incarceration in hospital wards and rehabilitation centres. She had been his constant companion when she was able to get away from ongoing investigations, helping him to maintain his cheery disposition despite everything.

Now he was at a trauma clinic. Was this just another box-ticking exercise? Even Ted seemed to be questioning what he was doing there. He was a serving police officer with many years' experience of dealing with horrendous crimes. He lived in a world where trauma was an everyday fact of life.

She knew that he would soon be asking her if he could come back to work, back to the world in which he felt most comfortable. And what was going to be her response? She couldn't afford to let her heart rule her head and would have to rely on medical advice to a certain extent. She had to be strong. And she had to make a decision which afforded him the comfort of being back in an environment he knew whilst at the same time not exposing him to any risks which might upset his total recovery programme.

These thoughts kept going around in her head as she continued through the countryside which had been dulled by the thick layer of cloud she had run into soon after leaving Eastbourne. She was now skirting round Mayfield on her way towards Frant. Soon after that, she would hit the outskirts of Tunbridge Wells before dropping into the morgue.

A gentle drizzle had turned to rain and, by the time Hunter reached the morgue, the raindrops were stotting off the road. Thankfully, finding a space in the visitors' car park was not a problem, and she pulled her jacket over the back of her head before scuttling across to the portico at the entrance to the pathology unit.

Sliding her ID card into the reader, she looked straight at the camera and waited the customary two or three seconds before the door clicked open. She walked along the corridor until she arrived at the pathology office but found it empty. Assuming that everyone was busy in the examination room, she retraced her steps to the scrubs room.

She opted for a Tyvek suit and, as was her custom, she pinned her hair up into an untidy bunch before cramming it under a scrubs cap. Slipping nitrile overshoes over her flatties, she picked up a mask on her way out of the room and wrapped the white bands around the back of her ears whilst tucking the mask itself under her chin.

The examination room was a hive of activity with all three autopsy tables in use at the same time, something Sarah had not seen before. As she entered the room, she made her way to the nearest of the tables where Dr Toby Swartzman was working. He looked up as she approached.

'Well, well, well,' he chortled, 'you're putting in an early appearance, Sarah!'

'And a very good afternoon to you too, Toby,' came the pithy response as Hunter moved round to join the chief pathologist at the end of the autopsy table. The body on the table in front of her had been badly burnt in the fire, its mouth open as if emitting a silent despairing scream at the point of death.

'A lot of them are like this,' Swartzman was saying as Hunter stared, fascinated and horrified in equal measure. 'There's considerable evidence of drug use – and probably abuse – in all the bodies we have so far processed. It's unlikely that many of them were actually conscious when they died but this chap looks as if he probably just woke up before his life was dramatically snatched from him.'

The door from the refrigeration room swung open and Norman Partington shuffled into the room closely followed by one of the mortuary assistants. An eminent pathologist of some distinction in his heyday, Partington had now retired but helped out at the morgue when golf and his social diary allowed. On seeing Hunter, he immediately came over.

'My dear Sarah,' he blustered, 'how lovely to see you here in our little ghetto. You've certainly excelled yourself this time. Poor old Toby's had trouble working out exactly how many bodies you've sent us, haven't you Toby?'

Swartzman nodded. 'Problem is that we've got so many different causes of death,' he added.

'That's right,' Partington continued, pointing to the body on the autopsy table. 'Some, like this poor chap, probably died because of the fire. But others were crushed to death under the falling masonry, and I've seen at least two who look as if they were hit by the aircraft.'

'We've had to call for reinforcements,' Swartzman continued, 'and guess who's putting in an appearance?'

Hunter looked across at Partington who simply raised both eyebrows.

'Is Ilona coming down?' Hunter asked, a note of excitement in her voice.

'Professor Ilona Jenkyns MBE to give her full title,' Swartzman replied.

'MBE?' Hunter exclaimed.

'Member of the Order of the British Empire no less,' Swartzman clarified.

'My God! When did that happen?' Hunter was shocked at the same time as feeling delighted for her friend and valued expert.

'New Year's Honours this year,' Swartzman continued. 'For services to medicine and pathology if my memory serves me.' Partington nodded his head in agreement.

'Well, that's great news,' Hunter gushed, 'and great news that she's coming here. When's she arriving?'

'Should be here tomorrow and then another day this week and a couple of days next week.'

Swartzman turned away and walked off towards one of the washing units which were arranged along the wall behind them. Partington now moved closer to Hunter, a conspiratorial look in his eye.

'The other matter we must draw your attention to, Sarah, is that some of the victims here are children.'

Partington had no doubt seen many harrowing sights during

his illustrious career but it was always difficult carrying out autopsies on children, and his voice had now almost dropped to a whisper. He looked at Hunter from under hooded eyebrows.

'I had heard that rumour, Norman,' she replied. 'Have we got a firm number yet?'

'Really difficult to say but I think I've seen three so far – there may be more. The problem is that they're not all complete so we're having to run multiple DNA tests to try and match up body parts which have been recovered from the scene.'

'Jeez,' Hunter sighed. 'Any idea at all about what sort of ages we're talking about?'

'Difficult to say precisely but probably between nine and early teens. Looks like a mixture of boys and girls. Now, they could all be the sons and daughters of some of the partygoers, but you know when something just doesn't look quite right …' His voice trailed away.

Sarah Hunter stared at the body on the table in front of her which was now being photographed by Toby Swartzman.

'How do you mean?' Hunter was intrigued.

'I don't know!' The old pathologist sounded flustered. 'Most of them look somewhat malnourished to me, and the ones that were wearing any clothes were not wearing designer labels like the majority of the deceased adults. It might be a bit far-fetched but it just looked to me as if the children didn't belong to the adults. So, could they have been brought in as entertainment for the partygoers' delight?'

'God, Norman, I hope you're wrong on that one,' Hunter exclaimed, 'but I can see where you're coming from.' A deep frown was etched on Hunter's forehead as the true horror of what Partington had just said started to deconstruct the picture she had built up in her mind about the last hours of Tideswell Manor.

Sarah was now absent-mindedly watching Swartzman as he busily recorded details of the cadaver on the autopsy table in front of him.

'I have also heard that the children and the other body parts assessed as being from young children were not all found in the same areas of the mansion,' Partington continued.

'Which means?' Hunter enquired.

'Well, if they had all been children of the adults, they might have all been in bed in the bedrooms or perhaps in somewhere like a dormitory. From the information we have, the bodies were located in different parts of the wreckage so they certainly weren't all together.'

The silence in the room was only compromised by the clicking of Swartzman's camera, the water gently sluicing through the drainage system under the autopsy tables and the quiet drone of refrigeration systems.

Hunter let out a long sigh.

'Okay, Norman, let's not detain you any longer but do let me know as soon as you find anything which is going to help us get a clearer picture of what was going on in the mansion.'

'Will do, Sarah.' And, with that, the pathologist stepped away to the autopsy table at the far end of the room on which two mortuary assistants were just placing another body.

Hunter turned to Swartzman.

'Okay if I use your office for a couple of minutes, Toby? Just need to make a call back to base.'

'No probs, Sarah. Be my guest.'

Hunter made her way out of the examination room and

into Swartzman's little office. Standing by the small window which looked out onto the autopsy tables, she dialled up Grace Kendall.

After a short exchange of pleasantries, Hunter cut to the chase. She explained the pathologists' confirmation that children were amongst the dead, and Norman Partington's hypothesis that they might not have belonged to the adults who were present in the manor.

'So, Grace, I want you to draw up names and details of all children currently on the missing list. Let's have all children up to the age of sixteen in Kent. Also ask Sussex, Surrey and Essex forces if they want to come in on this. It's clearly going to be very difficult to identify any of these kids so any solid info we can get should help.'

'Will do, Sarah,' Kendall replied. 'Is this a priority over everything or shall I continue my liaison with the air accident people as well?'

'Yes – we need to keep all channels of investigation open because I want to get as much information as soon as it's available. I don't want to be sitting around waiting for written reports.'

Hunter turned back to the little window just in time to see Swartzman pulling apart a charred set of ribs. She disconnected the call and turned away, a wave of nausea washing over her. She needed to get out of there.

7

Monday 27 April

It was only a short journey from the morgue back to Tonbridge police station at Pembury Road but Hunter seemed to have caught the traffic today. No doubt more unattended roadworks somewhere with diversion signs taking drivers to parts of Kent they never knew existed. At least the music on the radio was to her liking, and she turned the volume up to appreciate every note of the Massive Attack anthem, *Unfinished Sympathy*. She was addicted to the video on You Tube, always marvelling at how it seemed to have been shot in one take.

Eventually arriving at Pembury Road, Hunter made her way up to the Ops Room. Looking around the open-plan office area, she noticed that there seemed to be a rather sparse attendance today – was everyone out on calls? she wondered. She noticed that DS Angie Marshall was sitting at her desk, and wandered over to where Marshall was staring somewhat disinterestedly at a screen teeming with columns of figures.

'Monthly reports,' Marshall explained, presumably thinking that Hunter wanted to know what she was doing. But that was the last thing on Sarah's mind.

'A quick word, Angie,' Hunter said as she indicated the door out of the room. Marshall took the hint and followed her across the corridor and into a small meeting room, closing the door behind her.

'Not a great attendance today,' Marshall said as she propped herself against one of the desks in the room. As there were no chairs, Hunter had done the same which was a practical solution but not very comfortable.

'I'm sure they'd all be able to fully account for their whereabouts,' Hunter replied with a smirk. 'Anyway, Angie, I just wanted a quick word about the Tideswell Manor incident. It's really difficult not having Ted here and, as a consequence, I'm rather short on manpower. We've managed to get Elaine Jennings into an acting DS role but I still need more boots on the ground.'

'I can imagine how hard it is without Ted,' Marshall agreed. 'He's such a key part of the team. Anyway, I'd be happy to help if you need me for anything.'

'Thanks, Angie, but I was probably thinking in terms of a young DC at the moment. I need someone to do the leg work out at the crash site,' Hunter explained. 'I seem to remember you offering me Lisa Calder in the past because you were looking for something that she could really cut her teeth on. Was she also one of those youngsters who had a bit of an attitude?'

'Still has!' Marshall smiled. 'But she's a good kid really. Full of enthusiasm even if she does think she knows it all at the age of twenty-three. From what I've heard, Tideswell Manor might be a good testing ground for her.'

'Excellent!' Hunter was pleased that she had got another pair of hands who she could put with Jed Crowther at the mansion. 'Is she in today?'

'Sure is. She's just out collecting some papers from Sevenoaks magistrates but she's on the late shift so she'll be here until at least eight o'clock this evening.'

'Okay,' Hunter continued. 'While you're here, any idea where Rory Easton is? I just wanted to have a quick chat with him. None of my team have seen him for a few days.'

Marshall looked round the room, spreading her arms out and shrugging her shoulders.

'Not unlike him to be away on some secret mission,' Marshall explained. 'He normally stays in touch if he's away but not this time it seems. No one's heard from him for about a week. He's not over in Essex either – they've also been trying to track him down.'

'You've checked his home?' Hunter asked although she knew that Angie Marshall would have already done this. She was nothing if not thorough.

'Yep. Done that and spoken to his girlfriend. They have a bit of an on/off relationship so it's not unusual for her go without seeing him from one week to the next or longer. Anything I can help you with?'

'About six months ago, he gave us some useful information about how drugs gangs are structured, and I just need a bit more information as it looks as if Tideswell Manor was hosting some sort of drug-fest.'

'I'll see if I can find someone to get you that sort of information,' Marshall replied as she pushed herself off the desk. 'I know one of the guys who work in the County Lines & Gangs Team at Medway. Lives over this way somewhere – Tudeley, Five Oak Green? Somewhere like that. He could probably stop by on his way to or from Medway.'

'Yeah, that would be good if you could arrange something and let me know.'

Hunter also slid off the desk and moved towards the door.

'Shall I just collar Lisa when she gets in?'

'Be my guest!'

41

Returning to the Ops Room, Hunter took the chair next to Grace Kendall's desk as she needed to get an update on how her inquiries were progressing.

'What have we got so far, Grace?'

'Well, I've just come off a very long call with the air accident people who have been given details of the plane and the pilot by Biggin Hill, but they can't confirm these details to us until they have physically identified the plane which crashed into the manor.'

'And they, presumably, can't do that until it's safe to do so?'

'Something like that.'

'What about the pilot? Do they have ID on him or have we got to identify him first and then compare notes?'

Hunter was beginning to realise that the bureaucracy involved in any dealings with Government agencies was going to test her patience to the absolute limit.

'Well, something like that,' Kendall agreed. 'But I did manage to get them to give us a provisional name. Or, at least, the name that appears on the manifest for that flight. The name they have is John Smith.'

Hunter stared at Kendall, not quite comprehending what she had just been told. Was this some kind of wind-up?

'*John Smith?*' she asked incredulously.

'I know,' Grace replied. 'Sounds like we're being fobbed off or perhaps they can't divulge the name yet so it's common practice to just refer to a crashed pilot as *John Smith* until they are formally identified?'

'Or perhaps the name on the manifest really is John Smith. In which case…' Hunter's voice trailed away as the prospect of trying to find an identity for the pilot suddenly became a major problem.

'Well, the Civil Aviation Authority holds the register of all those who are qualified to fly in this country,' Kendall continued, trying to sound positive. 'I have already made contact with them and, thankfully, they appreciated that we had to move quickly on this so I'm hoping to get some information back first thing tomorrow.'

'Any idea of how many John Smiths are on their books?' Hunter asked with an air of sarcasm in her voice.

'Certainly more than one!' Kendall quipped as she changed the content of the screen in front of her to show a photograph of an aeroplane. 'I did, however, manage to twist the arm of the guy at Biggin Hill who said that the plane could have been a Beechcraft King Air 350. It's a twin turboprop aircraft with capacity for about eight passengers. Brand new will set you back the best part of six million quid. Second hand – probably three or four million. Good maximum speed and range. Would have made a big impression on the old walls of Tideswell Manor!'

'Any information about ownership?' Hunter asked, absent-mindedly imagining herself nestled into a luxury leather-padded seat on the aircraft as it sped her to a warm and sunny location, glass of champagne in hand.

'Not yet, but I'm hopeful that my new best friend at the CAA might get back to me tomorrow with that information.'

Hunter thought for a moment. There was something missing. A vital piece of information? What was it? Oh, yes…

'Did we get a description of John Smith from your contact at Biggin Hill?'

'Yes,' Grace replied, turning over a couple of pages in her notebook. 'Let me see…yes…that's right…CCTV wasn't working in the pilot's area.' She read some more of her notes. 'Yes…

our contact was on duty on the Saturday up to the time the airfield closed at 10.00 p.m. He said that the King Air came in quite late and that he completed the paperwork with the pilot. A swarthy well-built man, looked fit, smartly dressed, white short-sleeved shirt and tie. Aviator shades even though it was nearly dark outside. Pilot's cap on his head and rucksack on his back.'

'Anything else?'

'A mass of curly grey hair, apparently. The cap had given up the struggle of containing all the flowing locks which had been pulled together in a bushy ponytail. There were some tattoos on the man's forearms but the guy at the airport hadn't a clue what they depicted.'

They lapsed into silence, each with their own thoughts on the unfolding investigation. Eventually, Hunter leaned forward and put her elbows on the corner of the desk, cupping her chin in her hands, staring at a picture of the aeroplane on Grace's computer screen.

'What time is it now?' She stared at the bottom right-hand corner of the screen. 'Not even thirty six hours since the plane hit? And no one's asking *where's my John Smith*? Or *where's my six million pound plane*? You would have thought that someone, somewhere might have made an enquiry by now.'

Although Kendall was nodding, she was ready with a counter-argument.

'Perhaps they're not in the country,' she surmised. 'Perhaps the plane's owner and the pilot's family live overseas?'

'Or the plane's owner and the pilot are one and the same person!' Hunter was keen to conclude the list of valid alternatives.

They lapsed into silence again, the only sounds coming from the dull hum of traffic from the roundabout below them and the occasional raised voices from the few detectives who were still at their desks in the Ops Room.

Suddenly, Hunter took her elbows off the desk and sat back in her chair.

'Or…just suppose this *wasn't* a catastrophic accident!'

Kendall gave her a sideways glance. 'What? You mean that this was a deliberate act to kill many people which involved the actions of a kamikaze pilot?'

'Well it's *possible* isn't it?'

'Sounds as if you've been watching too many of those Nordic noir thrillers on BBC4 on a Saturday evening,' Kendall replied, smiling.

'Ha! Ha! Ha!' Hunter chuckled. 'Funnily enough, Ted suggested that it could have been a suicide mission. Are we, perhaps, in the middle of an epic drugs war with both sides trying to wipe each other out?'

Kendall looked askance at this suggestion. 'Surely not!' she exclaimed.

Hunter stood up to stretch her legs. Whatever the reason for the crash, she had to prioritise what she needed to do to get on top of her investigation whilst, at the same time, working out a plan for each team member.

She noticed that the clock on the wall was now showing a few minutes before 6.00 p.m. At that moment, the door to the Ops Room opened and Lisa Calder strolled in carrying a couple of box files. She went over to where Angie Marshall was sitting and dropped the files on her desk. After a quick chat, Angie directed her across the room to where Hunter was standing.

Calder was a little shorter than Sarah and was dressed in loose fitting clothes – a voluminous round-neck jumper over at least one T-shirt and baggy jeans with trendy slits in the knees. On arrival, she had been wearing a very old Barbour jacket which almost hid the knee slits. She had an engaging face and her eyes looked huge behind her round-lens glasses. A mop of mousey hair hung untidily around her shoulders.

Hunter suggested that they cross the corridor to the small meeting room where they perched on the desks so that they could have an informal introductory chat.

First impressions were favourable as far as Hunter was concerned although she found that Lisa talked rather a lot. She did toy with the idea of sending her down to the morgue for a couple of days which might quieten her down. But then she thought that might also put her off wanting to join the team. Perhaps it would be a better idea to let the girl get acquainted with the case first.

They wandered back into the Ops Room where Hunter noticed that Jed Crowther had just returned to leave some information with Grace Kendall. So, she immediately suggested that he take Calder with him when he returned to Tideswell the following day.

Crowther had reported that things were moving slowly at the mansion due to the many safety issues with the building. The Crime Scene Investigators had, however, been making progress but in a stop-start sort of way. They were also finding further evidence of a drug-fuelled party which had probably gone on and on until guests literally passed out wherever they happened to be in the building.

The fire that had raged following the rupturing of the aircraft's fuel tanks had accounted for a good deal of the contents of the mansion, and many of the bodies had been badly charred in the inferno. This might make identification tricky, Crowther had reported. But he had been happy to take Lisa back to site with him and made arrangements to collect her in the morning.

8

Tuesday 28 April

Acting DS Elaine Jennings had arrived early at Pembury Road in order to write up her notes following the previous day spent at the Tideswell crash site with the Search & Rescue teams. But she had been grabbed by the Desk Sergeant as soon as she walked through the door, and was now sitting in the rather grandly titled *Interview Suite*.

It was, in fact, an old storeroom at the end of the reception area on the ground floor of the police station which used to be packed to the gunwales with boxes of case records, all gently yellowing as time took its toll. However, with the coming of the digital age, these records had been loaded onto computer records and were now all stored at the Maidstone HQ.

The problem of what to do with the room had recently been solved by the decision to create a facility where police officers could meet members of the public who were not under suspicion for any criminal activity. The suite was different from the standard interview rooms located behind the front desk. For a start, the chairs were more comfortable and weren't screwed to the floor and the table had a wooden top rather than a sheet of cold metal. There was even a three-seater settee nestling under a window which had panes of frosted glass to prevent any surveillance from outside. In fact, the only active surveillance was carried out by a pair of wall-mounted cameras which relayed pictures but no sound to the viewing gallery attached to Interview Room One if required.

Across the table from Jennings sat Julie Buckley, her eyes red-rimmed as tears continued to flow freely, a box of tissues on the table in front of her. She was wearing a dirty and stained grey hoodie which was about two sizes too big for her. This covered a faded lime green round neck jumper which had long ago surrendered its shape, the neckline sagging alarmingly. Greasy and unkempt blonde hair hung straight down on either side of her face like a pair of limp curtains, a parting of dark roots evidencing its natural colour. Pudgy hands fiddled with the tissue box, cracked and dirty fingernails picking at the clean white tissues.

'So, when did you first notice that Rachael was missing?' Jennings gently enquired. Julie Buckley gave a sharp intake of breath – or was it a sob? Elaine wasn't sure but she waited patiently for an answer.

'Must have been Sunday evening when I got back,' Buckley replied, staring steadfastly at the table in front of her. 'Thought she was in her room so I went upstairs to see her but she wasn't there – and her bed hadn't been slept in.'

Jennings let the silence linger to see if Buckley was going to give up any further information but it soon became apparent that that was all she was going to say for the moment. Why had this woman waited thirty-six hours before reporting her daughter missing?

'Perhaps you can tell me when you last saw her,' Jennings enquired.

Buckley didn't answer immediately. Instead, she let her eyes roam around the room without ever looking at Jennings.

'Probably Friday morning when she went off to school,' Buckley finally whispered.

Jennings sat back in her chair. There was something not quite right here.

'Miss Buckley – Julie – can you explain how come you didn't see your daughter from Friday morning to Sunday evening?'

Buckley suddenly raised her head and looked straight at Jennings.

'I went away, didn't I,' she replied. 'I went a-sodding-way to get a break from everything. I couldn't take no more of her constant whingeing. Always things wrong with her or things wrong with me. I knew I should never have let her have that sodding phone. On it all the time, all that bloody social media rubbish. She's only just eleven for God's sake. The stuff she came out with – would have had my poor mother spinning in her grave. Got to the stage when I had to get away so I went down to Margate for a couple of nights. Stayed with a woman I used to work with. Went clubbing, drinking, and just had a good time. If Rach was so sure she could look after herself, then I thought this was the opportunity for her to try it out.'

Buckley lapsed into silence. Her eyes had returned to staring intently at the table top. Jennings just looked at her.

'Why haven't you reported her missing until now,' Jennings eventually asked.

'Because I thought she was with some of her mates and that she'd come back when she was good and ready.'

'But she hasn't come back, has she!' It was more a statement than a question but Jennings wanted to be absolutely sure. 'And, now that you've contacted all her friends and the school, I suppose no one's seen her. Right?'

Buckley nodded her head as more tears started to make their way down her face before dropping off her chin onto the hoodie. She sobbed gently and released a couple of the tissues from the box.

Whilst Jennings' first reaction was one of anger that a mother could be so stupid and uncaring to simply leave her child alone for over 48 hours, she could also imagine the frustration of trying to deal with a daughter who was probably old well beyond her years. And, although she didn't have children of her own, she knew the dangers that social media caused for unsuspecting children who were prime targets for grooming or sexting. Had Rachael been lured away by someone who had befriended her online for the sole purpose of exploiting her?

'So, she didn't go to school on Friday – you've checked with them?'

Another nod of the head.

'And she hasn't been in contact with any of her friends or other family members?'

'She ain't got no friends,' came the reply. 'Just that Linzi girl who's a real head case and another girl called Frizzy or something like that. Coloured girl. Just moved down here from Brixton or some such – Balham maybe.'

'Could she have gone to see her father?' Jennings enquired, more in hope than anything else.

'Doesn't know him. Neither do I for that matter.' Buckley paused as if questioning the accuracy of the response she had just given. 'Well, I mean I don't know *exactly* who her father is and, whoever it is, he's never taken any interest in her or anything. From what I can gather, she seems to think that not having a dad is cool – as if she's some sort of freak.'

Elaine Jennings groaned inwardly but pressed on.

'What about family?'

'Nah! They can't stand her! I tell you, she's got a right tongue on her. Used some words that even my sister's never heard of and my sister doesn't hold back when she's havin' a rant.'

Jennings could imagine. A Buckley family gathering sounded as if it was something to be avoided at all costs.

'Is there anything in her room that might give us a clue as to where she's gone?' Jennings asked, in hope more than anything else. 'Does she have a laptop or a tablet or any other electronic device?'

'Not likely!' came the reply. 'Can't afford nothing like that. She only got the bloody phone because Linzi passed her old phone on to Rach when her dad got her the latest new one. No, she does everything on her phone.'

It was clear to Jennings that Julie Buckley didn't actually know very much about what went on in her daughter's life and, whilst she accepted that Rachael could do pretty much everything through her phone, it was becoming a distinct possibility that there was another device – probably hidden in the girl's bedroom. She needed to take a look.

'Okay, Julie, we'll see what we can do to find your daughter but it would help us to get started if we could just take a quick look at Rachael's room. It'll give us more of a feeling of who we're looking for. If we can do that today then we can get on with looking for her.'

Buckley had stopped crying now and was looking at Jennings, suspicion in her eyes.

'You won't find nothing in there,' she said, airily. 'That girl doesn't keep anything. No dolls, no toys, never been interested. The only things she hangs onto are books. Rows and rows of books on her shelves. And lots of them snow things – you know, the ones you turn upside down and it starts snowing. They seem to fascinate her.'

'All the same, it would help if we could at least have a quick look,' Jennings reasoned.

There was silence in the room, the two women looking directly at each other.

'We can come now,' Jennings pressed on, keen to get the visit done while Buckley was still sufficiently distressed about her daughter's disappearance.

Buckley looked down at her fingers and then absent-mindedly scraped the dirt out from under one of her nails before flicking it across the floor. She sniffed, ran the back of her hand under her nose, wiped it down the side of her jeans, looked at the opaque windows and then up at the ceiling before focusing back on Jennings.

'Can you give us a lift then?' she asked as if the giving of the lift was a bargaining chip.

'Shouldn't be a problem,' Jennings replied. 'We can be ready to go in about twenty minutes.'

Julie Buckley nodded as the detritus from under another nail was jettisoned towards the corner of the room.

9

Tuesday 28 April

Sarah Hunter had spent an uncomfortable morning at the Maidstone HQ where she had been introduced to Margot Westwood, the ever so slightly severe PR expert. Hunter could immediately tell that Westwood was a civilian contractor. She was immaculately dressed in washed denim flared black jeans with a white cotton T-shirt under a pink boyfriend blazer. Her luxuriant auburn hair was swept back in a ponytail which was held in place with a classic barrette clip. She looked as if she had spent hours in make-up before coming to work, and her nails were freshly manicured.

Despite her reservations about PR, Hunter was quite drawn to Westwood. She always liked working with people who knew what they were talking about. People who exuded authority in their own subjects. Westwood had spent much of the morning explaining the importance of a good relationship with the press and how to determine what information to give out.

She had then set up a camera and had done a couple of imaginary interviews with Hunter. They had then watched these back with Westwood critiquing Hunter's performance. As she talked through the videos, she gave Sarah more tips about when to look at the camera, how to emphasise points, what to do with her hands, how to retain a sympathetic look and, above all, how to deal with inane questions without coming across as someone who has no time for the press.

Hunter had played along, still convinced in her own mind that journalists were nothing but a bunch of scribblers who only wrote what suited their own egos and agendas. And even that was sprinkled with a liberal amount of fantasy. But Westwood had made some interesting points which Sarah would certainly consider.

Once the PR session had finished, Sarah went in search of DCI Jack Pennington. It wasn't difficult to find the location of SCD as it always seemed to be taking up more office space every time she visited Maidstone. This phenomenon was obviously an indication of the sheer volume of serious and organised crime they were all dealing with in the south-east of England.

She couldn't see Pennington to start with but soon spotted him in conversation with a couple of uniformed officers. She took up position just inside the door of what was now a smart suite of offices and waited until he was free. While waiting, she checked her phone for messages and then scrolled on to a news channel to see if they were still reporting the plane crash at Tideswell Manor.

She was so engrossed in reading what journalists were reporting that she jumped when she realised that Pennington was standing right beside her.

'Hi Sarah,' he said with a broad smile, 'catching up on the news?'

'Sort of,' she replied rather defensively. 'Just trying to get a handle on how Tideswell Manor's being reported.'

'Probably not very accurately,' he suggested, 'but what on earth brings you to SCD on this late-April day?'

Regaining her composure, Hunter quickly told him about her session with Margot Westwood and then explained that Superintendent Eaves had insisted that they all work together on the Tideswell Manor plane crash.

'Yes, that's going to be a major investigation for us all,' Pennington noted, 'so it's great that we've got your team on the ground there. We're really short-staffed here what with all the stuff going on with these migrants who are now seemingly crossing the Channel at will in small dinghies. And we've got continuing problems with trying to deal with a huge increase in drug-related crime. These county lines gangs are growing ever-more sophisticated day-by-day. We just don't have the manpower to deal with it all.'

Sarah Hunter knew exactly what Pennington was talking about, and she empathised with the predicament that he was in.

'So, are we supposed to get on with the investigation at Tideswell Manor and just keep you informed?'

'I can't see how else we can do it, Sarah. We've worked well together before and I certainly don't feel the need to micro-manage you so, yes, just get on with the investigation and keep me in the loop.'

This was music to Hunter's ears as the thought of having to do everything through Pennington was not something she had been looking forward to – even though she did enjoy his company on the occasions when they had met outside of working time.

'Okay, that's good and certainly makes sense,' she said. 'Will you square this approach away with Eaves because otherwise she's going to keep bending Iversen's ear.'

'Yep, no problem there,' Pennington replied. 'Oh, by the way, any news of Ted?'

'Saw him yesterday. He's now at a trauma rehab clinic in Eastbourne. Not sure how long for but I would have thought that he should be allowed to go home soon – there's not much more they can do for him. Difficult to tell when he'll be fit for work but he might be able to get back to the station on a part-time basis in the next few weeks. He misses it very badly although he is sensible enough to know that he needs to take it one step at a time.'

'Well, give him my best when you next see him,' Pennington said as he raised his arm and waved to a new arrival in the suite of offices. 'Okay, that's my next meeting arrived so I'd better go. Keep in touch – and we must try for another dinner sometime.'

'That'd be good,' Hunter replied, 'and don't forget to tell Eaves!'

10

Tuesday 28 April

Elaine Jennings had collected DC Azzar Mishraz from the Ops Room on her way out of the station, and they were now standing in the chaos of Julie Buckley's small front room. For some reason there were two tumble dryers in the room along with a battered old leather three-seater settee and the biggest TV screen Mishraz had ever seen. Mops, brooms, buckets and other cleaning equipment was strewn randomly around the room. A scraggy ginger cat sat on one of the driers.

Buckley led the way to a steep staircase which she started to climb, indicating that the detectives should follow. Jennings was alarmed to find that there were no balusters on one side of the staircase and there was no handrail on the other side next to the wall. She, therefore, hugged the wall as she carefully placed her feet on the narrow treads.

They soon arrived at a small landing with a room to their right. Jennings assumed that this was a bedroom although its door was closed. Julie Buckley had, however, turned to the left and they found themselves in a narrow corridor with an open door at the end which led into the bathroom.

'This is her room,' Buckley said as she turned and opened the door to her left. She ushered the two detectives into what was clearly Rachael's room judging by the signage on the door. Beneath the girl's name were the words 'Do Not Enter' followed by a picture of a skull & crossbones.

The room was, indeed, rather spartan and Buckley hadn't been exaggerating when she had said that her daughter only seemed interested in books. Jennings counted four bookshelves, each crammed with books of all sizes. A fifth shelf above the books was crowded with the snow globes that Buckley had mentioned. They were mainly Christmas scenes but some contained models of people, buildings, trees and birds. She picked one up which contained a city scene with skyscraper buildings. Turning it over to create the snow effect, she noticed that the snow had been replaced with chunks of grey and black which gave an eerie effect to the model landscape. A label stuck to the underside of the ornament simply read '*Apocalyptic Nightmare*'. She put it back on the shelf, the grey and black detritus still falling onto the buildings.

'God knows what she sees in those,' Buckley was saying. 'Some of them are bloody spooky if you ask me. Anyway, I'll let you have a quick look around. I'll be downstairs if you need me.' With that, she backed out of the room.

Mishraz was now standing by the window in the small and rather airless bedroom. The sash windows rattled in their frames, the panes of glass yellowing around the edges and filthy dirty on the outside. He could only just make out the postage-stamp-sized garden at the back of the house. A train hooted as it passed unseen somewhere nearby - probably on its way out of Tonbridge towards London judging by the location of the terrace of houses.

'Okay, let's have a quick look around,' Jennings said as she and Mishraz slipped on their nitrile gloves to avoid contamination of the scene. 'You do the bed and the books, and I'll do the chest of drawers and the wardrobe.'

The two detectives knew that time was of the essence here. Ideally, they didn't want Julie Buckley coming back into the room while they were rummaging through her daughter's clothes and possessions so they had to be finished before she even thought of coming back to see how they were getting on.

Mishraz moved over to the single bed which was jammed into one corner of the room. He quickly ran his hands between the mattress and the base of the bed, pulling it out from the wall so he could make a thorough search. He also checked to make sure that there were no hidden drawers in the base before looking under the duvet and the pillows.

Jennings was also running her hands under items of clothing stored in the chest of drawers, making sure that nothing was wrapped in any of the folds. She was surprised to find that the bottom drawer was full of books. This girl was certainly into her reading, she thought as she felt around between the books to make sure that a tablet or i-pad hadn't been hidden there.

Mishraz had now started looking through the books on the bottom shelf as Jennings moved over to the wardrobe. Opening the doors, she saw a few items of clothing hanging limply from a single rail. There were shelves down one side which were stuffed with jumpers, tracksuit tops and bottoms, and what appeared to be dirty washing. The bottom shelf was jammed with an untidy mass of trainers of all different colours. She felt through all the clothing and then rummaged through the trainers. Nothing. Was this a fruitless waste of time? she asked herself.

'Something here, Elaine,' Mishraz whispered.

Jennings closed the wardrobe and stepped over to stand beside Mishraz who had a book open on the top of the chest of drawers. She could see that it was a book about volcanos but her eyes were drawn to letters and figures which had been written on a blank page between chapters.

'Looks like postcodes, dates and times to me,' Mishraz observed. Jennings had to agree and started to flick through the rest of the book. 'Nothing else in this one but I've seen some hieroglyphics in one or two other books. Can't tell what they mean though.'

'There's a drawer full of books down here,' Jennings said as she stood away from the chest. 'Think I'd better take a closer look at these but we really need to get a move on or she'll be back.'

Moving up to the next shelf, Mishraz started flicking through the books with greater urgency. Nothing on that shelf but, when he was about halfway along the next shelf, a slip of paper fluttered out of one of the books and landed on the top of the chest of drawers. This time, there was a list of single names with a set of numbers beside each name. Mishraz immediately thought they were telephone numbers but then realised that there were too many digits. He put the list to one side and continued flicking through the books.

Meanwhile, Jennings was carefully extracting the books from the drawer and was now flicking through the pages of each book before putting it back where it came from. She didn't really know what she was looking for but she was beginning to realise that the books couldn't possibly be reading matter for an eleven-year-old girl. Some of them were also in very poor condition and had probably been acquired as a job lot. But why?

She was mulling this over in her mind when she came to a hardback book with several elastic bands holding the covers together. She carefully released the bands before opening the book. There, sandwiched between its pages, was a battered old Nokia 3310. The screen was cracked in several places and the phone looked as if it had had a hard life.

'Gotcha!' she exclaimed, looking up to where Mishraz was staring down at her smiling. 'Right, we need to get this place searched properly,' she said as she finished putting all the books back in the drawer.

Mishraz had now got onto the top shelf of books and had just pulled down a great tome with 'The Complete Works of William Shakespeare' inscribed on its spine. He soon realised that the book had been tampered with when he found a secret compartment which had been crudely cut into the pages.

'Coke or heroin?' Elaine Jennings said as she leaned in to take a closer look at what Mishraz had found. They both stared at the little wraps of drugs which nestled in the cut-out compartment of the book.

'The brown wrap looks like heroin to me but the other's probably crack,' Mishraz replied as he got a pen out of his pocket and pushed the little parcels around in their hiding place.

'Okay, photograph it and then put it in an evidence bag,' Jennings instructed. 'You did bring them with you, didn't you?' Mishraz nodded.

'Better take that volcano book as well. I've also found a phone but it's probably not her everyday phone. Bag it anyway and then let's get out of here.'

11
Tuesday 28 April

Sarah Hunter decided on a lazy drive through the countryside on her way back to Tonbridge. She needed some time to think plus the fact that it was such a beautiful day. Kent always looked so lovely in the spring sunshine. So, she left Maidstone on the A26 which took her through Barming to the south of the hospital and then across Barming Heath, its views of the southern downlands already lifting her spirits.

On reaching Wateringbury, she decided to turn down towards the river Medway, eventually passing Nettlestead Place before arriving at the Hop Pole Inn. Here, she took the left fork in the road and was soon clattering over the level crossing outside Yalding station. The road then took her over Hampstead Lock and she followed the river until she arrived at The Boathouse. On the spur of the moment, she decided to stop so that she could enjoy a sandwich and a cool drink whilst watching the wildlife on the river.

After ordering a cheese & pickle sandwich and a glass of ginger beer at the bar, she took her drink outside into the sunshine and walked over to sit at one of the bench-tables overlooking Hampstead Weir. The noise of the water coursing through the weir allied to the sunlight dancing on the water was mesmeric, and Sarah Hunter found herself relaxing for the first time since she had heard about the plane crashing into Tideswell Manor.

Sitting with her back against the tabletop, she went through what the team knew about the incident – or was it, in fact, better to describe it as a disaster? She thought about this but couldn't decide. Perhaps she'd just refer to it as an incident for the time being. The word disaster had too many connotations of it being a catastrophe in which hundreds of people lost their lives.

Her sandwich arrived and she tucked into it with gusto, suddenly realising that it was ages since she had last had anything to eat.

They were, of course, extremely light on information and the job of rescuing all the bodies from the manor house had been halted so many times due to problems with the structure of the building. At least engineers had been working round the clock to make the building safe so that the grim task of searching for bodies could continue.

Sitting there in the sunshine, Sarah kept coming back to the same question that had been bugging her since Saturday – what could possibly have motivated someone to fly a plane straight into a building at full speed? Was the intention to cause the maximum amount of damage? Or the maximum number of casualties? Did the pilot know that the manor would be crammed with people enjoying a weekend in the country? If he or she had been on the original guest list, would they have been fully aware of the scale of the carnage they would be creating?

Hunter stared out across the water, her mind returning to 11 September 2001 when she watched, aghast, as the TV showed live pictures of two passenger jets flying into the twin towers of the World Trade Centre in New York. At the time, she wondered how anyone could have the nerve to fly an aeroplane at high speed straight at an immovable object.

She also recalled the incident when a young co-pilot

deliberately crashed a passenger airliner into the French Alps in 2015, killing himself and about 150 other people. She had been on a spring holiday in the south of France at the time, and there had been endless coverage on the local TV.

And now she was faced with trying to establish whether another pilot had deliberately flown an aircraft into a house full of people. She had to admit that it looked like there was probably more to this than simply a pilot losing control of the plane and nose-diving into an opulent country manor. There had been no mayday signal, and ATC had confirmed that they had lost contact with the pilot soon after the plane passed over Sevenoaks. The air traffic controller had confirmed that he could still see the plane on his screen but the pilot was not answering his calls. Perhaps the pilot had died of a heart attack at the controls.

Another thought burrowed its way into Hunter's thinking. She shouldn't discount the possibility that the pilot was female given their encounter with a female pilot by the name of Lulu Harrison in a previous case.

Her train of thought wandered to the unpalatable proposition that children were in the house and had died along with their parents. That was always assuming that they had come with their parents in the first place. What if they hadn't? Her eyes widened as she stared across the water at a couple of seagulls sitting on top of the weir. What if *unaccompanied* children had been there? *Why* would they have been there? Sarah Hunter had a particular aversion to any crimes involving children including those committed by children themselves.

She next turned her attention to the owner of Tideswell Manor. Grace Kendall had named the owner as Baz Biondi, one of the icons of British pop music in the 1980s. Sarah could remember dancing around her room to his number one hits which she recorded from the radio on a clapped-out tape recorder which her Gran had given her. She also recalled seeing him live at an 80s revival concert in London around about 2010 and remembered leaving the concert wondering what all the fuss had been about. But there was no doubting that Baz Biondi was an extremely wealthy man and she knew that Tideswell was but one small part of his global property empire.

At the moment, Biondi's whereabouts were unknown. He could, of course, be in the ruins of his own manor house waiting for the arrival of the pathologists to attach a label to his big toe prior to being transported to a cool fridge in the Tunbridge Wells mortuary. Or he could be out of the country and totally unaware that he no longer had a Palladian mansion in the Kent country-side. Hunter's money was on Biondi being found at Tideswell. He was well known for his love of partying and it was doubtful that he would have missed out on this weekend thrash.

Hunter determined that they would have to look into Biondi's affairs because, if it was him who was targeted, then someone had taken desperate measures to get rid of him. But they really needed to find out who was in the mansion at the time the plane struck. That might give them more clues about where to concentrate their investigation. Identifying the pilot would be top priority although Grace Kendall was already on to establishing the history of the aircraft and its flight log. They should have that information today so Hunter had a quick look at her phone to check for any messages. Nothing of any interest in her inbox so she would chase it up when she got back to the station.

Reluctantly, she got up from the table and retraced her steps to the car. She drove back to Hampstead Lock and then carried on to rejoin the Maidstone Road. At the roundabout with Seven Mile Lane, she decided to continue her ramble through the countryside so went straight across the roundabout and on to Hale Street. She was so busy turning over all the questions about the plane crash in her mind that she nearly missed the turning into Old Road and reckoned she had deserved the blare of the car horn as administered by the driver behind her.

She drove through the village of East Peckham and then turned onto Snoll Hatch Road which gave way to Addlestead Road before she joined yet another Tonbridge Road. How many Tonbridge Roads were there in Kent? she wondered. The next landmark she recognised was The Man of Kent pub which she remembered visiting with Ted Selitto in the early days of their working together. She was the new girl in town and he was out to impress her with his knowledge of country pubs. Happy days!

Eventually Tonbridge Road became Three Elm Lane and she raised a salute to The Carpenters Arms before she popped out onto the Hadlow Road and made her way back to the police station at Pembury Road.

12

Tuesday 28 April

Sarah Hunter got back to Pembury Road mid-afternoon and immediately headed for the Ops Room. It seemed quieter than usual for an afternoon shift so she was relieved to see Acting DS Elaine Jennings and DC Azzar Mishraz who were in discussion with DS Grace Kendall. In the far corner of the room, DC Jed Crowther appeared to be having an animated conversation with DS Angie Marshall and DC Lisa Calder. In another corner of the room, DC Carolyn Pennant was sitting on her own at one of the desks concentrating on information she was reading from a computer screen.

They had all become aware of Hunter's arrival in the room, and now responded to her hand signals as she ushered them towards the spare office across the corridor.

Once they had all squeezed into the room and the door had been closed, Hunter gave them a quick run-down of her visit to Maidstone, and the request from DCI Pennington that they should get on with the investigation into the plane crash but keep him and SCD in the loop.

'That's going to put a big workload on to us,' she told the team, 'but it should also help us to get things done without feeling that the powers-that-be are constantly looking over our shoulders.' She then asked Crowther to brief them on what progress was being made at Tideswell Manor.

'Things are moving reasonably well,' he reported. 'They've got tons of scaffolding up which is now supporting what's left of the structure, and the experts have declared that it is safe for everyone to be working in amongst the ruins. This will particularly facilitate the removal of the rest of the bodies. However, they do have to stop working from time to time so that the engineers can check their sensors to make sure that the supporting structure isn't about to collapse.'

'Okay!' Hunter sounded impatient. 'What about the plane?'

'I think it's going to be moved tomorrow morning. They've brought in some sophisticated equipment which has created a space between the tangled wreckage of the plane and the walls of the building which were virtually covering the fuse-lage. They're hoping to get it out in one piece but the fear is that the part of the building where the plane hit will collapse which could bring the rest of the mansion down. Anyway, once the plane's out and the building has been further secured, the Crime Scene Investigators will have much more room to work in.'

'Have the CSIs been excluded up to now?' Hunter asked.

'Seems that they have been poking about in the peripheral areas of the mansion but it hasn't been safe enough for them to operate within what's left of the actual building.'

After Crowther had finished his report, Jennings summarised the visit that she and Mishraz had made to the home of Julie Buckley earlier in the day.

'It looks like there's something going on with Rachael Buckley so we're examining some of the evidence we took away from the house earlier. We've got a phone which her mother knew nothing about so the techies are going to take a look at that. And I'm getting a warrant for a full-scale search of Rachael's bedroom. There are loads of books in there which could provide more clues as to what she's up to. She's also got a weird collection of snow globes, but at the moment we can't decide whether they are relevant or not. Seems a funny thing for a child to collect even though she seems to have an aversion to dolls and teddy bears.'

'And this girl's been missing since when?' Hunter asked.

'Well, we don't really know because her mother was away clubbing in Margate for forty-eight hours from Friday to Sunday. She only discovered the girl missing when she got home on Sunday evening and found that her bed hadn't been slept in.'

'And didn't report it until today?' Hunter asked for clarification.

'No. Usual story. Thought she'd turn up. Probably stayed at a friend's and had then gone to school as normal on Monday. I think it was when the school rang the mother to find out why Rachael wasn't at school that she started to get really worried but she still waited until today to come in here.'

'Anything else?'

'Well, our first thought was that Rachael might be involved in county lines drugs judging by the wraps we found in a hollowed-out book. We didn't have time to go through all the books or, indeed, to have a detailed look around the room so we don't know if there is any cash hidden there. But my money's on the phone being the 'line' to take the orders for drugs. It's often called the deal line. Rory Easton was telling me recently that one of the ways you could tell if children were getting involved with this sort of thing was an increase in anti-social behaviour. Well, from what Julie Buckley said, it seems that Rachael certainly ticked that box. We've yet to check on her attendance at school but truancy could be another indicator.'

'Okay, thanks for that Elaine. You and Azzar keep on with that one.'

Hunter looked round the room.

'Where is Rory Easton, anyway?' she asked. 'I haven't seen him for a while now and Angie says she hasn't seen him for about a week.'

'I haven't seen him since last week,' Kendall reported. The others shook their heads. No one had seen DC Rory Easton who was normally based at Tonbridge but occasionally worked on cases with the Kent & Essex Serious Crime Directorate. He was highly respected for his knowledge of how criminal drugs gangs are set up, and had helped Hunter and her team in past investigations.

'Okay, let's get on,' Hunter said impatiently. 'Carolyn, I want you to be our link to the pathologists. Stick with them and find out anything that's going to help us identify the bodies. Also, anything else that's going to help our investigation. Getting IDs is the main thing. We need to know exactly who was in that mansion.'

Pennant scribbled herself a note on her pad, her insides churning at the thought of being stuck at the morgue for days on end. She could only manage a weak smile when she looked up and saw that Hunter was still looking at her.

Sarah knew that her directive hadn't gone down well with Pennant but it was a matter of getting the best value out of the limited resources she had available to her. She knew the importance of identifying the victims of the crash at the earliest opportunity so she really needed someone to be on station at the morgue. With Jennings and Mishraz tied up with the Buckley case, Carolyn Pennant was the only other option.

She looked around the room, her eyes alighting on Crowther.

'Jed, I want you and Lisa to continue monitoring events at Tideswell.' Hunter told him. 'Report back on everything that's going on. Try not to be too much of a nuisance to the CSIs but, at the same time, we need to get their take on what they're uncovering. We don't want to be waiting for their report in order to make progress here.'

Crowther grunted which Hunter took to mean that he was happy with his assignment. Lisa nodded enthusiastically – a good sign, Sarah thought.

'You should also take some time to have a good look at the area around the crash site,' Hunter continued. 'Speak to some of the locals. Did they see or hear anything? Take a look at the flight path. Did the aircraft come in over the water? If it crossed land, is there any sign that bits were falling off the plane which would explain its loss of height and ultimate demise? I know that the AAIB will be all over this so you may have to cosy up to them in your search for quality information.'

Sarah knew that the Air Accident Investigation Branch was responsible for investigating all civil aviation accidents and serious incidents. She also knew that they already had a team at Tideswell Manor who were conducting their own investigation. Crowther would do well to get in with the AAIB team so that they could share information and, at the same time, he could build up his own bank of knowledge about the crash.

'Okay, Grace, what have you got for us?' Hunter asked, turning to DS Kendall who had been quietly making notes at one of the desks in the room.

'Well, I've been liaising with the AAIB who gave me permission to speak to Biggin Hill directly so I have managed to listen to the voice recording of the messages exchanged between the control tower and the aircraft. If you've ever listened to any communication between a pilot and an air traffic controller, the exchanges can best be described as anodyne. However, this was quite a short flight and, after three or four minutes, the controller noticed that the plane had changed course without seeking permission. It wouldn't have mattered if the course correction had been by a couple of degrees or so, but this change was in the region of forty degrees. The controller also noticed that the plane was losing altitude. On several occasions, he tries to make contact with the pilot without success. In the end, all he can do is watch his flight control screen as the aircraft continues to make more minor course corrections before losing more height and eventually disappearing altogether. It hit Tideswell Manor soon after that.'

'So, the pilot just stopped broadcasting did he?' Hunter enquired.

'Well that's what it sounds like – yes,' Kendall agreed.

'Could he have had a heart attack or some other catastrophic medical failure?' Pennant wanted to know.

'Early thoughts are that a heart attack may, indeed, be the cause so it will be important to retrieve the body and then get this confirmed through the PM. But my contact with the AAIB said that it was puzzling that the aircraft continued to fly, gradually losing height before burying itself in the manor house. He said it was almost as if it had been flown deliberately at the building. Which begs the question …'

'Fuck's sake!' Hunter exclaimed. 'I was only thinking about that earlier! You mean like that guy who slammed a passenger jet into a mountain a few years ago?'

'Andreas Lubitz,' Kendall said, reading from her notebook. 'Yes, that sort of thing.'

There was silence in the room.

'Well, I suppose it's a possibility,' Hunter eventually said. 'So, it's vital that they get the pilot out as soon as possible. And, Jed, it's probably more important that you liaise with the AAIB investigators who are no doubt searching for any parts which might have fallen off the plane. Perhaps there was a catastrophic equipment failure. Perhaps the comms system was only receiving from the tower so the pilot was unable to send a mayday. Perhaps he tried to land the plane but Tideswell Manor got in the way. Perhaps he was trying to land on Bewl Water but over-cooked it. Perhaps, perhaps, perhaps!'

She looked around the room. There were a lot of nodding heads, each member of the team gradually realising that they were going to have to dig deep to get clues which would help their investigation.

'Okay, Grace, what about the aeroplane?'

'From the limited information we have been given by the AAIB, the plane is a King Air 350 and is owned by Heragh Air Leasing, a company registered in Dublin.' Kendall was now reading from her notes. 'Even though it was owned by an Irish company, it was registered by the CAA here in the UK. Apparently, Ireland is one of the biggest centres for airline leasing in the world with many of the world's biggest airline leasing companies based there. Heragh is not a major player but seems to thrive in the small private jet sector of the market.'

Jed Crowther wanted to know a bit more about the aircraft which had flown into Tideswell Manor, either accidentally or on purpose. 'So, our aeroplane is owned by Heragh but will have been flown by whichever company was leasing it at the time. Do we know who that is?'

'Not at the moment, I'm afraid,' Grace replied. 'Protocol dictates that investigators must be absolutely certain of the identity of the plane and that the lessee must have been informed before official confirmation can be given. Normally, this doesn't take too long so I am expecting to get this information very soon.'

'And is there an identity for the pilot?' Crowther continued.

Hunter looked across at Grace and gave a slight nod of her head to indicate that she should take that question.

'Preliminary information is that the pilot was identified on the flight manifest as John Smith,' Kendall started, 'but we think it's unlikely to be his real identity. So, information gathered at the PM will be crucial. However, just in case he really is John Smith, the CAA are sending me details of all registered pilots with the name John Smith and we'll just have to check them out.'

'What if John Smith is not British and, therefore, not on the CAA register?' This time it was Lisa Calder asking the question.

Kendall flicked over a couple of pages on her notepad.

'As I understand it, a pilot from a country outside the UK is required to hold a licence or certificate issued by the International Civil Aviation Organisation otherwise known as the ICAO. This is then validated by the CAA for a limited duration during which time the pilot is allowed to fly within UK airspace. So, it would appear that if John Smith is not a British citizen, then his details should still be with the CAA.'

'And if he's not John Smith then presumably, whoever he is, his details will still have to be with the CAA,' Hunter surmised.

'Technically!' Grace concurred with a nod of her head.

'Okay, thanks Grace. We're obviously going to encounter problems in that direction but keep on it. When they get the body out of the plane, then stick closely with the pathologists and anyone else involved with identification.'

Hunter was keen to let them all get back to work so decided to bring the briefing to a close.

'There's clearly a lot of bureaucracy and red tape attached to investigations of this nature so we'll probably have to exercise a certain amount of patience. But do let me know if you feel that any one of these organisations is deliberately holding up the flow of information.'

Hunter looked round the room to see if there were any further questions but none seemed to be forthcoming.

'One final point before you all get back to your investigations,' she added before telling them about her meeting with Margot Westwood.

'So, the chiefs will be conducting any press conferences using information provided initially by us via SCD. All other press enquiries are to be channelled through Westwood. If you do get any requests for information from journos, and that may only be you, Jed, and you, Lisa, when you're out at the site, you must refer them back to me in the first instance. Do not enter into any discussion with anyone from any media outlet even if your paths have crossed before.'

There was a general nodding of heads. Hunter knew that most of her team had little time for members of the press corps so she was fairly confident that no one would be contacting anyone from the media – but she felt that she had to issue this edict all the same.

Bringing the meeting to a close, she watched as everyone filed out of the room. She turned and absent-mindedly wandered across to the window, her mind fretting over one unanswered question amongst many.

Where the hell was Rory Easton?

13
Tuesday 28 April

It was that time in the evening when fading twilight heralded the end of another long and exhausting day. Sarah Hunter was now thankfully on her journey home, picking her way through the darkening country lanes which would eventually deliver her to her little cottage.

She might have been driving home a little earlier had not DCI Alan Iversen put his head round the door of the Ops Room and requested an update as he was on his way out of the building. Mercifully, their impromptu meeting had not been either arduous or long, and had mainly been an opportunity for Sarah to bring her boss up to speed with developments over the last forty-eight hours. At least it would give him something to tell his bosses in the morning.

Whilst driving, Sarah had been busily reviewing and analysing the events of the past twelve hours during which her investigation had become a rollercoaster of a ride with one central question beginning to exercise her powers of detection – was this simply a tragic accident or was it, in fact, something far more sinister?

One way or another, it was still her job to work out what *had* happened at Tideswell Manor and who, if anyone, was directly responsible for all the deaths. After all, on joining the Police, she had taken the oath to, amongst other things, cause the peace to be kept and preserved and to prevent all offences against people and property. She had never forgotten that day when she had proudly proclaimed the oath in front of her fellow recruits as they had passed out of training college, and the words often gave her strength when she was feeling the pressure of an investigation.

She passed through the hamlet of Mockbeggar. Not far now.

Slowing to allow a huge four-by-four to pass by on the narrow road, her mind returned to the mansion. She needed to know more about this man, Baz Biondi, and his whereabouts. Was he now lying in a fridge at the morgue or was he sitting on a beach on the other side of the world watching the tragedy play out on TV? Was he responsible for the destruction of his own mansion or had someone else done it for him? And who were all those people who had been killed when the plane struck?

She was so deep in thought that she nearly missed the narrow entrance to the winding lane which led to her cottage. It was now almost dark and she was relieved when her headlights picked out a black mini which was partially buried in the foliage just off the tarmacked surface opposite her cottage. She drove on past it to a layby further down the lane where she carried out a very presentable three-point turn before returning and parking on an area of gravel just outside her front door. She could never face doing that manoeuvre first thing in the morning so she made sure that the car was always pointing in the right direction at the end of the day.

Sarah let herself into the small hallway and, after locking up the front door for the night, she made straight for the kitchen.

'You managed to get away then!' The cheery voice of Grace Kendall greeted Sarah as she flopped down on the carver chair at the head of the huge refectory table which was the centre-piece of her kitchen. Grace poured a generous glass of red wine from the bottle which stood beside the cooker and passed it across the table to her dear friend.

'*Finally*!' Sarah stressed the word as she had hoped to be here before now. But it was never easy when there were bosses who were always looking for progress updates and needed to be constantly briefed on the minutiae of an investigation.

Grace brought her own glass of wine to the table and slid onto one of the benches so that she was facing the cooker and could keep an eye on the three pans which covered much of the hob.

'Spag boll tonight, I'm afraid. Didn't have the mental capacity to consider anything more exciting. Only just managed to get to Chatfields before it closed.'

They clinked glasses and Sarah took a decent glug of wine before setting her glass down on the table.

A professional friendship between the two detectives had gradually become more than that over the last few months with Sarah and Grace enjoying each other's company away from the inquisitive eyes of their colleagues at the Pembury Road station.

The general guidelines were that relationships between serving officers were not strictly forbidden per se but that they might be frowned upon if the officers involved were at the same station and working together every single day. Sarah and Grace had discussed this at some length before concluding that they both felt that their work ethic would not be compromised by their relationship away from the work environment.

Grace had a small riverside apartment in the centre of Tonbridge but they generally preferred to meet at Sarah's cottage which was buried deep in the countryside away from prying eyes. In any event, Sarah much preferred sleeping in her own bed at night so it suited her that they should meet at her house.

Several months previously, an enjoyable evening at a local Thai restaurant had turned to acute embarrassment in Grace's apartment when the two women had allowed their pent up feelings for each other to boil over. In the ensuing passionate embrace, their lips had clashed in a fury of expectation as their hands tentatively explored and their bodies became tightly entwined. Until Sarah had suddenly extricated herself from Grace's arms before fleeing from the apartment.

After that, they had carefully avoided addressing the matter until one evening they had found themselves alone in the Ops Room. At Grace's suggestion they had talked through that fateful evening before both agreeing that it should not be a barrier to enjoying each other's company if that was what they wanted. And, as time had gone by, they had begun meeting at Sarah's cottage where they felt free from the shackles of their stressful working environment.

Neither Sarah nor Grace had had a previous relationship with a woman before, but they soon became willing companions. They had, however, both agreed that they would prefer their relationship to be more platonic than anything else and, although they slept together in Sarah's huge bed on the nights when they were with each other, there was nothing more physical between them than a kiss and a cuddle before sleep took its natural course.

Hunter had kicked off her flatties and had just taken a second glug of the red wine when her phone started to vibrate on the table in front of her. She glanced at Grace and shrugged her shoulders before picking up the phone and looking at the screen. Caller ID was Jed Crowther so she decided to take the call.

'Sorry to call you late in the evening, ma'am,' he started, 'but there's been a bit of a game changer down at Tideswell. The rescue services have managed to partially release the aircraft this evening so that the medics could get to the pilot. But when they got into what was left of the cockpit, there was no pilot.'

Hunter wasn't quite sure that she had heard Crowther correctly.

'No pilot?' she questioned, trying to sound calm.

'No pilot!' came the reply.

'Fuck's sake! Are they completely sure about that?' she asked, now staring at Kendall who was sitting with a quizzical look on her face.

'Apparently the cockpit was virtually destroyed in the crash but there are no signs of human remains in the wreckage. There's also no sign of a body in the rest of the fuselage. In short, it looks as if the plane crashed into the mansion without anyone flying it.'

'Bloody hell. That really is a game changer!'

Hunter's mind was racing as she tried desperately to see where this news might be taking her investigation.

'Okay, stay on this, Jed. Are you at Tideswell?'

'Not quite,' he replied. 'Thought I'd get down there and get as much intel as I can. I'll text you when I get more updates.'

'Yes, good,' she replied, 'or call me if it's easier. Don't mind what time it is – I probably won't be sleeping anyway. We desperately need to know what happened to the pilot.'

Disconnecting the call, Sarah continued staring at Grace Kendall.

'Would you bloody believe it? There's no pilot on board the crashed plane.'

'I rather gathered that,' Grace replied. 'And there's absolutely no trace of a human being in the whole of the aircraft?'

'That's what they're saying. Did he know that the plane was doomed so he just jumped out? Could have been quite close to the crash site if it was a genuine emergency and he thought he could survive the fall. Perhaps over forestation or over Bewl Water itself?'

'Presume the AAIB will be getting a search organised,' Kendall said as she got up from the table and crossed the room to retrieve her laptop from her rucksack. 'Let's see if I can get a satellite image of the area so that we can have a look at what terrain the flight path might have covered?'

She soon found a map of the area around Tideswell Manor, and they both sat back staring at it.

'Well, that gives us a big clue,' she said, looking across at Hunter.

'Hmm!' Hunter was still staring at the screen. 'So, there's something wrong with the plane, the pilot's lost control, he's losing height and possibly power, he realises that the plane is doomed but he knows he's near Bewl Water so he manages to make a course correction. Once over the water, he takes his chance and jumps for his life before the plane reaches land again. The plane continues to fly on, gradually losing height until it crashes into Tideswell Manor which just happened to be in the way.'

'But, if the plane was in trouble, why didn't he at least make contact with the guy at Biggin TC?' Kendall asked. 'As I recall from listening to the tape, the controller kept trying to contact the plane but there was no reply from the pilot. I think the first recorded non-response transmission was when the plane veered onto a different course just past Sevenoaks.'

'He must have still been in the aircraft at that point,' Hunter surmised, although she knew next to nothing about flying and certainly nothing about how a pilot would have to react in an emergency.

Lost in thought, they both continued to stare at the screen, the image of Bewl Water depicting the gnarled root system of an old oak tree.

'So, are we back to thinking that the pilot deliberately crashed the plane into the mansion?' Hunter had an uncomfortable feeling that this scenario was quickly becoming more likely. 'Of course he doesn't answer ATC because he's setting his own course and nobody can do anything about that. He follows the countryside down towards Bewl then sets his sights on Tideswell before parachuting out of the plane and landing in the water. The plane then flies on and splatters itself all over the mansion. Job done!'

Grace gave Hunter one of her quizzical looks, left eyebrow arched. Had she taken leave of her senses? Perhaps she had been watching too many James Bond movies.

'Sounds like the advert with that man who delivered the milk chocolates,' Kendall quipped, getting up from the table and moving over to the cooker. 'Anyway, how does the pilot get the plane to fly directly at Tideswell if he bails out?'

'I don't know!' Hunter was becoming frustrated about her lack of technical knowledge. 'Could he have used some sort of guidance system so that the plane was guided to the mansion? He knew what height it would be at when it was over the water so he jumped at the appropriate moment, probably with a parachute, and in the knowledge that the plane would fly on to its destination because it was being guided there.'

Grace was stirring the contents of one of the pans, deep in thought.

'If you're right,' she eventually said in response to Hunter's hypothesis, 'the guidance system as you describe it would probably have needed some sort of receiver at the mansion that the plane could lock onto in order to guide it to its destination.'

'Blimey! Hadn't thought of that,' Hunter replied. 'So, the pilot could simply switch the plane onto auto-pilot which then somehow transmitted signals to a receiver on the ground? And would the receiver then guide the plane to the intended crash site? No idea!'

'Well, if you're right, the AAIB guys will no doubt find a transmitter in the wreckage of the plane.' Grace leaned across the table to rescue her glass and took a sip before turning back to the cooker hob.

Hunter was sitting back in her chair, thoughts swirling around in her head. If this was, in fact, a carefully planned attack which had the sole purpose of killing innocent people, then they were looking for a mass murderer. But who had Baz Biondi crossed that would want to wreak such dreadful revenge? They urgently needed to establish whether Biondi was buried in the rubble or whether he was elsewhere. It was now over forty eight hours since the plane had struck and the 1980s rocker had yet to break cover.

Surely he would have heard about the demise of his precious mansion if he was still alive?

14
Wednesday 29 April

It wasn't often that Sarah Hunter found herself in a quandary. She didn't like quandaries. The uncertainties. The dilemmas. What should she concentrate on? She knew that Toby Swartzman was already having to consider alternative accommodation for all the bodies which had been taken from Tideswell Manor to the morgue, and that identification had become a slow and laborious task. Carolyn Pennant was quite capable of keeping an eye on what was going on at the morgue so Hunter didn't need to be there as well.

Should she be initiating a search for the pilot? Or was that a job for the AAIB? Or were they only interested in finding out why the plane crashed? Well that should be straightforward, she thought facetiously, because no one was flying the bloody thing! Anyway, could the pilot have survived a fall from the aircraft onto water? It might have been possible with a parachute, she reasoned. And if he did jump with a parachute, surely someone must have seen him?

God! She needed Ted Selitto here to help her get her thoughts into some semblance of order.

She had endured a restless night, busily turning all the information over in her mind following Crowther's revelation about the pilot. Grace had said that she would be prioritising the lists which Elaine Jennings had lifted from Rachael Buckley's room. They had to mean something, and the sooner they could understand the significance of the information, the sooner they could perhaps find the girl.

On her way along the corridor to get a coffee, she fished her phone out of the pocket of her jeans and was just about to call Crowther when it sprang into life in her hand. Incoming from Elaine Jennings.

'How's it going, Elaine,' Hunter snapped, immediately regretting her insensitivity.

'Not very well, I'm afraid,' came the reply. 'Looks like someone's beaten us to it. They've also given Julie Buckley a hell of a beating. Medics think she might not pull through. Currently being blue-lighted to hospital. We'll take a good look around here but the CSIs have had to send for reinforcements.'

'Shit!' Hunter replied. 'That's all we need.'

'The search team got here nice and early but found the front door open,' Jennings continued. 'Buckley was lying in a pool of blood with serious head injuries. Looked as if she had been subjected to a good kicking as well. The girl's room has been ransacked and much of the rest of the house has been trashed. Azzar's doing a bit of house-to-house with the immediate neighbours, and I've sent for some of our uniformed colleagues to see if anyone in the street saw or heard anything.'

'Okay, stay with it.'

Hunter disconnected the call. Now she had to deal with an attack on a woman who had reported her eleven-year-old daughter missing. An incident which appeared to be completely unrelated to the crash at Tideswell Manor.

Back in the Ops Room with a cup of coffee in hand, she took a seat next to Grace Kendall and stared vacantly at the two screens on Grace's desk whilst filling her in on the phone call from Jennings.

'Anyway, have you managed to have a look at the info from

the Buckley house?' Hunter was keen to get on so that she could get away from Pembury Road and make herself useful either at Tideswell Manor, at the morgue or even at the Buckley house. She did need to keep a handle on how the identification process was going so perhaps she should be at the morgue.

'Yes. That book on volcanos was quite a find!' Grace was saying. She activated the cursor and a picture of one of the pages in the book appeared on the screen. She enlarged the area of the page which clearly had a child's handwriting on it.

'We've got postcodes, dates and times. The postcodes aren't all local to Tonbridge but the areas look as if they can be easily accessed by rail from Tonbridge. Although the times don't differentiate between a.m. and p.m. it seems sensible to assume that they are between six o'clock in the morning and six o'clock at night. Many of the dates are weekends although some are on weekdays. We'll need to check with the school to see whether the girl was absent on those days.'

'So, what are you thinking?'

'I reckon that she's been running drugs to people in these postcode areas, and that these are dates and times for the drop-offs. Most of the dates have now passed but there are a couple in the near future.'

Sarah Hunter wished that she knew more about how county lines worked but, for now, she would just have to rely on instinct and common sense.

'So, she gets this information from the phone and writes it down in her volcano book,' Sarah hypothesised. 'She's then got to get supplied somehow and then takes whatever public transport she can get to make the deliveries.'

'Yes, but don't forget that she's disappeared so she might be holed up with someone who will drive to every drop,' Kendall interjected. 'Anyway, one of the dates is tomorrow. Postcode's in the area of the High Street in Ashford. That's all pedestrianised if I recall so there may be some CCTV in operation there. Trouble is, we don't really know what the girl looks like. The photo that Elaine got from the mother is almost worse than useless.'

'Yeah, but two people dealing might stick out like a sore thumb, particularly if there aren't many people about,' Hunter surmised. 'But, presumably, these drops *have* to be made – some of these people are desperately dependent on the drugs. Perhaps we should get someone from the local nick to take a look. You've got a time haven't you?'

Kendall nodded.

'Do you know anyone down there?'

Kendall nodded again.

'Good. When's the other one?'

'Saturday. I think it says TN33 0AE which means that it is another High Street, this time in Battle.'

'Ah, over the county line!' Hunter exclaimed. 'Better get in touch with Hastings and see if they can take a look. We don't really want to send plain clothes down there in case they're asked to answer questions about why we're operating on their patch. All it needs is one nosey Traffic guy.'

'Interesting choice of locations,' Kendall remarked, sitting back in her chair. 'Both High Streets have numerous little alleyways leading off them which gives great cover for the drops to be made. Might be difficult to see exactly what is going on without completely blowing one's cover.'

They sat in silence for a minute or two as the Ops Room

started to fill up with officers who were now returning from early morning calls.

Eventually, Hunter let out an extended sigh.

'We still need a better description of the Buckley girl,' she concluded. 'Don't they still do individual end-of-year pupil photos at primary schools?'

'Possibly,' Kendall replied. 'I'll chase up on that.'

They lapsed into silence again but it wasn't long before Hunter seemed to tire of further discussion about Rachael Buckley's disappearance.

'Perhaps the girl has simply left home!' she exclaimed, getting up and grabbing her coat off the back of the chair.

15
Wednesday 29 April

When they had arrived at Julie Buckley's house, Jennings and Mishraz had ducked under the crime scene tape as they stepped through a gap in the white wicket fence which ran across the front of the terraced house. A uniformed PC had made a note of their names before pointing to a box beside him.

'Overshoes, gloves and masks must be worn inside,' he had informed them before confirming the imminent arrival of the CSIs.

The detectives had pulled on the overshoes, slipped their hands into the clammy embrace of the nitrile gloves and looped the masks behind their ears. They had then ducked under another strand of crime scene tape and were now once again standing in the doorway of the front room of the house.

'No sign of forced entry,' Jennings observed as she looked back towards the open front door.

If it were at all possible, the room was even more chaotic than it had been on their first visit. The doors of the tumble driers had all but been wrenched off and their contents had been scattered around the room. Foam padding was spewing out of jagged slashes in the settee's covering The TV was sitting at a drunken angle on the floor next to one of the driers, a huge crack spreading across the screen. It was clear that this room had witnessed an orgy of violence.

Jennings noticed a smear of blood across the wall to her left as she eased her way into the next room. Damage was extensive in this room, and she soon realised she was walking on broken glass as she crunched her way towards the kitchen. This was where Julie Buckley had presumably been cornered like a frightened animal. However, she hadn't had the wherewithal to either fight or escape judging by the amount of blood which covered the floor and the single worktop. Blood-soaked kitchen knives told their own sorry tale.

'Okay, let's get upstairs before the CSIs get here,' Jennings murmured as she turned back towards the steep staircase that would take them up to the girl's bedroom.

The scene which greeted them at the top of the stairs wasn't much different to the carnage downstairs. The room to the right of the staircase was, indeed, another bedroom which had now been well and truly ransacked. They quickly moved on to Rachael's room which, not surprisingly, had also been trashed. It was doubtful that any of the snow globes were still in one piece, and all the books had been flung to the four corners of the room. The shelves had been reduced to matchwood.

The bed had been stripped, and there were great gouges in the mattress where the stuffing had been unceremoniously pulled out. Drawers had been removed from the chest and clothes had been scattered on the floor. The wardrobe had similarly been emptied.

Jennings stepped into the room and then stopped. She put one arm out to prevent Mishraz from going any further.

'Look at the chest of drawers,' she commanded. 'Are my eyes deceiving me or is that bottom drawer still in its place?'

'Sure looks like it,' he replied.

They both inched their way across the room trying not to step on any of the evidence. It certainly looked as if the drawer hadn't been opened. Mishraz squatted down in front of the chest. The drawer above the bottom had been removed altogether and the one above that was hanging open, clothes spilling from it. But the bottom drawer hadn't been moved.

'Must've got interrupted,' Mishraz suggested as he gently eased the drawer open. Jennings squatted down beside him and they both stared at its contents.

'Looks pretty much as we left it,' Jennings noted as she reached in to pick up one of the books. Opening it up, she remembered that its pages had been hollowed out and she had removed a couple of wraps of what had looked like cocaine.

'Okay, Azzar, let's have a quick look through these books before the CSIs get here. I'm not interested in cash or wraps – we can leave that to forensics. But it would be great if we could find another phone. That's what we really want.'

Mishraz nodded as Jennings stood up and looked at the devastation around her. Stepping away from the chest of drawers, her foot kicked something that skittered across the floor and crashed into the skirting board. Looking down, she saw that it was a tiny model of a reindeer which had been covered in white paint to represent snow. Tiny particles of fake snow lay on the floor alongside the smashed glass dome, the liquid pooling around it.

Jennings stared at the floor around her, at the smashed and broken snow globes which had disgorged their contents in this frenzied attack. Were these little ornaments of any significance or did the girl just like them? She couldn't see how they could have any relevance to a county lines gang. Had they been given to her in exchange for drugs? Surely not! They had no intrinsic value. Perhaps they had some coded meaning. What was the name on that one she had seen on her last visit? *Apocalyptic*

Nightmare? What on earth could that be code for? No, it would be best to get them tested by forensics and then review their significance. At least she had taken a photo of them all sitting on the shelf during her last visit.

There was a sudden commotion downstairs which, Jennings suspected, heralded the arrival of the CSIs, their cases of scientific kit crashing against walls and furniture as they tried to negotiate the tiny confines of the house. She left Mishraz in the bedroom and carefully descended the steep stairs, attracting the attention of Crime Scenes Officer Donny Campbell as she reached the bottom step.

'Hello, Elaine, didn't expect to see you here,' he said brightly as he looked for somewhere to put all the equipment he was carrying.

'Just having a quick look round before you guys start covering everything with the magic dust,' she replied, smiling. 'Looks like you'll need to concentrate on the kitchen through there. In fact, it looks like the victim was only assaulted downstairs – nothing upstairs to indicate that she was up there when she was attacked.'

'Okay, sounds good,' Campbell replied, eventually finding a space just inside the kitchen to rest the cases he had been carrying.

'Blimey!' he exclaimed as he cast his eyes around the little room. 'And you say the woman's still alive?'

Jennings detected a tone of incredulity in Campbell's voice.

'Well, she was last time we heard,' she replied.

'Certainly a scene of torture which we don't see too often these days. They've even laid out all the bloody implements for us,' he commented as he wafted an arm over the worksurface.

'Oh well, better get started. Anything else?'

'Yep. The daughter's bedroom. Looks like she could be involved with county lines. We've already found some wraps, cash and a mobile. Anything else would be a bonus although the room may have been cleaned out by the gang that almost killed the mother. Hopefully, you'll get some good prints and anything else will be a bonus.'

'Right, we'll take a look at that,' Campbell grunted as he popped the latches on one of the crime scenes cases, opening it up to reveal an array of small bottles of powders and liquids.

'One other thing you could take a look at,' Jennings continued. 'The girl had a collection of snow globes. Most of them are now smashed on the floor. Can't work out if they're significant or not. Perhaps you could run some tests on the contents or what you can find of the contents. You might also want to check for any loose floorboards.'

At this point, she noticed Mishraz standing on the bottom stair. He flicked his head towards the front of the house and then headed for the entrance.

'Okay, I'll leave it in your capable hands, Donny. When can we expect the report?'

'Couple of days.'

Jennings gave him a thumbs-up before creeping back through the house towards the front door. She took her over-shoes, gloves and mask off and tossed them into the bin by the door. Mishraz was already on the pavement outside the house, and she joined him as they walked towards the car. As they got further away from the house, he made a point of patting his pocket.

'Found another one!'

16

Wednesday 29 April

Puddles of black water stretched across the ground towards what remained of the grand entrance to Tideswell Manor. The air was still redolent of the smell of burnt materials, and there was also an underlying odour which reminded Sarah Hunter of the tragedy of a house fire which she had investigated whilst in the Met. The smell of burnt flesh held a special place in the sensory memory banks of every police officer who had ever attended a crime scene involving fire and human beings.

The sun was shining through the ruins in front of her which brought a somewhat ethereal beauty to a scene of such devastation, and she shaded her eyes as she continued her inspection of the site accompanied by the Crime Scenes Manager, Beth Dench.

'The problem we've had with the structure,' Dench was saying, 'is that it was already in quite an advanced state of decay. Many of the beams were rotten and the huge pillars holding the building up had suffered extensive erosion over the many years they had been in place. It might have looked good from the outside but, within the four walls, it was a disaster waiting to happen. The arrival of the aircraft was a bit like lighting the blue touch paper.'

They negotiated their way around an enormous skip which was being winched into place on the back of a skip loader lorry ready for transportation back to the forensics labs in Maidstone.

'When the aircraft hit,' Dench continued, 'it had the similar effect of taking one of the bottom cards out of a house of cards – the whole lot collapsed in on itself. In fact, not unlike those horrendous images of the World Trade Centre towers when they collapsed in 2001. This has meant that we have had an unimaginably difficult job to prise all the levels of the manor apart in order to search for bodies. Those on the lower levels were simply crushed to death, and those on the higher levels were consumed by the fire. I doubt that anyone stood a chance of escape.'

The sound of masonry drills echoed through the eerie emptiness of the building as they got closer, and Hunter could see banks of floodlights set up around the area to make sure that nothing was missed. The crime scene investigation team, dressed in their all-white protective clothing, were painstakingly removing the rubble and constantly checking for any signs of life or any evidence that might provide more clues to what actually happened here. Suddenly, a klaxon sounded and the drilling ceased. Everyone stopped working and stood still.

'That's a signal that either a noise has been heard or something has been noticed which requires immediate investigation,' Dench whispered as they reached the edge of the scaffolding which now surrounded what was left of the mansion. They stood and watched as three CSI technicians converged on an area of masonry which had been recently worked on. After a few minutes, one of them looked up and made a hand signal whereupon the klaxon sounded again and the drilling restarted.

'False alarm!' Dench exclaimed with a sigh.

They walked on down one side of the building, keeping outside the line of scaffolding, and then turned the corner so that they were now at the back of the mansion. Two portacabins had been placed about fifty metres from the rear entrance, and there were three forensic tents with a Kent Police logo emblazoned on each.

'We're pretty much 24/7 here so one of the cabins is our office and the other affords space for resting and sleeping. Haven't tried the sleeping accommodation myself but the team seem to think it's okay.'

'And the tents?' Hunter asked although she suspected that she already knew the answer.

'They're the first port of call for any bodies which have been recovered,' Dench continued. 'We've got some basic equipment in there which we can use to prepare them for the journey to the morgue. It just helps Dr Swartzman and his team who are on the receiving end.'

Turning towards a gaping hole in the rear of the building, Dench beckoned Hunter to follow her as they entered what had probably been the kitchen area. They picked their way through piles of rubble and larger sections of masonry which could have once formed the outside wall around the rear entrance to the property. There was water everywhere and, looking up, Hunter could see stubby joists of blackened wood which had once held the upper floors in place. She was thankful that she was wearing the hard hat which Beth Dench had given her when she arrived at the site.

Apart from assuming that they had just come through the kitchen area, it was difficult to picture exactly what part of the mansion they were now in. The sound of the masonry drills was a lot closer so she assumed that they must have reached the reception rooms. At that point, the klaxon sounded again and silence descended on the ruins. Hunter looked around her, in awe of the scale of devastation. Her mind was desperately trying to picture what the mansion must have been like in its pomp, and the people who must have enjoyed its hospitality over the centuries.

Eventually, the klaxon sounded again and the masonry drills resumed their cacophony of noise.

A white-suited technician in hard hat and facemask was beating a path towards them through the piles of rubble. Judging by the size of the individual, Hunter guessed it would be Jimbo Carrigan, one of Dench's CSI officers, and she wasn't disappointed when he pulled the mask down so that it was under his chin and offered her a flamboyant greeting, almost bowing in the process.

'It's been a while, Jimbo,' Hunter agreed. 'Prism Theatre last year?'

'Sure was!' Carrigan nodded as he turned to address his boss.

'You know we talked about the possibility of there being a cellar underneath a building of this age?'

'That's right,' Dench agreed. 'Most big country houses had cellars in which to store food and wine plus other household goods. They could keep everything cool for a start, and it helped to mature the red wine and port.'

'Well, we originally thought that its entrance might be somewhere in or near the kitchen but we had no luck there,' Carrigan continued. 'Anyway, the boys are currently drilling in what we are thinking is a large vestibule or reception area. You know, where we looked at the ruins of the staircase yesterday. And they're detecting a change in the way the sound of the drilling is coming back at them. There appears to be some hollowness underneath the stuff they're clearing.'

'Sounds interesting, Jimbo. Can we come through for a look?'

'Be my guest.'

Carrigan looked the two women up and down to make sure they were wearing all the requisite safety gear and then signalled for them to follow him.

Once they were in the area where the staircase used to be, he sounded the klaxon which brought the drilling to a halt.

'Okay guys, we've got DI Hunter with us today,' Carrigan noted, as he addressed his colleagues. 'She's the SIO on this case and is interested in our theory about location of a cellar. Can we go back to where we think it might be?'

The drilling team moved across to what, Hunter thought, certainly looked like the ruins of a rather impressive staircase. If anything, they appeared to be going behind it but she couldn't be sure bearing in mind that it was difficult to judge the layout of the floor.

Without any signal from anyone, they just got on with drilling in the area that they thought might uncover the entrance to a cellar. Sarah Hunter looked on, a knot beginning to form in her stomach. In her experience, cellars always provided nasty surprises and she was certain that this one would be no exception.

It didn't take long before the technicians had managed to clear enough masonry and other debris away to reveal the entrance to what looked like the top of a set of stone steps. The only problem was that the flight of steps had been completely filled in with one of the huge stone pillars. This discovery brought about a halt in drilling activities whilst they decided what to do about clearing the entrance to the cellar.

Hunter and Dench had been standing well away from the

work which was going on but Sarah had noticed some twisted metal which the technicians had already moved to one side, no doubt in readiness for it to be transported back to the Maidstone labs. There was something about its shape which was puzzling the DI so she beckoned Jimbo Carrigan over.

'Have you taken a look at that lump of twisted metal?' she asked as he approached.

Carrigan turned to look at what Hunter was pointing at.

'No,' he replied. 'Not even sure where it's come from.' He wandered over to where he could get a better look at it, and Hunter also crossed the broken up masonry to stand next to him. Carrigan unclipped a pair of reinforced safety gloves which were hanging from his Tyvek suit and slipped them on before attempting to move the metal object.

'Blimey, it's got some weight to it!' he exclaimed although he eventually succeeded in pulling it free of some of the rubble which had built up around it. The three of them stood and assessed the significance of what was now lying in front of them.

'Well, it's certainly a door.' Beth Dench was the first to say what they were all thinking. 'But a reinforced metal door – steel probably. That's why it's so heavy. Looks like three locking points – the handle's sheared off as well.'

Hunter squatted down to take a closer look at the underside of the door and then wished she hadn't as a searing pain shot up her left leg from an injury she had sustained to her ankle the previous year. She wanted to know if the handles on both sides of the door had sheared off so she felt around its underside. Once she had found what she was looking for, she stood up and turned to the others.

'Smooth surface on the other side – no sign of a handle.

Which can only mean one thing.'

'The door could only be opened from out here,' Beth Dench finished the sentence for her.

'Which also means that we're probably not going to like what we find when we finally get down into the cellar,' Hunter said, looking wistfully back to its stone-covered entrance.

17

Wednesday 29 April

Johnnie Arcane drew a lung-full from a freshly lit Gauloise cigarette before exhaling a cloud of thick blue smoke through his nostrils. He had always liked the smell of the French cigarettes – a mixture of burnt rubber and the chaos of the Paris metro. And he still got a little light-headed if he smoked too many in a short space of time.

Although Gauloises were no longer available over the counter in the UK, he knew where to get them – and he even treated himself to the occasional trip to Paris on Eurostar where he would head straight for the Boulevard de Clichy or the back streets around La Pigalle. After enjoying some of the delights on offer in this seedy corner of the French capital, he usually filled his half-empty holdall with all the Gauloises he could get hold of before taking a cab back to Le Gare du Nord for the journey home.

Arcane by name. Arcane by nature. Johnnie was known to very few people – and understood by even fewer. He was a mysterious, secretive manipulator who operated in a clandestine way which helped him to cover his illegal activities. He had liked the word '*arcane*' as soon as he had spotted it in a dictionary – and he had liked the ascribed meaning even better because it perfectly described the person he was. He liked to be mysterious. He was secretive. He also liked the word 'clandestine' although he'd had to look that one up too. Yes, that was him as well.

Today, he had travelled down to Bayham Old Abbey from

his base in the Medway towns. He was driving an old Citroen Nemo van which had been knocking around his cousin Dingbat's yard for a few years. Dingbat always insisted that the Nemo was ideal for low profile journeys such as today's trip into mid-Kent. Deciding to take the main roads all the way, he was relieved that neither of the two police cars that passed him seemed remotely interested in what he was doing on the road. Must have been the sign painting on the back of the van – '*NHS Medical Supplies in Transit*'. Always worked a treat.

Exiting the A21 at the end of the Lamberhurst bypass, he had driven past The Brown Trout before turning onto Furnace Lane and out into the country. He liked this part of Kent and had always wanted to come here to take a good look around. But, as with a lot of the things he wanted to do, there never seemed to be the hours to spare.

He was now parked up on a little postage stamp of gravel not far from the ruins of the old abbey. It was a warm and sunny spot and he could just see the disjointed outline of the ruins in the distance. He had considered taking a closer look but eventually decided that he wasn't interested enough in the history of the place. Better to just rest his back against the rear doors of the van and enjoy the sunshine. And the sweetness of the Gauloises.

His thoughts turned to the reason for his journey today, and the unexpected request from one of his most trusted lieutenants that they have a face-to-face meeting.

Gav was a hard-nosed bastard with a vicious temper which sometimes caused even Johnnie to be wary of him. He held the lines for one of Johnnie's largest county lines gangs which covered a considerable area of north and west Kent. Not only did he deal in drugs but he also sold weapons and was heavily into sexual exploitation. But he had recently seen his market share take a tumble as a new gang had started to muscle in on the area in which he operated. His usual enforcement methods were also being met with a vicious resistance so that Gav was having to think of new ways of keeping his punters under control. That and the fact that there had been some supply problems. So, he had demanded a meeting with Johnnie to discuss the situation. It was as if Gav held Johnnie singularly responsible for the problems he was facing.

Johnnie was already aware of the supply problems, particularly for the new drugs on the street. That had brought about an automatic increase in prices. And, if the prices went up, a marked increase in violence would be just around the corner. The scale of the violence would depend on how long the restrictions in supply lasted. But there was little he could do about that in the short term. They would all just have to find a way to adapt to the situation and hope that normal service could be resumed as soon as possible. But he also knew that there would be casualties along the way.

Johnnie was just thinking of lighting up another Gauloise when he heard a vehicle approaching, its engine spluttering as it bounced over the uneven track. Peering around the side of his van, he watched as an ageing Toyota Hilux lumbered onto the gravel, an orange light swivelling round drunkenly on the roof above the driver's compartment. As the engine was cut, the vehicle involuntarily jerked forward another couple of feet. No doubt it was still in gear, Johnnie surmised as he observed the driver jumping down from the vehicle before turning and launching a vicious kick at the side panel.

'You're a fucking heap of shite!' he shouted at the vehicle before stomping off to the back of the Hilux. Meanwhile, the orange light continued to strobe listlessly in the bright spring sunshine.

Johnnie broke cover and wandered over to the Hilux just as its driver reappeared at the other side of the vehicle.

'Having a bit of trouble, Gav?'

'Got this heap of shite from one of my bruvs didn't I. Thought the cops wouldn't notice it, you know, with its orange light an' all. Looks like I'm on a fucking call-out or something important. But I didn't realise it'd be such a pig to drive. That Boris Johnson's got a lot to answer for – making me drive around in a fucking rust bucket like this!'

Johnnie wasn't sure that it was all the ex-Prime Minister's fault that Gav was driving an ancient Hilux – at least 'ancient' based on its registration plate. But even that probably wasn't the plate originally issued for the vehicle.

Gav was still staring at the Hilux – a naked fury in his eyes. Although he had been born and bred in south London, Gav's parents were originally from Jamaica. His father was a Rastafarian and had always assumed that Gav would follow him into the faith. When Gav was old enough to understand something about Rastafarianism, he was quite taken with its traditions. He liked the way they grew their hair and beards, and the way they dressed. He particularly liked the rastacaps and started to grow his hair so that he could fill out the headgear like his father who had long dreadlocks and a huge black beard.

Over the years, however, Gav had developed a skin problem on his scalp which had resulted in his hair being frequently razored off so that he could get treatment. This meant that his rastacap often looked like an unoccupied tea-cosy as it lay flat on the top of his head, its sides drooping down over his ears. But no one would dare poke fun at his precious rastacap.

At six foot five inches, Gav was still an imposing figure with biceps the size of proverbial tree-trunks. His arms were covered in a frightening array of tattoos. On one, there was a skull sitting in the middle of a huge spider's web with the spider exiting through one of the skull's eye sockets. Under this, the tattooist had made out that the skin of the arm had been peeled back to reveal a claw hammer. The other arm sported guns, knives, hand-grenades, and other items of weaponry all intricately portrayed in a sickening montage.

Johnnie looked across the gravel at the man he considered to be his most loyal dealer. But he could also be the most difficult to get on with.

'OK Gav, let's cool it on the Hilux. You said you wanted a meet. I'm here. What do you want to talk about?' Johnnie hadn't got all day and, in any case, he was well off his normal territory and always felt uncomfortable when visiting a dealer's neighbourhood. He also didn't know Gav very well – more by reputation than anything else. And, if only half the things he'd heard about him were true, he needed to be very careful.

'It's this fucking supply problem!' The rastacap had now slipped down almost over Gav's eyes so it was a bit like talking to a woolly hat. Johnnie groaned inwardly at the situation he found himself in.

'Yeah, Gav, we're all in it. Bolloxed us for the moment, but we'll get used to it. You'll just have to find ways of dealing with your punters if they start threatening to go elsewhere. Adapt and move on – that's what they say. Anyway, that's a problem for your runners isn't it? They're just going to have to start thinking of new ways to get the gear out on the street and get the punters paying the prices.'

'Are you going to be able to sort out our supplies an' all?'

'Don't you worry about that, Gav. You just make sure your runners are keeping the punters happy. The market won't go away. But it's going to be tough. Prices will probably have to rise. Maybe not so much money around. More debts.'

'Yeah, well I know how to deal with that!' Gav snarled, his top lip almost turning in on itself.

Johnnie had seen images of the torture which Gav personally handed out to those who crossed him – beatings, burns, hot water scalding, knife wounds. Mostly uploaded to the Dark Web just so others could wallow in his sadistic practices but also to warn his punters what could happen to them if they dared to consider finding another supplier.

He turned away to look back down the track that they had both driven along to reach this godforsaken place.

'Anyway, I've got another prob!' Gav bent down to pick up a piece of gravel before throwing it in the direction of a blackbird which had landed on the top of a nearby fencing post. The bird was never in any danger but took the decision to fly away as a precaution.

'One of my runners has fucking disappeared and the pigs have found her stash. Fucking mother reported the kid missing so they sent a couple of woodentops straight round and started searching.'

'What did they find?' Johnnie asked. Although this was not really his problem, it always paid to get good intel if the police were starting to uncover parts of his empire.

'Don't know exactly. Me and my boys went in this morning before the men in white suits got there. We had to shut the fucking bitch mother up. Her screaming was getting the neighbours interested. Anyway, we found a few wraps and some money but no phone. Unless the girl's got it with her, that could give us a real problem.'

'Hmm. And what am I supposed to do about that, Gav?'

'Just letting you know, Johnnie. We could also be losing some punters if we can't find that phone. As I said, there's plenty of others dealing on our streets. Sales go down, we've got less to pass on.'

Johnnie studied his fingers before scratching at a scab on the back of his right hand which eventually started to bleed. He raised the hand to his mouth and sucked the fresh blood.

'No, Gav, you don't seem to understand,' he said, still licking the wound and without looking up at the wanna-be Rastafarian. 'You pay me what we've agreed I get. It's not my problem if you can't get the cash in. You'll just have to get it from somewhere else.'

He finally looked up and gave Gav a withering look.

'You know what happens when I don't get what I want, don't you Gav?'

Both men stared each other in the eye before Johnnie went back to sucking the back of his hand.

'To be honest, Gav, I don't give a flying fuck that a schoolgirl's gone missing. Or that you might have lost a phone. Or that you might lose some punters. Or even that your money might be down. We have a deal, my friend, and I expect you to keep up payments. Do I make myself understood?'

The sun continued to shine down from a clear blue sky. There was a smattering of birdsong in the air. Otherwise, silence prevailed.

'Crystal,' Gav eventually declared with an iciness in his voice. 'Absolutely crystal.'

18

Wednesday 29 April

While the Crime Scenes team had a think about how they were going to clear the entrance to the cellar, Sarah Hunter took herself off for a walk around the outside perimeter of Tideswell Manor.

Looking past the portacabins, she noticed a number of motorhomes which had been parked in a circle around a huge picnic area. It reminded her of some of the old cowboy films where the wagons rolled onto a camp site and congregated around a central fire. Fast-forwarding about 150 years, these state-of-the-art homes on wheels faced on to an area which was crowded with tables and chairs of all shapes and sizes. As she got closer, she realised that the vehicles were a mixture of luxury motorhomes and Winnebagos.

Knowing very little about this sort of vehicle apart from the pain of being stuck behind them on the winding country lanes of Kent, Sarah took out her phone and googled the make and model of the motorhome nearest to her. She scrolled down until she came to a picture which was a close match to the vehicle she was looking at – and then just stared at the screen. The price tag for this motorhome was shown as being £485,000. She was astonished.

Moving towards the centre of the circle and carefully avoiding the tables and chairs, she now discovered that the vehicle owners weren't short of cooking facilities – barbeques, ovens, small fridges which were linked to generators, a range cooker with six hobs powered by bottled gas. All mod cons here, she thought, before moving across to one of the Winnebagos.

An awning was deployed from the side of the vehicle affording cover for a door which was located behind the driving compartment. Sarah pulled down the door handle and, to her great surprise, it opened. She peered into the interior and then stepped up into what was clearly the lounge area. Situated immediately behind the driver's compartment, there were two armchairs and two leather settees which faced each other across the width of the vehicle. Turning to her left, she saw a dining table with four chairs which was opposite a set of kitchen cupboards, a small range cooker, a double sink with mixer taps and an American-style fridge. A large television screen was attached to a wooden partition that separated the kitchen area from the sleeping quarters which comprised one large double bed. Further to the rear of the vehicle, Sarah could see a well-appointed bathroom with shower unit, another double sink, a fully functioning toilet and what was probably a bidet.

It was some piece of kit, she thought. But... but... it was filthy!

Retrieving some Tyvek gloves from the back pocket of her jeans, Sarah slipped them on before drawing her index finger across the top of the dining table. She could easily see the track her finger had made through what appeared to be dust and congealed fat from the cooking area. There were burn marks on the edges of the table and, as she looked around, she noticed similar marks on the settees and on the armchairs. She assumed that these had been caused by lit cigarettes or, perhaps, by reefers or other smoking materials. There were also scorch marks dotted all over two partially threadbare rugs which had been carelessly thrown between the two settees.

Moving over to the kitchen area, she opened some of the cupboards which were well stocked with plates, cups and glasses. She turned the sink taps on to check that water was actually running, and had a quick look in the cupboard under the sink. She then opened the fridge and immediately wished that she hadn't. Not only did the rancid smell of gone-off milk turn her stomach but the sight of the racked shelving sprouting a black mould made her quickly slam the door and take a step backwards.

Deciding to have a closer look at the sleeping accommodation, she again noticed cigarette burns on the furniture, on the floor mats, and even on the bedding. She bent down to open the top drawer of one of the bedside cabinets.

'Well, what have we got here?' she murmured under her breath.

The interior of the drawer was cluttered with much of the paraphernalia associated with drug-taking – syringes, blackened spoons, a couple of boxes of matches and a lighter. There were also lengths of rubber tubing some of which looked as if they were stained with blood. She could also see a few wraps of crack or perhaps heroin but she certainly wasn't going to pull them out for closer examination at this stage of their investigation.

Carefully closing the top drawer, she pulled open the middle drawer where she found some more drug-taking gear - a few bottle tops, a bundle of pre-cut squares of foil, a box of straws all of which had been cut in half, and some razor blades. There were packets of prescription drugs, mainly sleeping pills, and a number of prescription inhalers. Rather incongruously, a suspender belt was wrapped around some of the inhalers, and other items of lingerie seemed to have been stuffed into the drawer as if it had another function as a laundry basket. There was nothing that gave Sarah to believe that these items of clothing were clean.

She closed the drawer and reached down to the bottom drawer in the little cabinet. Locked!

She bent down to look at the lock built into the drawer and quickly realised that she might have seen a key to fit the lock. But where had that been? She walked back out to the kitchen area and looked at the range of cupboards. Was it here? Eventually, she opened one of the cupboard doors and reached up to remove an orange glass from the middle shelf. She placed it on the worksurface before tipping it up and watching as a key slid out of the glass. She then returned to the bedside cabinet.

After unlocking the drawer, she removed it from the bedside table and placed it on the bed for a closer inspection. Finding that it was packed with what appeared to be clean lingerie, she gently worked her fingers through a colourful array of lacy garments before deciding to leave the whole thing to the Crime Scenes team. She lifted the drawer off the bed and was just about to replace it in the cabinet when she came to her senses.

The drawer was surely far heavier than the sum total of all the wispy knickers, thongs and bras she'd just been handling. So, she put it back on the bed.

Gradually removing the contents, she soon came across the reason for the extra weight. Lying in the bottom of the drawer, and pushed right to the back was a heavy-duty supermarket plastic carrier bag. Sarah knew immediately what she was looking at but couldn't resist gently dragging the tips of her fingers across the surface of the bag. She could almost feel the cold steel of the gun through the Tyvek material and the plastic.

She would have to get the CSIs to immediately start searching these vehicles. Meanwhile, she moved back into the main living area of the vehicle and started opening drawers and cupboards, looking for any other evidence of the drug-taking which must have gone on in this Winnebago. There was some more paraphernalia in the kitchen drawers and, for some reason, blackened spoons had been returned to the cutlery drawer.

Having one last sweep of the inside of the vehicle, she jumped down onto the grass and pushed the door shut. She then moved back to the centre of the circle of vehicles and called Grace Kendall.

'Have you got all these registration numbers?' she asked Grace as she scanned all the expensive motorhomes facing her. It was at that point that she realised that two of them had foreign registration plates – one from France and the other from The Netherlands.

'Yes, I've got those,' Grace replied. 'Following up has been a bit slow due to a change in some of the working practices at the DVLA.'

'There are a couple of European plates here too,' Hunter continued.

'Yep, got those too but, again, it's been slow progress. I'm hoping that there will be something back tomorrow but everything seems to be running slowly at the moment. Rumours of a cyber-attack are gathering pace!'

'Okay. But I'm particularly interested in one of the Winnebagos.' Hunter read off the registration number. 'See if you can get some identification on the owner of this vehicle. It looks as if the home address will need a visit as a matter of some urgency.'

'Will do. And before I forget, Angie has arranged for that guy from the drug squad to drop in early tomorrow morning – around 6.30 a.m. if that's okay with you?'

'Okay, Grace, I've got no problem with that. Have you heard from Jed recently?'

'Last I heard, he and Lisa Calder had been checking the flight path between the edge of the water and the mansion. Sounds as if it's been slow-going as the terrain is very wet and a lot of it is inaccessible. Jed was thinking of getting a boat and taking a look at things from out on the water. You should give him a call – he's probably not a million miles from where you're standing.'

'Yeah, I'll do that. Think I'll be here until it gets dark this evening so I'll just go straight home. It'll save the detour back to Tonbridge.'

Sarah disconnected the call and was just about to put the phone back in her pocket when the screen lit up with an incoming call from Beth Dench asking her to get back to the area around the cellar. They had encountered a problem.

Entering through the rear of the mansion and then picking her way across the cracked and broken masonry, Hunter eventually reached Dench and her team. She noticed that Jimbo Carrigan was now sitting in the driving seat of a pick & carry crane, and that some robust lifting straps had been wound around the first section of the smashed pillar which was obstructing the entrance to the cellar.

Her first instinct was that the crane was not fit for the purpose of picking up the heavy section of pillar. And she was proved right as she watched the rear of little crane rise into the air as it tried desperately to lift the stone.

'We'll have to get back to the crane people for something bigger,' Carrigan said to Dench as he turned the ignition off and stepped back onto the crushed masonry.

'How long is that going to take?' Hunter asked, becoming increasingly concerned that there might actually be some people trapped in the cellar.

'They're pretty good,' Dench said, referring to the company which had provided a range of cranes for the rescue work. 'They've only just taken one of the bigger mobile machines away so we might be able to get them to turn round and come back this evening or overnight. Let's try and get the cellar open by tomorrow noon.'

Hunter always liked to have a plan so she nodded enthusiastically. 'Sounds good!'

Carrigan re-joined the team which was still involved with breaking up the fallen masonry and picked up one of the drills.

As the noise of drilling started up again, Hunter beckoned Dench to follow her back to the rear entrance of the building. They walked out towards the portacabins.

'There's a Winnebago over there that I'd like you to take a look at in what's left of this afternoon if possible,' Hunter said, pointing to the motorhome she had been in earlier. 'There's a gun all wrapped up in one of the bedside cabinets. Bottom drawer – it's got a key in it.'

Dench raised her eyebrows. 'A gun? That doesn't bode well for what else we may find in the other vehicles.'

'Agreed!' Hunter replied looking over to the circle of motorhomes. 'In fact, sooner rather than later we'll need to take a look at all these vehicles as it's unlikely that their owners will ever return to reclaim them.'

'Well, we had sort of ring-fenced them for further investigation once we'd made progress in the main house,' Dench said, removing her mask and breathing in some fresh air. 'We carried out a cursory inspection to make sure that there was nobody aboard any of the vehicles. We also collected some DNA samples which have gone down to the morgue. But that's about it – no in-depth examination yet. So, we'd better move that back up the priority list if we're going to start finding guns and ammunition.'

'And I noticed that there are a couple from Europe – France and Holland,' Hunter pointed in the vague direction of the two vehicles. 'Any problems with accessing them?'

'Shouldn't be if their owners can be identified from the mansion. And, as this is a crime scene until proved otherwise, the vehicles cannot be removed until they have been ruled out of the investigation.'

'True – but we still need some confirmed identities so that we can get in touch with our friends in Europe.' Hunter knew that this would become a bureaucratic process so she was glad that she could rely on Grace Kendall to sort out all the paperwork. That woman had the patience of a saint, she thought.

Dench was fiddling with her phone.

'About another ninety minutes of daylight I should think so we might as well keep going with the masonry drills. I'll probably take a look at the Winnebago with Jimbo. Do you want to be here when we open up the cellar?'

'Definitely! Count me in for that,' Hunter replied. 'By midday tomorrow you said. I've got a dawn briefing so I'll get down here around ten.'

'That should be good. We have a daily safety inspection

118

first thing and then we'll need to get the new crane set up. It'll probably have an operator who'll need to be inducted onto site. All these things eat into the timeframe. But around ten should be fine.'

Sarah Hunter returned to her car and phoned Jed Crowther who answered almost immediately. As Crowther and Calder were still in the area, Hunter arranged to meet them in the car park of the Dale Hill Golf Club in half an hour.

Next, she called Jennings to get an update on Julie Buckley and a progress report on the CSI investigation at the Buckley house.

Julie Buckley was still alive – just. She was in an induced coma, and all sorts of machines were keeping her vital organs working. Jennings had taken the decision to post a police guard on her just in case anyone had the idea of coming back to finish her off. There was still no sign of Rachael and no one had heard anything from her. No phone calls, emails, cheeky text messages – nothing.

'CSIs found another couple of phones and some more wraps so those have gone away for analysis,' Jennings continued with her report. 'I've asked for a by-return service from the Techies given the grievous situation the mother and daughter are in so we should hopefully have something tomorrow.'

Sarah Hunter still couldn't see any connection between the Buckleys and Tideswell Manor so she suggested that Jennings continued with her investigation as a separate entity for the time being. She also suggested that Jennings and Mishraz should attend the briefing in the morning with the DC from the drugs squad.

'It's an early start but this guy knows exactly what's occurring on the streets of Kent and South London. We also need to have this knowledge. It could provide some new thinking for the Buckley case.'

Jennings sounded keen to attend and, after some further discussion about the availability of the CSIs report, Hunter disconnected the call and headed off in the direction of Dale Hill Golf Club.

19

Wednesday 29 April

She has lost all track of time.

The once-dim lighting has been extinguished in the corridor. There is no sound apart from a constant drone of machinery which reminds her of the time men were digging up the road near her house.

The air has become fetid with the stench of human excrement. She once dared to try and find a toilet but was driven back to the tiny room by the filthy state of the hovel in which she was now incarcerated.

The bodies of men and women were slumped on the floor of the narrow corridor. She didn't know whether they were even still alive. Attempts to get the main door to open had stopped a long time ago. There is no food or water – or any fresh air. It seems ages since she was brought in here, since she was thrown onto this dirty bed, since she had wrapped her arm round the girl with the frizzy hair.

But what was the girl doing here in this room?

Last time she had seen her, the two of them had been dancing to loud music in a room full of men and women who were trying to dance with them. Hands had been reaching out to touch her near-naked body. Some wanted to do more than just touch. Hands were everywhere. But neither she nor her friend seemed to have the will to complain. They had danced with a freedom that had overwhelmed them. They had been powerless to stop the heinous defilement of their young bodies.

After that, her mind has become a confused jumble of

terrifying images right up to the time the man came into the room and roughly threw her onto the bed.

Since then, she has remained in the room – in her prison cell. She has had to pee on the floor in a corner of the room. But even that has stopped. She is very thirsty. Her lips are dry and cracked. Her throat is sore.

She raises her arms but can't see them in the darkness. She knows that they are covered in bruises with bracelets of dried blood circling her wrists where the restraining cords have broken the skin. She can feel the rough needle marks in the crooks of her arms. Her memory doesn't want to go there but the images flash across her brain nevertheless.

She allows her fingers to gently explore her naked body. She winces time and again as, even with her own soft touch, the venal bruising and cracked ribs are evidence of the feral treatment she has had to endure.

She can't bring herself to touch her body below the waist. She is deeply ashamed of what has been done to her. The way these men and women have subjected her to such a long and enduring ordeal of depravity.

Tears start to flow freely – some pooling in the lobes of her ears, others simply cascading onto the filthy sheet below. She screws her eyes tight shut trying to blot everything out of her mind.

She instinctively snuggles closer to, and almost under, the larger body of her best friend.

Not for warmth because the body is cold.

But because she is terrified about what is going to happen to her.

20

Thursday 30 April

Sarah Hunter had gone to sleep feeling as if she was swimming in treacle such were the complexities of the investigation at Tideswell Manor. It was four days since the plane had ripped the heart out of the old manor house but their investigation still had very little to show for itself. Even though the rescue teams were working around the clock, there had been endless delays whilst the disaster site had been made safe only for the delicate clearing work to come to a complete halt every time a new health & safety issue came to light.

But, on this bright sunlit late April day, Sarah had woken with the lark feeling fully refreshed and energised. Slipping quietly out of the bed so as not to wake Grace, she headed for the bathroom. She showered enthusiastically, spinning the controls between hot and cold water which seemed to add to the buzz she was feeling. Draped in a towel, she then tiptoed across the bedroom, picking up items of clothing as she went, and clambered down the stairs into the open plan living area.

Flicking on the gas fire to take the early morning chill off the room, she dressed quickly before removing her shower cap and pinning her hair into an untidy bundle on the back of her head.

Hearing signs of movement upstairs, she busied herself in the kitchen pouring orange juice and cutting slices of sour-dough bread for toasting. She put out plates on the table along with the butter dish and a newish jar of Carver's Whisky Mac marmalade before switching the kettle on and getting mugs out in readiness for their first coffee fix of the day.

There was normally time for a little light conversation at the breakfast table, and this morning was no exception. Sarah had given Grace her assessment of the complexities of crane operations with particular reference to the demonstration she had witnessed the day before. It had been an education for her to understand the level of planning which had to be completed before any heavy lift could even be contemplated.

With the dishes filed away in the dishwasher, both women headed for the door and into their respective cars for the journey back to Tonbridge. Sarah would always get into the station first as Grace invariably parked her car back at her flat before walking the half mile to Pembury Road.

Sarah and Grace now sat in a small meeting room along with Angie Marshall, Elaine Jennings and Azzar Mishraz. They had been joined by Jed Crowther and Lisa Calder. Also in the room was DC Jordan Wright, a member of the County Lines & Gangs Team based at Medway.

Whilst Angie Marshall made the introductions, Sarah gave Wright the once over. He certainly looked the part, she thought. Shaven-headed with a gold stud in his left ear, he had a good covering of designer stubble across his face and round his neck. He was wearing a Kent Police issue black T-shirt that was struggling to contain a muscular upper body which Hunter assumed had been developed through hours spent in the gym. And, at around six foot three, he towered over her.

After giving a short introduction about the team he worked in at Medway, Wright got straight to the task of explaining how county lines gangs worked.

'Very simply, a county line is a drug-dealing network,' he

told the assembled detectives. 'They are normally run by dealers who are based in cities and who are distributing drugs to a customer base in smaller towns. Here in Kent, the dealers are mainly based either just in or close to the London area so getting to them will often require us to work with the Met and with the Transport Police.'

'How do the drugs actually get sold?' Kendall wanted to know.

'Through phone-dealing lines with crack cocaine and heroin being the most popular. Profits from a single county line are staggering. Could be anything up to around half a million a year.'

Hunter and Kendall looked at each other. Sarah knew that these gangs made vast sums of money, but she had never realised that it was quite so much.

'So, who is actually making this sort of money?' Sarah asked. 'You see, this is where I get a bit confused about who is doing what. Dealers, distributors, runners, line-holders – all these terms we keep hearing. But, presumably, there has to be some sort of organised structure.'

'Okay!' Wright realised that perhaps he needed to go back to basics in terms of the way in which county lines were set up. 'At the top of the pile, we have the dealers. County lines drug dealers are a sophisticated, organised and incredibly violent group of individuals and each gang will vigorously defend its area.'

'So, you're not really going after the dealers because they operate in our major cities and are being monitored by the city police?' Hunter had really intended this to be a statement but it came out as more of a question.

Wright nodded.

'And, in any event, they don't often leave the city if ever,' she continued. 'But have you got the means to maintain intel on what they're up to?

Wright nodded again.

'Yeah, we pretty much know about the gang leaders through our city colleagues. The biggest problem we have is when a rival gang tries to break into an established dealer's area. That is when the violence reaches new levels as the established dealer makes absolutely sure that rivals are driven away never to return. Some of this extreme violence has even resulted in rivals being murdered – normally either shot or stabbed to death. But, with many of the biggest dealers not being hands on and hardly ever being seen by us, we have very little to pin on them. They're almost untouchable unless we get really lucky.'

Wright looked round the room as seven attentive faces stared back at him, hanging on his every word.

'What we're really after is grabbing the people who are bringing the drugs into our area,' he continued. 'We need to get hold of the distributors who are supplying the runners with drugs. Distributors are also known as line holders, and we want to take out the people who are holding the lines because not only are they the biggest threat but they're also harder to replace. They can be in control of several lines and several runners so it would take out more people in the long run.'

Hunter shifted uncomfortably in her chair. This was a very sophisticated enemy which was blighting the lives of millions of people.

'Runners are the most junior and the most exposed members of the county lines network,' Wright continued. 'They will each have at least one phone and each phone will have a nickname. The nickname helps those in the chain above to build their brand but hide their identity. When we are able to get hold of one of these phones, we normally hope that the data from the phone will help us to identify the distributor.'

Hunter looked over at Grace Kendall who was furiously making notes, listening to every word Wright had to say.

'With county lines there's no mates, no friendship. There's no respect, just deadlines. If you don't meet the deadlines, that's when the violence starts. Runners are doing all the donkey work and taking the risks. They're mainly doing wraps and the people higher up the line aren't going to care if one of them gets caught – they'll just move on to the next poor sod. There's no ethics to it.'

'So, what exactly is your role in the team,' Hunter wanted to know.

'As a Disruption Officer, part of my job is to gather as much information as possible in order to start an investigation. We mainly do this by going out and picking up the runners who we know are supplying the drugs. They're quite easy to spot as they tend to use roads or areas where there is good access to a network of alleyways. Shopping centres are also popular places for dealing. Users go to these centres, do their shoplifting and then sell the goods on so that they have the cash to buy the drugs. Once we start getting good information, we can start an investigation into the identity of the line holder.'

'How many county lines do we have in Kent?' Kendall asked, barely looking up from her notes.

'We're estimating between forty and fifty but there could be as many as two thousand in the UK as a whole,' he replied.

'We're hoping to get the Kent numbers down by about a quarter this year but it's a tough ask.'

'So, would you say that the phones are the key to cracking these gangs?' Hunter asked, feeling herself becoming immersed in the dark and sinister world of street drug-dealing.

'Well, a single phone is certainly the source of considerable intel about a dedicated county line,' Wright responded, 'and we do tend to concentrate on trying to seize the phones so that we can extract all the information. Ultimately, we hope that the data on the phone will lead us to the distributor.'

'And, as each phone has an identity, the runner will know which distributor they are dealing with?' Hunter asked, just to make sure she understood.

'Yeah, pretty much. Some of the runners keep the phones in plastic folders along with its identity name. Occasionally, they also include the distributor's name which makes life a bit easier.'

There was a pause while the detectives took in the information Wright was giving them. Elaine Jennings was trying to catch his eye.

'I've heard that runners can be very vulnerable people,' she asked. 'Is that a generality?'

Wright nodded. 'Yes. Vulnerable people are often coerced into selling or distributing drugs by those higher up in the county lines network – the younger they are the easier it is for the gangs to groom them. We're always looking for vulnerability when deciding which lines to target. If you've got a young child, a juvenile or a vulnerable young adult as a runner, you're more likely to get better intel.'

'We've had reports that there are some supply problems at the moment. Will this have an effect on your activities?'

Kendall asked, at last looking up from her notes.

'Dealers and distributors will probably have to change the way they operate,' Wright agreed. 'We've been told that some have embraced the new drugs which are easier to supply right now. We also had some intel yesterday that one of our known runners had heard that some of the supply problems may have been caused by the plane crash at Bewl Water. It seems some of the distributors may have been wiped out in that.'

The detectives looked at each other as they grasped the consequences that this may have for the county lines network.

'One thing's for certain,' Wright continued, 'people with an addiction always need to feed that addiction. Their addiction will not suddenly go away just because there's a supply problem or the supply line's been wiped out. The only thing that will change is that prices will have to go up. And, if prices go up, we know that violence normally also increases. But criminals will quickly adapt to new circumstances, and we don't expect it'll be long before it's back to business as usual.'

He looked around the room.

'One of my colleagues has a great way of summing up what we are all involved with. It's not a war because a war ends. It's just a constant battle.'

Jordan Wright had had to get away at 8.00 a.m. as he and a couple of colleagues were on a stake-out in the Rochester & Chatham area. Before he left, Elaine Jennings brought up the subject of Rachael Buckley's disappearance and the discoveries they had made at her house.

Wright had expressed the view that it did sound as if Rachael might have become a runner. The poor relationship with her mother and the fact that there had never been a father figure in her life meant that she could very probably be classified as 'vulnerable' which left her open to grooming by one of the gangs. The fact that they had discovered some phones in the house was of great interest to Wright who insisted that his team should take them over as their technical guys were more likely to make sense of the information which was bound to be stored on the devices.

Sarah Hunter could see the logic in this but was keen that the information could be shared by both interested parties in case it gave any pointers towards where Rachael might be. They were in the middle of a misper investigation after all. Wright seemed to be happy with that arrangement.

They had talked about the drugs found in Rachael's room but Wright didn't appear that interested and suggested that they were destroyed in the normal way unless, of course, they were needed for any criminal charges. Similarly, any cash found in the property was of no consequence. He was only interested in phones and hard evidence.

Sarah Hunter had thanked him for his time and they had all swapped visiting cards with Grace suggesting that she should be the principle point of contact if they had any further questions. That was all agreed and Jordan Wright had gone off to his stake-out in the north of the county.

As the team was all assembled in one place, Hunter suggested that they had a catch-up before they continued with their own lines of investigation. But, no sooner had she asked Jed Crowther to bring them up to speed on the tracking of the plane than her phone started thrumming in her pocket.

Beth Dench.

She swiped the screen to answer the call.

'Hi Beth. Have the risk assessment people finished already?'

'Sure have. Crane's in place so we're ready to go in as soon as you can get here.'

'Okay. On my way.'

21
Thursday 30 April

Stopping off at one of the CSI vans, Sarah Hunter slipped into a set of white coveralls, tucked her hair under a white safety helmet and wrapped a pair of ear defenders around the back of her neck. She also hung a pair of safety glasses around the front of her neck before pushing a pair of nitrile gloves and a face mask into the pockets of the coverall. Even though she was wearing an old pair of trainers, she slipped protective over-shoes on before entering the rear of the building and making her way towards the sound of the masonry drills.

Beth Dench and Jimbo Carrigan were standing beside a huge mobile crane which had been jacked up on its four outriggers. The crane operators were standing next to their machine, and other members of the CSI team had gathered to watch the removal of the pillar and any other obstructions which might have fallen into the area around the cellar entrance.

'Hi, Sarah!' Dench called over as Hunter made her way across the uneven rubble. 'Pretty much ready to go here. Okay with you?'

'Yes. Let's get on with it,' Sarah replied.

One of the crane crew stepped forward. 'Masks and goggles on in case something doesn't go to plan,' he instructed them.

The rest of the crew then took up positions around the pillar and began the process of attaching a set of chain slings which were hanging from the boom of the crane. Once these were in place, one of the crew jumped up into the operator's cabin and fired up the engine.

Two of the crew stood either side of the pillar making

exaggerated hand signals to the operator as the boom started to take the strain. Hunter watched, fascinated. She didn't think she had ever been this close to a major lift before so she was interested to see the techniques being used.

Eventually, the pillar started to ease out of its resting place. Dench tugged at Sarah's elbow to suggest that they should move a little further back.

They could now see daylight beneath the pillar as the crane operator started to manoeuvre the boom to the side of the cellar entrance, its cargo moving slowly but steadily to the area which had been identified as a landing site.

Once the pillar had come to rest on the ground, the crew detached the chain slings and then started the process of wedging the monstrous piece of stone into place.

Getting the thumbs up from the crane operator, Beth Dench and Sarah Hunter picked their way across the rubble to look down at the entrance to the cellar. They could see that there was still a long way to go in terms of clearing the entrance. Other large pieces of stone and masonry had been wedged into the stairwell and stood in the way of any effort to open the door, the top of which they could just make out.

The crane operator had joined them and was now pointing into the stairwell.

'We can get that lot shifted, no problem,' he said without looking at either Dench or Hunter. 'Shouldn't take too long.'

And he was right. Very soon everyone was staring into an empty stairwell and at another huge silver coloured door which guarded the entrance to the cellar.

'Spotted the next problem?' Beth Dench asked no one in particular.

'No door handle,' Hunter replied, still staring at the door.

'Looks like there was more than one,' Dench said, pointing at the door. 'See the bottom of the door. There's a lever handle just above ground level. It's the sort of handle you'd see on a ship's door, and there would have also been one at the top but that's been knocked off. Looks like we'll have to cut our way in. Jimbo!' she called over to Carrigan. 'Have we got the oxy here?'

'In the van. I'll get it.'

Hunter gingerly made her way down the stairs, carefully picking her steps through rubble and bits of masonry which still littered the area. On reaching the door, she could see where the handle had sheared off when the pillar fell into the stairwell and she could also see the twisted bit of metal sticking out from under a couple of bricks in front of the door. The lever handle which was still attached at the bottom of the door looked as if it was in the 'locked' position but she would leave that to the CSIs to sort out.

She made her way back to the top of the steps just as Carrigan arrived with all the oxyacetylene cutting equipment and immediately got started on the task of freeing the door.

Aware that her phone had been vibrating in her pocket, Hunter now retreated towards the back of the mansion and saw that caller i/d was Jed Crowther. She poked the screen to return his call.

'Ma'am, looks like we may have found something here,' Crowther informed her, sounding slightly breathless.

He and Lisa Calder had just had a look around the Bewl Water Outdoor Centre and had spotted two CCTV cameras which covered the area of water that was used for sailing and other water sports. One camera focused on the inshore area and the other seemed to cover a much wider area of water away from the shore.

'There's a guy in the office here, and he's now getting on with finding the CCTV feed for Sunday morning,' Crowther informed his boss. 'Lisa's very persuasive!'

Hunter smiled to herself. 'Sounds good, Jed. And you think the cameras will show us something?'

'Our thinking is that one of the cameras may have picked up the plane as it came in over the water. Lisa's convinced the pilot would have baled out over water and I tend to agree with her. The guy here said that he's done some base jumping and that, if the pilot could have got out at 1,000 feet, he'd still have about ten seconds to deploy his parachute. So, we're hoping to get this theory confirmed through the CCTV.'

Hunter was impressed with their level of enthusiasm but her many years' experience of CCTV was that it never gave you either what you expected or exactly what you wanted. It was often a source of huge frustration and disappointment. But, not wishing to dent their enthusiasm, she wished them luck and asked for a report as soon as they had completed the viewing.

Making her way back towards the cellar, Hunter could see that the oxyacetylene equipment was being removed from the stairwell as Beth Dench called her over.

'We're pretty much ready to open up now so masks, gloves and safety glasses on please. And keep your hard hat on at all times,' Dench instructed. 'Jim and one of the lads will open the door up and then we'll go in and see if anything's been going on.'

Hunter nodded, a couple of butterflies starting to spread their wings in her stomach. She had a particular aversion to cellars, especially if she had absolutely no knowledge of what she was going to find inside them.

Using a couple of crowbars to give them purchase on the heavy door, Carrigan and his colleague gradually eased the door open before staggering backwards, holding their hands to their faces.

At first, Hunter couldn't understand what was going on until the stench of putrefaction suddenly hit her – an invisible cloud of noxious gases which wrapped itself around them all. Even though she was wearing her mask, she instinctively put her hand to her face to cover her nose and mouth before craning her neck to try and see past Carrigan into the darkened cellar.

'Jesus Christ, Jim, get that fucking door shut!' Dench shouted down to the two men. Once the door had been closed, everyone exited the stairwell.

Without wasting any time, Dench rattled off a string of instructions to the other CSI officers about getting the emergency services back to Tideswell as well as listing the equipment she would need – preferably by yesterday. She then turned back to Hunter.

'You'll probably need to leave us to handle this, Sarah. Fuck knows what we're going to find in there but I can guarantee that none of it's going to be pleasant.'

'I'll be okay, Beth,' Hunter replied. 'I need to see exactly what's been going on here with my own eyes. If I'm going to find who is responsible for all this carnage, I need to see everything. Let's go!'

Dench simply shrugged her shoulders before turning to the stairwell. One of her team handed her a couple of powerful torches. She passed one to Hunter as Carrigan and his colleague levered the door open again. This time they were ready for the stench which washed over them as they inched towards what looked more like the entrance to a dark sarcophagus.

Sweeping their LED powered torchlight over the entrance to the cellar, Dench suddenly put her arm out to prevent Hunter going any further. Her torch beam had picked out two bodies on the floor just inside the door. She crouched down and carefully felt for the carotid artery to establish if there was any sign of a pulse.

'Nothing here,' she murmured as she stood up and shone her torch beam into the blackness in front of her.

Having stepped over the two bodies, Dench again stopped in her tracks. 'My God!' she exclaimed.

Sarah was now standing next to Dench as they played their torch beams over bodies which were bestrewn all over the passageway in front of them.

Dench instinctively crouched down and started desperately searching for any signs of life. Hunter had meanwhile spotted a door which was standing ajar just beyond where Dench was frantically checking one of the bodies. Carefully stepping over two more bodies, she pulled the door fully open and shone her torch around the room. All she could see was an empty bed and a lightbulb hanging from the ceiling. There was the all-enveloping stench of urine and faeces pervading every corner of the room.

Noticing that all the doors seemed to open out onto the passageway, she crossed to another on the opposite side which also stood slightly ajar. Pulling it open and shining the powerful beam into the little room, she almost gagged on the putrid smell of death which permeated the air from the enclosed space.

Hurrying across the cobbled floor, she suddenly slipped on the wet surface and crashed into the bed before her knees hit the unyielding stones below. Despite the pain, she pulled herself up on to the mattress and shone her torch onto the naked body of a dark-skinned girl. She was lying in the foetal position with knees drawn tightly up to her chest, her young eyes staring sightlessly towards Hunter and beyond. Sarah instinctively leaned over and felt for a pulse, but it was a futile gesture as life had long-since drained out of the poor girl.

Sitting back on her heels to look at the body, Hunter guessed that she was no more than eleven or twelve years old. But how on earth had she ended up in this squalid location where life had drained out of her in the most awful circumstances?

She played the torch beam around the dark, windowless room and was just about to make her way back to the passage-way when she suddenly realised that there was another body on the bed, sheltering behind the dead girl. Moving round to the other side of the bed, Hunter saw the naked body of a white girl which was jammed so close to the dark-skinned girl that she was almost underneath the body.

Again, Sarah's first instinct was to feel for a pulse. She reached under the girl's neck and then leaned in closer. Was that a very faint heartbeat she could feel? Leaning in even closer, she tried to see if there was a breath coming from the girl's mouth. Hard to tell. She lifted her arm up and searched for a pulse at the wrist. There it was again! But extremely weak.

Hunter dashed back into the passageway and was relieved to find Jimbo Carrigan outside the room.

'Jim, quick! There's a young girl in here,' she said, beckoning him into the room. 'I'm pretty sure that there's a faint pulse.

Doubt she's got long to live unless we can get her to the medics straightaway. Can you get her out of here?'

Carrigan quickly took some evidence shots of the scene before helping Sarah to uncouple the two bodies. He gently carried the white girl towards the stairwell. On the way, he passed Beth Dench who had now almost made her way down to where Hunter was standing.

'My God! This is gross,' Dench whispered as she caught up with Sarah. 'Never seen anything like it. These people had no chance. No air, no water, no food, no nothing.'

'We need to look into all these rooms,' Sarah insisted as she flashed her torch towards the end of the passageway. 'Two more to go.'

Dench reached for the handle of the door immediately to her left and pulled the door open. Their senses were now inured to the malodorous environment they found themselves in, and they quickly entered the room. Again, there was a large double bed but this time the body of a young boy lay amongst the tangle of soiled sheets which covered a mattress. His hands and feet had been loosely tied to the top and bottom bars of the bedstead. Dench quickly assessed the body for any signs of life but there were none.

'Probably something to do with the ligature around his neck,' she said after completing her examination. 'He's been dead for some time.'

Hunter was beginning to feel weak and helpless. Not only had many people died as a direct result of the aircraft crashing into the mansion, but they had now found someone who had probably been murdered before the plane had even hit the building. However, now was not the time for reflection. They had to conclude their search of the cellar, and Beth Dench was already back out in the corridor pulling at the last door.

Locked!

She pulled at it again just to make sure.

'There must be a key here somewhere,' Dench hissed, the tension in her voice evident.

Standing back from the door, they both shone their torches onto the surrounding walls – looking for any clue which would help them to get into the room.

Hunter wasn't quite sure what they were looking for and was relieved when Dench suddenly squatted down and started agitating one of the bricks with her fingers. She eventually managed to prise a half-brick out of the wall. Putting her hand into the hole she had created, she finally produced a key which she showed to Hunter.

No words were spoken between them.

There was just an overriding shared need to get the door open, discover the contents of the room and get out of this hell hole.

The key turned easily in the lock, and the door handle responded to the pressure Dench applied before she slowly pulled it open.

They both stepped across the threshold of the room, shining their torches into its dark depths. And then froze, a rising tide of fear threatening to engulf their senses as they studied the terrifying spectacle which had been arranged in front of them.

22
Thursday 30 April

The centrepiece of the room and, indeed, the only item of furniture was an enormous wooden throne chair which had been placed on a huge stone plinth. The overall effect of this was to raise the throne towards the low ceiling so that Hunter and Dench had to look upwards to take in the whole horrific spectacle.

A naked woman was seated on the throne chair. Her wrists were lashed to the arms of the chair and her ankles were securely fastened to its legs. Her feet didn't come anywhere near the ground which gave Sarah an idea of the size of the throne.

As they started to take in the scene in front of them, Hunter realised that the woman had a razor-wire ligature around her neck which was attached to a hook in the ceiling above her. Dench had also spotted it. Any movement of the woman's head would most likely have been the cause of the necklace of dried blood which now adorned her neck. And it seemed probable that this laceration had spawned the rivulets of blood which had their confluence between her breasts. But was this what had killed her? Hunter wasn't sure.

A long mane of once-elegant copper red hair had now lost its lustre in the damp atmosphere of the room, and strands of knotted straggly hair hung limply over the woman's shoulders partially covering her breasts. Flicking the torch beam further down the woman's body, Hunter was able to pick out severe bruising around her lower abdomen which extended towards her pelvic area.

But Sarah's attention was inexorably drawn to the woman's eyes. She was fascinated that they seemed to stare back at her with an unreal intensity. What was it that was creating this illusion because the woman was quite obviously dead? And then Sarah suddenly realised what she was looking at, and a violent shudder convulsed her whole body.

In the powerful torch beam, she could now just make out tiny strands of skin which lay across the tops of the woman's eyeballs. This uneven red fringe was all that was left of her eyelids. It looked as if the lids themselves had been chewed away and, as Hunter stared in disbelief, a beetle crawled out of a gap at the corner of the eye socket before picking its way across the eyeball. Sarah winced as the beetle continued its journey down the woman's nose before disappearing into her partially open mouth.

Wanting to drag herself away from this horrific spectacle but fascinated by it at the same time, she watched as the head of a snake suddenly appeared through the curtains of hair on the woman's right shoulder, its forked tongue sliding in and out of its mouth as it slithered across her neck. Hunter was rooted to the spot, her muddled brain taking in the morbid beauty of the reptile's black, yellow and red banding whilst, at the same time, reminding herself that she was terrified of snakes.

Without thinking, she nudged Dench to get her attention but then realised that the CSI Manager was similarly staring at the snake with an expression of dread fear.

The snake lazily continued its journey over the woman's body, the head disappearing into the shadows behind the throne, its long body still slithering across the woman's neck.

Another forked tongue appeared through the tangle of the

woman's hair, the yellow head of the snake in stark contrast with the copper red. Sarah almost gagged as its head seemed to disappear between the woman's legs but was relieved when she located it slithering into the darkness behind the throne chair.

Being in a room full of snakes *and* a dead body was probably up there as her very worst nightmare, and Hunter had to snap herself out of it.

Instinctively, she now dropped to her haunches, the beam of her torch sweeping the ground around the plinth. She was appalled to see more snakes either coiled up in repose or lazily winding their way through the ornate carvings of the throne.

She was just about to stand up when she noticed dots of blood on each of the woman's legs. Would the snakes really have attacked her, she wondered. Based on what little she knew about snakes, it seemed improbable. Didn't they only bite if provoked? So, if these were not snake bites, had the woman been attacked by another creature which might also be lurking in the shadows behind the throne?

She swept the torch beam around the area once more, stopping to watch a scorpion scuttling around in the shadows, its segmented tail curved over its back, the stinger at its end. Was that responsible for attacking the woman? If not, was there something far deadlier lying in wait for her should she venture further into the room?

The level of terror she felt was now at maximum.

Leaping up, she grabbed Dench by the arm. 'Come on Beth, we're out of here, *now*!'

They quickly retreated to the corridor, Hunter more or less dragging Dench by the arm. It felt as if the CSI manager had been screwed to the floor, mesmerised by the hideous tableau in front of her. Once they were outside the room, Hunter turned and allowed her torchlight to scour the cobbled floor to make sure that none of the reptiles had shown any interest in leaving the room with them. She then slammed the door shut and turned the key.

Both women stood facing each other, their torch beams pointing aimlessly at the ground around them. Slowly coming to their senses, they gradually became aware of a huge amount of activity at the other end of the passageway and turned to see that arc lighting had already been installed as medics moved amongst the bodies. Were they still looking for signs of life or were they just preparing for transportation to the morgue? Hunter couldn't be sure.

She turned back and flashed her torch beam along the last few yards of the passageway but all she could see was concrete – concrete walls and a concrete ceiling. Thankfully, there were unlikely to be any more unaccounted-for horrors in this cellar.

It was time to get out of this hell on earth, to stand in the open and to breathe in fresh air.

23

Thursday 30 April

The heel of an Adidas trainer ground the dogend into an ugly smear of black ash and tiny flecks of unsmoked tobacco. Another Gauloise had bitten the dust.

Johnnie Arcane looked out across the Thames Estuary towards Thurrock on the north bank with the Queen Elizabeth II bridge away to his left. He was sitting in what loosely passed for a beer garden behind The Fo'Castle Arms toying with the last dregs of a glass of Diet Coke, the ice having long since given up the ghost.

Of course, the beer garden wasn't really a garden at all. It was an area of ground which had been carpeted with bitumen before various bench-tables had been randomly distributed across it. But it was clear that no one was being paid enough to keep the so-called 'garden' clean as there were discarded bits of food lying under some of the tables, splodges of tomato ketchup under others, and even the remains of a broken glass under another. Empty crisp packets and other discarded detritus had caught on the wire fencing and rustled in the sea breeze. An occasional seagull swooped in to assess what was on offer but soon decided that there were better pickings to be had elsewhere.

The only thing the garden did have going for it was that it was quiet. And Johnnie liked somewhere quiet when he was doing business. Particularly if the business required him to think. Thinking was the problem for Johnnie who saw life predominately in black and white so any deviation from a straight choice of two options normally became a problem.

Earlier in the day, he had received a tip off from his mate, Vinnie. Being a self-confessed loner, Johnnie didn't normally form associations with people but, over the years, Vinnie had become the one person he could trust. The one person who wouldn't try to screw him on a deal or throw him under a bus when the heat was on. Vinnie had messaged him to say that there was someone who was keen to discuss a business proposition with Johnnie and, as Johnnie always liked to discuss business propositions, he had agreed to a meeting. If Vinnie thought it was a good idea, that was good enough for Johnnie.

So, he had arrived at The Fo'Castle early in order to case the joint and make sure that they could do business without too many distractions. The beer garden seemed ideal as its filthy state appeared to be a deterrent to punters wanting to sit outside and, in any case, a chilly breeze was now blowing up from the east causing the rustling of the empty crisp packets to intensify. An occasional smoker slipped out of the pub for a quick nicotine fix but, otherwise, the beer garden was deserted.

Johnnie was just contemplating another quick Gauloise before Vinnie's contact arrived when the door to the pub opened and a tall man descended the three steps into the beer garden. Looking across at Johnnie, he negotiated his way through the jungle of bench-tables until he arrived at the one Johnnie had selected for their meeting.

'You Arcane?' the man grunted.

Johnnie took that to be a question so nodded. 'And you are?' he asked.

'You can call me Maddox,' the man replied before folding himself into the bench opposite Johnnie.

Maddox was certainly tall – well over six feet in Johnnie's

estimation. And well-built. He had huge shoulders and a thick neck which attested to many hours spent in the gym. He sported a full set of black designer stubble which blended in with a head of jet black close-cropped hair. A pair of sunglasses was wrapped around the top of his head, there was a diamond stud in each ear, and a heavy metal chain hung from his neck. He was dressed all in black with a black bomber jacket keeping out the cool of the breeze. But it was the blue eyes which Johnnie had particularly noticed. They seemed to bore into his skull with their intensity.

Johnnie offered his visitor a Gauloise but the offer was rejected with a shake of the head as both men sized each other up. Johnnie lit one anyway and, turning his head away but keeping his eyes fixed on Maddox, he exhaled a long stream of sweet-smelling tobacco smoke.

'How d'you know Vinnie?' Johnnie asked casually.

Maddox stared at Johnnie. 'Known him years – since we were kids,' he replied, shrugging his shoulders. 'We've always looked out for each other.'

Johnnie could imagine. Like himself, Vinnie didn't do friends or acquaintances and, if he did, he certainly wouldn't mention them to anyone. Which was probably why Johnnie had never heard the name Maddox in all the years he had known Vinnie.

Maddox continued.

'Vinnie said that you might be interested in getting on board with some fentanyl if the price is right and we can get the supply chain right.'

Johnnie had heard about fentanyl and the potential for making him shedloads of money. But he had also heard the downside that users had to be supplied more frequently in order to maintain their levels of dependence. It had also been reported in the USA that even small doses of the drug could be fatal when mixed with heroin, a view that had been substantiated by a much higher death rate amongst users. However, if only a small amount of the drug was going to make him lots of money, he was very interested.

'Yeah, I might consider it,' Johnnie replied, trying to sound calm and in control although his elation about finding something that would send his bank balance into the stratosphere was making him feel good inside. But could he simply turn a blind eye to the number of fentanyl-related deaths which might result from him supplying the drug, or would he have to factor this in to any decision-making process?

'Tell me about what you're offering,' he said, needing to hear more.

'Okay. The thing to remember about fentanyl is that it is a highly addictive synthetic opioid. It's often mixed with either heroin, or cocaine, or meth to make it more powerful, even more addictive – and more dangerous. It's been reported in the States that one kilo of fentanyl can be cut and turned into 50 kilos of another saleable drug on the street.'

Johnnie's eyes nearly popped out of his head as his mind frantically tried to calculate the riches this could bring.

'However, a fentanyl high lasts for a shorter period of time if you compare it with just taking heroin in its pure form. So, people who are addicted have to use it several times a day. This means that they'll have to be supplied more frequently. That could impact on your supply chain and also on the ability of your runners to manage the increased number of drops.'

Johnnie listened intently. He was hooked. His mind was

whizzing through the positives and negatives of getting seriously involved with fentanyl.

'The other thing you're going to have to get right is the mixing,' Maddox continued. 'A few grains of fentanyl will make you high, a few too many may well kill you. Mixing fentanyl with anything will make the user a fentanyl addict and, if they don't have the right level of tolerance to the drug, it's probably going to kill them anyway.'

'Okay!' Johnnie said after a brief pause. He had finally spotted a downside to the proposition and needed to explore this.

'I can see a problem here and that is the ability of our punters to afford to go from, say, two supplies per week to six or even seven. They won't have the cash for that.'

'Yeah, well that's down to how your dealers carry out the enforcement, isn't it?' Maddox raised his eyebrows in a supercilious manner. 'Users will always find the cash if you've got the right enforcement in operation.'

Although Johnnie considered himself as a hard-nosed bastard who had been personally responsible for any number of injuries to any number of human bodies, he had to give some serious thought as to whether he wanted to become ultimately responsible for wantonly killing people. But Maddox was right. Good enforcement should avoid too many bad debts although you couldn't enforce payment of a debt if the punter was dead – unless you went after the family.

Johnnie tried to swallow but his mouth was dry. He would rather not continue with that train of thought.

'Okay, where do we go from here?' he eventually asked.

The two dealers then spent the next hour thrashing out the details of a plan for supplying fentanyl. Maddox offered to give Johnnie a lesson on how to mix the drug with heroin so as to avoid too many fentanyl-related deaths, and Johnnie was pleased when they managed to reach an agreement on price. This venture would, indeed, make him very rich.

The minute the deal was agreed, Maddox stood up to leave. He disengaged himself from the bench-table and looked down at Johnnie.

'Never forget, my friend,' he said menacingly, peering down his nose at Johnnie, 'we also do not tolerate bad debts – or any debts!'

With that, he turned and walked back into the pub. Johnnie stared after him.

'What the fuck?' he exclaimed before releasing another Gauloise from the crumpled pack.

The first lungful of nicotine was always the best.

24
Thursday 30 April

Sarah Hunter stood in a patch of sunlight which shone in through the burnt rafters of the mansion out of a clear blue sky. Looking up, she watched a jet's vapour trail develop across the sky, the aircraft hurrying its passengers to some exotic destination no doubt. Did she wish she was on it? She certainly needed time to be alone and to think. She continued watching as the trail dissolved into fluffy white clouds which eventually dispersed on the high-altitude winds.

In front of her, medics and crime scene investigators jostled for position on the narrow staircase which led down into the cellar. Stretchers bearing the dead were being taken out to the portacabins at the rear of the building where she assumed that one of Toby Swartzman's team was readying them for transportation to the morgue. She saw Beth Dench in conversation with the Health & Safety officials, a lot of arm waving probably indicating that she was giving her views as to the conditions underground.

The unveiling of the horrors in the cellar had put beyond doubt any other conclusion than that many reprehensible acts were routinely enjoyed in this place by a select group of individuals who had no respect for human life. In some ways, Sarah was satisfied that those in the cellar had died a slow and painful death whilst the rest of them probably didn't realise what had hit them. But the presence of children was causing her considerable discomfort as this had clearly been a much more sinister gathering than a simple weekend '*bring the family*' party in the countryside.

She was pleased to be away from the melee of activity where she could at least start to gather some of her thoughts. But she just couldn't get the image of the dead woman out of her head. Who on earth had wanted to stage such an exhibition and what was the reason behind it?

She felt her phone vibrating in her pocket so she reached inside her Tyvek suit to release it from her back pocket.

'Yes, Grace,' she answered, trying to sound calm but with her stomach still churning.

'Just to let you know that there have been a few developments so I was wondering when you would be back here,' Kendall asked.

'Any headlines amongst these developments?'

'Looks like Baz Biondi is out of the UK at the moment,' Kendall continued. 'We're trying to find out how and when he travelled and, more importantly, where he is now.'

Hunter felt a little deflated. Part of her had expected Biondi to be amongst the ruins of Tideswell Manor but now it seemed that he was not only still alive but he was also possibly out of reach, hiding in another country. Was that because he had prior knowledge of a suicide mission to destroy his mansion?

'Okay,' Hunter replied. 'Anything more on the plane or the mysterious John Smith?'

'Slow progress but I think Jed and Lisa may have spotted something on the CCTV. Are you on your way back here?'

Hunter desperately wanted a little time to herself so she told Grace that she would be back later, and to organise a team meeting for 5.30 p.m. Cutting the call, she looked around for Beth Dench but now couldn't see her amongst the white-suited forensic investigators. Perhaps she had gone back into the cellar, Sarah thought. So she made her way back to where she had originally entered the building, signed out and dumped all her protective gear in the bins which had been provided.

Getting into her car, she just hoped for some good music on the radio to help her relax a bit as she still felt like a tightly coiled spring. Chris Rea's *On the Beach* had the effect of transporting her to a faraway place as she drove away from what had become a grotesque monument to depravity in the Kent countryside.

Whilst talking to Grace Kendall, Sarah had decided to go straight home, get showered and pick up a change of clothes. She wanted to rid herself of anything to do with the foul cellar under the floors of Tideswell Manor.

Slowing to allow a huge four-by-four to pass by on one of the narrow country roads, she allowed her mind to return to the cellar and, in particular, to the room with the woman tied to the throne chair. It was a vision that was unlikely to leave her for many weeks and months – if ever.

It now sounded as if Biondi had escaped this atrocity so it was suddenly even more important to find out the identities of the dead and where had they died - in the cellar or upstairs in the mansion when the plane struck. Were Biondi and his cronies somewhere else, perhaps watching the tragedy play out on TV news programmes?

Arriving at her cottage, she made her way straight to the kitchen and, standing in front of the washing machine, she undressed before pushing every item of clothing into the drum and closing the door. After inserting the powder ball and switching the machine on, she ran up the stairs heading directly for the shower.

With questions spinning around in her head, she turned the water temperature up to 'hot' and selected the 'power shower' option. She stood under the jets of water as they began the task of erasing some of the memories of her ordeal from her mind and body.

Picking up the soap which Grace preferred to use in the shower, she scrubbed at her arms and legs in an attempt to drive out any lingering traces of the cellar.

Question: who was the woman in the throne room?

She then repeated a gentler cleansing process with her own scented shower gel, feeling better as the foamy soapiness washed from her body.

Question: who was the young girl who may have survived her ordeal?

She then hung her head under the shower, making sure that the water could get to every inch of her scalp, washing away some of the sickening sights she had witnessed.

Question: why were there no handles on the inside of the cellar door?

Towelling herself dry in the bedroom, and combing her wet hair in front of the floor length mirror, she quickly dressed before reaching for the hair dryer.

Question: why was Baz Biondi not at the party at his own mansion?

Back downstairs, she toasted two slices of bread and took a yoghurt out of the fridge.

Question: who had orchestrated the plane crash – and why?

Sitting at the table, she mulled over the events of the last few days whilst eating her meagre rations. Eventually concluding that her investigation was still very much behind the eight ball in terms of solid evidence, she left the cottage and drove back to Pembury Road for the late afternoon team meeting.

25

Thursday 30 April

As she wandered up the stairs to the Ops Room, Sarah Hunter felt her phone vibrating in her pocket. Looking at the screen she was slightly puzzled by the 'Private Number' notification on the screen but decided to answer it anyway.

'DI Hunter!'

'DI Hunter,' repeated a voice. 'You don't know me but my name is Rocco Vance, editor, chief reporter, cook and bottle washer of *News Notepad*. It's a young and upcoming online news blog for Kent and East Sussex.'

Hunter's heart skipped a beat. The dreaded press!

'How did you get my number?' she asked.

'Just rang Maidstone. Spoke to someone in PR. Margot, is it? Can't recall her surname but she seemed happy to give me your number.'

Hunter was riled. She disliked the smug tone of Vance's voice. He sounded as if he believed that he had got one over on her and that he was now in control of their conversation. Would that Westwood woman really give her number out to any Tom, Dick and Harry claiming to be from the press? She would have to find the answer to that question at the earliest opportunity but, for now, she tried to adopt a more conciliatory tone.

'Okay, Mr Vance. How can I help you?'

'Well, I was hoping that we could meet to discuss the tragedy at the house at Bewl Water. You see, I'm trying to put together a blog post with video about the crash, and I thought that my readers might benefit from the inclusion of an interview with the Senior Investigating Officer.'

'How do you know that I am the SIO?' Hunter asked.

'That was the easy part,' Vance replied. 'Just asked the guy at the end of the drive.'

Sarah's eyes rolled towards the ceiling. Why couldn't uniformed officers keep their bloody mouths shut for one moment?

'Well, I can't really see a need for us to meet, Mr Vance,' she said, hoping that she could end this call soon. 'Most of the detail about the crash as we know it is already in the public domain. We are simply following up all leads which will help us to positively identify all the victims. We will also have to await a report from the AAIB about possible cause of the crash. So, it's all pretty mundane police work. I wouldn't have thought that it would be of much interest as a video blog post.'

There was silence on the line. In her dreams, Sarah had hoped that they had been cut off but she then heard Vance clearing his throat.

'I had also hoped that we could meet to talk about the discoveries in the cellar and, in particular, the woman in the room full of snakes.'

Sarah felt as if someone had poured a bucket of ice cold water down the back of her T-shirt. Her stomach churned at the mere mention of the woman. But how on earth did this man know about something they had discovered only a few hours ago? Was there a leak amongst those in her team? Surely not! But she now knew she had to tread very carefully.

'I'm afraid that I'm not at liberty to discuss our ongoing investigations until all the victims have been accounted for,' she parroted with a formality that might even have impressed Westwood.

'Oh, come on Inspector,' Vance persisted. 'I know that something was going on in that cellar. But, if you don't want to help me then my only other option will be to publish what I know which may not be an accurate representation of the actual situation. Surely you would have a preference for allowing the public to at least understand the lines of your investigation. And it would give you an opportunity to perhaps reach out to them for further information about the crash or the crash victims.'

Hunter was aghast at the thought of going on camera with this man, and she was still desperately trying to work out how he had gained some knowledge of the cellar – and, particularly, the throne room.

'And this would be a hell of a scoop for *News Notepad*,' Vance continued. 'The syndication of an interview with you would help us to continue operating in the dog-eat-dog world of news gathering and information. And it would be a great opportunity for the police to appeal directly to the public for further information about this tragedy.'

'Okay! Okay! I've heard enough!' Hunter desperately wanted this phone call to end. 'I'll have a think about it and let you know. How do I get in touch with you?'

'I'll text you my number,' Vance replied.

'Just so that you are aware,' Hunter continued, 'all information about the cellar is strictly off limits for the time being as this is most definitely a criminal investigation. So, I am not at liberty to discuss it with you. But we may be able to do something which will help your blog post and which also aids our investigation. I'll, therefore, have a think about it and be in touch.'

'Don't leave it too long!' Vance exclaimed. 'Things move very quickly in the process of dissemination of information these days.'

'Thank you for letting me know that, Mr Vance,' she said before flicking the red circle on the phone's screen.

She stood staring at the phone for a few seconds after the call had ended, almost dropping it when it vibrated in her hand with an incoming text. Vance had sent his phone number.

26

Thursday 30 April

To Sarah's surprise, DCI Alan Iversen was in attendance at her late afternoon meeting with the team. She was just preparing to start the meeting when he sneaked into the room and stood at the back, giving her a perfunctory nod of the head as if to say that he was only there to listen. Anyway, that is what Sarah took it to mean.

'Okay, everyone,' she started, 'it's already been a long one for all of us so I don't want to delay you from getting some rest as you'll need to be ready to get going again bright and early tomorrow.'

She looked round the room. Everyone looked reasonably bright eyed but that was probably more to do with the fact that they were still in the relatively early days of what could turn out to be a long and difficult investigation. So, where to start. Her eyes alighted on Acting DS Elaine Jennings.

'Right Elaine, the Buckley missing daughter case. How's that going?'

Jennings had her notebook to hand and, although she fiddled with it and turned a few pages over, Hunter could see that she was on top of her investigation as she never once actually looked at the notes.

'Well, Julie Buckley is still touch and go. They had a couple of emergencies with her during the night but managed to stabilise her on each occasion. We certainly can't get in to see her and one of the nurses we spoke to said she doubted that Julie would pull through.'

Jennings fiddled with her notebook again.

'We have, however, made some progress in the hunt for her assailants,' Jennings continued. 'There was so much blood around the scene of her assault that it became transferred to Rachael's room by the assailants. This allowed the forensics team to get a couple of quite presentable prints which they are now working on.' She looked across at DC Azzar Mishraz. 'Do you want to cover the phones, Azz?'

'Yeah, sure!' Mishraz replied. 'In all, we found three phones in the daughter's bedroom. They were all pretty bashed up – cracked glass mainly which made it difficult to see what was on the screen. But they still worked. We gave two of the phones to Jordan Wright to let his team see what information they could get from them, and we have kept one for ourselves. They were all ringing off the hook, particularly the one we kept. Just shows you the number of punters the girl must have been supplying. I've spent some time this afternoon with the techie boys downstairs trying to see if there were any clues which might suggest where Rachael may have gone.'

Hunter butted in. 'And I presume that there was nothing that was immediately going to help us.'

'Well, there was nothing which immediately gave any clues about her whereabouts but we did make one interesting discovery,' Azzer continued. 'Jordan Wright told us that all the phones used in county lines normally have names to identify the name of the line. It didn't take me long to establish that the name on the phone we have is *AXTON* so that must be the identity of one of the lines. I then remembered where I had seen that name before. It was on a label attached to the bottom of one of the snow globes in Rachael's bedroom.'

Jennings took up the story. 'So we went back to the house and had a word with the CSIs. They were just starting to bag and label what was left of the snow globes so we had a look through all the bits and pieces they had and, hey presto, *AXTON* was amongst them. What's more, it was intact. Apparently a feared warmonger from one of the X-box games. Quite why someone would produce a snow globe containing the character of a warlord is anyone's guess. But it does indicate that perhaps all Rachael's county lines were named after snow globes.'

'But I thought you told me that she had loads of snow globes,' Hunter asked, recalling their discussions of a couple of days ago.

'She did,' Mishraz replied, 'so I looked back at the photos I took when we first got into the room and noticed that, whilst they were all crammed onto one of the shelves, there were four which stood on their own at the end of the shelf. Our thinking is, therefore, that she was working on four lines which means that one of the phones is unaccounted for.'

'And that could have been found by the assailants or she could have taken it with her when she disappeared,' Hunter hypothesised. 'Was there anything from house-to-house?'

'Sounds as if the mother and daughter spent much of their lives shouting and screaming at each other,' Jennings continued. 'The closest neighbours did hear a bit of a commotion yesterday morning but just assumed that it was yet another argument. Someone further down the road had been out early on a dog walk and was passed by one of those Hilux vehicles favoured by people in the building trade. Apparently going like the clappers. Otherwise, nothing much worth reporting.'

'Get a photo of a Hilux and send the uniforms back to see if they can jog a few memories,' Hunter said, not believing that nobody else had seen a vehicle of that size, even at that time in the morning.

'Will do, ma'am,' Jennings responded. 'Otherwise we're making a nuisance of ourselves with Jordan's techies and with our own. If you don't keep on their backs, they get easily distracted. Hopefully, we should get some intel from them tomorrow.'

'What about drugs?' Hunter asked, wanting to know the scale of Racheal Buckley's supply line.

'Well, we found at least forty wraps of cocaine – if not more. And a solid ounce of heroin. So, she was being kept busy.'

'Good, Elaine. And keep up the pressure on the techies.' Sarah looked around the room but Jennings wasn't quite finished.

'There is one other consideration,' she began. Hunter raised an eyebrow but nodded as if inviting Jennings to carry on.

'Well it's probably a bit of a long shot but, as you know, one of the first things we did was to go round the hospitals to see if anyone of Rachael's description had been admitted. We talked to all hospitals in Kent, East Sussex and East Surrey but drew a blank there. However, that was before the girl from Tideswell Manor had been admitted. Do we know anything more about her?'

Sarah Hunter felt a little tingle of excitement. 'I don't even know which hospital she's in,' she said, looking round the room.

'She's in Pembury,' Grace replied. 'And I think Julie Buckley's still there as she's too ill to be moved.'

'Well, that's a very interesting thought, Elaine. Get on to that first thing in the morning. I don't think we have a medical report on the Tideswell girl, do we?' Sarah said, looking over to where Grace was sitting. Her gaze was met with a shake of the head.

'We took some items for DNA testing when we were at the house so I'll see if we can get a test sorted out.' Jennings wasn't anything if not thorough, and Hunter knew that she would get the DNA testing done come hell or high water. Could there be a link between Julie Buckley and the girl at Tideswell? Hunter looked over to Iversen who was nodding enthusiastically.

'Okay, Jed you're next.' Sarah had one eye on the clock and really wanted to let everyone get off home at a reasonable hour. 'Last time we spoke you had discovered some CCTV which might be useful.'

'Yes, ma'am.' Crowther reported without the use of notes. 'Lisa and I have spent most of the day looking at CCTV footage from two cameras mounted on the shoreline near the Bewl Water Estate Office. Seems they are mainly used to keep an eye on all the activities going on at the outdoor centre. Sailing, windsurfing, canoeing – that sort of thing. Quality's not bad but low sun is a bit of a problem early in the day. They seem to keep the equipment well-maintained and the glass in the boxes had recently been cleaned. So, overall, the recorded feed from the cameras was pretty good quality.'

'And what has been going on?' Hunter asked.

'Well, their system has two settings.' Lisa Calder had now taken up the narrative. 'It's motion-activated during the hours of darkness which basically means that it will only record when activity is detected. From daybreak, and during all the hours of sunlight, it becomes a continuous video recording system. This means that the Estate Office can maintain real-time security surveillance over the waters at the north end of Bewl Water.'

'It took us a bit of time to locate the tape for last Sunday,' Crowther was consulting some notes, 'and when we did get there we had a bit of difficulty finding the correct time slot because there was a fault with the timer. Thankfully, the guy knew what he was doing and found the right images for our time window of seven o'clock onwards.'

'Sounds interesting,' Hunter interjected. 'But it sounds as if these cameras had a limited field of vision if they were essentially to monitor windsurfing or canoeing close to the shoreline.'

'That's what we thought to start with but the pictures showed almost a panoramic view of the north end of the water.' Crowther turned to Grace Kendall. 'Grace, we arranged for the tape to be emailed to you. Has it arrived yet?'

Kendall spun the cursor around the screen before confirming that the email had arrived. She turned the screen so that it was facing more into the room as the team shuffled around so they could all take a look.

'Great! It should be loaded at the time of the incident so if you just play it from here,' Crowther instructed.

At the click of the mouse, a vista of water glinting in the morning sun appeared, a clearly-defined shoreline running up the left of the screen. In the distance, an area of forestation looked as if it came to the edge of the water.

'Any minute now,' Crowther said, almost in a whisper.

They all watched as a black smudge shot across the water in the top half of the screen. Just as they were trying to decide what they had just seen, there was a disturbance in the water near the area of forestation.

'Can you re-run it please, Grace,' Crowther asked.

Now that they all knew what they were looking at, eight

pairs of eyes concentrated on the original smudge followed by the disturbance in the water. When they had all had a chance to view the CCTV footage for a second time, Lisa Calder continued.

'Our thinking is that the smudge or blur or whatever you like to call it is the shadow of the plane which must have been quite close to the ground by this stage. And that the disturbance in the water is actually a huge splash as the pilot hits the water. The only caveat to that assessment is that it's difficult to see any evidence of a parachute, possibly because of the sun glinting on the water.'

Hunter was unsure about the evidence of a splash. It seemed too indistinct and, apart from anything else, it was quite a long way from the camera that recorded it. In fact, if the camera itself hadn't been so clean, she doubted that they would have even seen the splash. She made her misgivings known to Crowther.

'Well ma'am,' he responded, 'we did talk about this with the guy from the office as both Lisa and I thought that there could be creatures in the water that might break the surface from time to time. He said that he didn't think there were any which could make that sort of a disturbance to the water's surface so it had to be something else.'

'Could it have been a section of the plane falling into the water?' Carolyn Pennant had been carefully studying the images on the screen. 'Perhaps the aircraft really was in trouble with bits falling off it. Did the pilot have no alternative but to bale out? Either coming down on the water or on the land.'

Everyone was still staring rather blankly at the screen where Grace had paused the tape.

'Well, that's a good point Carolyn,' Hunter replied, moving

away from the screen and propping herself against the edge of one of the desks. 'However, we haven't yet had any reports that the plane had suffered a catastrophic failure or that pieces of the aircraft were found on the ground between the water's edge and the manor house. I would also suggest that, if the plane really was in trouble, the pilot wouldn't already be kitted out with a parachute. So, if he did bale out, we would presumably be looking for his body unless he survived a fall into water.'

'Yes but, if he did survive,' Lisa Calder countered, 'he would have either been picked up by a boat or he would have got to the shore and gone to get some help. Instead of which, he's simply disappeared.'

There was a cough and the clearing of a throat at the back of the room.

'However, in the other scenario, the pilot may well have planned to jump when the plane was over the water,' Iversen intervened, 'so the smaller smudge could well be a parachute in which case we should probably be searching the area of forestation which comes down to the water's edge in that part of Bewl.'

'Yes, I had thought of that, sir,' Crowther replied. 'In fact, we should probably be searching the length of that north shore so Lisa and I are going to have a scout around there first thing tomorrow.'

Iversen nodded, gave a thumbs up sign to Crowther and looked over to Sarah. 'Sorry to butt in!'

She smiled.

The meeting carried on with Carolyn Pennant giving a detailed account of progress or, rather, lack of it at the morgue. However, the pathologists had indicated that they might be able to start identifying those bodies discovered in the cellar as they had not either been crushed to death or incinerated. In fact, they were quite well preserved and cause of death was fairly easy to ascertain.

There was then just time for Grace to give a quick update on the identity of the plane, the pilot and her discussions with the AAIB all of which were proceeding at a snail's pace much to the frustration of all concerned. She also gave an update on the search for Baz Biondi.

'At the moment, we think that he is out of the country but we can't seem to find out where,' she informed her colleagues. 'I have been promised more information tomorrow so I'll let you know as soon as it comes in.'

Sarah then moved to close the briefing.

'Okay, guys, tomorrow's a key day for our investigation when we need to make a decisive move forward. Getting some solid information from at least one of our channels of inquiry will give us a chance to start to unravel what is gradually becoming a complex case with several strands to it. So, early night tonight and early start tomorrow.'

But, as she watched them file out of the room, she wondered if they really would be able to make any serious progress tomorrow. There were so many unknowns, and it was becoming increasingly difficult to see where her investigation was going.

The pangs of self-doubt were starting to take over from the positivity which she had felt earlier in the day.

27

Friday 1 May

The village of Underriver lies about 3 miles to the south-east of Sevenoaks. A road known simply as Carters Hill runs through the village and then climbs towards One Tree Hill, a National Trust area of outstanding natural beauty with panoramic views over the Weald of Kent. This was a popular spot for walkers and others who simply wanted to feast their eyes on the stunning scenery which was all around them.

Sarah Hunter had only been dozing when the call had come in that there had been a multiple shooting at the local beaty spot. Apparently, a young couple looking for a quiet spot in which to improve their knowledge of each other had stumbled on an abandoned London taxi cab with three bodies inside it. This report had then been investigated by a vehicle from Traffic Division, and the officers confirmed that there had, indeed, been an incident at One Tree Hill.

As Grace hadn't been staying over, Sarah had decided to take a quick shower and then hit the road, heading towards Sevenoaks in the dead of night. The clock on the dashboard now showed 02.36 a.m. as she drove past The White Rock Inn in the centre of Underriver, its windows in darkness, the last of the drinkers long gone home to their beds.

In her headlights, she could now see that Carters Hill had been closed at its junction with the road which leads down to Underriver's cricket club ground, about 250 metres past the pub. A 'Police No Entry' sign had been positioned in the middle of the narrow road, and blue and white barrier tape had been strung across the road. She slowed to a halt as a uniformed constable wearing a high viz jacket stepped out of the shadows and made his way to her car.

She thought that she recognised the constable from the Tonbridge station but wasn't sure so she showed him her warrant card anyway.

'Any trouble?' she asked as the constable shone his torch onto the card and then quickly across her face.

'Not really,' he replied. 'Just some smart arse who tried to blag his way through. Actually mentioned your name. Said he was meeting you at the top of the hill. Turns out he couldn't provide ID and, as you weren't here anyway, I told him to take a hike which he wasn't very happy about. Apart from that, very little traffic at all as you would expect at this time of night.'

Hunter was intrigued yet concerned that someone would be trying to blag their way into a crime scene by insinuating that they were meeting her. How did they know that she would be coming to One Tree Hill? Or had they just taken a punt that she would be here? Come to think of it, how did they even know that a crime had been committed here?

'Did you take the number of the vehicle?' she asked, hopefully.

'Certainly did, ma'am,' the constable replied, pulling a notebook from one of the pockets inside the high viz. He tore a page out of the notebook and passed it through her open window.

'Thanks very much,' she replied. 'I'll follow this up. Well done!'

The constable smiled, stepped back from the car and moved the sign to the side of the road before lifting the tape and allowing Hunter to continue her journey up Carter's Hill.

Arriving at the public parking area at the entrance to One Tree Hill, she eventually decided to park at the end of a line of cars and crime scenes vehicles which stretched along the road beyond the car park. As she started to walk back to the crime scene, a car door opened in front of her and Elaine Jennings stepped down onto the road.

'Thought you might like some company, ma'am,' she said, stretching her back as if she had been sitting in the car for a while.

'Thanks, Elaine. But how did you know I'd be here?' Hunter sounded puzzled.

'In my Acting DS role, I've asked for all emergency calls to be notified to me in case I feel that we need to be involved. Doesn't happen very often but I assumed that you would attend this one so I thought I'd come along to see if I can be of any help.'

Hunter was impressed. 'Two pairs of eyes will no doubt be better than one,' she observed as they set off along the road.

They soon reached the car park where the CSI team were making notes, photographing, measuring and collecting as much evidence as they could find. Banks of LED floodlights had been set up around the whole area providing the sort of clinical stark lighting favoured by crime scene investigators.

The centrepiece was a modern black London taxi cab which sat forlornly at one end of the car park, its doors hanging open, its occupants already zipped into body bags for their trip to the morgue. It was an eerie yet somehow ethereal sight.

She soon spotted Beth Dench and then stopped dead in her tracks when she saw who she was talking to.

What on earth was DCI Jack Pennington doing here, and

how had he managed to get to One Tree Hill before her? She was just thinking of making herself scarce and taking a look at the taxi when Pennington noticed her and cut away from his discussion with Dench.

'Morning, Sarah!' he chortled as if it was quite normal for them to meet up at three o'clock in the dead of night. 'Looks like the shootout at the O.K. Corral has come to Kent!'

Hunter surveyed the scene before responding. 'Maybe, but Underriver, Kent, is hardly the same as Tombstone, Arizona, even on a hot day!' She smiled whilst Pennington looked slightly bemused.

'Hi, Sarah,' Dench interjected before the conversation could get any more ridiculous, and then turned towards Jennings. 'Morning Elaine. Thought I saw you arrive a little earlier. We've got the crime scene pretty much secured so I'll happily talk you through it if you'd like to follow me.'

Dench led them across the parking area, carefully avoiding an array of small cones and other coloured markers which littered the ground around them. She stopped once they had got to the other side of the area.

'Right. There was a 999 call at about 10.45 p.m. The local Traffic boys took a bit of time getting here as they were attending a ruckus at a house just south of Tunbridge Wells. Anyway, they managed to secure the area once they had got their heads around what had happened and our duty team arrived on site about an hour later. They've been working to get the three bodies moved to the morgue, a job which has now been completed. I think Norman Partington's still here doing some measuring so you should be able to catch him before he goes home to his bed. And, as you can see, we have one black

London taxi cab which will be eventually transported to our yard at Maidstone.'

'Any ideas about who the victims are?' Hunter asked, more in hope than anything else.

'The cab was positioned where it is now with both rear doors and the driver's door open. Two bodies were in the back of the cab and the driver was half in and half out of the vehicle. Could have fallen out when the door was opened from the outside. All three were men. The two in the back were probably IC 1 – you know, Caucasian and from northern Europe but one could have been from southern Europe. The pathologists might be able to be more specific. The driver was an IC 3 – probably from a Caribbean background; more particularly Rastafarian. It helped that our search of the area produced a rastacap which could have become dislodged from what was left of his head when he fell out of the cab.'

'And all shots were fired through open doors?' Jennings asked. 'No sign of bullet holes in the bodywork of the cab?'

'That's what it looks like,' Dench replied. 'Which also seems to suggest that there were two gunmen. However, the driver was shot twice in the back of the head with the bullets leaving a large hole in the Perspex panel between the passenger compartment and the driver.'

'So, you're inferring that the driver was shot by one of the passengers?' Hunter enquired. She was always fascinated by the way Beth Dench and her team almost brought crime scenes back to life.

'That's the clear inference from looking at the evidence,' Dench replied, 'although, rather puzzlingly, we couldn't find a weapon. The man seated directly behind the driver had a holster strapped to his body but no sign of the firearm which went with it. We'll be able to tell more when ballistics take a look at all the evidence but, at this stage, I'd say that two gunmen approached the cab and shot the two passengers inside.'

'Surely one of them could have shot the driver,' Jennings speculated.

'My money's still on the driver being shot by the passenger sitting directly behind his compartment. I suppose it's possible that one of the gunmen could have fired a shot from inside the cab to make it look like the driver was killed by one of the passengers. But two bullets exited the cab high up the windscreen and the blood spatter on the windscreen is consistent with the bullets exiting the top of his forehead. This would indicate that the shots had been fired from a low position, like someone leaning forward in the seat and firing. In any case, there would have been no reason for the gunmen to take the trouble to shoot the driver from inside the cab when they could easily get to him through his window.'

The detectives stood mulling over the information they had just been given.

'The other thing we found in the cab was a mobile phone,' Dench continued. That got everyone's attention. 'Looks like it was in the driver's hand when he was blasted from behind. We'll get our techies to take a look at it. Now, let's move over to that area of yellow cones.'

They all moved about ten yards from where the cab had been positioned, and now stood almost in the middle of the parking area.

'That dark patch on the ground is dried blood,' Dench said, pointing at the ground. 'Looks like a significant spill in anyone's language. Our view is that one of the gunmen suffered gunshot wounds and collapsed right here. He must have then been dragged to another vehicle. You can just see two lines in the dried mud where his heels would have scraped along the ground. There's also a trail of blood leading to where the other vehicle must have been parked. We've been working on lifting tyre prints from the area over there with the blue cones but the vehicle must have taken off at speed with tyres spinning and churning up the earth.'

'Are you going to be doing the rounds of the hospitals, Sarah?' Pennington asked, his eyes roaming over the ground around him.

Hunter was a bit taken aback by this question.

'I'd rather assumed that you would be arranging that as it seems to be your investigation,' she replied, trying to tactfully imply that his presence here was certainly an indication that he was laying claim to the case.

'Not this one. I only came over because there's been a series of gangland executions in the London area and I wanted to see if this bore any similarity to the incidents we're investigating.'

'And does it?'

'That'll depend very much on what forensics, ballistics and the pathologists come up with. On the face of it, this looks like part of a bitter feud with one side knocking out some key personnel on the other side. The only slightly puzzling aspect is why one of the passengers killed the driver. You would have thought all those in the taxi were on the same side.'

Hunter wandered back to where the taxi had been parked.

'And this hasn't been moved?' She just wanted to confirm that the cab had been parked facing along the road towards the village of Seal and the busy A25 road.

'No, that's where we found it,' Dench confirmed. 'Listen guys, I've got to get on so I'll let you have an interim report as soon as possible.'

Hunter could sympathise with Dench. She would have deadlines to meet and was, therefore, keen not to spend too much time ruminating on hypotheses which were yet to be backed up by hard evidence. She watched as Dench strode off to the periphery of the parking area and joined a small group of white-suited crime scene investigators who seemed to be comparing notes they had on their clipboards.

'How're you getting on out at Tideswell Manor?' Pennington asked as they picked their way across the parking area and back to the road. 'I read your last report. God only knows what's been going on there right under our noses. Now you've got a plane without a pilot and the owner of the mansion is on the missing list.'

Thank goodness Pennington had got her report, Hunter thought. Well done, Grace, for writing and sending it. In Sarah's mind, the fact that she had not had much input didn't really matter in the great scheme of things. As long as he was still happy for her to just get on with the investigation – that was all that really mattered.

'We're hoping for something back from the pathologists very soon, and it looks like we were able to rescue a young girl alive from the wreckage. As long as she pulls through we may have a witness. We're also pulling out all the stops in our search for Baz Biondi as, apart from owning the mansion, there is a growing suspicion that he may well have been involved in its demise.'

'Oh? How come?' Pennington asked.

'Well, it doesn't look as if he's in a fridge at the morgue so why hasn't he surfaced to lay claim to what's left of his property? This plane crash is national news and has been well reported on the web so it's gone round the world. Yet we haven't heard a squeak from Biondi let alone a visit. Don't you think that's rather odd?'

Pennington took time to mull this over before eventually responding.

'Do we have any idea about where he might be or what his most recent movements have been?'

Elaine Jennings took this opportunity to update Pennington on the work Grace had been doing to trace Biondi. 'As far as we know, he's not here in the UK at the moment. We have, therefore, been trying to check all his known overseas residences which hasn't been easy due to the complex security barriers which some of these mega stars put in place to keep their lives private.'

'Meanwhile, a drug-fuelled orgy takes place at his mansion which is only brought to an end when four tonnes of aircraft engineering brings the whole lot tumbling down,' Hunter summarised. 'Surely, he must have known about this gathering. It's inconceivable that it could have taken place without his knowledge. But who are or, rather, were those attending? Are they all dealers and distributors? Is Biondi the top man? I had a look in one of a bunch of Winnebagos which were parked behind the mansion. Not only was there a reasonable stash of Class A but there was also at least one firearm.'

'Doesn't sound like a get-together for members of a county lines group,' Pennington commented. 'They'd be too busy killing each other rather than partying the night away. But they could have all been there for some sort of assessment by Biondi's cronies. If he really is controlling some huge drug empire then perhaps he needs to recruit people further down the food chain from time to time. Of course, he doesn't want to be there himself so he hands the reins to his principle dealers who pick those that they want to work with. One thing I would guarantee is that Biondi would have known the identity of every single person present at Tideswell.'

The three detectives had slowly wandered along the road and were now standing by Hunter's car.

'Well it looks like I've got a mountain to climb if we factor in this little lot,' she said, pointing back towards the parking area. 'And before you go, what do you know of Jordan Wright?'

'The guy at Medway?' Pennington asked. 'Yeah, solid performer. Tough cookie when he's in the field by all accounts. Gets his man if you know what I mean.'

Hunter could imagine. 'And any news on the whereabouts of Rory Easton?'

Pennington visibly stiffened at the mention of Easton's name. He looked around the darkness that surrounded them as if scouring the shadows for someone who might be spying on them.

'No more questions today, Sarah,' he said with an air of finality before turning and walking away.

28

Friday 1 May

Eschewing the temptation to allow herself to catch up on some sleep, Sarah Hunter had set the alarm for 07.00 a.m. after returning home from One Tree Hill. She had then fallen into a fitful sleep whilst her overactive brain tried to work through the detail of the crime scene she had just attended.

She had found the sound of the alarm a merciful release from her mental torment, and had then taken a long hot shower to get herself ready for whatever the day had in store for her.

The traffic had been unusually light for a Friday morning so she had immersed herself in some of Diana Krall's music, particularly enjoying her version of *Walk On By*. As she negotiated the Vauxhall roundabout before heading off along Pembury Road, she had turned the volume up at the point where Ms Krall's eloquent piano playing once again dominates with a greater urgency. It seemed the perfect musical background for a lovely sunny May morning.

She parked in her usual space just as the music faded at the end of the track and, still humming the tune, she made her way up the steps to the front door of the station.

'Morning, ma'am!' The bright and breezy greeting echoed around the empty reception area as Hunter made her way across the floor to the security door.

'Morning Trevor,' she replied, acknowledging the greeting from Sergeant Trevor Arnold who seemed to be on the early morning shift today. 'Nice and quiet for you at this time of day. Is it like this every day at this time?'

'Can't complain. I can get some of the paperwork done before the great and the good of Tonbridge think we're open,' Arnold mused whilst deftly folding the morning paper which had been lying open in front of him and sliding it onto a shelf beneath the desk.

Hunter hadn't missed the attempted sleight of hand. 'I see what you mean about the *paperwork*!' she quipped.

She could, however, empathise with what the Desk Sergeant was saying. Although Tonbridge was a town, it had something of the way of life of a large village with many of the inhabitants knowing each other or, indeed, being related to each other. Sarah knew that Arnold and his colleagues in uniform were often required to officiate at inter-family feuds, many of which ended up in the reception area at the station.

Removing her pass from her pocket, she was just about to swipe it through the reader on the wall next to the entry door when Arnold called over again.

'Before you go up, ma'am, there's someone to see you. I've put them in the Suite. Most insistent they were.'

Sarah frowned.

'You'd better not be winding me up, *Sergeant* Arnold!' she replied disparagingly. Arnold simply pointed towards the Suite, at the same time waving his hand to indicate that she should check out who her visitor was.

Mentally ticking off all the things she had to do today, she crossed the reception area before barrelling through the door into the Suite. And stopped in her tracks. Staring at the man sitting at the table in front of her. She took two steps backwards to close the door behind her before walking over and sitting in the chair across the table.

'May I ask what the hell you are doing here?' She didn't know whether she was angry, elated, disappointed, exulted or simply completely baffled.

'Thought you'd be pleased to see me, boss!'

Ted Selitto sat opposite her, his eyes twinkling above the line of the surgical mask which covered the lower part of his face and neck. His dark glasses sat on the top of his head.

'But what *are* you doing here, Ted? You're supposed to be in that trauma clinic down in Eastbourne.'

'I know, and I'd probably still be there if it wasn't for the fact that the clinic is keen to reduce the number of its inmates. Something about adopting a new set of protocols so I volunteered to leave. They carried out some sort of assessment and, after talking to my medical people, they decided that I could go as long as I took things very easy.'

'So you came straight back here to a major disaster investigation! You call that taking things *very easy?*'

'Boss, I need something to get my old brain back into gear. It's a bowl full of stodge up here.' He pointed to the sides of his head.

Hunter sat back in the chair just staring at him. In the darkest hours and days when she had sat at his bedside and held his hand for hours on end, she had longed for the day when he would be back at the station. And now here he was! What was not to like? But, was he really ready to return?

'How did you get here?' she asked without really thinking about what she was saying. Her mind was in turmoil just wondering how much value he could actually be to her investigation. She would have to be keeping a constant eye on him, checking for any signs that his recovery was regressing, making sure that he wasn't doing too much.

'Cab,' he replied. 'Cabbie wasn't too keen to start with but when he found out I was in the job, he took the fare. He'd recently retired after thirty years with our old friends at Hantspol and had moved to Eastbourne. Quickly became bored stiff with retirement so he took up taxiing just to get him out of the house. We had a good old natter on the journey. I took his number just in case we ever need a civilian with a bit of knowledge.'

Sarah rolled her eyes at this suggestion knowing just how difficult it could be for a retired officer to get back into the groove of a major investigation.

'Didn't you think it might have been better to go home first and then think about coming in here?' she asked. 'Or perhaps calling me first?'

Selitto looked down at the table, his eyes suddenly looking rather sad.

'No! Okay! Sorry!' she spluttered. 'I shouldn't have said that. Of course it's absolutely fantastic to have you back here. You must do what you think is best for your recovery. And, if being in here is best for that, then fine. We can certainly use another pair of hands.'

'No doubt you're dealing with that plane crash,' Selitto offered. 'A lot of legwork needed on something like that. I can help Grace with the hard yards on checking and re-checking the intel.'

'Yes, yes, yes!' Sarah sighed in a deprecating manner.

They lapsed into silence, looking at each other across the table. Sarah was in two minds about how much help Selitto would be to Grace on the deskwork. He was more of a field operator – best when out collecting evidence and catching criminals. They worked well together as a partnership, spear-heading investigations, putting in the long hours, separating the wheat from the chaff.

In many ways, Sarah was relieved when she heard a knock on the door. She got up and went to open it.

'Come in! Come in!' she beckoned as Elaine Jennings stepped into the Suite.

'Morning, Guv!' she exclaimed as she spotted Selitto sitting at the table.

'Good to see you, Elaine,' Selitto replied. 'Thought I'd better get back here before they confirmed you as my permanent replacement!'

'That'll be the day,' she joshed before turning to Hunter.

'Sorry to interrupt, ma'am, but I've just had a call from the crime scene technicians and they're just finishing up at One Tree Hill. Did we want to get up there before they leave and have a look at the place in daylight?

'Jeez,' Sarah murmured, 'have we got time to do that?' Then, as if answering her own question. 'I suppose we ought to have another look in the natural light. Okay, Elaine, get a car organised and I'll meet you outside in five minutes.'

As Jennings left the room, Hunter returned her gaze to the man sitting opposite her.

'Well, Ted, it seems I have no choice,' she said as she sat back in her chair. 'You'd better get yourself upstairs and installed with Grace. She'll certainly welcome an extra pair of hands but you must tell us if you start to feel unwell. You must be honest with yourself, and with me.'

'Yes, boss,' he replied as he got to his feet and shuffled out of the Suite. They crossed the now busy reception area and

Sarah swiped her card on the reader to let him into the inner sanctum of the station. Grace could deal with reactivating his pass later. On her way, she had noticed that he had left his suitcase behind so she asked the Desk Sergeant to arrange for it to be taken upstairs.

With feelings of self-doubt and foreboding about the wisdom of letting Selitto come back quite so soon, Sarah turned and walked out of the building to wait for Jennings.

29
Friday 1 May

Despite the jets of hot water pounding onto his scalp and body, and a liberal use of shower gel, he just couldn't shift the feeling that he was still covered in blood. Using an old scrubbing brush he had found under the sink in the kitchen, he scrubbed and scrubbed until his skin was almost raw.

Johnnie Arcane had never seen such a quantity of the red stuff before. And it seemed to just keep on flowing despite his best efforts to stem the bleeding.

That bastard Gav! He'd told him to keep the fucking phone on silent. But when Johnnie gave the signal as he walked across the car park, he could hear the trill of the message alert tone in the cab. Not surprising the guys realised that something was up. Gav deserved the bullet in the back of his head. Fucking idiot!

Johnnie also castigated himself for being slow to get round to the other side of the vehicle, and started to scrub with renewed vigour. Just that split second delay had allowed the guy with the gun to send a fusillade of shots in the direction of Stryker Stone who had spun away from the door frame just as Johnnie managed to pull the other door open and silence the bastard.

Wrenching the shooter out of the dead gunman's hand, Johnnie had then opened the driver's door to make sure that Gav was dead. He had then reached into the cab and collected the phone which was sitting in its holder attached to the dashboard. Running back round the cab, he had found Stryker lying in a pool of blood. He had dragged the heavy, unresponsive body to the car and then had great difficulty getting it onto the back seat. This had been such a monumental effort that sweat had soaked through his clothes by the time he had got the car started, and he had then set off at speed along the lane back to the A25 at Seal.

To begin with, he had driven aimlessly, his mind analysing what his next moves should be. In the original plan, he would have taken Stryker back to Wouldham where he'd left his car and then got himself back to Chatham. But he'd had to change the plan and try to get his accomplice to a hospital without attracting attention. Although he knew he would risk being seen by CCTV, he didn't think that there would be many people around at that time of the night. But, otherwise, he just couldn't think what else to do with Stryker. In fact, he wasn't even sure if the man was still alive.

So, he had unceremoniously dumped the body by the road-side close to the Medway Maritime Hospital in Gillingham. He had found a section of pavement which wasn't overlooked, and had propped Stryker up against a rubbish bin in the hope that he might be noticed by someone.

He had then headed back to Rochester but needed to get rid of the car so called up one of his dealers who also ran a garage doing dodgy MoTs and insurance quotations. The dealer, known only as 'Spanners', arranged to meet Johnnie in a narrow lane off Blue Bell Hill where they swapped cars. He also handed over the phone he had taken from the dashboard of the cab in the full knowledge that it would be crushed to about one tenth of its original size and distributed in landfill many miles from Kent.

Dawn was starting to break over the River Medway as Johnnie had driven home to St Mary's Island to the north of Chatham. He had immediately stripped and set fire to all his clothes in the incinerator he kept in his secluded garden. It had some fancy chimney which cut down the smoke so he hoped that he had not attracted any attention at that time in the early morning.

Eventually, the hot water started to lose its effect. Johnnie stepped out of the shower, towelled himself down and wandered through into the bedroom. He flopped down on the bed and stared at the ceiling even though the floor-to-ceiling windows in the room gave a panoramic view across the Medway to Hoo Marina – a magnificent sight at any time of the day or night, and in any weather.

Johnnie's mind was in turmoil. Too many loose ends. Too many 'what ifs'. They had definitely hit the right people. That bloody Frenchman had been sniffing around his area for a while now. Thank goodness Stryker had managed to *off* him before he himself had got hit, Johnnie thought. He didn't know who the other guy was who'd killed Gav but he had a right posh shooter which had now been placed in the secret wall safe located behind a false panel in his garage. He had also rigorously cleaned the guns he and Stryker had used. These had also been stored in the safe and would be returned to their owner later today.

Although the loss of Gav was going to present him with a problem, he reasoned that Gav was totally responsible for the fact that Stryker was unlikely to survive which meant that he had lost two of his main dealers in one night. To lose one might be classified as bad luck, he reasoned. To lose two looked like sheer fucking carelessness. Did he have replacements he could immediately call on? Or was he going to have to get back on the road himself? He mulled this over as his eyes searched the ceiling for answers to his questions.

Suddenly, Johnnie sat bolt upright on the bed.

Maddox!

Fuck! He had to get back to Maddox!

He swung his legs onto the floor and padded over to the built-in wardrobe where he quickly dressed in a T-shirt and beach shorts before standing in front of the window, staring at the River Medway and Hoo Marina.

Shit! How could he manage the introduction of fentanyl and everything that went with it without Gav and Stryker? Would he have to shift it through their dealers and runners himself? Fuck! Did he even know who was in their lines? Did he know enough about how they operated? And who was going to do the cutting?

He knew some of Gav's gang so he could probably get something set up with them. But Stryker's chain of command was a bit of an unknown. He always kept himself very much to himself, and ruled with a rod of iron. His name had derived from the Stryker saw much used by pathologists on dead bodies whereas Stone mainly used his Stryker saw on live bodies. '*Keeps them on their toes*' was his mantra even though some of them ended up without toes.

But Johnnie couldn't miss the opportunity that Maddox was giving him. He stared at the yachts tied up on the marina across the river at Hoo. He would certainly be able to afford at least one of those once he got distribution of the fentanyl going. Even if he had to do more leg work than he originally envisaged, he was not going to let the absence of two of his lieutenants get in the way of him, Johnnie Arcane, making himself a fucking stash.

He smiled as one of the yachts broke free from the confines of the marina and set a course towards the Thames Estuary.

'One day that'll be me,' he whispered under his breath. 'Captain Johnnie!'

30

Friday 1 May

'Died at 06.32 this morning.'

The voice of DC Azzar Mishraz cut through the noise of the traffic around them as Hunter and Jennings drove back to Pembury Road.

'Seems she had another cardiac arrest at around 04.00 a.m. from which she never recovered. They just couldn't get her back this time.'

Jennings was driving on the return journey from One Tree Hill and was concentrating on keeping her distance from a truck full of scaffolding poles which didn't look as if they had been properly tied down. Hunter was staring out of the passenger window at the little shops and pubs of Hildenborough as they passed through the village.

Now she had yet another murder enquiry on her hands. Julie Buckley would be the fourth body delivered to the morgue today, and it wasn't even ten o'clock.

'Okay, Azzar, sorry to hear that.' She paused as Jennings slammed on her brakes to avoid the scaffolding wagon which had suddenly made a violent left turn without any indication. The faulty brake lights didn't help.

'We've got the number recorded,' Jennings said, tapping the dashcam in front of her.

Hunter went back to staring out of her window. 'Azzar, are you still there?'

'Yes, ma'am.'

'What about the girl?'

'Making progress is all I'm being told. However, we have managed to get a DNA test done and that has been sent off for analysis. I also persuaded the people here to get some prints so we can see if that can help us with identification. I've arranged to get them sent electronically to the CSI office so they should have them today, hopefully.'

'Sounds good. If we can just find out who she is and see how she fits in with all the others who were at the mansion, then we might be getting somewhere. Are you still at the hospital?'

'Just leaving. I think Grace needs help back at base.'

Hunter wished him well and disconnected the call. They were now passing Tonbridge School in reasonably light traffic.

'Initial thoughts about One Tree Hill?' Hunter asked Jennings who was watching the traffic build up in front of them as they crossed the bridge over the Medway.

'Gangland feud,' Jennings replied. 'Once we know who they are, we might know more. But the London cab rather gives it away, doesn't it. A day trip out to Kent, never to return. Could this be one for Jordan Wright and his team?'

'Yes, I was thinking the same,' Hunter agreed, even if she hadn't actually been thinking along those lines. But now Jennings had mentioned it, there was some scope for developing the idea further. She also needed to decide where her priorities lay. The wreckage of Tideswell Manor still bore testimony to the fact that her investigation was yet to get off the ground. She reasoned that she couldn't get very far unless she knew who all the bodies belonged to but she seemed to have been distracted from keeping on top of the identification process. Perhaps she should pay a visit to the pathologists this afternoon.

As Jennings searched for a parking space in the underground

car park at Pembury Road, Hunter felt her phone vibrate in her pocket. She pulled it out and swiped the screen to reveal a text message.

Can I be at front of Q for briefing on 1 Tree Hill?

It wasn't signed but Hunter knew exactly who the sender was. This was getting beyond a joke, she thought as she got out of the car.

The Ops Room was a busy place this morning as Hunter and Jennings threaded their way between the myriad of desks to the far end of the open-plan office where Grace Kendall sat at her workstation, her two screens creating a wall between her and the rest of the room. Alongside her, Ted Selitto sat in one of the office chairs which was an unusual sight as his normal preference was to lean against the wall and look out of the window. The two detective sergeants were deep in conversation.

'Is it a private party or can anyone join?' Hunter asked as she flopped into a chair on the other side of Kendall. She left Jennings to go and find her own chair. It would be a good initiative test for her given the chronic shortage of seating options in the station as a whole.

'Anyone with any idea of what we're dealing with is welcome here,' Grace replied rather wearily.

'Ah! Have we found a few more blind alleys?' Hunter asked, leaning over for a closer look at the screens.

She had hoped that today would be what she had once heard referred to as *moving day* in an investigation. It had been on a training course where the trainer, a fanatical golf enthusiast, had made an analogy between 'moving day' in a golf tournament and one specific day in each investigation. That day when some of the leads which were on the fringes of consideration started to become central to the investigation while other hitherto strong leads started to fade away. Sarah just felt that the term resonated with how she saw investigations progressing.

Was it too much to expect that, after five days, they should feel as if they were getting somewhere?

'It's just taking a bit of time dealing with the AAIB,' Grace said, interrupting Hunter's thoughts about progress. 'The crash at Tideswell has been classified as an accident which is a description that seems to cover a multitude of sins. It can be where a person suffers a fatal or serious injury, or the aircraft sustains damage or structural failure which adversely affects its performance, or where the aircraft is missing or they know where it is but can't get to it.'

Selitto got up and moved his chair to the side of the desk so that he could see Sarah Hunter more clearly. 'They've got the plane back at their hangers at Farnborough now so the investigation is underway,' he informed the new arrivals. 'But it's not like us dealing with Beth and the CSI crew. You know, when we just rock up and expect to get information even if they haven't completely finished their investigation. This is all much more formal. There are lines of reporting. But Grace has made some progress by sweet-talking one of their guys who now seems to be on our wavelength and is feeding us occasional bits of information.'

'Yes, we are at least getting some intel which is probably of more value to our investigation than to theirs,' Grace said, taking over the commentary from Selitto. 'One thing that we have learned is that there are no traces of blood in the wreckage which would indicate that the pilot exited the aircraft before it crashed. We've already identified that as a possibility so this seems to confirm that either the pilot deliberately set the plane on a collision course with the mansion before ejecting himself from the aircraft or he jumped because he had lost control. We have yet to get any indication as to whether the aircraft was faulty, and it may take some time before the AAIB are able to give us any technical information.'

'Okay,' Hunter said after taking a few seconds to consider the possibilities. 'Here's what I'm thinking. The pilot jumping out of the plane makes far more sense in the scenario that the crash at Tideswell was a deliberate act. He knows what he's going to do, he's prepared, he's got a parachute, he's trained in base-jumping, he's fit and he's confident. If he wasn't all those things and he was simply flying an aircraft which had got into difficulties, he would desperately try to overcome the problems and fly the thing to safety. He would be communicating with the air traffic controller on the ground, he may even be patched through to someone with intimate knowledge of the aircraft he was flying so he could get some suggestions. He wouldn't just give up and jump out into the blue yonder without a parachute.'

They all considered this assessment of options for a moment.

'You also hear about hero pilots who manage to steer doomed aircraft away from inhabited areas,' Jennings commented. 'If the plane was in trouble, it seems an incredible coincidence that its flight path managed to pick out the only building within a radius of two or three miles.'

There was a rousing cheer at the other end of the office. A bunch of their colleagues obviously celebrating a breakthrough in an investigation, something that Hunter thought was a long way off in hers.

'Remember we spoke to that retired airline captain when we were looking for more information about the helicopter crash?' Grace chipped in. Selitto's ears pricked up at the mention of the helicopter in which he had nearly lost his life. He had fortuitously fallen from the aircraft as it took off before plummeting to the ground seconds later. In the ensuing investigation, Grace had engaged the services of Captain Richard Donaldson who had provided some technical input about the crash. This had enabled Hunter's team to complete a full assessment to establish why the crash happened and to apportion blame for the disaster which had killed nine people.

'Have you been in contact with him, Grace?' Hunter asked, recalling the clarity with which the retired captain had spoken. He had made everything sound so straightforward.

'I actually called him yesterday in anticipation that we may need to pick his brains,' Grace replied, 'and he said that he would be in Tonbridge today having lunch with an old flying colleague. He said he'd drop by before going to meet his friend.'

At that moment, Azzar Mishraz entered the room followed by a tall, silver-haired man smartly dressed in an open-necked checked shirt, double-breasted navy blue blazer, tartan slacks and a pair of slip-on brown suede shoes. Hunter instantly recognised Donaldson and got to her feet to welcome him with a handshake.

'Good morning, Captain,' she said with a smile.

'Ah, Detective Inspector, nice to see you again,' Donaldson replied.

'I think you know most of the team from last time you

were here,' she said as she waved an arm towards Jennings and Mishraz, 'but not this one.'

Selitto made his way around the desk and shook Donaldson's hand.

'No, we've not met but I'm mightily relieved to see you back in the land of the living,' Donaldson smiled. 'I got the distinct impression it was touch and go at one stage.'

'So they tell me,' Selitto responded, 'but here I am back where I belong.'

Mishraz had miraculously managed to find a chair for Donaldson who sat on it and then wheeled himself to a position beside Grace. Selitto re-took his seat and Hunter sat on the other side of Donaldson. Jennings and Mishraz stood although their eyes constantly roamed the room, searching for any chair which might become vacant.

'So, what have you got for me this time?'

31
Friday 1 May

'As you know, we're investigating the plane crash at Tideswell Manor,' Grace began. 'I mentioned on the phone that, when they pulled the plane out of the wreckage of the building, there was no sign of the pilot. As time goes by, it's becoming increasingly clear to us that there are potentially two scenarios here. The first is that the pilot deliberately flew the plane at the mansion but baled out some distance before it hit. The second is that there was a mechanical fault and that he jumped seconds before it hit the building, possibly when he saw Bewl Water ahead of him.'

'We have problems with both scenarios,' Hunter took over. 'If it really was an act of premeditated aggression, how could the pilot guarantee that the plane would hit the mansion? And if there was a technical fault and he just jumped, we don't believe that he would have survived. Yet no bodies have been fished out of Bewl Water to our knowledge.'

Grace had opened a photograph giving an arial view of the mansion with the aircraft embedded in it which had been taken by a Kent Police drone soon after the crash. Donaldson leaned forward to study the evidence.

'Hmm! That's fairly well plumb in the centre of the building isn't it?' his comment eventually turning into a question. 'Pretty much a *bullseye* in any other language, wouldn't you say?'

'So, are you inferring that we should draw a conclusion from the angle at which the aircraft hit the building?' Hunter asked, hoping that she had correctly understood his insinuation.

'Well, yes,' the Captain replied. 'It looks to me as if the aircraft has hit the building at what's called the desired mean point of impact. This is a precise point, like you would have on a target or something similar, which is selected as the centre for impact. In most cases, this description would be associated with weapons but it can be used for other analogies involving something hitting a target.'

'But, how could the aircraft be guided to the precise point of impact without a pilot being at the controls?' Hunter asked.

'Ah, well, that's where it becomes a little more complicated,' Donaldson replied. 'There would have to be some direct communication between the aircraft and the building or its immediate surrounds. Most airfields use one of two types of navigation systems which you may have heard of. There's the VOR system and the ILS system. VOR stands for VHF Omni-directional Range and is a type of short-range navigation beacon which emits a signal that is sent in a straight line. This means that its use may be limited by line of sight. Pilots are able to fly towards the VOR beacon from a certain direction and be fairly confident of their position. The only reason I have for anticipating that this system was not the one used is because a VOR beacon is quite a large piece of equipment which would have to be in close proximity to the landing point.'

'Is this one here?' Grace asked, pointing to the screen nearest to Donaldson.

'Yes, that's it,' he replied, taking a look at the screen. 'Bet you haven't seen one of those in the grounds of Tideswell Manor. It would certainly be noticeable.'

Everyone shuffled around to take a look at the screen before Donaldson continued.

'So, it's far more likely that some sort of instrument landing system was set up. That's the ILS system I mentioned earlier. Virtually all major international airports I've flown into had an ILS for approach which allowed us to fly the aircraft all the way to the runway without even needing to see the ground around us. The ILS consists of two radio beams which project from the area around the runway up into the approach path. The first signal is the localiser which normally radiates from antennae which are located at the end of the runway. This is more for direction and tells pilots where the aircraft is in relation to the centreline of the runway. The second signal comes from antennae to the side of the runway which guides the aircraft down vertically to the correct touchdown spot.'

Everyone seemed totally engrossed in what Donaldson was telling them and, in no small measure, also horrified as it dawned on them that they could be investigating a pre-meditated mass murder.

'Now,' Donaldson continued, 'the equipment needed in the scenario of the aircraft hitting the building would be a couple of antennae positioned on the ground. It is feasible that one of them could have been located in the house or it could be located on the ground behind the building in line with the flightpath the aircraft was on. The other will have been located to the side of the building in the grounds. There would then have to have been a receiver in the aircraft itself. I think I've got a picture of one of these antennae.'

Donaldson started scrolling through some photographs on his phone.

'Yes, here we are.' He passed the phone to Hunter who then shared it with the others.

'One other thing you should bear in mind,' he continued while they all had a look at the sort of equipment which they would now have to start looking for. 'If some sort of ILS was set up at your crash site, then it will be much smaller than we have at international airports, and the equipment may not even look like the photos on my phone. And you should probably tell the boffins at the AAIB to be on the lookout for some sort of transmitter capable of sending a signal to lock on to the antennae in or near your building.'

'When you say much smaller,' Jennings interjected, 'surely the antennae are still going to be reasonably sizeable pieces of kit given their function. Or are you suggesting that they can be dramatically reduced in size so that they can be hidden from view or camouflaged in some way. Given the area of ground around the mansion, and the fact that quite a lot of it is given over to woodland, would the antennae have to be in the open or could they be in the woodland?'

'Based on the scale of the landing area, I think that the antennae would have to be in the open although perhaps they could also function on the edges of the woodland. Wherever they are placed, they will still have to have the capacity to send the two radio beams which are required to provide the necessary guidance. The more I think about it, the more I believe that one of the antennae would not have been placed inside the mansion because, apart from anything else, it would look completely out of place. So, you should concentrate your search in the area behind the building and to the side of it.'

'Just one other question, sir.' It was Mishraz this time. 'Have you ever heard of a pilot exiting a plane without a parachute even if he did think it was about to crash? In fact, what would you do?'

Donaldson thought for a moment.

'That's an interesting question,' he finally replied. 'What would I do? I suppose that if I knew that the aircraft couldn't be saved and I saw a stretch of water coming up, I might be tempted to make a jump for it. But, in reality, I think I would be so engrossed in trying to avoid a crash that I would just stay in my seat. I'm sure that most pilots think that they have the ability to overcome malfunctions on an aircraft. And there is a definite unwritten rule to try and avoid any casualties on the ground. Which normally means staying with your machine until the very end. But an interesting and thought-provoking question.'

There were a couple of other questions from the team about the strength of the radio beams before Hunter decided that she was not going to get anything more from this encounter. So, she thanked Donaldson for his detailed briefing and for explaining complex technology in a language that they could all understand.

'My pleasure, Detective Inspector,' he replied rather formally. 'I just hope that this helps you to track down the mastermind behind this dreadful slaughter. Believe me, you are looking for someone with no scruples or morals, and someone who has access to modern technology and knows how to use it. I don't envy you one bit in your search for the perpetrator. A very dangerous person indeed.'

32

Friday 1 May

Much against her better judgment, Hunter had eventually given in to Selitto's pleadings and allowed him to accompany her to the morgue if only to enable her to get on with her day. She was already well behind the schedule she had set herself which only served to irritate her even more. Having got gowned up in the expectation of visiting the examination room, they now found themselves confined to the pathologists' office

'We're just doing a bit of a deep clean,' Dr Toby Swartzman sighed as he shuffled some of the papers around on his desk. Sarah was never sure if he was ever on top of what was going on at the morgue on a daily basis, but she did have some sympathy for him at the moment with the number of bodies which had been shipped in and out over the last few days.

'Well, it's not really a *deep* clean as such,' he continued. 'Should be finished any moment. We have to get these things done pretty much to order. You know, get the box ticked. Otherwise we'll fail an inspection and get closed down for a few days. You can imagine the chaos that would ensue if that happened. It's bad enough as it is at the moment without losing vital hours.'

Hunter found herself nodding in agreement although she didn't really have any interest in the Chief Pathologist's domestic arrangements. She got up to glance through the small window that looked out on to the three autopsy tables which made up the centre of the examination room. There didn't seem to be much going on so she assumed that the cleaning may have already finished. On the other side of the room, an open doorway led into the refrigeration area, and she saw Norman Partington in conversation with Professor Ivana Jenkyns.

'I see Ivana's still here,' she said as she turned back from the window and leant against the wall.

'Yep. La Jenkyns is still helping us although she is only coming down from London for the odd day here and there,' Swartzman replied, looking up from his paperwork. 'Two days this week which has been a great help. She's actually about to start on that woman you found in the cellar. Goodness knows what we're going to find there. Took them an age to get her out. There were some very dangerous creatures in that room. I mean, most of them could have given you a one-way ticket to any of the tables in there.' He waved his hand in the general direction of the examination room.

The phone on the desk buzzed. Swartzman gave it a suspicious look before lifting the receiver.

Hunter re-took her seat next to Selitto. 'You alright?' she asked him.

'Yeah, good thanks boss. It's just great to be back in places I know so well. It's all I've been thinking about over the last weeks and months. I can feel it doing me good just being here.'

'Okay, we're back in business,' Swartzman announced. They filed through into the examination room and were joined by Partington and Jenkyns who both made a fuss of saying hello to Selitto and welcoming him back. Jenkyns in particular had kept a close eye on his progress from her position in the Home Office, and she now expressed how pleased she was to see him back. Partington was his usual ebullient self and just managed to hold himself in check as he was about to give Ted a thump on the back, deciding instead to shake him warmly by the hand.

'Right,' Hunter said, bringing everyone back to the reason for her visit. 'We are getting fairly desperate for some identification data on those you have been processing here.'

'Have you been inundated with calls?' Jenkyns asked.

'There has, obviously, been a reasonable level of enquiries but not as many as you would get if there had been a fatal accident involving many innocent members of the public,' Hunter replied. 'We're pretty sure that those in attendance at Tideswell were all drug dealers and distributors from far and wide. They were either with their partners, or they were accompanied by someone they knew well. Whilst they may have other family members waiting for them at home, those other family members may not want to draw attention to themselves by contacting us. So, they'll probably rely on their normal sources of information to keep them updated. The press have reported that there were no survivors and, as far as I'm aware, that is still the case except for the girl who we found alive in the cellar. She's making some progress by the way.'

'Well, we certainly haven't seen any live ones round here!' Partington quipped. 'But we've had a devil of a job trying to get anything to help with identification although we have managed to get DNA from some of the victims. For others, we've had to rely on prints from fingers that had not either been burnt to a cinder or flattened or simply destroyed.'

'Yes, we've been working closely with forensics and the CSIs on the testing,' Swartzman continued, 'and we've started by trying to match the deceased with the expensive array of vehicles which are parked at the back of the mansion. I was hoping to have some news on that today but nothing so far.'

Hunter wasn't sure that this would help them very much. 'Just so as you know, we have encountered some difficulty in establishing ownership of those vehicles. Unfortunately, it hasn't been quite as easy as just ringing the DVLA and giving them the registration number. But your initiative should, hopefully, help in some way. What about the people in the cellar?'

'Most of them died through oxygen starvation,' Jenkyns confirmed. 'Hypoxia by any other name. That's where the body can't take in oxygen, and normally oxygenated blood can't be provided to the brain. This can very quickly be fatal which has clearly been the case here.'

'Could they possibly have survived until we got to them?' Hunter asked no one in particular, and then seemed to answer her own question. 'Probably, if they had simply sat still and preserved their oxygen. But their frantic efforts to break out of the locked cellar clearly exacerbated the situation and quickly reduced the oxygen levels.'

The pathologists were all nodding.

'Of more concern is the fate of the two youngsters,' Hunter continued. 'We have done a preliminary search of missing persons records in Kent and the Sussex/Surrey area. There are some possibilities but we really do need the DNA results. And I'm presuming that their deaths were not simply down to oxygen starvation.'

'Afraid not,' Swartzman said, looking round at Jenkyns and Partington. 'It won't come as any surprise to you, I'm sure, but they had suffered extreme sexual violence which may have left them too weak to survive the reduction in oxygen levels. The girl who you found is lucky to be alive if she has anything like the injuries which the other two had suffered. So, we can do our reports and draw our conclusions on the two kids but presumably there will be nothing for you to investigate as all the potential suspects are dead.'

They stood in silence, each contemplating Swartzman's words. The only sounds were the humming of the refrigeration systems and a tap dripping into one of the stainless steel sink units.

Hunter eventually broke the silence. 'So, that leaves us with the woman on the throne chair.'

'Yes, I was just about to start on her when we had to adjourn for the deep clean,' Jenkyns said, giving Swartzman an accusatory glance.

'Don't look at me,' he said, defensively. 'It's not my fault that we had to stop when we did. Anyway, it's probably some procedure dreamed up by your department.'

'Touché!' Jenkyns replied, smiling. 'I'll take that as a compliment.'

'Could we just have a look at her if you're going to be getting the body out anyway?' Hunter asked, a thought suddenly beginning to burrow its way into her brain.

'Sure!' Jenkyns turned and called out to Joe, one of the mortuary assistants, who was in the refrigeration room. He quickly appeared with a body bag on a gurney, and he and Jenkyns transferred it to one of the autopsy tables. They then gently unwrapped the body and released it from the confines of the bag before Joe retrieved a head rest from one of the units along the side of the room and carefully placed the back of the woman's head on the rest. A sheet of gauze-like fabric was stretched over her face but, otherwise, her naked body lay on the autopsy table under the intense lighting of the examination room.

'No other injuries?' Hunter asked, her eyes roving over the body, expecting to at least see some signs of bruising.

'Doesn't look like it, does it?' Jenkyns replied. Having snapped on a pair of surgical gloves, she now lifted the woman's arms up to check for bruising on their undersides.

'Okay, let's have a look at the face,' Hunter said although a little voice inside her head was asking if this was really a good idea. She already knew the hideous sight that awaited her.

Jenkyns carefully removed the fabric to reveal the woman's face and the dead eyes which stared straight up to the lights above the table, unblinking. They really were the stuff of nightmares. Now that Hunter was much closer to the woman than she had been in the cellar, she could clearly see that the eyelids had been coarsely chewed by an unknown predator leaving tiny strands of skin and the occasional eyelash which were clearly visible against the white of the sclera.

Selitto suddenly took a step forwards, muttering something under his breath and pointing as he shuffled up to the table. He looked down at the woman's face, lowered his head as if to take a closer look, but then pulled away and shuffled on to the foot of the table.

Hunter watched him closely, ready to pull him back if the need arose. The pathologists looked concerned. The tension in the room was palpable.

Eventually, Selitto gripped the end of the autopsy table and let out a loud sigh as he hung his head, staring at the floor.

'Those eyes,' he whispered.

No one moved.

'Those eyes,' he repeated.

The pathologists looked at each other, frowns on their faces, trying to understand what Selitto was saying. The only person who wasn't frowning was Sarah Hunter. She suddenly realised what Selitto was looking at. Something he had seen in his recent past which had left an indelible imprint on his brain.

'It's her!' he exclaimed as his voice became louder. 'I tell you, it's her!'

Hunter moved to the foot of the table and put an arm around Selitto's shoulders. He almost collapsed into her but remained standing as he lifted his head, staring again at the body in front of him.

'The woman in the helicopter?' Hunter gently asked.

Staring at the woman, Selitto seemed to be having difficulty getting his thoughts in order but eventually he slowly nodded. 'It's her,' he repeated.

'Okay, let's get you out of here,' Hunter said, guiding Selitto away from the body and around the other autopsy tables until they had exited the examination room and returned to the pathologists' office.

She sat him down in Swartzman's chair because it had arms and was more comfortable. After getting him a glass of water, she returned to the examination room. The pathologists looked anxious as she made her way towards them.

'Is he going to be alright?' Jenkyns asked.

Hunter sought to alay their concerns. 'He'll be fine. He's just had a bit of a shock at seeing someone from the darkest recesses of his nightmares. It's bringing back painful memories for him which, in a way, is good as it will help him to recover from the ordeal he's been through.'

The pathologists still looked puzzled; Norman Partington particularly looked uncomfortable with what he had just seen.

'So, does Ted actually know this woman?' he asked.

Hunter was now standing at the top of the autopsy table, looking directly down at the head of the woman.

'He doesn't actually know her,' she informed them. 'But he knows who she is. She very nearly killed him. The body in front of us is very likely to be that of Samantha Frobisher, a truly venomous assassin.'

33
Friday 1 May

The discovery that Samantha Frobisher was probably the woman who had been incarcerated with various reptiles and arachnids in the cellar at Tideswell Manor could be considered as an unexpected bonus for Sarah Hunter and her team as they had failed to apprehend Frobisher before she had fled the country. True, they had identified her as the probable assassin but she had slipped through their fingers in the end.

Failure was not a word which Hunter liked to have tagged to her name, and there were extreme mitigating circumstances surrounding the *failure* to apprehend the assassin. She often lay awake at night wondering where the woman was, all too readily picturing her lying on a sandy beach in the Caribbean blowing raspberries in the direction of the Kent police force. But how come she had now turned up dead in a room full of dangerous predators?

Having dropped Selitto off at the street level entrance to the Pembury Road station, she was now sitting in her car in the car park staring at the concrete wall in front of her, fingers tapping tunelessly on the steering wheel.

Did Frobisher know Biondi? The woman had been locked in a room in the cellar. It did not seem that the partygoers had access to this room which meant that it was unlikely that she had arrived as a guest of whoever was organising the party. So, she must have been put in there before the party started. Had Biondi incarcerated her in the cellar and left the reptiles and the garotte to do the rest? And, if so, was it to wreak some kind of terrible revenge? But why? What connected Frobisher to Biondi?

Hunter's train of thought was interrupted by her phone emitting an impatient buzz.

Someone waiting 4 U here. Suggest U hurry. Gx

Intrigued to know who her visitor might be, Hunter texted back that she was on her way before heading for the stairs which would take her to the first floor.

Throwing open the door to the Ops Room, she looked across to Grace's corner but couldn't see anyone sitting with her. Fortunately, Grace had spotted Hunter's arrival and quickly signalled that the visitor was in one of the meeting rooms. So she crossed the corridor and entered the room nearest to her.

Jordan Wright was standing at the far end of the room looking out of the window. He spun round as soon as he heard Hunter enter the room.

'Good afternoon, ma'am,' he formally addressed her. 'Sorry to arrive unannounced but DCI Pennington contacted me to get down here like yesterday. It seems that we might have a problem with crossover into a covert operation we are involved with.'

That was all Sarah needed. A covert operation going on right under her nose with none of the parties involved having mentioned it to the others. Happened all the time, she told herself, but at least someone seems to have seen sense in this instance.

'Okay, Jordan,' she replied. 'How do you want to play this?'

'DCI Pennington has asked me to give you a heads up about

our operation on the understanding that he doesn't want you to share any of the details with your team just yet.'

'What about with my DCI?' she asked. 'I'm not beholden to DCI Pennington, you know. There is another line of command here.' Hunter was damned if she was going to be dictated to by the suits in Maidstone and, although she had a good working relationship with Pennington, her allegiances would always be to Iversen.

'Whilst I obviously can't give you orders, it may be best for the operation if you could just keep the information I'm about to give you to yourself for the time being.'

Wright was certainly a confident officer but protocol didn't seem to be his strongest suit. It was often the case with detectives who spent most of their time in the field on a very long lead from their controller. She often likened it to one of those extendable dog leads – the dog could be completely out of sight yet the walker still held the lead in their hand.

'I think I'll be the judge of that but rest assured that your operation won't be compromised by anything I may do or say.' Hunter was not going to have anyone telling her what to do or what not to do when it was her investigation. She took a huge amount of pride in being Senior Investigating Officer of all the cases she worked on, and it was not a position she would easily relinquish

'Thank you, ma'am.'

'Right. No doubt this is about One Tree Hill,' she said, staring straight at Wright. She was pleased to see that she had caught him ever so slightly off guard.

'Yes, ma'am,' he replied. 'We are targeting a dealer who is running one of the biggest county lines in Kent. Taking him out would have the potential to close the operation down altogether which would be a significant achievement. We have an ongoing undercover operation which is a sting by any other name. One of our officers is setting this guy up to buy a quantity of Class A. We think that the dealer we are interested in may have been at the shoot out on One Tree Hill although we have no proof at the moment.'

Hunter was interested but sceptical as she had already heard that clues to who had shot the two passengers in the taxi were proving to be scarce. Beth Dench and her team had scoured the area but there was little for forensics to get their teeth into. Her attention had now turned to the techies who were examining the phone found in the driver's hand.

'How have you been able to make a link to your man when forensics are still struggling to find anything that links to a suspect?' she asked.

'There was a body left on the pavement outside the Medway Maritime Hospital in Gillingham at around midnight last night,' Wright replied. 'Gunshot wounds. Probably bled to death. He's been identified as Charles Stone. Known as Dancer to his friends but also known as Stryker Stone. Of interest to us as he's a close associate of the guy we're targeting.'

'Are you going to tell me who this suspect is?' Hunter asked, fully expecting identification of the man to be covered by a 'D' notice or whatever they were called in modern parlance. Her father had always referred to 'D' notices with nothing but scorn as it meant that he couldn't talk freely about cases he was involved with.

'Our target is a man by the name of Johnnie Arcane,' Wright continued, showing no sign that he was giving her anything but general information. 'He's based on our patch so we can normally keep an eye on him. But, as with all these guys, they have a whole raft of people doing their dirty work which makes it very difficult for us to stick anything on them. That's why the sting on Arcane is so important and why we would prefer to hear from you as soon as you think that he might be involved with anything you are working on.'

Hunter took her time to consider what Wright was asking for. She doubted that Arcane had anything to do with the Tideswell Manor investigation, but he could have been involved with the One Tree Hill incident – quite possibly having been there in person. Therefore, he would be a person of interest for that investigation.

'How soon are you planning to execute the sting?' she asked.

'Just as soon as we can get it all ready,' he replied. 'These things take a lot of planning and must be done correctly if we are ever going to get a conviction. Bear in mind we're going to supply him with a Class A drug and then nick him for possession and dealing. That should get him a life sentence if we're lucky. But we have to be very careful to distance ourselves from being involved in the actual supply chain otherwise any case against him could be thrown out.'

Hunter could see the dilemma that Pennington and his chums in the drugs squad had. The route they had decided to follow in order to take Arcane out was fraught with the danger that it could all come to nothing in the courts. She could already foresee an argument raging as to whether their operation was really a sting or whether it was entrapment. A smart KC claiming that his client had suffered entrapment would be more than capable of getting any of the charges thrown out of court.

Silence filled the room as Hunter considered her options.

'Okay. This is the way we can work together. As it's highly unlikely that your Johnnie Arcane had anything to do with the plane crash at Tideswell, we'll simply continue investigating that as a separate matter. We're also investigating the shootings at One Tree Hill so we'll keep you in the loop about what we turn up there. As you presumably know, there was a large patch of blood at the scene which could be your man Stone. Who should Beth Dench liaise with in order to confirm this?'

Wright thought for a moment and then gave Hunter a name. She wrote it on a pad she found in a desk drawer along with a mobile number which Wright read out from his phone.

'It certainly looked like there were two gunmen at the scene and, if one of them can be confirmed as Charlie Stone, then the other could very well have been Arcane. We'll have to see what other clues we can find and we'll keep you informed of anything which looks of interest.'

She tore the top two pages off the pad and crudely folded them before shoving them into the back pocket of her jeans. She looked over at Wright who was now perched on one of the desks near the door.

'Are we done here?' she asked.

34

Friday 1 May

Despite a raised eyebrow stifling a 'what-was-that-all-about?' enquiry, Grace Kendall pointed Hunter to the unoccupied chair which was next to her desk. It was still warm so someone was going to be unlucky when they came back from wherever they had nipped off to, Hunter thought. She could see Ted Selitto on the other side of the room in conversation with Angie Marshall so he hadn't been sitting on it. That was fine then – the rest of them were young and fit enough to stand, she thought.

Still processing the information which Jordan Wright had just given her, Hunter was slow to realise that Kendall was keen to show her something on her computer screens.

'Sarah, are you listening to what I'm saying?' Kendall fretted. 'I think I might have something that's going to interest you.'

Hunter put thoughts of Johnnie Arcane to one side and smiled at Kendall as if inviting her to continue.

'See this photo here, it's the latest we've got for Baz Biondi. He's at a reception in London for an up and coming pop group. Taken about five weeks ago. One of the few I've seen where he genuinely seems pleased to be looking at the camera.'

'Perhaps he knew the photographer,' Hunter suggested. 'I read an article not so long ago which reported that some of the 'A' list stars in the music industry wouldn't even leave their houses unless their chosen photographer was going to be at whatever function they were attending. They didn't want any old snapper taking less than flattering photographs of them.

For these people, vanity knows no bounds.'

'Perhaps,' Kendall replied, 'but now look at this.' Another photo of Biondi appeared on the screen but much less clear and slightly grainy. It could only have been downloaded from CCTV.

'Okay. CCTV image. But where was this taken?' Hunter asked, unable to define the background.

'At the boarding gate for a flight which he took on Sunday week ago,' Kendall informed her.

'Shit!' Hunter exclaimed, suddenly taking a close interest in what Grace was saying and leaning in towards the screen. 'Well, it's definitely him. Sunday week ago you say? What was that? Sunday 19 April? Probably five days before the start of the party. Where was he going?'

'The picture was taken at the boarding gate for a flight to Hamilton which is the main town of Bermuda.'

'How the hell did you get to know that he was going to Bermuda?' Hunter asked, excited at seeing the picture on the screen but also amazed that Grace had managed to track Biondi down.

'Well, I didn't actually know where he was going, just that he was going somewhere. Spoke to one of those entertainment reporters I used to know on the Evening Standard. She quite often writes stuff about Biondi and told me that he had an overseas trip planned around that date. Didn't have much detail but she said that he invariably flew from Gatwick because he couldn't stand the journey to Heathrow – far too many hold ups and missed flights. Anyway, she also said that he nearly always travelled to islands in the Caribbean so I have literally spent hours begging airlines for passenger lists of flights to the Caribbean from Gatwick not to mention the hours it took to persuade Gatwick to release some CCTV.'

'Yes, I can imagine. Not the most helpful in the world but not too bad once they understand why you need the information.' Hunter continued staring at the two images of Biondi on Kendall's screens.

'Having spent hours scanning passenger lists, I eventually found him on the flight to Bermuda. But, interestingly, I didn't catch him on CCTV until he was boarding at the gate. Perhaps I just missed him at check-in and passport control.'

'Doesn't really matter,' Hunter summarised, 'because that's our boy on his way to sunny Bermuda.'

'It doesn't stop there,' Grace continued, 'because he returned only a few days later.'

'Oh?' Hunter sounded surprised. 'So, he wasn't exactly going for a holiday then. More likely some sort of business arrangement. No doubt he's got some of his ill-gotten gains stashed away in a Bermuda bank which no one's ever heard of – or has access to.'

'Interestingly, I was able to pick him up at passport control when he got back to Gatwick.' Grace gave the mouse a couple of clicks and another picture of Biondi morphed onto the screen in front of her.

'Hmm,' Hunter sighed. 'So, he's here in the UK after all.'

Grace manoeuvred the mouse and the cursor flew around the screen until a new grainy CCTV photo appeared. It was Biondi again.

'Okay, what's he doing now?' Hunter asked. 'Paying for his parking?'

'Not exactly. Look at the date at the top of the screen.' Hunter did as she was told.

'Twenty-fourth. Bloody hell. That was the Friday before the plane crash.'

'Quite right. This is Biondi back at Gatwick checking in for a flight to Antigua,' Grace continued.

'Fuck's sake! He does like to get around,' Hunter mused. 'So he is out of the country or has he already returned?'

'Well, this is where it gets really interesting,' Grace replied, at the same time lowering her voice and putting up another CCTV image of Biondi. 'This is him immediately prior to going through security. You know, where they look at your boarding card and passport.'

Hunter nodded although she couldn't remember the last time she had flown anywhere out of the UK so her knowledge of current airport procedures was sketchy to say the least.

'So, what does he do now?' she asked. 'Go through security and head for the departure gate?'

'Yep, that's pretty much it,' Grace replied. 'He could stop for a coffee or a drink in the bar or even do a little shopping. But the general idea is to get to the departure gate on time. The big problem we have is that he didn't board that flight to Antigua.'

'*What*?' Hunter exclaimed.

'I've exhaustively reviewed all CCTV of passengers boarding the flight at the departure gate and Biondi isn't one of them,' Grace continued. 'When you're hunting someone through CCTV, you pick up little nuances about their stature, the way they walk, the way they do things like wait in a queue. You know – head up or looking at the floor. And I can say, hand on heart, that he did not go through the gate and onto the aircraft.'

'Could he have turned round and gone back the way he came in?' Hunter asked, trying to think of why he might have deliberately missed the flight.

'Checked all that,' Grace replied. 'You can get back out but there is a process you have to go through which carefully records details of passengers returning to the landside of an airport. Biondi did not make that journey.'

'So there was an empty seat on the aircraft, and no one has any idea where Biondi is.' It sounded more like a statement from Hunter but she was only trying to summarise the situation for her own sake.

'I'm afraid it's not quite as straightforward as that,' Grace continued. 'I got talking to someone in the airline's technical team who told me that CCTV operates on board the aircraft on all flights. He accessed the flight Biondi was supposed to be on and, with the knowledge of which seat he was booked into, we watched as a man who was clearly not Biondi sat in his seat.'

'Perhaps he had swapped with Biondi,' Hunter challenged. 'Perhaps Biondi had gone to sit somewhere else. Or perhaps he gave the air crew the eye at the door of the plane and wangled his way into the cockpit with the pilot.'

Grace gave Hunter a quizzical look over the top of her spectacles.

'Okay, okay, I get what you're trying to tell me.' Hunter sounded exasperated. 'He didn't take the flight. So, where does that leave us?'

'Ah, but that's where you're wrong,' Grace continued. 'According to the airline, Biondi was on the flight. The guy who sat in the seat Biondi was booked into had a boarding card and passport in the name of Baz Biondi.'

Hunter froze, staring in disbelief at Grace, her mouth open, no words forthcoming. Eventually, she pulled herself together.

'For fuck's sake, Grace, what the hell's going on?' she exploded. 'So, we've now got someone impersonating Biondi. Why? To make everyone believe that Biondi took that flight?'

'Presumably,' Grace agreed. 'Someone clearly didn't want to draw attention to the fact that the real Biondi wasn't travelling.'

'Jeez! So, what have we got now? A kidnapping?' Hunter swivelled round to look squarely at Grace. 'Don't tell me we've got a fucking kidnapping as well as everything else that's going on?'

Grace started to manoeuvre the cursor around the screen, clicking here and there, watching as CCTV pictures came and went. Hunter leaned back in her chair, clutched her hands behind her head and stretched her spine. All her thoughts were on Biondi's disappearance.

She released her hands and leant forward, elbows on the desk in front of her, head cupped in her hands. A CCTV image of Biondi was on the screen in front of her.

'Seen that one,' she said. 'Passport control on the way in from Bermuda if I remember.'

'Yes, correct,' Grace commented. 'But sometimes you need to study these sort of shots to see if there's anyone else you should be noticing.'

'And is there?' Hunter wasn't sure she wanted to play this game as she had better things to do with her time. But Grace wouldn't normally get her to look at something unless she thought that it was critically important. So, she kept watching the screen.

'Well, I was looking at the people immediately behind

Biondi and, although you can't really see their faces, there's a woman and two men who look as if they might be with him.'

Hunter screwed her eyes up to try and make the CCTV image clearer. She could see what Grace was getting at. There were others around Biondi who could also have been with him.

'So I went back to my contact at the airline.' Grace was saying, 'and asked him if he had some CCTV from the flight back from Bermuda. After a while, he was able to identify Biondi's seat number and he sent over this image.'

The image came up on the screen and Hunter leaned in for a closer look. It certainly looked like Biondi. He was sitting in an aisle seat, the middle seat was vacant and a woman was sitting in the window seat to his left. Both looked tired and devoid of facial expression, and it was difficult to tell whether they already knew each other or whether they had just encountered each other as they boarded the flight. But that wasn't what had grabbed Hunter's attention. She suddenly looked wildly around the room. Where was he? Still with Angie Marshall.

'Ted!' she shouted across the room. 'Here! Now!' For a moment, everyone seemed to stop what they were doing and turned to stare at Hunter. But almost immediately they returned to their work and their conversations as Selitto ambled over.

'Yes, boss? What is it?' he asked.

She got up from her chair. 'Sit there and tell me what you can see on the screen,' she commanded.

Selitto sat down as he had been bidden and stared at the screen. A deep frown started to crease his forehead as he leant forward to take a closer look at the screen.

'No!' he muttered to himself. 'No! Surely not! No! Can't be! It simply cannot be!' Although he was shaking his head, he hadn't taken his eyes off the screen. 'But…' his voice trailed off.

'It could be her, couldn't it,' Hunter encouraged him. 'From where I'm sitting, it certainly looks like our girl.'

Selitto peered at the screen, deep in thought. His hands were in his lap, one hand squeezing the fingers of the other, the knuckles white.

Hunter looked across at Kendall. 'Is this the only shot we've got?'

Grace fiddled with the mouse whilst looking at her other screen. Eventually, she found what she was looking for and transferred another image to the screen Selitto was looking at. As the new image replaced the one he had been concentrating on, his eyes lit up.

'That's her!' he declared, a degree of certainty now in his voice. 'That is most definitely her.'

Hunter moved to stand behind him and looked down at the screen.

'Do we have a name, Grace?' she asked.

'This seat was assigned to a Donna Hicks,' Grace replied. 'Travelling on a British passport. That's all we know about her at the moment. There are others by the name of Donna Hicks on the PNC but we can't discount these people unless we simply go by age.'

'Okay, what have we got here?' Hunter asked no one in particular. She had suddenly been presented with a scenario which she could not have imagined in her wildest dreams and which had added another layer of complication to her investigation.

'I'm not sure that it looks as if they know each other,' Grace offered, 'but then there's something that's making me think that they're definitely travelling together. It doesn't look as if they just happened to board the same plane and then found that they were sitting next to each other.'

'So, has Biondi gone off to Bermuda with the express intention of bringing Frobisher or whatever her name is back to the UK?' Selitto was getting into the swing of the investigation now and had summed up what the others were thinking.

'But why?' Hunter sighed.

'Perhaps she wanted to return,' Grace suggested. 'Perhaps she was fed up with lying on a sandy beach in the sun all day. Perhaps she wanted to benefit from whatever protection Biondi could offer, particularly if she felt vulnerable.'

'In which case, this begs the question as to whether Biondi bankrolled her murderous spree in the first place,' Hunter said. 'But why would he be interested in facilitating her return? Surely he would just pay for the plane ticket and await her arrival. He wouldn't travel thousands of miles just to pick her up.'

As usual, Sarah Hunter was trying to get into the minds of the people involved. Assuming that the woman in the picture really was Samantha Frobisher, deadly assassin of this parish, did Biondi have another job for her? Had he flown out to Bermuda to persuade her to take on this other job? Had he had to plead with her? Did she set the bar high in terms of payment? They didn't look like friends or acquaintances so they could only be discussing business. Yet, twenty four hours after this CCTV image was collected, Biondi had disappeared from sight in the departures lounge at Gatwick Airport. And a few days later, Frobisher had turned up dead in the cellar of Biondi's mansion.

'Look at the two men in the row behind,' Grace continued. 'Now look at the shot of Biondi at passport control.'

'Hmm. Looks like the woman's sandwiched between them and Biondi,' Selitto observed. 'Bodyguards?'

'That's my feeling,' Grace said, agreeing with Selitto's suggestion. 'I'll see if I can find out their identities but it may not be of much use to us if they're travelling on false papers.'

Hunter wandered over to the window. She looked down onto the traffic slowly making its way out of Tonbridge, the drivers with thoughts of what they had planned for the weekend.

Things weren't looking too good for Mr Biondi, she thought.

35
Friday 1 May

It hadn't been a good day. Nothing seemed to be going right. Lack of sleep hadn't helped. Johnnie Arcane had so much on his mind that he felt his head was about to burst open.

First up, he had been hugely frustrated by the wheels given to him by his mate on Bluebell Hill. In the rush to get rid of his own car, he hadn't immediately appreciated what a heap of shit the replacement vehicle was. Not only did it sound as if someone had nicked the catalytic converter, but the gears crunched almost every time he changed up or down. He was thinking of taking it back to get a roadworthy replacement but then tempered his enthusiasm in case the cops were snooping around. You could never be too careful.

Then he'd had to get to a housing estate in Bobbing to drop off some gear and pick up some cash before going on to meet a couple of runners who had called Stryker Stone's phone earlier. Even if Stone was still alive, he wouldn't be back on the road for many months so Johnnie would just have to cover for him. That was the problem when you only had two or three people you really trusted, he thought. Lose one of them, and you had to put yourself out a bit to keep the show on the road. Lose two and you were bolloxed.

The two runners had suggested meeting in the car park of a crematorium which Johnnie was initially wary about. However, on getting there he found that there were plenty of parking spaces away from the two chapels of rest. He eventually found their green Toyota Aygo slewed across two parking bays, its front buried in a small privet hedge.

There were two of them in the car. Johnnie doubted that the driver was anywhere near the legal age for driving on a public highway – for a start, he could hardly see over the steering wheel. And it quickly became apparent that he was dealing with a couple of gobby little scrotes. Where *did* Stryker Stone get his runners from? No wonder he had got himself one of those mortuary saws. It was the only sort of language these two would understand.

Eventually getting them out of the car and then persuading them to part with some cash, Johnnie handed over the gear they had asked for. He also warned them that they would be dealing with him from now on and, if they thought that Stone was tough, they had seen nothing yet. But the warning seemed to have fallen on deaf ears as the two of them were laughing as they skipped back to the Aygo.

Glad to be on his way again, and with the car lurching out of the crematorium like a sick dog, Johnnie headed towards the Isle of Sheppey, choosing to stay on Sheppey Way so that he could cross the River Swale via the Kingsferry Bridge. He had always had a fascination with this bridge as its centre section operated as a vertical lift when marine craft needed to pass through. He was half hoping that he might get there today and find that the lift was in operation but, as he approached the bridge, he realised that he would have an uninterrupted passage across to the island. Probably for the best – he had a lot to get done in what remained of daylight hours.

Taking a cross country route, he headed for Leysdown-on-Sea and eventually onto the road to Shellness Beach which ran along the shores of the Thames Estuary. In the distance, he could see the sentry-like turbines of the London Array wind farm, the rotors turning at some speed in the windy conditions. The road then headed inland away from the sea before becoming little more than a rough dirt track. This would be a test for the shit car, he thought. But the vehicle managed the terrain reasonably well and Johnnie was soon parked up in the corner of a field. The rest of his journey would be on foot so he got out of the car and immediately wished he had brought a windproof coat. His tracksuit top was not going to give him much protection from the wind which was sweeping across this desolate part of Sheppey.

Collecting a holdall from the back seat of the car, he set off along an ill-defined pathway, stumbling over large tufts of grass, his eyes streaming in the onslaught from the wind. Eventually, he reached the sea which was crashing onto a stretch of beach divided by a series of groynes. Continuing along the beach, he kept an eye out for the marker which would point him towards his destination. And there it was. A small cairn built from large pebbles with edges smoothed by the tides over hundreds of years.

Johnnie turned inland again but it was only a short walk until he came across a caravan nestling amongst the scrubland which abutted the beach. Behind the caravan was a wooden shed painted green so that it blended in with its surroundings. In front of both structures was the empty hull of a boat which was never likely to sail again judging by the holes below the waterline. He could hear a generator purring away in the background, and wisps of smoke were escaping from a small chimney on the roof of the caravan.

He was expected, and the man he had come to see was out of the caravan before Johnnie had even reached the boat. He beckoned Johnnie towards the shed before slipping inside.

'Close the door,' the man said in a wheezy, breathless voice. Johnnie did as he was told and then found that the two of them were standing in the shadows of bright LED lighting that lit up a workbench which ran along one side of the shed. Tools of all shapes and sizes were clipped into place on the wall behind the workbench. On the other side of the shed were two large safes and some other heavier machinery. An old metal 20-litre jerry can stood behind the door and a cable leading from the generator had been fed through a crudely cut hole in one of the wooden wall panels. The whole place had the heady aroma of creosote, lubricants and petrol.

Johnnie had been here on several occasions but it never ceased to amaze him how organised this workshop was. He loved just standing there and marvelling at the selection of tools which all had their own hook or clip on the wall. It was also the remoteness of the location and the continual sound of the wind whistling around the structure which added to the sense of adventure he always felt when visiting Judson.

Known in the criminal fraternity simply as Judson, he was one of the best armourers in the south of England with an impressive array of arms for any occasion. There wasn't much Judson didn't know about firearms of all shapes, sizes and ages, and anything he didn't know wasn't worth knowing. Although it was a bastard of a journey to get to this workshop, Johnnie knew that it was always worth it to make sure that he had the best tools for his trade.

'What you got, son?' Judson asked, peering at Johnnie

through huge round eyeglass spectacles. Grey hair leaked out from under the rim of an ancient oily black flat cap, and there was at least a week's growth of grey and black stubble covering the man's face. He wore a lumberjack shirt which had had the collar unceremoniously ripped off it, and an oil-stained waistcoat which, rather incongruously, sported a gold watch chain across its front.

Today, Johnnie needed to get rid of the gun he had used to kill the man in the taxi, whoever the hell he was. It was a gun which Judson had supplied so, in Johnnie's mind, it was coming home. He had also brought with him the gun which Stryker Stone had used to kill the other man in the taxi. He laid both firearms out on the workbench, removing their oily rags as he did so.

'These been fired, have they?' Judson asked, picking up one of the guns. It was the one Johnnie had used at One Tree Hill. He nodded as Judson held it up to the light for a general inspection.

Returning the gun to the workbench, he picked up the other firearm and turned it over in his hands, making sure that the safety catch was on. Holding it up to his eyes, he looked down the barrel before giving it a closer inspection.

'And this one, you say?' he asked.

'Also fired.'

While Judson continued his inspection, Arcane opened up his holdall and removed the gun he had taken from the victim in the taxi. He laid the greasy cloth on the workbench and peeled back the material to expose the gun. Eventually, Judson looked across at the third firearm.

'Also been fired but no other details about it or its owner.'

Although it was a half-truth, Johnnie wasn't going to give the old armourer any more information than he had to.

'Hmm. A Ruger. Expensive piece of kit.' The armourer reached across and almost reverently caressed the weapon before lifting it up and turning it over in his hands. Johnnie looked nonplussed.

'Okay, what do you want to do with it?'

'That's not for me, Judson. If you want to take it then please – be my guest. Otherwise, can you scrap it. Or do you want me to get it melted down?'

Judson removed the magazine from the gun before pulling the barrel slide back. He then pulled the trigger. It gave a satisfying click.

'Okay, leave it with me, son. Be a shame to destroy this little beauty. Not for cash mind. I'm just taking it off your hands as a favour.'

He laid the Ruger on the workbench. 'You wanting anything else while you're here?'

Johnnie never felt secure unless he had easy access to a firearm so he now spent some time looking at a selection of weapons which the armourer retrieved from one of his safes. Eventually, he settled on a Glock and paid Judson the going rate. There was never much point in negotiating with armourers – they always had the upper hand as far as Johnnie was concerned.

He wrapped the Glock in a cloth which Judson had provided and placed it in the holdall. The armourer opened a metal cabinet inside the safe and drew out two magazines of ammunition for the Glock. These also went into the holdall. Johnnie then pulled a roll of twenty pound notes from his pocket and counted off a number equivalent to the price they had agreed.

As he handed them over one by one, Judson checked them to make sure that he wasn't being given notes with consecutive numbers. Finally, they shook hands before Johnnie left the shed and started the trek back to his car.

Mission accomplished, he thought as he walked back towards the beach, turning left at the cairn. But getting tooled up was the least of his worries. And he completely failed to spot the man in a full SAS woodland camouflage outfit who was snuggled down into the scrubland which bordered the landside of the pathway.

36
Friday 1 May

It had been a long day and some of the team were looking distinctly frayed around the edges. They could all do with a break from wrestling with the complexities of the investigations that were ongoing at the moment.

Sarah Hunter was pleased to see that Carolyn Pennant was in the Ops Room. She hadn't seen Pennant when she had visited the morgue earlier during the day but had found out that Elaine Jennings had asked her to keep an eye on Rachael Buckley now that the girl was conscious. The Acting DS wanted to be able to get to talk to the girl as soon as she was fit enough to have visitors.

Her phone vibrated in her pocket. She looked at the screen. Rocco Vance was nothing if not persistent. She let it ring out to voicemail. Not now, Rocco. Not now.

Earlier on, she had insisted that Ted Selitto went home to his apartment in Sevenoaks. He wasn't keen to go but she had put her foot down and commanded that he should leave the station. She would have taken him herself if she had the time but, in the circumstances, she got one of the drivers from Traffic to drop him at home. Someone from one of the other apartments had been keeping the place ticking over while he had been away so he should have had no trouble settling back in. Sarah, herself, had been round there a few times over the months just to check things out but the place required very little regular maintenance.

Jed Crowther and Lisa Calder had arrived in the Ops Room looking somewhat battle scarred. There were scratches and spots of dried blood on their arms where the vegetation in the woodland area they had been searching on the shores of Bewl Water had fought back. In fact, Calder looked as if she had caught the sun so perhaps she had been engaged in searching a more exposed area. They were in conversation with Azzar Mishraz who now seemed to be working with Elaine Jennings on the One Tree Hill shooting.

Her troops were thinly spread across a number of seemingly unrelated incidents but Hunter was beginning to get a feeling in the pit of her stomach that they might not be quite as unrelated as she had initially thought. So, she was reasonably pleased when Iverson stuck his head round the door of the Ops Room and nodded for her to join him. She arrived in the corridor as he was opening the door to one of the meeting rooms, and he beckoned her to follow him.

'A quick word before you go, Sarah,' he said, sitting on the corner of one of the desks.

'Oh, I wish,' she replied. 'Can't see me leaving here any time soon.'

'Okay, a quick word before *I* go,' he smiled. 'Mrs Iversen's turn to host the village Bridge evening so it's a three-line whip for yours truly. Anyway, never mind that.' He got up and shuffled over towards the window. Sarah made herself comfortable behind one of the desks, arms resting on the wood veneer, fingers interlocked, thumbs unconsciously tapping each other.

'I was reviewing your caseload earlier and concluded that you're way short on numbers for all the stuff that's going on,' he opined. 'So, I hope you don't mind but I've stuck my oar in, pulled rank, and demanded Stuart Crosby's immediate return from Canterbury.'

Sarah was gobsmacked. Whilst she respected Iversen for all the support he gave her, he was a stickler for procedure and doing things by the book. The old school training, as he would put it.

'Thank you, sir,' she replied, not really knowing what else to say. Crosby was a good, solid operator and could go far. He had been getting some experience in the Serious Crime squad so would be ideal for Hunter's ongoing investigations. Plus, he already knew most of the team from when they worked together on the harrowing sex trafficking case. He had more of a cerebral approach to the job, often able to think three or four steps ahead whereas some of her team were through the door without even thinking what might be on the other side.

'He should be with you over the weekend,' Iversen informed her. 'By the way, have you been in touch with Pennington lately?'

'He was up at One Tree Hill when we arrived last night. I must say I was surprised to see him and I still can't think why he would have wanted to be there. Unless the people in the cab were of interest to him.'

Hunter had been chasing an idea around in her head that Pennington knew more than he was prepared to let on about the shooting. He seemed to have become very adept at being in places either just before or just after serious incidents. But he wasn't someone who wanted to get his own hands dirty by taking on the investigations. He would simply farm them out to people like Hunter with a '*keep me informed*' tag attached.

'He's working with Medway on some major drug-related investigation,' Iversen continued. 'Has he mentioned it to you?'

No he hadn't, Hunter thought. But someone else had. Should she tell Iversen about the visit from Jordan Wright? *Could* she tell Iversen about the visit from Jordan Wright? On the basis that Iversen probably knew as much about the investigation as she did, particularly if he had been talking to Pennington, she decided to keep her own counsel whilst hoping that this decision didn't come back to bite her.

'No, he was a bit evasive when we met him,' Hunter eventually replied. 'But we certainly got the feeling that something was going on.'

'Well, there's definitely something going on but exactly *what* is anyone's guess,' Iversen continued. 'Any news on the identities of the victims at One Tree Hill?'

'Not yet, sir, but we have had a bit of a breakthrough this afternoon.' Hunter then brought Iversen up to speed on their theory that Biondi had travelled to Bermuda to escort Samantha Frobisher back to the UK. She also covered Selitto's recognition of Frobisher in the morgue and the fact that Biondi appeared to have disappeared whilst taking a flight to Antigua.

'You can't just disappear in a place like Gatwick Airport,' Iversen remarked, 'it's pretty much got wall-to-wall CCTV.'

Whilst Hunter agreed with her boss, the fact of the matter was that Biondi had not been seen again after going through security.

'Grace is continuing to work through hours of CCTV to see if she can spot him, but you can imagine that it's not easy with that number of people flowing through the airport all the time.'

Iversen thought about this then changed tack.

'By the way, I was speaking to that Margot PR person at Maidstone the other day. She told me that she had been dealing with all the nationals on the Tideswell crash although there doesn't seem to have been a huge amount of interest since the crash itself. Even Kent Online seem to have gone quiet on it. Have you had any approaches?'

Hunter wasn't sure that she wanted to tell Iversen about the call from Rocco Vance, particularly because she hadn't followed it up. However, it was probably something that she should mention so she recounted the call and the fact that Vance knew about the snakes in the cellar.

'Hmm. How on earth would he have known that?' Iversen wondered out loud, casting a glance out of the window. 'Surely no one in your team would be talking to the press, let alone a one-man blogging outfit.'

'I would certainly hope not,' Hunter replied, an air of indignation in her voice. 'I also doubt that he would have got anywhere by talking to the crime scenes and forensics teams which then leaves us with the uniforms. Unfortunately, they seem to be incapable of keeping information to themselves and seem all too ready to blurt it out if anyone comes asking. The only other possibility is that Vance has used subterfuge to obtain information, and someone has been suckered into telling him things they shouldn't have done. Anyway, I will speak to him soon, particularly as Margot gave him my contact details in the first place.'

Iversen frowned.

'What? He phoned her up and she just gave him your number so that he could make contact with you direct? That's not how she operates. She would never give anyone your number unless you had asked her to do so. You'd better check that out with her but, in discussions I've ever had with her,

237

she has always alluded to herself as being the *gate-keeper*. She won't let anyone from the press talk to an investigating officer unless she has briefed the officer concerned in the first place.'

Hunter was annoyed with herself for not having contacted Margot Westwood as soon as she had taken Vance's first call. She had thought at the time that it was odd that Westwood would just give out her number to anyone who rang up purporting to be from the press. But it was the old story for Sarah – there had been something more important to deal with at the time so calling Westwood had been put on the back burner.

'And did you say that this is some sort of news blogger?' Iversen continued.

'Yes, I think he called it an online news resource for Kent and Sussex.' Hunter was desperately trying to remember what Vance had called it. Notebook News? Noteblog News? She thought it had the word 'note' in it somewhere, then she remembered. 'News Notepad,' she blurted out. 'That's what it's called. *News Notepad.*'

'Never heard of it,' Iversen sighed, looking at his watch. 'Okay. I'd better get going. I'll be around over the weekend so just give me a call if you need anything. It's always good to have an excuse to get out for an hour or so.' Hunter noticed a mischievous twinkle in his eye as he pushed himself off the wall. 'It's about time we had something from the CSIs, isn't it?'

Hunter had also been thinking along those lines. 'Probably tomorrow,' she replied. 'Hopefully that will give us the impetus to move things along.'

Following Iversen's departure, Hunter had called Jed Crowther and Lisa Calder into the meeting room for a quick end-of-the-day debrief on their search of the woodland area north of Bewl Water. As it had become more and more likely that the pilot had baled out over the water, and because a body had not been recovered from the water, the hunt was on for evidence that he had come ashore.

'We've got two areas of search, ma'am,' Crowther was saying. 'The main one is Chingley Wood which goes right down to the water's edge in places. There are crude paths as well as recognised footpaths criss-crossing the wood but, once you're off the path, the vegetation is pretty dense. And it's making it very difficult for us to make progress. The other area is known locally as Thieves Wood although it's a bit further back from the water's edge and the pilot would have certainly risked being seen by anyone who had been at the Outdoor Centre at that time in the morning.'

'Presumably you've got some help.' It was more of a state-ment from Hunter as she assumed that Crowther would have taken a vanload of uniforms with him to Bewl Water.

'Not that many,' Calder replied. 'In fact, we could only get three guys today and that was for only two or three hours. We have requisitioned for some more tomorrow.'

Hunter was impressed that they were planning to continue their search into the weekend. But she wanted to know where they were searching.

'Well, we started by assuming that he would want to come ashore with the maximum amount of cover from prying eyes,' Crowther replied, 'so we've concentrated on the area where the treeline comes right down to the water. Needless to say, it's a pig to get to and once you're in the thick of it, it's easy to lose your bearings. It's mixed woodland with lots of tall thin trees growing close to each other and loads of undergrowth which invariably catches your feet and ankles.'

'But it would make a great place to hide a parachute,' Calder butted in. 'In fact, it would make a great place to hide anything, including a body. We have been keeping that in mind as he may have been badly injured after going into the water but managed to get ashore before collapsing in the wood.'

'Yeah, we can't rule anything out,' Crowther agreed, 'but at the moment we've come up with zilch.'

Hunter didn't want to discourage them in any way but she was also conscious that two of her precious resources were essentially unavailable because they were undertaking a search which really should be undertaken by the uniformed section of the force, or even by accredited members of the public – perhaps a local ramblers group. After all, they were only really looking for a parachute, weren't they?

'Okay, if you want to have another go at it, let's get that done tomorrow. If you don't find anything, then we'll have to think of a Plan B as I'll need you to help in other areas of this multi-faceted investigation.'

They both nodded and left the room. Hunter stared at the closed door. Iversen was right. She had to get in touch with Margot Westwood as a matter of some urgency.

37

Saturday 2 May

A brisk south-westerly had sprung up during the night, and it was now driving curtains of rain against the front of Hunter's cottage, rivulets of water streaming down the window. Sarah sat at the kitchen table, mesmerised by the sound of the wind and the noise of the rain, trying to make sense of the jumbled thoughts that were going around in her head. She hadn't had a bad night but it had seemed to be a pretty dreamless sleep that she had eventually fallen into.

A steaming cup of coffee suddenly appeared in front of her as Grace slid into the seat at the head of the table. They had shared scrambled eggs on toast for breakfast as well as a couple of hot cross buns which were past their sell-by date but seemed perfectly edible once they had been toasted.

They had discussed their plans for the day with Grace deciding to go back to the station to continue her search for Biondi. She had received some new CCTV footage late on Friday and needed to spend time looking through it. Hunter had a visit planned to the CSI labs in Maidstone where Beth Dench and her team were ready to go through some of their findings.

'Is Ted going with you?' Grace asked as she finished her coffee.

'Well, he's going but not with me. He was absolutely insistent that he should be there for the debrief so he'll be taking a taxi.'

'Did you say Stuart Crosby might be in today?' Grace asked.

'Iversen said he might be but who knows?' Sarah replied with a resigned tone. 'If he does make an appearance, can you just get him up to speed as quickly as possible and then the three of us can have a chat when I get back.'

Her phone buzzed on the table in front of her, its screen lighting up with a message. Picking up the phone, she stared at the words, a knot quickly tightening in her stomach.

Going live tmrw with or without yr input – yr choice

She got up from her chair, pushed the phone across the table to Grace and went to stand by the window, watching the rain as it continued to batter what was left of the spring flowers in her tiny front garden.

'You're going to have to confront this, Sarah,' Grace said, trying to get the right inflexion in her voice so as to avoid making it sound as if she was telling her friend what to do. 'You'll only end up taking it out on yourself if he publishes something which is plainly detrimental to our investigation.'

Sarah continued looking out of the window, hands stuffed into the pockets of her black jeans, furiously chewing her lower lip. Eventually, she turned and wandered back to the table.

'You're right, of course, and I'll call him when I've finished with Beth Dench. In the meantime, perhaps you could take a look at *News Notepad*, just in case there's a good reason why I shouldn't be calling him. Find out what sort of stuff they blog about, who's reading it, what sort of people are commenting, that sort of thing. When I get back to the office, you can give me the heads up and then I'll call him. In the meantime, I'll reply to his text saying that I'll contact him later.'

'Sounds like a plan,' Grace agreed as she got up from the table and put their cups in the sink. 'Better get going.'

By contrast, Johnnie Arcane didn't have a plan. He was just cruising aimlessly around. Rudderless. He had completely lost direction. His brain was fizzing, but he just didn't have answers to the two central problems which were foremost in the maelstrom of activity in his head.

Why had Gav been such a dickhead? Why hadn't he had that phone on silent? The trouble Johnnie had gone to in order to get the phone for him in the first place. He'd set it up with reduced illumination on the screen so that Gav could still see the message from Johnnie without the passengers being aware that something was going on. He had muted the sound and told Gav to use his own phone if he wanted to make calls.

But, for some reason, Gav had unmuted the sound which had then alerted the two bastards in the taxi to the fact that something was up. The carnage that followed had left Stryker with wounds he was unlikely to recover from, and Gav himself with his brains splattered all over the taxi's windscreen.

Right now, Johnnie was in Chatham trying to deal with his next problem which was also a question. Where the fuck was Vinnie? His life-long friend and soulmate had disappeared just at the time he was needed the most. Not answering his phone, not replying to text messages, not been seen in any of his usual haunts. Johnnie had even done the unthinkable and had actually driven past the block where Vinnie had a small one-bedroom flat. No sign of the man or his van. So Johnnie was now reduced to walking the streets of Chatham, which had always been Vinnie's territory, hoping to perhaps catch a glimpse of the man himself.

He was negotiating his way along the bustling High Street and had just passed The Pentagon shopping centre when he thought he caught sight of the back of his friend's head about 100 yards in front of him. He suddenly lunged forward towards the retreating figure and immediately collided with a woman carrying several Primark shopping bags.

'Oy! Watch where you're going, arsehole!'

Johnnie muttered a terse '*fuck you*' which only served to unleash a lengthy foul-mouthed tirade from the woman. Trying to get away from her, he stumbled on but had now lost sight of the person who could have been Vinnie. Exasperated, he collapsed into the waiting arms of one of the chairs set out on the paved area in front of a coffee shop. Meanwhile, the woman projected one further volley of invective in his general direction before turning and storming off up the street.

God, what a mess, he thought.

He stared at the ground, once again carefully replaying every second of the encounter on One Tree Hill. As he and Stryker crossed the parking area, he had sent a message to Gav as planned on the special phone he had given him. On receipt of the message …

He felt a tap on his shoulder. Swivelling around, he found himself looking up at a lanky young man dressed head to toe in black with a small black apron draped around his hips.

'Can I get you anything?' the young man asked. 'Coffee or another refreshment. Something to eat perhaps, or some biscuits?'

'Double espresso with hot milk will be fine,' Johnnie replied and went back to his private brainstorming session. The waiter sped off to get the order made up inside the shop.

At least he still had Stryker's phone which he now took out of his pocket. He held it in his hands almost under the table top as if protecting it from any prying eyes. He scrolled through the list of contacts but none of the names made any sense to him. In fact, some of the names didn't even make sense. *Noddy the Nonce*. How was he supposed to know who that was? He checked the recent call log but, again, he had no idea who these people were. *Sickbag*. Who the hell would call themselves Sickbag?

Perhaps Gav's phone would be more useful. But hold on a minute! If he had given Spanners the phone he had given to Gav in order to receive his signal, where was Gav's phone? He had simply taken the phone off the dashboard, never thinking to look for another phone. Idiot! Had Gav kept his phone in his pocket? Had he even taken it with him? Of course he had. Wouldn't go anywhere without it. In which case, it would now be in a lab being dismantled. Shit!

Johnnie decided that he'd been a bit hasty giving the phone to Spanners for liquidation. Surely he hadn't destroyed it yet. He took his own phone out of his pocket and called the mechanic. Had he still got the phone from last night? Yes, he had. Great! Johnnie would come over immediately to collect it. Was he really sure he wanted it? Yes, yes, yes! Even though it was now roughly one square inch of plastic and techno-wizardry?

Johnnie disconnected the call and stared disconsolately at the blank screen. Nothing was ever straightforward, was it?

The waiter arrived with his espresso and milk before scurrying back to the safety of the shop. Reflecting on his own stupidity for not searching Gav's pockets, Johnnie absentmindedly poured the milk into the espresso before realising that he had poured so much that the cup of black coffee had turned a very pale brown. He could hardly taste the coffee.

Perhaps he should ditch the phone he now held in his hand. But that was impossible because it was the only way Maddox could contact him. Contact with Maddox was a one way street. Johnnie had not yet been given the means to make contact with Maddox. And Maddox was only going to contact Johnnie when he was good and ready to do so. If Maddox had no means of contacting Johnnie, the whole deal would be off and Johnnie would have pissed his deposit up against the wall.

And then there was Vinnie to worry about. Where the hell was he?

38

Saturday 2 May

Parking her car in a designated visitor's space at the back of the CSI labs which were tucked away in a corner of the Kent Police HQ in Maidstone, she dialled the number she had been given earlier in the week and just hoped the woman would answer her call on a Saturday.

'Hello, Sarah!' Margot Westwood's voice sounded more plummy on the telephone than it did in real life, and probably wasn't helped by the faint buzzing on the line. Hunter had decided to give Westwood a call before she started her meeting with Beth Dench, and was relieved that she had managed to make contact with the PR guru straightaway.

'Hi, Margot,' she replied airily. 'Sorry to call you on a Saturday. Are you able to talk now or shall I call back later?'

Westwood laughed. 'Believe me, Sarah, this is also a twenty four/seven job just like yours. Our top brass need to react to press enquiries at a moment's notice irrespective of the time of day. There's all hell to pay if I'm not there to get the whole show on the road. So it's easier to just keep the phone on and answer all the calls.'

Hunter was impressed. She was starting to relate to this woman.

'Anyway, what can I do for you? I'm sure you haven't simply called to discuss the price of fish!'

'That'll be the day, Margot,' Hunter replied. 'No, I wanted to run the name of a journalist past you to see if you had heard of him. The name's Rocco Vance who claims to run a news blogsite called *News Notepad*. Said he had spoken to you and you had put him on to me.'

There was silence and Hunter wondered if the call had been cut off but she could still hear the faint buzzing. 'Are you still there?' she asked.

'Yes, Sarah. Sorry. Just thinking.' There was another snippet of silence before Westwood responded.

'Hmm. Something's not quite right here, Sarah,' Westwood began. 'I'm pretty sure that I've never heard of *News Notepad*. Some sort of blogsite you said? And the name, Rocco Vance, isn't ringing any bells with me. Did you say that I told him to call you?'

'Affirmative!'

'In that case, I can be pretty certain that I have never heard of him or his blogsite.'

'And how can you be so sure?'

'I would never give a journalist your number unless I had contacted you beforehand. Data protection and all that. But even if we didn't have all this DP stuff, I'd still want to clear it with you before handing out such details.'

It was Hunter's turn to take a moment's silence while she processed this information. Who *was* this guy? And how had he got her number? And how did he know so much about what her investigation was uncovering?

'Okay, let me start from the beginning on this one and see if you've got any ideas of what is going on here.' Hunter then related all she knew about Vance and his blogsite which admittedly wasn't much. She also told Westwood that Vance had known about the body in the snake room within two or three hours of the discovery being made. He had then texted her about the shootings at One Tree Hill while Hunter was still getting up to speed with her investigation. And now he was proposing to go ahead with some blog about her investigations with or without her input.

Westwood was thoughtful.

'There are a couple of issues here aren't there,' she began, 'quite apart from how he came by your phone number. The one that screams out to me is that you've got a leak somewhere. Possibly someone quite close to your investigation. The other issue is motivation. What is his motivation? Is he on a mission to bring you crashing to earth? Or is he some sort of do-gooder who has an axe to grind with the police and you just happen to be conveniently in the crosshairs? Or is he, in fact, simply a young journo trying to make a name for himself by creating an online newsfeed and looking for a big news story in his home county of Kent?'

If she was honest with herself, it was the fact that Vance had got her phone number which was causing Hunter the most concern. But Westwood had raised the spectre of a leak within her close-knit group of officers which was a possibility that she had also thought about but which she had dismissed out of hand.

'So, there's no other way he could have got any information through your PR set-up?' Hunter asked, hopefully.

'I'm afraid not, Sarah,' Westwood replied with some conviction. 'We run a very tight ship anyway. There's only myself and my two assistants and they wouldn't have access to that information without coming to me.'

'No one else he could have contacted who would have given out my phone number?' Hunter asked, knowing that she was clutching at straws here.

'Not unless he's called someone at Tonbridge and misrepresented himself and his intentions.' Westwood's tone was slightly defensive but she seemed content to shift the potential for any leak to have come from Tonbridge rather than Maidstone.

'Hmm. Always a possibility, I suppose,' Hunter conceded. 'Okay. Any tips on how I should deal with him and his threats?'

'Well, you could either tell him to publish and be damned or take the more conciliatory route by asking him what it is that he wants to get out there. I doubt that he's got much coverage so he'll probably be hoping that a bigger fish will pick up whatever the story is and run it on a regional basis whereafter it may be picked up by someone with national coverage. Somewhere along the line, we would pick it up anyway and, depending on what the subject matter was and how it reflected on the Kent force, we would either let it go or try and spike it.'

Hunter was feeling increasingly uneasy about what the content of this blogpost could be, particularly if it showed that she and the team had acted in an inappropriate manner in some way.

'And you'd need to find out how he got your number,' Westwood continued. 'Use that information as some sort of bargaining chip. You'll help him with his story if he spills about who told him your number. He might not come across on this but we really do need to know so that we can plug that hole for the future.'

'Okay, thanks for that, Margot.' Hunter had just noticed the time on the car clock and realised she was now late for her appointment with the CSIs. 'My DS is checking out *News Notepad* as we speak and I'll probably give Vance a call when I get back to the station.'

'Good luck! And let me know how you get on.'

The buzzing stopped. The line went dead. Hunter looked ruefully out of the window at the brick building in front of her. Vance was like a boil which needed to be lanced as a matter of some urgency.

39

Saturday 2 May

Sarah Hunter exited the lift on the third floor of the CSI building and walked across the small reception area. Looking up at the camera above the door into the main lab, she waited for the green light to appear and then heard a click as the door opened out towards her.

'Hello, Sarah. Thought we'd lost you!' Beth Dench welcomed her with a smile. 'Come in, come in.'

'Yes, apologies for being late but there was a call I just had to make,' Hunter mumbled as she walked across the threshold into the main lab.

'No problem,' Dench continued as she led the way to the meeting room. 'It's given us an opportunity to have a catch-up with Ted. It's good to have him back on the team after all this time.'

Hunter was pleased to hear that her DS had already arrived which meant that they could start the briefing straightaway. On entering the room, she nodded a greeting to Jimbo Carrigan and Donny Campbell before taking the seat next to Selitto. Campbell poured a mug of coffee from a flask on the table and put it in front of her.

'You got here, then,' Hunter smiled as she gave Selitto a sideways glance. She then removed her phone from the pocket of her jeans and laid it on the table in front of her. Dench took a seat on the other side of the table so that she was looking directly at the two detectives. She had a laptop open in front of her. The two CSI officers sat to her left and there was a screen on the wall to her right.

'Okay, let's get started,' Dench suggested. 'Shall we look at the crash site first?' Hunter nodded. An arial view of the remains of Tideswell Manor appeared on the screen as Carrigan took up the commentary.

'The force of the aircraft hitting the building combined with the collapse of the upper floors and the resulting fire meant that there were no survivors. The exact number of bodies will be down to the pathologists to confirm but, by our reckoning, there were at least twenty-five plus some minors. There was significant evidence of drug-taking in the house, and our view would be that a considerable amount of alcohol had also been consumed judging by the number of empty bottles that were strewn around the grounds outside of the building. Goodness knows how many more there were amongst all the smashed glass we found.'

Another picture flashed up on the screen.

'This is a section of the ground floor which we managed to uncover, and you can see that it was one of the few areas not affected by the fire. You'll also see that it's carpeted and, indeed, it appears that the mansion was carpeted throughout with no expense being spared on the quality of the carpeting.' Carrigan pressed a key on his tablet and the screen divided into quarters. He then activated a digital laser pointer and its little red arrow drew everyone's attention to various marks on the carpet.

'We've forensically examined sections of this carpet and others like it,' he continued, 'and have found traces of Class A drugs. This darker patch here is probably red wine, this one over here is undoubtedly urine and the other patch at the bottom left of the screen is vomit. What you can't really see in the photo bottom right are small shards of thin darkened glass which could be from a crack pipe.'

'One discovery we've made,' Dench said, taking over from Carrigan, 'is that some of these marks were not made in the days leading up to the crash. They are older which indicates that this sort of party was probably a regular occurrence. It also indicates that no one really bothered to clear the place up. Which might bring into question whether Biondi ever went there himself. Or was it only used by an itinerant set of druggies who would just turn up when they fancied having a rave and shooting up? Presumably Biondi still owns it?'

Hunter had assumed that Grace would have checked ownership but made a note on her phone to check. 'As far as we're aware he's still the owner but I'll get Grace to confirm.'

Dench invited Carrigan to continue. 'We also found seven adults and three minors in the cellar along with the woman who had been locked in one of the rooms. It is clear from our investigation that the rooms in the cellar were used for vile and degrading sexual activities, mainly involving children or young adults. The bedding, such as it was, provided clear evidence of sexual activity with stains of bodily secretions on the sheets along with blood and sweat. The occupants of the rooms had either urinated on the floors of the rooms or on the bed where they lay. There was evidence of some faeces under two of the beds but, again, we are not convinced that they were that recent.'

Hunter stared at the screen. This was hard going, she thought.

'We spent some time examining the entrance to the cellar,' Carrigan was saying. 'The puzzle was why the door only had a handle on the outside. This meant that the cellar could only be accessed from within the mansion or, to put it another way, no one in the cellar could escape. We also found that there had been an intercom system which presumably allowed people in the cellar to be released if the door had been shut. The door itself was made of steel with internal reinforcing and an insulated core, presumably to prevent the spread of fire. It had a thickness of around seventy millimetres with overhanging flanges on all four edges to provide additional security. We'd normally expect to see this sort of door in gun rooms or cash rooms, or even in panic rooms. Anyway, it seems to have been closed at the time of the plane strike and the falling masonry essentially sealed the cellar so that it became some sort of sarcophagus. Not even the Greek god, Atlas, would have been able to open that door from inside the cellar.'

Beth Dench then changed the picture on the screen to show the room in which the woman now suspected to be Samantha Frobisher was found. There was an audible intake of breath from Ted Selitto as he leaned forward, peering intently at the screen.

'Jeez!' he muttered under his breath whilst, at the same time, shaking his head. The woman's eyes were wide open, staring sightlessly across the room.

'Once we'd had all the creatures removed and managed to get to the body, it seemed likely that she had probably died of an overdose. Although the garotte was fairly well embedded into her neck and had probably severed the carotid artery, the lack of blood suggested that this occurred post mortem. But the antecubital areas of both her arms were like pin cushions.'

Selitto turned to Dench, a frown creasing his forehead.

'Sorry, Ted, the inner parts of both forearms. You know, where they mainly take blood from when you go for a blood test. There are extensive puncture marks on her arms which, in our view, are more likely to be where substances were injected into the body rather than evidence of multiple extractions of blood. Toby Swartzman and his team will be able to give you much more chapter and verse on this but it didn't look to us as if she had died as a result of being bitten by a snake.'

Hunter decided that she wasn't too fussed about how Frobisher had died. The fact that she *had* died was all that mattered. In the meantime, she was trying to fit a couple of pieces together in the Frobisher jigsaw. The woman arrives back in the UK on the Thursday and is then found in a sealed cellar a week later. In the intervening period, she has clearly suffered abuse, she has probably been stuffed full of Class A drugs and has been left to die with a garotte around her neck. Somebody clearly didn't like her, but was that somebody Baz Biondi? He had certainly accompanied her back to the UK but what happened after they left Gatwick Airport? She would need further information on time of death from Swartzman before going much further with this train of thought.

Dench put a picture on the screen showing the camper wagons and Winnebagos parked at the back of the mansion. She then pointed the red arrow at one of the vehicles and Hunter immediately recognised it as being the one that she had taken a look at.

'That's the one you had a look in isn't it, Sarah?'

'Certainly is,' she nodded. 'Did I disturb some of the evidence?'

'No, nothing like that. I only knew it was the one you had been in because I found the gun.'

Hunter nodded and smiled, remembering the gun wrapped in a heavy-duty plastic bag and hidden at the back of one of the drawers in the sleeping quarters.

'Anyway, of greater importance,' Beth continued, an air of excitement in her voice, 'is that we've been able to match the prints in the vehicle to two of the bodies in the cellar.' Police-style mugshots of a man and a woman appeared on the screen. Hunter stared at the crude photos. So, these were the two people who lived in that hovel where the dust stuck to the grease or the grease stuck to the dust. Did it matter what stuck to what? she wondered. It was still revolting.

'This is Leif van Donk and his wife, Romy. They're both Dutch nationals but seem to spend quite a lot of time travelling around Europe. They pitch up here in the UK from time to time, and the pictures and prints came from an arrest at Dover Docks in 2015 when a small amount of cannabis was found in their vehicle. Looks like they had forgotten to take it out of the vehicle before leaving home. A fine and a record although there is a note on the file to the effect that they're suspected of being high up in the pecking order of one of the biggest drug gangs in the Netherlands.'

'And the gun?' Hunter asked.

'Hmm, the gun,' Dench sighed and then paused. 'Recently fired I'd say, so we've sent it off to ballistics. We also found quite a lot of Class A plus amphetamines, barbiturates and cannabis. Mind you, we had to take the vehicle to pieces to find it so it was very well hidden.'

'Any others?' Hunter asked although she wasn't holding

out too much hope that Dench had identified everyone in the cellar.

'We were able to match prints in another of the vehicles on the site,' Dench continued. More mugshots appeared on the screen. 'This is Joos and Bibi Eikenboom. They have a conviction in this country for importation of pornography. We also have an identification for the third person who was sharing their Winnebago.'

A photo of a glamourous woman appeared on the screen. Probably in her thirties, she had long blonde hair swept back to reveal an attractive face, large eyes, a sensual mouth and alluring cheek bones. She was wearing a low-cut chiffon top with a good deal of cleavage on show. Pouting at the camera with rosy red lips, she certainly had the air of a film star or, at least, a wannabe film star.

'Presumably not a police mugshot then,' Hunter observed dryly.

'No, we found the photo in the Winnebago,' Dench replied. 'Meet Isabella Langenberg otherwise known to her fans as *Blaze*. She's a porn actress and has a police record here for exposing herself in public. Reading between the lines, it looks as if she was caught *in flagrante* with a couple of male performers while making a movie on Wimbledon Common. Donny's done a bit of investigating and it seems that she normally appears in hard porn movies along with any number of sexual deviants. Some of the movies also involve kids. We found a couple of LED lighting panels on tripods in the corner of one of the rooms in the cellar. A bit like the gear we use to light a dark area. There were other lighting panels and two cameras in the Winnebago so she and the Eikenbooms were clearly involved in movie-making while they were here.'

'No sign of drugs, then?' Hunter was starting to wonder at the scale of what had been going on at Tideswell Manor right under their noses.

'Nothing of any note,' Dench replied. 'A few tablets which are probably Es and a couple of wraps of heroin. We also found a small pistol but it hadn't been fired in an age. In fact, we could hardly get the safety catch off. No, I think they were all simply there for the porn so I imagine that the two other adults in the cellar were probably also there for the filming. We have been able to tag them to a very upmarket motorhome which is registered in France but nothing on the PNC to link them to any previous convictions in the UK.'

Hunter slumped back in her seat.

'Bloody hell,' she muttered, continuing to stare at the image of Isabella Langenberg on the screen. 'What a mess.'

40

Saturday 2 May

It hadn't been difficult following Johnnie Arcane. Not only because the target seemed totally oblivious to the fact that he was being shadowed but also because he seemed to be completely unaware of the people around him in a busy shopping precinct on a Saturday morning. He gave the appearance of being utterly lost in his own thoughts.

DC Abigail Knight had taken a seat on one of the many benches which had been laid out along the pedestrianised part of the High Street in Chatham to give shoppers the opportunity to take a break from the arduous business of shopping. From where she was sitting, she had a perfect view of the coffee shop and of her target who was now surreptitiously scrutinising one of the two phones she had watched him pull out of his jacket pockets.

Known as Abbie to her friends and colleagues at Maidstone Police HQ, Knight had been in the Serious Crime Directorate's surveillance team for the last two years and loved the challenges she faced on an almost daily basis. Mostly working alone, she was used to long hours in the cramped environs of her car so it made a nice change to be sitting outside today, particularly as the sun was shining.

She was wearing what she often wore on stakeouts – a black long-sleeved T-shirt under a rather tatty woollen hoodie and dark navy jeans with trendy slits at the knees. Her long jet black hair was pulled through the clasp at the back of an NYC cap and she was wearing a pair of well-worn dark blue trainers.

Nothing flashy. Nothing that would draw attention to her being anything but a young woman out for a stroll round the shops on a Saturday.

Knight had already taken a number of photos of Arcane walking through the town and then sitting outside the coffee shop. She had even managed to get a few shots of his altercation with the bag lady. This evidence was immediately encrypted and transmitted back to her controller in the SCD suite at Maidstone.

Strangely, for a target who the police considered important enough to be assigned a dedicated surveillance officer, Arcane seemed to be blissfully unaware that he was under scrutiny. As Knight continued watching, he put a mobile phone back into one of the pouch pockets on the outside of his denim jacket hoodie and then produced another phone from one of the inside pockets. That was three phones so far, she thought. He punched in a number on this phone then held it to his ear. After about five seconds, he snatched it away from the side of his head and stared at the screen before jamming the phone back into the inner depths of the jacket.

Abbie Knight was used to recording every activity and movement made by her targets without getting too close to them or, indeed, letting them get out of her sight. Her controller reckoned that she had a photographic memory on account of her ability to recall even the most minor details. And her memory was now busily storing details about these phones.

She was just reaching into her shoulder bag for a bottle of water when she heard the faint sound of a ringtone and watched as Arcane searched for one of the phones secreted in his jacket. Eventually identifying the miscreant phone, he jabbed a finger at the screen and then held the device to his ear. Whatever he was being told made him suddenly look up and take account of his location. He glanced up and down the precinct a couple of times before his eyes finally alighted on something behind him to his right. Knight craned her neck to see what had got Arcane's attention but could only make out the Waterstones shop front which was immediately in her line of sight.

The call was quickly ended as Arcane stood up and tossed some coins onto the metal table in front of him. The waiter made a surprisingly quick appearance and was counting the money as Arcane stalked off. Knight stood up and slung her bag over her shoulder, slipped her sunglasses on and did some window shopping as she watched her target cross the precinct and head up a narrow alleyway between two of the shops. This was what she hadn't been able to see although she was relieved to find that a number of people seemed to use it as a means of getting to the precinct.

She quickly had Arcane in her sights up ahead, a reasonable number of people between her and her target. Soon she noticed that the alleyway was starting to become wider and that the pedestrians in front of her were no longer providing sufficient cover. She, therefore, moved to the side of the path and slowed down. She now realised that the alleyway had opened onto a car park for disabled drivers, the extended spaces all clearly painted out on the tarmac. Out of habit, she counted out twenty bays and then decided that only eleven of them were occupied.

Stopping to lean against a wall, she took her phone out to make it look as if she was making a call so she could watch Arcane make his way across the car park. Judging by the way he was studying each car, it was clear that he was looking for a particular registration plate. Eventually he stopped behind a black Mini which was parked in the shadow of a large tree. Taking a furtive look around, he moved towards the car, slid into the passenger seat and pulled the door shut.

Knight pushed herself off the wall and followed an elderly couple who were slowly making their way across the car park. She made a mental note of the registration number as she approached the Mini, and also noticed that it had tinted windows. As she walked past the vehicle, she realised that the driver's door was open, a heavily tattooed arm tapping against the door sill, a cigarette jammed between finger and thumb. She could hear voices but couldn't make out what was being said. She was, however, able to find a shaded spot behind another car from where she took a few shots of the Mini and, more importantly, the driver's arm.

Realising that she was now at the end of the tarmacked area, she moved further into the shadows and sat on a low wall while she waited to see what happened next. She didn't have to wait long as Arcane was soon exiting the Mini and heading off back the way he had come. Knight managed to get a couple of shots of her target leaving the car and held back for a few seconds, waiting until Arcane had re-joined the throng of people using the alleyway.

By the time they got back to the shopping precinct, Arcane had one of his phones clamped to his ear and was looking around as if he was being given instructions about where to meet someone. He had stopped in front of the Pentagon Centre so Knight decided to position herself on a bench about fifty yards away from where he was. After a lot of hand and arm gesticulations, Arcane pocketed the phone and started walking towards her. She immediately dropped her head and pretended to be typing a text message, the peak of her cap covering her face.

Eventually daring to look up, she saw her target peering up at windows above some of the shops. And before she could properly follow his gaze, he had dived into a mini supermarket selling everything for one pound or less.

She wasn't far behind him and, once inside the shop, she was relieved to see Arcane speaking to one of the shop assistants. She quickly grabbed a shopping basket before noticing that this was something her target hadn't done. Although the shop was quite busy, the narrow aisles helped her to keep him in sight as he started to wander towards the back of the shop. Suddenly, he stepped sideways and disappeared through a door marked 'Staff Only'.

In all her training, Knight had been taught never to be alarmed if the unexpected happened, so she made her way to the back of the shop, all the time keeping the 'Staff Only' door in her line of sight. There were a number of tall cage trollies lined up along the back wall of the shop, each one piled high with goods waiting to be put on empty shelves. She carefully surveyed the scene before finding what she was looking for.

The fire exit for the shop was a set of double doors and was probably also used for bringing stock onto the premises. The fact that it was currently obstructed by the trollies was of no consequence to Knight at this moment, but it did indicate that her target was likely to be still on the premises.

Looking around, she noticed that there only seemed to be one shop assistant on the floor and he was helping a customer.

One of his colleagues was manning the till at the front of the shop so Knight decided to quickly test her theory about the 'Staff Only' door. She nonchalantly made her way towards it, taking a couple of items off one of the shelves and putting them in her basket.

Stopping for one last quick glance to see if anyone was watching her, Knight reached for the door handle just as the door burst open and a man was unceremoniously ejected into the shop, losing his footing and sprawling on the floor.

'And don't fucking come back here with that heap of shit ever again!' From her position behind the open door, all that Knight could see was a brown hairy hand with forefinger pointing down towards the figure lying on the floor. The door was then slammed shut and she heard feet stamping their way up an uncarpeted set of wooden stairs.

Feeling slightly exposed now that the door wasn't offering something to hide behind, Knight pulled back towards the next aisle but kept watch as Johnnie Arcane got back on his feet and then hustled his way to the front of the shop and out into the precinct. Her speed of reaction was such that she managed to take some shots of him getting to his feet and then leaving the shop. She was just about to follow when she noticed what looked like two confectionary wrappers on the floor where Arcane had fallen.

Checking that no one was watching her, she photographed the two wrappers where they lay on the floor. She then whipped a pair of nitrile gloves out of her back pocket and snapped one onto her right hand, all the time scouring the shop to see if anyone was watching her. She bent down to pick the wrappers up and then shuffled to where the cage trollies still obstructed the fire exit.

Peeling the glove off her hand so that it created a sealed unit around the wrappers, she placed the little parcel gently in her pocket. Finding her way back to the aisle from which she had gathered the two items that were now in her basket, she returned them to their rightful places before making her way to the front of the shop. She dumped the now empty basket on the pile by the door, and strolled out into the fresh air.

Once outside the shop, she looked for her target but he was nowhere to be seen. No problem, she thought as she walked over to one of the benches opposite the shop. Reaching into her pocket, she pulled out the little pale blue package and examined it. Crude it may be but it should preserve any evidence to show who had had their grubby little fingers on these wraps, she thought.

With her vast experience of policing the drug culture which was prevalent on the streets of Kent, Abigail Knight knew that each wrap contained around a third of a gram of heroin. She also knew that her next report would inform her controller that it was likely that Johnnie Arcane was dealing on the streets of Chatham.

But why?

41
Saturday 2 May

The flask had been replenished and they all sat round the table with mugs of steaming fresh coffee. Selitto had done some exercises to help with the rehabilitation of his fractured left leg, and the CSI officers had prepared the next set of visuals for their briefing. Beth Dench had gone out into the lab to make a phone call.

Sarah Hunter sat at the table watching the activity going on around her without actually taking any notice of what everyone was doing. She was in her own little bubble trying to get to grips with the wickedness of these perverted thugs and the degradation they had wrought on young people just getting started in life. In many ways it was probably a blessing that two of them hadn't survived, she miserably concluded.

Her musings were disturbed when her phone buzzed and a message flashed up on the screen.

Chute found in Chingley Wood. Area sealed. CSIs on way.

Hunter smiled. So, they were right to spend all that time searching the area around Bewl Water, and now they knew that the pilot had most likely survived. He had, therefore, become a person of considerable interest.

Beth Dench returned to the room. 'Did you get that message, Sarah?' she asked, retaking her seat.

'Sure did,' she replied, still looking at the brief message on her phone.

'Annalise Vardy's on her way there now with a small team,' Dench continued. 'Have you met her yet?'

Hunter didn't think that she had met Vardy before so shook her head.

'Annalise will take a look at the area to see if there's any evidence that the pilot was injured and then try to see how he made his getaway from the wood – unless, of course, anyone finds a body in the meantime.'

Selitto had retaken his seat and looked at the message on the screen. He gave a thumbs-up sign to Hunter.

'Okay, let's move on to the Buckley house,' Dench said, looking over towards Donny Campbell. 'We are, of course, now treating Julie Buckley's death as murder and our investigation has been raised to that level.'

Campbell tapped a key on his laptop and a visual showing a blood-bespattered kitchen appeared on the screen.

'Julie Buckley was attacked with several of her own kitchen knives which were stored in a knife block located on the work surface next to the sink. I had originally surmised that she had been tortured as all the knives had been removed from the block and were covered in blood on the worksurface.' The visual on the screen changed to show what Campbell was referring to. A blood-soaked knife block lay on its side on the kitchen work surface, its contents lying in little puddles of blood where they had been discarded.

'It is our belief that only one blade inflicted the wound that actually killed the victim and it is likely that it was eight inches long. As there was no knife with an eight inch blade either on the kitchen work surface or in the house, I had to conclude that the attacker had removed the murder weapon from the premises. We've checked drains in the vicinity but nothing found so far.'

The next visual was a photograph of a kitchen carving knife with a black handle and a shiny silver-coloured blade. 'This is probably what we're looking for. The knife block is one of the best sellers at the cheaper end of kitchen equipment ranges, available everywhere. It holds five knives with the eight inch blade being the biggest. If it's any consolation for the victim, none of the knives we have processed were sharp but you can still do a lot of damage with a blunt knife.'

Hunter shifted uneasily in her chair. This looked a lot like mindless violence simply for the sake of inflicting maximum pain for no gain until, in a final fit of rage, the most destructive of the weapons is used to snuff the victim's life out.

Two new visuals appeared on a split screen. 'Now, on the left, you'll see an overturned straight-backed chair. There is evidence that, at some point, the victim had been restrained – probably manually - in this chair. On the right, you can see a small patch of blood on the hardwood floor which indicates the area where the victim would have hit her head in the event that the chair had been pushed over. This leads us to question whether there was any original intention to kill her as they may have only intended to rough her up whilst one of them searched the girl's room. However, once they couldn't find what they were looking for, things got nasty. Julie Buckley was clearly a fighter, and there is evidence of her blood spatter in both the kitchen and the adjoining sitting room. But the overriding evidence points to assailants losing their cool and running amok when they couldn't find what they came for.'

Hunter studied the visuals on the screen. 'What about the girl's room?'

Another visual appeared showing the shambles which the room had been left in once it had been searched.

'As I think you already know, we only found one phone in the bedroom,' Campbell said, looking over at Hunter who was avoiding eye contact and concentrating on the screen. 'Whereas we might have expected to find more if this girl was involved in county lines.' Sarah thought of responding but then decided to just leave the matter. The phones collected by Jennings and Mishraz were already being taken apart and she would very soon have the information she needed.

Realising that Hunter wasn't going to rise to his challenge, Campbell continued. 'Rachael Buckley collected snow globes which she kept on a set of shelves in her room. Many of these were smashed when the room was ransacked, probably stamped on because the Perspex domes are reasonably tough. Anyway, some survived and three of these had the name of the snow globe printed on the bottom.'

The next visual showed the snow globes with the names of the items printed on the underneath of the base platforms.

'These are all from a range of globes known as *Apocalypse*. This is where the sparkly white snow is replaced by chunks of grey and black. They typically depict a cityscape which has been devastated as a result of a nuclear disaster or some other disaster such as a zombie plague.'

Beth Dench looked across the table at Hunter and Selitto. 'The point we're drawing to your attention is that it seems a strange sort of thing for an eleven year old child to collect. But there could be some symbolism or coded messages in the written description for each globe. Or perhaps we're trying to read too much into it?'

'That's interesting,' Selitto butted in, peering over the top of his mask at the visual on the screen. 'We've been thinking along the same lines. All the names start with the word *Apocalyptic* after which we have *nuclear*, *plague* and *zombie* which we thought could be codenames for county lines connections. Could they be the names of the phones? Could a dealer have been giving Rachael one of the snow globes each time he gave her a new phone so that she could remember the name of the phone line?'

Hunter looked across at the CSI team.

'Although it sounds a bit far-fetched, I certainly think that the idea has merits so we're following up with the techies who are dealing with the phones. By way of a peace offering, we sent one of the phones over to the drugs squad at Medway – they were fairly insistent. So, I presume you'll get your own people to look at the phone you've got here, Beth?'

Dench indicated that they would get that organised when this briefing was finished. The next visual showed a book which had been hollowed-out leaving a cavity into which little wraps of drugs had been placed.

'As you're already aware, drugs were predominately kept in books where the pages had been hollowed-out. They were kept in the bottom drawer of the chest of drawers in the girl's bedroom.' Campbell consulted his notes. 'There were a few of these books which we have assumed were kept on the shelves above the chest but they contained no drugs either wrapped or unwrapped. The cavities did, however, show traces of having contained drugs at some point in time.'

'Yes,' Hunter interjected. 'Our guys felt that the books were either for storage or for transporting the drugs. Even an old book with an elastic band round it wouldn't arouse any suspicion. So, the books were good for keeping the gear away from her mother and for taking it to the drops. Did you find other information jotted down in any of the other books?'

'We found some,' Campbell replied. 'Postcodes and dates. I'll email the information over to Grace Kendall if you like.' Hunter nodded a silent 'thank you'.

'Yes, her bedroom was a right little treasure trove,' Beth Dench summarised, 'but you'll be more than interested to know that we found a couple of partials at the Buckley house. And we've now managed to analyse these with what I can only describe as remarkable results.'

This announcement perked Hunter up and Selitto was also staring at Dench in eager anticipation.

'In fact, we could hardly believe it ourselves so we had to test and re-test to make absolutely sure. In the end, we could draw no other conclusion than that one of the thugs at Julie Buckley's house was one of the men who were shot dead on One Tree Hill.'

'For fuck's sake!' Hunter exclaimed. 'Are you absolutely sure?' Her mind was frantically processing this information, trying to work out the crossover between both events.

'The prints at the Buckley house match those of the taxi driver so we can identify him as Gavinder Ramdeen. He operates a number of county lines gangs out of South-East London and is well known to the Met. An impressive record of drug dealing and mostly mindless violence.'

'And the other two in the taxi?' Hunter asked, already

beginning to realise why Pennington had been so quick off the mark in getting to One Tree Hill.

'Nothing on them as far as we can see although they may be French.'

Hunter raised an inquisitive eyebrow, inviting Dench to continue.

'Some of the clothes they were wearing had labelling in French and were likely to have been purchased in France. We could, of course, speculate that the clothes were actually purchased in the UK from a shop specialising in French designer clothing but, for my money, the two men in the taxi either had been resident in France or still lived there.'

'So, what the bloody hell were they doing at One Tree Hill?' Hunter snapped, frustration beginning to raise its ugly head again.

'Well, that's your department, Sarah,' Dench replied with a smile, 'we can only tell you what they did whilst they were there.' Hunter was unimpressed with this response and stared at Dench for a few seconds longer than she had intended.

Another visual flashed up on the screen and Donny Campbell continued the briefing.

'This is the body of the man who was sitting in the seat behind the driver as we found it. You can see that his body has turned to face the door on the other side of the vehicle although we know that he was shot through the doorway immediately to his right. We can only, therefore, assume that he had turned towards whoever had killed his colleague and didn't realise that there were two of them. When he heard his door open, he probably only had a split second to turn his head, not his whole body, before he was shot although it's doubtful that he even saw the person who pulled the trigger. He did have a shoulder holster but we didn't find a weapon so can only assume that one of the assailants took it.'

Both Hunter and Selitto looked puzzled. There seemed to be rather a lot of imponderables in Campbell's explanation of what happened. Such as, who else had the passenger been firing at? Why hadn't the other passenger tried to defend himself? Without looking at each other, they both independently decided to let Campbell continue with his commentary in the hope that it would all become clearer.

A couple of clicks of the mouse heralded the arrival of a picture of a firearm on the screen.

'This is a Smith & Wesson M&P Shield pistol. A nine milli-metre weapon with a small magazine. Easy to conceal and, in this case, it was being carried in the jacket pocket of the other passenger in the taxi. We suspect that this may have hindered his ability to quickly respond to the attack on the taxi as there is evidence that the gun got caught up in the lining of the pocket.'

Dench pulled her chair up to the edge of the table and folded her arms in front of her. 'For what it's worth, our combined opinion is that the two passengers only came to the rendezvous armed because they always carried weapons. The fact that one of them couldn't even get his gun out of his pocket in time seems to indicate that he wasn't expecting trouble. It also seems conclusive that there were two gunmen as the two passengers were not killed with the same weapon.'

'I think we also concluded that there were probably two gunmen,' Hunter intervened but Dench continued as if Hunter had never spoken.

'So, the scenario we're working on is that the first shots killed the driver and were fired by the man sitting in the seat directly behind him. Meanwhile, someone opens the nearside rear door and shoots the other passenger but is then, himself, shot by the guy who killed the driver. That would also explain the blood on the ground between where the taxi had stopped and where we assume another vehicle had come to a halt. If that is how it happened, then there must have been an accomplice who opened the offside passenger door and shot the driver's killer. Now we have one of the gunmen who's seriously wounded and bleeding out on the ground between the vehicles. His accomplice, therefore, has to drag him across the car park to their vehicle before they can make a getaway.'

Silence fell on the room as Campbell changed the visual on the screen to show the taxi standing with the driver's door and the two passenger doors open.

Hunter leaned forward on the table to take a closer look at something. 'What is becoming a bit of a puzzle is why the driver was killed by one of the men he was transporting in his taxi. Was he armed?'

'We found a six inch blade tucked into the carpet under the driver's seat,' Campbell replied, 'but this is probably standard practice for cabbies in London. We didn't find any other firearms apart from the one we found on the body of one of the two passengers. But we did find this clutched in the hands of the driver.'

Campbell changed the visual on the screen to show a cheap pay-as-you-go Nokia 110 mobile phone.

'Looks fairly new,' Selitto observed.

'Almost brand new if you want my opinion,' Campbell replied. 'Not a scratch on it and, in fact, it still had the plastic film stuck to the screen.'

'Hmm,' Selitto murmured. 'Don't suppose you've managed to get a techie to have a quick look yet, have you?'

'I was lucky to get one of them interested in giving it a quick scan on the promise that it was unlikely to have been used,' Campbell replied.

'And?' asked Selitto.

'And it had only been used once. To receive an incoming text message. Just the single word *NOW*. Timed at 22.27 on Thursday. The day of the shootings at One Tree Hill.'

42
Saturday 2 May

Picking up the A206 near Greenhithe and then negotiating the double roundabout by the Hilton at the Dartford Crossing, Johnnie Arcane headed for south-east London.

His route took him past the dramatic mosaic structure of three fish which stood in the middle of the roundabout marking the entrance to the town of Erith. The structure had always fascinated him and often served as a distraction when he should have been concentrating on his driving. Today was no exception and the howl of a triple airhorn from an impatient driver in a small red Skoda jolted him from his reverie of the local landmark. It was probably lucky for the Nissan driver that Johnnie didn't see the accompanying middle finger salute.

Now heading in a more northerly direction onto Eastern Way, he kept a look out for the exit slip road which would take him to Thamesmead. This is where it always got tricky for Johnnie. He could never remember if he was able to leave Carlyle Road and drop down into the labyrinth of little streets which were almost underneath the main drag into central Thamesmead or whether he should go on towards Bentham Road and then find an exit. In the end, he spotted a way off the main road and into a maze of modern terraced houses. The area was festooned with cars – cars on drives, cars outside lock-ups, cars on the road. There were also green waste bins as far as the eye could see.

Johnnie slowed in order to get his bearings before eventually managing to find a parking space which was not either in front of a house or blocking the entrance to a lock-up. He didn't notice that the motorbike which had been following him at a discrete distance had now pulled up behind several other cars, a position from where its rider could observe his every move without fear of being noticed.

Turning the engine off, Johnnie sat in the car not wishing to draw any further attention to himself. The weather had taken a turn for the worse and there were now large splodges of rain spattering the windscreen. That suited Johnnie as the rain would provide him with that extra bit of cover.

Peering through the rivulets of water which were now running down the window beside him, he reflected on what he had so far managed to achieve today. He wasn't finding it easy working with Stryker's dealers who spent most of their time whingeing about the quality of the gear. He knew this was an old tactic aimed at getting the price down but he wasn't having any of it. These people had to understand who they were now dealing with and the consequences for falling out of line. He was going to have to teach those bastards in the mini supermarket a fucking lesson. Perhaps a session in Stryker's infamous torture chamber would bring them into line. He was not going to be pushed around by anyone, particularly a couple of Asian arseholes. He would make them learn respect.

After about ten minutes, the rain started to ease off. Taking this as a cue to get on with the purpose of his visit, Johnnie reached into the storage compartment in the door beside him and pulled out a keyring which had three keys attached to it along with a key fob. The fob simply showed the number 'thirty-one'.

Eventually, he got out of the car and, tugging his baseball

cap down so that it almost covered his eyes, he walked across the road into one of the alleys which ran between blocks of the terraced houses. This brought him into a courtyard at the back of the houses which had other alleyways running left and right behind the blocks. Following one of these round to his right, he soon came to a high wooden fence which had a gate built into it. A figure '*three*' and a figure '*one*' had been crudely burned into the fence, and Johnnie used his height to stretch an arm over the gate to release the bolt on the other side. Not very secure, he thought, but at least it had a chance of stopping the local kids getting in.

The gate opened on to a small garden which had been almost completely paved over. There were thistles and other thuggish weeds growing out of a narrow strip of earth on one side of the garden where the paving didn't quite meet the side fence. Assorted greenery, moss and other weeds were growing freely between the paving stones, and a badly misshapen rotary washing line stood drunkenly near the back door into the house. A black plastic bin was on its side behind the gate.

Johnnie picked his way across the paved area, unlocked the door and stepped into one of Stryker Stone's hideaways. Closing it behind him, he found himself in a surprisingly modern kitchen with units which looked almost brand new. He didn't remember them from his previous visits and simply assumed that it must have been a debt that Stryker had called in. No doubt the supplier had been in the last chance saloon. Johnnie smirked. Stryker was all heart like that!

He walked on and peered into the only other room on the ground floor. As usual, it was piled high with junk. There were packing cases crammed full of what looked like bedding, a set of bunk beds, two bicycles, standard lamps, table fans, pedestal fans, an old washing machine, an ironing board. Shaking his head, Johnnie closed the door. He climbed a set of uncarpeted stairs which led onto a small landing. Another room full of junk was off to his left and a bathroom to his right.

There was a fusty smell in the house indicating that it probably hadn't been occupied for some time. In the bathroom, he turned on the cold tap in the sink and stood back as it choked and spat brown water. He reached up to a bathroom cabinet on the wall to the right of the sink and removed a small key from a mug which was also home to a family of toothbrushes.

A surprisingly modern bath was rammed into one corner of the room but there was no overhead shower. The bath itself had a very ornate wooden panel surrounding it which gave the appearance of being an integral part of the bath but also looked completely out of place.

Johnnie, however, knew that it wasn't part of the unit and that it could be removed from its position if you knew how the release mechanism worked. He also knew that there were other treasures in this house if you only knew where to look.

He remembered when the house had been acquired by Stryker who had wanted a bolt hole in south-east London where he could store *stuff* as he put it. The junk that was now crammed into the two rooms bore testament to the *stuff* he had collected over the years, much of it never likely to either be used or, indeed, to be of any use to anyone. Stryker had also wanted a place where he could bring runners and dealers to teach them a lesson which they would never forget.

Moving back downstairs, Johnnie returned to the room off the kitchen and, squeezing between several boxes of tiles and other bathroom paraphernalia, he reached a locked door. He quickly opened it using one of the keys on the ring, and now found himself in a small windowless space. He flicked the light switch and cast his eye over the area in front of him.

Stryker had created what he candidly nicknamed his torture chamber by erecting a false wall across the room next to the kitchen and incorporating the small entrance hall at the front of the property. Another door opposite where Johnnie stood opened into the garage. But, in the space between the two doors, there was a lifeless atmosphere - a testament to the quality of the soundproofing which Stryker had installed. His victims could scream all they liked. Not even a gunshot could be heard outside the four walls.

A faint whiff of human excrement mixed with bleach hung in the air. The walls had been painted in a dark brown, almost sepia colour. Johnnie could see dark stains on the flooring which hadn't been completely removed, and there were some dark spots on the walls which also hadn't been cleaned off properly. The single metal chair which was screwed to the floor in the middle of the room bore further evidence of what had gone on in this room, and camera equipment stood idle in one of the corners.

Johnnie could just picture it. The car with the unsuspecting occupant drives into the garage. Door closes. The victim is hauled out of the car and into the soundproofed room. The chair is waiting. The implements of torture are waiting. The camera is set up and recording every movement.

His mind went back to an occasion when he had been present at one of what Stryker called his retribution sessions. A scruffy, malnourished man in his early thirties had been mislaying cash and drugs, and Stryker had had enough. In a three-hour ordeal, the man was beaten with various objects, scalded with boiling water, and had cuts inflicted on his body which were then burned with a blow torch. And all the time Stryker was spinning the chamber of a revolver, putting the barrel to the man's temple and pulling the trigger. A video of the torture was then uploaded onto the Dark Web as some sort of weird warning to others.

Johnnie had marvelled at Stryker's patience. If it had been him, he would have simply made sure that the gun was loaded.

He shook his head as if to disperse the thoughts of all the times he had been in this hell hole and walked over to what looked like a panel of dimmer switches on the far wall. Pressing the third knob from the left, he heard a click. With his fingers still holding the knob he turned to look at the chair. He then very slowly rotated the knob and watched as the chair started to tip backwards, a small section of the floor still attached to its legs.

Once the chair was all but horizontal, Johnnie knelt next to the secret compartment which had been uncovered. Looking down at the top of a steel floor safe, he produced the key he had taken from the bathroom cabinet and inserted it into two holes on the top of the safe. Twisting the key to the left, he freed the security plate to reveal a small combination lock. Entering the six-number code, he twisted the handle and pulled the lid of the safe towards him.

The minute he had the safe open in front of him, Johnnie knew he had a problem. For a start, there didn't seem to be anything in it. He scrabbled around getting his phone out of his back pocket before finally persuading the torch to work.

Shining it into the safe, he was appalled at how little cash there was inside it. Hardly believing his eyes, he thrust his hand into the void and felt into all four corners. He then sat back on his heels looking at its meagre offerings.

There was a roll of ten pound notes, a roll of twenties and a roll of fifties. Just one of each. He counted the money out. He then counted it out again but still couldn't make it more than £2,500. Shit! That was never going to be enough to pay Maddox. Surely Stryker had more than this. There were some small bags of what Johnnie assumed was heroin and cocaine, some wraps all ready to go, and some Es which had been wrapped in clingfilm to make them look like tubes of mints.

Johnnie tossed the drugs back into the safe, pocketed the cash and spun the combination lock before replacing the security shield. Pressing the dimmer switch to return the chair to the upright, he turned the lights off and headed back upstairs to the bathroom.

After a couple of fruitless attempts, he managed to release the bath panel and then groped around the space under the bath. Eventually locating the loose floorboard, he plunged his hands into the cavity, tension mounting, sweat starting to drip from his forehead. Where the fuck was all Stryker's money? The question kept playing around in his head as if on repeat.

Finally, he sat back on the bathroom floor staring at another £1,200 in used notes. Less than four grand altogether, he thought. Shit! He needed more than that simply to stand a chance that Maddox might start a supply line. He stared into the space under the bath, not knowing what he was looking for but having a suspicion that he was missing something.

There was something about the bath that didn't look quite

right. Did it have a false bottom? He got onto his hands and knees and started tapping the inner surfaces of the tub. It certainly sounded like a steel construction. He felt the underside of the tub and gave this a few taps. There was a dull sound like he was tapping on plastic. A false bottom perhaps?

Johnnie started to run his hands around the bottom of the tub until he eventually felt a tiny catch between the tub and the wall. Releasing the catch, the false bottom dropped onto the floor along with the items it was concealing.

Due to the position of the secret compartment, Johnnie could only rely on what he could feel with his fingers. Eventually he sat back, his eyes lighting up at the sight of the five firearms lying on the floor in front of him. The Sig Sauer was certainly brand new as was one of the Rugers. Johnnie could see that the other Ruger, the Glock and the Smith & Wesson had all been fired but perhaps not more than a couple of times.

Having a reasonable knowledge of the market price for these gun models, he did a quick calculation in his head.

Making sure that he hadn't missed anything, he allowed a thin smile to start playing on his lips. He was pretty confident that he now had the wherewithal to get started with Maddox. All he had to do was persuade the old armourer or one of his mates to come across with the readies because these were high quality firearms.

Make no mistake.

43

Saturday 2 May

On arrival back at Pembury Road, Sarah Hunter took the stairs two at a time leaving Selitto to trudge wearily up the two flights which would take him to the Ops Room. On arrival in the room, he could see his boss already sitting with DS Grace Kendall in the far corner. He made his way across to Kendall's desk, grabbing a chair on the way.

'Teas, coffees?' he offered. Tea for Kendall, a cold bottle of water for Hunter. Selitto sloped off towards the kitchen.

Hunter's ingrained impatience was at a high level. She fidgeted with her phone in one hand whilst mercilessly twiddling several strands of hair through the fingers of her other hand.

'Okay, Grace, what have you got on this newspaper guy?' she rasped, her voice sounding almost hoarse. She suddenly felt very thirsty. The atmosphere in the crime scene lab always made her thirsty. Probably something to do with the dry air bubble they seemed to always work in.

'Not been easy,' Grace started, 'mainly because it hasn't been going for more than about nine months. Rocco Vance has a LinkedIn page which doesn't look as if it's been updated since he started the news blog. He graduated with a 2:1 in Broadcast Journalism from Nottingham Trent in 2008 and then went into a number of regional newspapers starting with the *Nottingham Post*. He must have then moved to the south west as he spent some time on the *Western Daily Press* before moving to the *Coventry Telegraph* and then the *Stoke Sentinel* which is where he would have probably learned all about online news broadcasting. Then he moved to London working with one of those online local news groups before seemingly setting up his *News Notebook* venture towards the end of last year.'

'Okay, so he knows his way around digital news media, or whatever you call it, but what is this notebook venture?' Hunter was sounding more exasperated by the second and it was probably fortuitous that Selitto arrived with the drinks. She leaned over and grabbed the bottle of water before snapping open the dispenser and drinking greedily.

Grace resumed her report. 'All I've really managed to establish so far is that it doesn't seem to be a straightforward news blog. They seem to latch on to major stories and then develop comment around what they see as the issues of the day. So, for example, one of the hot topics is the migrants crossing the Channel in small boats. There's plenty about that and, whilst there are editorials about the numbers and what happens to the migrants once they've been brought ashore, Vance is also keen to go *off piste* and give his own view of the situation thus inviting other comments, some of which make uncomfortable reading. He's also blogged about Border Force checks at Dover following Brexit and, at the other end of the county, he has been looking at plans for development of the green belt. So, it's not a straightforward news reporting outlet.'

'More like news reporting with attitude,' Hunter commented. 'Have we got any idea of readership or whatever you call it in blog speak?'

'Well, we don't have access to the website analytics right at this moment but we could set something up if you wanted to investigate further,' Grace informed them. 'I've shown the site to one of our techies and she thought that it probably only had a fairly limited readership judging by the number of comments posted. She said that the number of page views per visit is a metric which can quantify the success of the blogpost with the unofficial average being two pages per session. The goal is to increase this by keeping users engaged and nurturing their interest so that they start to look at more pages. It's once the blogpost gets past a certain level of usage that advertising starts to kick in but it doesn't look as if Vance is anywhere near that yet.'

'So, we're not exactly dealing with the Press here,' Selitto interrupted, 'but we are dealing with someone who has a digital news outlet through which he tends to give his own take on topical stories and then invites comments. Presumably this approach has the effect of skewing the original story because the reader has moved into the realm of potential fantasy dressed up as truth.'

Hunter and Kendall looked at each other. His long recuperation hadn't blunted Selitto's ability to get to the nub of the matter, and he was now questioning whether Hunter really should be talking to someone who was probably not going to accurately represent any information that she passed on.

Taking another glug of water, Hunter eventually spoke. 'I hear what you're both saying, but it still concerns me that Vance seems to know things almost as soon as we do. I really need to try and find out what his objectives are with the Tideswell story and, if possible, how the information is getting to him. And how he got my phone number.'

'Well, he's not going to go away so I suggest you get onto him if only to stop him wasting any more of our time.' Grace felt as if she was also talking on behalf of Selitto who was nodding his head. 'If he's going to start blogging stuff which helps our investigation, then all well and good. But, if he's just going to snipe from the side lines, then we probably need to be aware of him and keep an eye on how he reports the investigation.'

'Yep, you're right,' Hunter replied, a hint of resignation in her voice.

Having gathered up her bottle of water, Sarah Hunter was now installed in one of the empty rooms across the corridor from the Ops Room. She accessed Vance's number and initiated the call, feeling the need to be formal when he answered.

'Mr Vance, this is DI Hunter, Kent Police. I'm in receipt of a text message which intimates that you would like to talk to me about an incident that is currently under investigation.'

'Yes, I know who you are. Your name's come up on my screen.'

Ignoring his arrogant attempt at humour, Hunter continued. 'Mr Vance, I am a very busy person. You have already told me that you have information regarding an ongoing investigation. It concerns me that this information is not in the public domain which would indicate that you have obtained it by nefarious means. You have now sent me a text message which basically says that you are going to publish and be damned. In other words, you don't care that what you are publishing probably hasn't got a scintilla of truth in it. This, in turn, makes it difficult for me to have any meaningful discussions with you as a journalist.'

There was a pause before Vance answered.

'Well, I thought you might like the opportunity of saying something about your case before I went ahead and published the facts as I see them because, from where I'm standing, the public has a right to know what's been going on at Tideswell Manor.'

Was there a trace of an Australian accent in his voice? she wondered. Would that explain his rather direct style of communicating?

'But what would you want me to say, Mr Vance, bearing in mind that we do not wish to currently divulge details of our investigation?' Hunter knew that this wouldn't shut him up but she had to make sure that he clearly understood the constraints she was under when giving out information.

'Yeah, but you wouldn't want me to publish anything that might mislead the public, or which might give the impression that Kent Police don't have a scooby doo about what they're investigating. I mean, you'd have to say that a load of druggies and kids locked up together in a cellar with a room full of snakes would make quite a sensational story!'

It certainly would, Hunter thought, and it would be even more sensational given your evil twist on it no doubt.

'Mr Vance, your simplification of the facts is commendable but, without detail, your story would be sensationalism at its worst. What we are doing is forensically sifting through all the evidence in order to build up a picture of how these people died, why they died, and why they were trapped in the cellar in the first place. It's what we do. It's called police investigation work. And it won't be helped by someone like you expressing your own, totally unfounded, assessment of the tragedy.'

There was another pause although Hunter doubted that Vance had dropped off the line.

'What about the guy that owns the place? The eighties rock

star? Biondi? Are you talking to him as part of your enquiries?'

'All in good time, Mr Vance,' Hunter replied, trying not to give the game away that they hadn't got a clue where he was. 'All in good time,' she repeated as if to convince herself that they would be talking to him very soon.

'Okay. Are you making a connection with the plane crash and the shootings at One Tree Hill?'

The question slightly blindsided Hunter as she thought he only wanted to talk about Tideswell Manor. And she hadn't really got round to considering whether the two incidents were related.

'Although our investigations are continuing into the incident at One Tree Hill, we have not yet established any link to Tideswell Manor. But you will, of course, respect that we are in the early stages of assessing the evidence.'

'Are you in a position to name the occupants of the taxi yet?'

Again, Hunter was initially taken aback that Vance knew about the taxi but then reasoned that word of the shootings might have quickly circulated around the small village of Underriver. Any journalist worth their salt would have probably been able to access basic information just by turning up at the local pub. She chose her words carefully.

'As I have said, it is too early for us to make any comment about this incident.'

'Oh, come on Detective Inspector, can't you at least entrust me with some information that I can use in my news blog? You never know, one of my readers might have just the little snippet of information which you are looking for in order to complete the jigsaw.'

This was just the opening Hunter had been waiting for.

'And why would I want to entrust you with anything, Mr Vance? You have already lied to me once so why should I believe anything that you might say during this call? Indeed, I am beginning to wonder why I am even talking to you!'

There was a further pause. Hunter hoped that Vance was digesting her assault on his integrity.

'So, all I can conclude from this conversation is that you as Senior Investigating Officer are unwilling to co-operate with the press and that you have no information to give us.'

Hunter rolled her eyes. It was like trying to deal with a spoiled child.

'That is not the case, Mr Vance, and you know it.' She was desperately trying to avoid showing her annoyance and decided to end the call with a placatory gesture in order to dampen his enthusiasm for vilifying her in his blog. 'I am prepared to come across with some information once I've identified exactly what it is that we are dealing with here. There's a lot of evidence which we're having to examine and it may be some days before we are able to complete a detailed picture of what happened at Tideswell Manor and at One Tree Hill. Once I've something to tell you, I promise I'll give you a call. In the meantime, I can't stop you publishing whatever you want to. But, if you're hoping that your channel of communication with me stays open, I can only suggest that you publish exactly what I've told you. And, if you want to make sure that you are publishing the truth, you are at liberty to tell your readers that I, as SIO, do not currently believe that there is a connection between the plane crash at Tideswell Manor and the incident at One Tree Hill.'

'Okay, I appreciate that,' Vance replied. 'I'm still going to do something on Tideswell Manor because I think it's a big story and it's already got national coverage. But I'll make sure that I clearly state your position at this stage in the investigation process. If I get any feedback which looks interesting, I'll get in touch with you. I'll then, hopefully, hear from you once you're able to circulate more information. Perhaps we might even be able to meet sometime.'

'Let's not get ahead of ourselves, Mr Vance. And just remember the golden rule. Never lie to me again. I'll know if you do. I'm clever like that. Goodbye for now.'

Hunter poked the red circle on her phone and the call was ended. She pushed herself off the desk she had been perched on and went across to look out of the window. She drained what was left of the water in the bottle as she looked down on the Saturday afternoon traffic trundling around the roundabout below her, vehicles making their way into and out of the town centre. Thank God that was over, she thought.

Time was marching on.

44

Saturday 2 May

Grace Kendall had managed to secure one of the large meeting rooms over the corridor from the Ops Room so that they could at last have a central point for their investigations. Angie Marshall had helped to scrounge some furniture and Kendall had set up the old crime wall which looked almost new after a rub down with some washing-up liquid. Azzer Mishraz had said that he would come in later that afternoon to help with making sure that all the IT and phone connections worked, and one of Angie Marshall's team had been tasked with setting up a small stationery store in the room.

'Excellent,' Hunter murmured. Having a dedicated Major Investigation Room for her team was so important because it meant that they had a focal point for communicating with each other. Also, having a functioning crime wall helped everyone to think through all the evidence, particularly when it all started to link together. Hunter liked nothing more than when she was able to start drawing lines which showed how people or places or incidents were related to each other.

'In fact we could probably get in there right now,' Kendall added, picking up her laptop and leaving the Ops Room.

The new MIR wasn't exactly opposite the entrance to the Ops Room but a little further along the corridor towards the front of the building. Selitto noted that it was also further away from the kitchen!

Hunter and Selitto entered the MIR and took their seats around the desk where Kendall had already activated her laptop. They could now continue their discussions from where they had left off.

'Before you bring us up to date, Grace, I'd say that it's looking increasingly likely that all the incidents we are dealing with are linked in some way.' Hunter then summarised all the information they had got from their visit to the forensics labs at Maidstone whilst Grace made copious notes on the pad she had brought with her. The edited information would then be added to the crime wall so that a picture of the investigation would start to emerge and evolve.

'So, one of Julie Buckley's killers was shot dead at One Tree Hill.' It was more of a statement from Kendall rather than a question. 'And we know the identity of the victim?'

'We do but we need to get more information from the Met about him and who he has been running with,' Hunter said, wanting to make sure that Kendall realised that they knew very little about Gavinder Ramdeen. 'Apparently he's got an impressive record of drug-dealing and violence.'

'Seems to me that we really need to try and identify the other two in the taxi,' Selitto chipped in, partially hidden from Hunter by unconnected computer equipment which had just been dumped on the desk. 'Forensics seem to think that they could be French.'

Grace looked up from her note-taking. 'French?' she asked. 'What makes them think that?'

'As far as I could gather, it was their clothing more than anything else. They think that the clothing had, in all probability, been bought from boutique shops in France rather than from a French clothing outlet in the UK.'

Kendall fiddled with the mouse sending the cursor on her

screen into overdrive as she sought to reference how this information impacted on the work she had been doing.

'Okay, we may have something here,' she eventually informed them before rotating the laptop so that all three of them could now see what was on the screen.

'Remember I pointed out the two men who seemed to be an ever-present in the CCTV images of Biondi and Frobisher on their journey back to the UK?'

Hunter and Selitto nodded, recalling yesterday's briefing.

'Well, having spent more hours poring over CCTV feed from the airport, it now looks as if the same two men who accompanied Biondi on his flight back from Bermuda on Thursday 23 April also accompanied him on his original flight to Bermuda on Sunday 19 April.'

A CCTV image showing Biondi at the departure gate was now on the screen. Two men stood behind the ageing rocker, almost either side of him. There was no doubt that they were the same men who had stood behind him in the passport queue a few days later.

'Okay, Grace, I agree. It's the same guys. But who the fuck are they? His own personal security service, perhaps? Or security guards provided by a record company in case any fans recognised Biondi and started trying to grab him? Or something else?'

Hunter's voice trailed off as she suddenly realised that Kendall hadn't finished yet. There was more to come.

'Remember I showed you CCTV images of Biondi going through Security on Friday 24 April when he was down to take a flight to Antigua?'

The others nodded. Hunter had a horrible feeling in the pit

of her stomach that she knew what was coming next.

A CCTV image showing Biondi at the Security checkpoint was on the screen. The date in the top left-hand corner showed Friday 24 April. Two men stood behind Biondi. If anything, they looked more menacing than before and were certainly taking much closer order on the man in front of them.

'Looks like he had the same accompaniment for the Antigua flight,' Kendall pointed out, 'but none of them made it to the plane. The two men disappeared just as Biondi did the minute they got into the departure lounge.'

Hunter sat back in her chair, arms folded, eyes fixed on the CCTV image of Biondi.

'Thoughts, Ted?'

'My immediate thought is that they don't look very friendly,' Selitto observed. 'If they were some sort of personal security force or they'd been provided by the record company or whatever, there would've probably been more of a dynamic between the three of them. But there's nothing. Same on the flight back from Bermuda when they're sitting behind Biondi and Frobisher. You just get the feeling that they're the gaolers. They've got the invisible handcuffs on the two in front of them.'

Hunter got up and walked over to the window.

'So, let's get this sequenced,' she started in an attempt to get everything straight in her head. 'Worst case scenario. Someone wants Frobisher out of the way. Problem is they don't know where she is. But they do know someone who does know her whereabouts. So, they get Biondi to lead them to her and then get her back to the UK. For all we know, Biondi may be trying to save his own skin here and Frobisher thinks that he is luring her back to the UK to do another job. She doesn't even clock the two men who are shadowing her on the flight. But, once out of Gatwick Airport, the gloves are off and she's banged up in the cellar at Biondi's place.'

'Hmm! I'm not sure about some of that,' Selitto said looking across the room at his boss. 'I mean, would Frobisher come back to the UK that easily? My money would be on Biondi leading the heavies to her. They then took over and probably threatened her with grim descriptions of what would happen to her if she didn't return to the UK with them. Probably roughed her up so that she clearly got the message that staying in Bermuda was not an option. I wonder if there's any evidence in the post mortem report of her being knocked about. Have you seen it yet, Grace?'

Kendall shook her head. She hadn't seen it and made a note to follow up with the pathologists. Meanwhile, Selitto continued to give his take on what he had seen.

'It didn't look as if she and Biondi had much to say to each other on the plane. In fact, I'd go as far as to say that they may never have met until this point. If Biondi had simply taken the two thugs to where he knew she was staying, he could have remained in the background while they took her down.'

Sarah Hunter was beginning to feel somewhat jaded by the continual need to hypothesise. The facts appeared to be clear but, when they didn't seem to make sense, the only option was to derive some meaningful interpretation by relying on an informed imagination. They simply didn't have enough information, and were relying principally on what they could read into grainy CCTV images.

'Okay, let's look at what we do know,' Hunter continued in a resigned tone. 'Frobisher returned to the UK either of her own free will or under duress and was then killed at Tideswell Manor. From the CCTV, we know that Biondi travelled back to the UK with her which would indicate that there is some association between the two of them – or at least they knew each other.'

'I'm not so sure that they did know each other.' This time it was Kendall who was casting doubt on Hunter's assertion that Biondi and Frobisher were known to each other. 'Looking at the CCTV on the plane, Frobisher looks like someone who doesn't know who's sitting next to her. You know what it's like when a stranger sits next to you on a plane. You sort of lean away from them trying to avoid any contact whatsoever. That's how she looks in the CCTV image.'

'Okay, so she didn't know him,' Hunter conceded, an air of frustration creeping into her voice. 'But they were each being separately controlled by the two heavies because they stayed pretty much together as a foursome for their journey through the airport at Gatwick.'

'Yes, I'd have to agree with you there,' Kendall replied although Selitto was now shaking his head.

'If these guys have taken Biondi all the way to Bermuda just to identify Frobisher then he must know Frobisher by sight,' Selitto reasoned. 'But that doesn't necessarily mean that Frobisher knows him by sight. Perhaps she only ever spoke to him by phone. If she was receiving instructions from him to carry out killings to order, perhaps he only communicated with her by email and put money in her bank account when the jobs were done.'

Hunter was becoming frustrated with this line of attritional thinking as it didn't seem to be getting them anywhere. Indeed, was it relevant? she asked herself. Kendall noticed that Hunter was losing interest in the discussion so she sought to move things on.

'I do have some new information which I've got from the very helpful security team at Gatwick,' she said, immediately grabbing their attention. 'I didn't know it myself but there is a separate facility for those travelling by private jet which circumvents the need to use the commercial flight terminal. This got me wondering if the trip to Antigua was, in fact, going to be by private jet.'

Hunter was now intrigued and had retaken her seat at the desk.

'Apparently, soon after you pass through security, there is an exit from the departure lounge to the outside world. You can only use this exit if you have the correct identification papers but anyone using it would not be picked up by CCTV in the departure lounge.'

'So our guys headed straight for this exit,' Selitto commented. 'Very clever!'

'We can only assume that's what they did,' Kendall continued,' but what we do know is that they definitely used this separate lounge facility.' Another CCTV image came up on her screen clearly showing Biondi accompanied by the two thugs. This time they appeared to be in a smaller space although the background was not well defined. But they were clearly presenting themselves at another desk, this time with one of the thugs taking charge.

'So, someone sent a private jet to collect them and whisk them off to Antigua,' Hunter mocked. 'As you do!'

'Not quite, Sarah,' Kendall responded icily. She was

becoming exasperated by the negativity which Hunter was showing. 'There were no private jets leaving for Antigua on that day. In fact, at the time Biondi was captured on CCTV, there was only one private jet leaving within a window of four hours. And that was going to Nantes.'

'*Nantes*?' Hunter exclaimed. 'As in Nantes in northern France?'

'The very same!' Kendall calmly confirmed the information she had been given.

'Well, that's a bit of a come down from Antigua. But why would they be going to Nantes?' Hunter's question hung in the air. 'Unless… Oh shit! I bet that's not far from Bréhat.'

'140 miles as the crow flies, which it probably did,' Kendall replied.

'Jeez, that puts a completely different spin on this entire investigation,' Hunter declared, wondering if her head could cope with any more complexity.

45
Saturday 2 May

The early evening sunlight filtered through the trees as Sarah Hunter drove up Carter's Hill and past the car park at One Tree Hill which was still cordoned off, the yellow crime scene tape fluttering in the gentle breeze. She slowed so that Selitto could take a look at the scene of the shootings but then increased her speed as she became aware of a very impatient motorist behind her.

They passed Sevenoaks Preparatory School before descending into Godden Green. Indicating that she would be turning left, Sarah was relieved to see that there was a parking space on the forecourt in front of The Bucks Head. She swung the car into the space and watched as the motorist behind her picked up speed as the car headed off towards Seal. *Idiot*, she whispered under her breath.

It had been a long and arduous couple of days and, although they had seen a lot of each other, Sarah felt that she had not properly connected with Selitto since he had turned up at the station unannounced. Was it really only thirty six hours ago? It felt more like half a lifetime.

They walked up the steps into the pub and made their way across to the bar. A couple of early evening drinkers were sitting further along the bar seemingly engaged in earnest conversation. Others were at tables dotted around the lounge and there was a sudden roar of laughter from the back of the pub which Sarah presumed was where the beer garden was. She went off to investigate while Selitto waited for the barman to finish serving another customer.

Once armed with a pint of Guinness and a pint of Spitfire, and his pockets bulging with two packets of cheese & onion crisps, he made his way somewhat unsteadily to the back of the pub and out into the garden.

Hunter had found a table in the shade and Selitto deposited the glasses on it. He then made a fuss of shaking beer off his hand after he had managed to spill some from his own pint when he had tripped on the step up to the grassed area. Miraculously, nothing had escaped from the pint of Guinness which Hunter was quick to seize, taking a long draught of the black stuff before greedily licking her lips to ensure that she hadn't missed any of the creamy head.

Selitto sat on the bench attached to the table, not bothering to swing his legs over it. He took a couple of gentle mouthfuls of the golden ale and then let out a long contented sigh.

'The times I have dreamed of this moment,' he said staring into the depths of his pint. 'And now here we are. God, it's good to be back!' He took another mouthful of the beer, savouring its taste before swallowing.

'Well, it hasn't been much fun for me either,' Hunter replied, teasing him by lowering her eyelids and pouting. 'And my metabolism just hasn't been the same without the salt & vinegar crisps!'

Selitto nearly choked on his beer before putting his glass back on the table and taking the two packets of crisps out of his pockets. 'Seems I've been away too long.'

Hunter picked up one of the packets. 'Cheese & onion?' she exclaimed. 'Have we moved into the realms of fine dining?'

'I'm sure they'll have the same effect,' he replied. 'Probably taste the same as well.'

They both laughed at their poor attempt at humour as Hunter tore her way into the packet. They both knew that such moments were few and far between during intense investigations such as the ones with which they were currently involved.

'So, everything okay at the flat?' Hunter asked, pushing strands of loose hair behind one ear before attacking the bag of crisps with renewed vigour.

'Yep,' he replied, 'my neighbour's been in and out all through the time I've been away. Gave her a call on Thursday and she organised someone to go in and give it a deep clean. All in good working order, stuff in the fridge, even a couple of cans of beer bless her. Pile of post although most of it can be shredded. Clean sheets on the bed and new soap in the bathroom. Even a new tube of toothpaste. Couldn't have asked for more. I'll have to get her some flowers or something.'

'Good to know that you can still rely on the decency of neighbours,' Sarah said as she shook the remaining crisps into the palm of her hand before stuffing them into her mouth.

They lapsed into silence with Hunter experiencing a slight feeling of unease. Even though she had worked closely with Selitto ever since she had arrived in Tonbridge, and despite many hours helping him with his recovery from injury, she suddenly felt as if they were starting their relationship all over again. Being in each other's company seemed to lack the spark that it used to have. Or was she just being hyper sensitive? Maybe it was just a natural reaction to being jogged out of a routine and having to, once again, get used to being around each other in a working environment. She should snap out of any negative thoughts, she chided herself. Stop over-complicating things.

'So, are you really thinking that everything's connected up?' Selitto asked as he tore into the second bag of crisps. 'I mean the disappearance of the girl, the plane crash and the shootings. Are they all linked?'

Hunter was going to have to pick her words carefully if she was going to fulfil her promise to Jack Pennington via his messenger boy Jordan Wright.

'At the moment, I can't see that the plane crash is linked to anything,' she replied, fiddling with her glass on the table. 'That seems to be a whole separate ball game, some sort of act of revenge. But revenge for what? Biondi's certainly involved but what has he done to upset someone to the extent that they want to fly an aeroplane into his pile of bricks in the Kent countryside?'

'That's more like retribution if you ask me,' Selitto replied. 'Some sort of punishment inflicted as vengeance for something Biondi must have done.'

'Revenge or retribution, it doesn't really matter. The pile of bricks is now a pile of rubble and many people have lost their lives as a result. We still have to find out why.'

Hunter drained the last of her Guinness and pushed her glass across the table which Selitto took as his cue to return to the bar. Whilst he was gone, she took a look around the garden, enjoying the colourful borders and the greenery surrounding her.

'What I don't get,' Selitto started as he put two half pint glasses down on the table, 'is why the taxi driver appears to be linked to the killing of the Buckley woman?'

'That's certainly exercised my mind,' Hunter said as she pulled the glass towards her and had a mouthful of cold Guinness. 'I can only think that it is a drug-related connection. The evidence seems to point to the girl being involved with one of the county lines gangs so, inter alia, the shootings down the road from here are probably also connected with county lines.'

Would it be easier to develop this line of thinking with her DS if she mentioned the visit of Jordan Wright? Hunter wondered. And, in particular, if she told him about the identity of Johnnie Arcane? Or perhaps leave Arcane's name out of it? Then another thought came into her head.

'Strictly between you and me, and this is *not* to go any further, I think the big hand of SCD is at work somewhere amongst all this. Pennington seems to be very interested in what we're up to, and he was pretty cagey about why he was one of the first on the scene at the shooting. I also happen to have had a visit from one of his minions to tell me something of what they're up to but, reading between the lines, it looks like they've got another stake-out going on. The guy they're targeting could just be involved in the incidents we are dealing with.'

'Shit!' Selitto exclaimed. 'Good luck to whoever's doing the staking out. It didn't do their last one much good. Surely they're not going to risk any more surveillance officers being sent home in a body bag are they?'

Hunter was reminded of the gruesome news that one of their colleagues from surveillance had turned up with a bullet through his temple and his tongue cut out whilst trying to infiltrate one of the continental drugs cartels. She had no doubt that Pennington's team would take a lesson from this and would not be risking any further lives no matter how tempting it was to get someone behind enemy lines.

'Let's just say that, if they manage to confirm that this guy they're interested in was at One Tree Hill, then there is a tenuous link to the Buckley house.'

'But not to Tideswell Manor.' Selitto sounded as if he was trying to convince himself that they were dealing with separate criminal incidents.

'Not Tideswell,' Hunter confirmed.

They both lapsed into silence again, each considering the overlap of the various cases. Selitto had a puzzled look on his face.

'You know, I've always wondered who that Frobisher woman was really working for. The nights I've been lying awake in bed just trying to figure it out. And then I see her sitting on a plane with Biondi. It just doesn't make sense to me. Was she actually working for him?'

'That's a question we'd all like answered, Ted. Truth is we're running out of people who are still alive to answer it.'

But something that Selitto had said had started a new train of thought for Sarah Hunter. She stared into the distance, trying to grasp the coattails of her new thinking as she watched a group of four people get up from their table and head for the confines of the lounge bar.

'What if Biondi's the real top man in the county lines pyramid here in the south of England? What if he ultimately controls all or most of the lines? What if someone wants to take his empire over? What if that someone has been trying to get established in the UK for years? What if that person is Pascal Hennenbont?'

Selitto stared at her. 'Are you serious?'

'Yeah, deadly serious. I'm still trying to make it all fit together in my mind. But, say Hennenbont saw an opportunity by piggy-backing onto those guys in Guernsey. That would have given him the opportunity to start flooding the market by getting his stuff onto the beaches so that it could be taken away by helicopter and delivered to his dealers. But Frobisher fucked that plan up by killing the helicopter pilot and causing the helicopter to crash thus ruining plans to distribute the drugs. Hennenbont could well be on a mission to destroy Biondi.'

'Jeez! That's some thought process,' Selitto commented. 'So, he arranges the destruction of Biondi's headquarters but not before finding the assassin and locking her up in the cellar and pumping her full of God knows what. Then he takes Biondi off to his own HQ off the Brittany coast – no doubt never to be seen again. Bloody hell. You could have something there.'

Hunter was licking the final crumbs from the crisp bag which she had shaken into her cupped hand. 'Okay, it's a thought in progress. Let's get back to it tomorrow.'

Walking back through the pub, they put their glasses on the bar, wished the barman a good evening and made their way out to the car. As Sarah Hunter plipped the key fob to open the doors to the car, she knew that she had a lot of thinking to do this evening if she was ever going to knock these ideas into shape.

46

Sunday 3 May

Like the delicate misting from a scent bottle, there was still a very light drizzle in the air and the ground underfoot bore the evidence of how it must have rained overnight in the location around Bewl Water. Sarah Hunter had arrived at a small clearing in Chingley Wood which had been turned into a holding area for the Crime Scene Investigation vehicles and equipment. She changed into her hiking boots at the back of her car and then went off to see what protective clothing was required today. A yellow sou'wester rain hat might be a good idea, she thought.

After going through identification formalities with the CSI officer who was in charge of access to the scene, Hunter discovered that there were no mandatory protective clothing requirements so she simply headed for the pathway which the officer had pointed her towards. Blue police incident scene tape had been draped across the foliage beside the path so she followed the tape until she eventually caught sight of the water to her right. Soon after that, she arrived at a clearing which had a pile of logs stacked along one side of it. She could see a small group of white-suited CSI officers to her left so she headed in their direction.

Looking up and seeing Hunter approaching, one of the CSIs broke away from the others and walked over to meet her.

'DI Hunter?' Sarah nodded. 'My name's Annalise Vardy. I'm the CSI Manager for this site. I've recently moved into Beth

Dench's team at Maidstone. Sorry that you've had to join us on such a dreich morning.'

Hunter knew that Dench liked to mobilise small dedicated teams of CSI officers in the field because she felt that it helped to improve response times. The change had been well received by SIOs like Hunter who normally required results, or at least a detailed report, by yesterday. She knew that Beth had been looking for another manager so she was pleased to have the opportunity of meeting Vardy for the first time. They shook hands.

'Are you from north of the border, then?' Hunter asked as they took a few steps towards the main area where the CSI's were concentrating their search for clues.

'Are you referring to my use of the word *dreich*?' she replied. 'Good heavens, no! Yorkshire born and bred. I just read somewhere that it was Scotland's most popular word. And in any event, the type of rain we've got today is known as *smirr* north of the border which sounds far more apposite than drizzle.'

Hunter wasn't going to argue. 'So, what have you got so far?'

'Seems your man managed to pull himself out of the water, came up the path over there and into this clearing where he dumped the parachute behind that pile of logs. There was also what's referred to as a container which incorporates a harness. This is what he would have had strapped to his body and what would have held the chute.'

'What about the chute itself?' Hunter asked.

'Well, it's fairly typical of the ones they use for base jumping. They're actually called canopies in the fraternity. The one that we've found is a high spec canopy which is produced by a well-regarded French company.'

'Really?' Hunter sounded intrigued.

'Seems a lot of the technical design is carried out in the French Alps where base jumping is hugely popular, and then the canopies themselves are made in the Czech Republic. Not cheap either.'

'So, this is a Czech-made canopy available to buy all over the world?' Hunter enquired, needing to establish that it wasn't only available for purchase in France or the Czech Republic.

'I imagine so,' Vardy replied, 'probably available on the Internet for a start. But I'm pretty sure that this one came from France.'

Hunter gave her a look which was half frown and half raised eyebrow.

'Yes, we've found a label sewn into the lining which identifies it as being the property of a sky diving club based in Chambery, south-east France. Travelled through there once – very close to the French alps. It's also got an airport which does flights to the UK in winter.'

'So, do we think that matey-the-pilot comes from round there and flew his plane from Chambery to Biggin Hill?' Hunter was trying to determine whether this was significant or if further supposition would just take them down a blind alley.

'Afraid I'm not paid to think, DI Hunter. Beth Dench tells me that's your job. All I can tell you with any degree of certainty is that the canopy is likely to have come from France. Whether matey-the-pilot, as you put it, also comes from France is another matter. He could have picked this equipment up anywhere.'

'You're right,' Hunter conceded. 'Interesting fact to know but probably irrelevant. By the way, feel free to address me as Sarah.' Vardy nodded. 'So, anything else I should know about?'

'Well, as you can imagine, everything's very wet so we've carefully packed it all up for transportation back to the lab where we can get it dried and see if there is still any evidence on it. Might get a print or two but don't get your hopes up. We're also looking at a potential trail away from here. If we're right, it looks as if he damaged one of his ankles. May even have broken it. But we've found some footprints that look as if they were made by someone who was shuffling along, possibly dragging one of their feet.'

'Interesting,' Hunter commented although she realised that they were talking about an event which had occurred a week ago. To say the trail was cold was probably an understatement.

'If we're right on this and we've been following the correct trail, this guy may well have been picked up by a motorbike. There's another tiny clearing over there where the footprints and dragged foot seem to stop.' Vardy pointed in the direction of the route Hunter had followed earlier. 'We've got some good impressions of the tyres which may help to identify what sort of bike it was, but that's probably going to be about all unless we can find anything that really helps us to identify the pilot.'

Hunter let her eyes roam around the clearing, imagining the pilot reaching this spot and deciding that it was the ideal place to dump his gear. But why dump it if he was going to get a lift on a bike? Why not take it with him? Perhaps he was quite badly injured to the extent that carrying the gear was impeding his progress. Maybe he thought that no one would bother looking for him here.

'Are you suggesting a trawl around local A&E departments?' she asked.

'Depends how bad it was,' Vardy replied. 'Trouble is, if the ankle is badly broken, the medics often keep you in so that they can pin it or plate it straightaway. Highly doubtful that our man would bother with all that so I'd say it would be a fruitless exercise contacting the local A&Es.'

'Okay, Annalise, I think I'll leave you to it. Let me know if you find anything else of interest. At the moment, we have no idea as to the identity of the pilot and little idea of the motive behind the destruction of Tideswell Manor. So, anything you can help us with will probably be a bonus.'

'Ma'am!' A shout from one of the CSI officers who was now standing beside the pile of logs. 'Over here!'

Annalise Vardy immediately turned and started walking towards her officer. Hunter thought she might as well find out what was going on so she followed the CSI Manager. The officer had dropped to his knees and was pointing to an area behind the logs. Vardy and Hunter bent down and peered at what the officer had uncovered.

'Two cigarette butts,' the officer advised them. 'Quite recent. You can see where they've been stubbed out on one of the logs.'

'Anything else?' Hunter asked.

'They're the Gitanes brand,' the officer continued, 'mainly sold in France and not available to purchase in the UK.'

Yet another French connection, Hunter thought.

'Okay, bag them up and we'll take a closer look back at base,' Vardy instructed her officer.

'Anything else for me?' Hunter asked as she and Vardy watched the officer begin the delicate process of bagging what could be vital evidence.

'Nothing that should delay you for the moment,' Vardy replied. 'Our initial report should be ready late tomorrow if you want to get a Zoom meeting organised.'

Hunter thanked Vardy for her assistance and said she'd get one of her team to arrange the Zoom meeting. She then made her way back along the path to where she had left her car.

There was much to ponder.

47

Sunday 3 May

The drizzle, or *smirr* as she now preferred to call it, had turned to more persistent rain as Sarah Hunter got back to her car. She rued the fact that she had tied the laces of her hiking boots with double knots which were fiddly to undo in her hurry to get into the car and escape the rain. Finally sitting behind the wheel, she ran her fingers through her hair and felt a drop of water skitter down the back of her neck.

There was no doubting the links to France which had been uncovered by the CSIs but was that the real hard evidence she would need to prove that the destruction of Tideswell Manor had been orchestrated from outside the UK? Along with the various suppositions which they had already scraped together, the case for even thinking that the incident was connected to Hennenbont looked weak. They needed something far more tenable.

Her phone started to vibrate in her back pocket. Jiggling about in her seat to retrieve the handset before the call went to voicemail, she ended up answering rather breathlessly.

'Hi Sarah. You alright?' came the rather worried sound of DCI Jack Pennington's voice.

'Yeah, fine thanks,' Hunter replied. Without thinking, she pulled down the sun visor and checked herself in the mirror before coming to her senses and mentally scolding herself for doing something so out of character. She then glanced at the clock on the dashboard. What was he calling for at this time on a Sunday?

'Okay, great,' Pennington continued. 'I'm not sure where you are or even what you're doing on this damp Sunday morning but it would be great if you could get yourself over here to HQ in Maidstone. We've got a situation going on and we're going to need your help with it.'

This rather took Sarah by surprise. She knew that Grace Kendall had planned to be at Pembury Road all morning, and they had toyed with the idea of having a pub lunch somewhere. But the weather might have put paid to that idea so they would probably just end up in the MIR further examining the evidence which they had so far collected. A rather thankless task given the fact that they hadn't really unearthed any game-changing evidence in either case.

'Well, I'm at Bewl Water at the moment,' Hunter replied. 'We've found some base jumping kit and other evidence that would indicate that the pilot successfully managed to bail out of the aircraft before it smashed into Tideswell Manor. Something else which seems to point to our man across the Channel but nothing conclusive yet.'

She didn't want to say much more at the moment as she hated just passing on bits and pieces of information. Far better to give Pennington a full debrief when she was absolutely sure of how all the evidence fitted together. And it didn't really sound as if he had called to discuss Tideswell Manor anyway so Sarah decided that her best tactic was simply to wait for Pennington to continue.

'Yep, thanks for that Sarah but we've got something for you which is more connected with the One Tree Hill incident. Things have become a bit complicated to the extent that we now need to involve you in our plans which necessitates you being here for a briefing.'

She wondered if Iversen was aware of this approach or, indeed, whether Pennington had any plans to make him aware, even retrospectively. And she didn't seem to have the authority to use the information she had been given by Jordan Wright so she might as well go along with Pennington's request if for no other reason than to find out what was actually going on in his world of subterfuge and bluff.

'Okay, Jack,' Hunter replied. 'I should be with you in about half an hour depending on the traffic.' She didn't wait for his response as she disconnected the call and peered at the clearing through thin rivulets of rainwater which had started to run down the car's windscreen.

What was Pennington up to with the One Tree Hill killings? Why had he sent his messenger-boy Wright to give her a smattering of information when he could just as easily have done that himself? She sat in the car, reviewing everything she knew about the One Tree Hill incident but failing to come up with a solid link to Tideswell Manor apart from a hunch that there might be a French connection. With an audible sigh of resignation, she decided that there was only one way to find out so she started the car and made her way out of Chingley Wood before heading off towards Maidstone.

48

Sunday 3 May

DC Abigail Knight was rueing her choice of mode of transport today but, at the same time, congratulating herself on being even more invisible than she normally was.

She had been a biker girl at heart for as long as she could remember. Her father had an affinity with motorbikes, and had even made a little side car for his princess to sit in when he took her out for runs at the weekends. Once she had reached her teens, he had bought her a motorcycle of her own which she would ride offroad near their home. And, as soon as she was old enough, she had begged and borrowed enough to buy herself something with two wheels. However, her penchant for bikes began to fade once she discovered the thrills of fast cars although, more recently, she had returned to her previous love of biking. Having saved as hard as she could, she had now managed to acquire a Kawasaki Ninja which was her pride and joy.

Today, she was once again trailing Johnnie Arcane and, having studied the weather forecast, she had got herself dressed in as much black wet weather gear as she possessed. She had reached St Mary's Island early and made sure that he was still at home. She had then taken up position in an unoccupied car port where she could keep an eye on Arcane's apartment block and keep the rain off her back.

She hadn't had to wait too long before Arcane appeared and got into his car which was parked in the road opposite where she was positioned. Once they were on the road travelling away from St Mary's, Knight kept a decent distance behind him in the sure knowledge that she would be able to catch up quickly if he suddenly took an unexpected turn.

Once out of Chatham, Arcane had taken the A2 down to the Key Street roundabout before following the Sheppey Way to Bobbing. Knight held back and watched as Arcane visited a couple of houses in Bobbing. She kept a photographic record of these visits for future reference and then followed Arcane as he joined the A249 for the journey across the new Sheppey bridge crossing.

She now had a pretty good idea of where they were headed and realised that she would eventually become very exposed on the isolated roads on the north-eastern coast of Sheppey. Thankfully, the weather had really closed in and she had taken the precaution of turning all the Kawasaki's lights out. It wouldn't impede her vision but would improve her invisibility.

As they approached the eastern end of the island, Knight saw Arcane's brake lights in the distance as he turned off the road to the right. She hung back, cutting the bike's engine.

Arcane soon reappeared on the road, shrugging himself into a long trench coat as he stepped onto a grassy pathway and kept walking. Knight didn't dare turn the bike's engine back on so she pushed the Kawasaki along the road to where Arcane had abandoned his car. She found a small car park which was cut into the field and, according to the sign at its entrance, was designated for people visiting the Swale Nature Reserve. There were a few other cars in the parking area none of which were parked uniformly so she propped her bike on its stand behind a huge Land Rover, well out of sight of Arcane's car.

Exiting the car park, she quickly realised why Arcane had

parked there. Having read something about the Shellness Estate in the past, she recalled that it was a small gated community which hides behind fences and barriers deterring visitors from outside. She now saw one of these barriers spread across the road with the word '*Private*' emblazoned on it in red paint. Looking to her right, she saw the figure of Arcane following a pathway which was taking him alongside the estate towards the very eastern tip of the island.

Knight surveyed the terrain and realised that she could still watch Arcane from a distance if she headed across the scrub-land which was now separating them. Sooner or later, Arcane would meet up with the coastal path which would enable her to get a bit closer.

Peering through the gloom and the incessant drizzle, Knight continued to watch her quarry as she charted a course through a mixture of bracken, heather and gorse. Ahead of her, Arcane was already trudging along the chalk-strewn coastal path.

Suddenly stopping to pull the collar of his trench coat right up to his ears, he took time to have a good look around him. Although he probably wouldn't have been able to see her in the stooped position she had adopted, Knight was taking no chances and immediately hit the ground. Raising her head up, she watched as Arcane took out his phone and appeared to make a call. However, he didn't seem to have made a connection as he was soon looking at the screen before putting the phone back in his pocket. Knight ran off a few shots on her phone and then got back on her feet once she was sure that Arcane had resumed his walk.

She watched as he came to a halt again before leaving the path and walking inland away from the beach. As she already had a good idea of where he was headed, she allowed herself to lose sight of him as she clambered into deeper undergrowth and started to circle around until she found herself at the back of a small clearing. Peering through the gloom, she recognised the old caravan and the dark green shed from surveillance photographs she had studied the previous day. They wouldn't have been visible from the coastal path, she thought, and probably not even from the air. Keeping well out of sight, Knight watched as Arcane picked his way around an empty boat hull which had been abandoned between the caravan and the path.

He then crossed a clearing where tufts of green grass sprouted from cracks in the chalk rock and started knocking on the caravan door. When he got no response, he walked over to the shed and started hammering on its door. In frustration at not getting a response, he pulled and pushed at the handle of the door but his efforts were to no avail.

'Come on, you silly old fool,' he bawled, 'get the fuck out here!'

He clomped back to the caravan and gave the door a mighty pummelling before standing back and surveying both structures. Silence hung in the air, only broken by the sound of the wind rustling the vegetation and waves rolling relentlessly onto the beach.

There was clearly no one here.

Knight fired off a few more shots on her phone as Arcane started to vent his rage on anything which came within his orbit. Roaring a string of expletives at the top of his voice, he kicked at the ground sending pieces of chalk flying. He also kicked at the shed door before again pummelling his fists on the caravan door. Eventually he aimed a kick at the empty boat hull but this was clearly made of sterner stuff as he immediately started hopping around on one leg whilst trying to grab hold of the other leg with both hands. All the time, Knight's phone camera was recording the activities for posterity.

Circling back through the undergrowth, and now being quite a distance from the coastal path, Abigail Knight watched as the forlorn figure of Johnnie Arcane dragged himself back towards his car.

He hadn't been able to get whatever it was that he had gone there for, and that information would be of huge importance to her controller. She hung back in the gloom but didn't have to wait long before Arcane's car drove out of the car park and sped off back along the road towards Leysdown.

Finally allowing herself to stand up straight, she entered the car park and reunited herself with the Kawasaki. Propping herself against the seat, she got her phone out and called her controller.

49

Sunday 3 May

'Biggin, this is Golf Papa Mike Kilo November ready for take-off. Kilo November. One-two-zero, level three zero. Thank you and have a good day.'

DS Grace Kendall had pasted together the two transmissions made by the pilot of the doomed aircraft, and she was now playing them to herself in the MIR. She had awoken during the night with the thought that perhaps listening more closely to the voice of the pilot might help the identification process. But exactly what was she looking for? she kept asking herself. Was it to see if there was a clue in the accent? Were there any intonations she should be concentrating on? Was the pilot using accepted pilot-speak if ever there was such a thing? She played the loop again through the set of expensive headphones which she had retrieved from her apartment earlier.

And then, without even thinking, she played it again.

She was concentrating so hard on listening to the voice that she got a bit of a shock when the stout frame of DS Ted Selitto suddenly appeared in front of her.

'Morning Grace,' he chortled when he saw the look of surprise on her face. 'You putting in a full weekend as well?'

He ambled across the room and looked out of the window at the gloomy weather before making himself comfortable behind the desk directly opposite Grace. A steaming mug of coffee had already been placed on the desk and he now extracted a *pain au chocolat* from the brown paper bag he had brought with him.

'No rest for the wicked as you well know, Ted,' she replied, sliding the headphones off her head so that they now encircled her neck. 'Anyway, I thought that you were still supposed to be taking it easy.'

'Sitting around at home trying to take it easy does my head in. I need to be where the action is, to feel part of the team, to get the adrenaline rush of nicking criminals.'

'Well then, perhaps you could help me with the identification of the pilot.' Grace went on to tell Selitto about her hunch that the voice of the pilot might give them a clue as to his identity, and she played the recorded loop she had been listening to.

The first time Selitto heard it he simply asked her to play it again. By the end of the second playback, his elbows were on the desk and he was forward in his chair straining to listen to the voice. After the third play, he sat back in his chair, elbows on the arms of the chair, fingers steepled under his chin.

'I think you might be on to something there, Grace,' he eventually remarked. 'One of the numbers doesn't sound quite right. Is it the *zero*? Also, would he really say have a *good* day? Isn't the phrase have a *nice* day used internationally? Which might mean that he is trying too hard to sound British and thinks that we would say *good* instead of *nice*.'

'That's interesting, Ted, because I thought one of the numbers didn't sound right – but it wasn't the *zero*.' She played the recording again. 'But I can see what you're getting at. I also think that the intonation of the letter O is quite harsh.'

She played the recording yet again.

'Hmm. We really need to be talking to one of those forensic speech analysts.' Grace had managed to sum up what Selitto had been thinking to himself.

'Beth Dench will be able to put you in touch with one of those,' he replied. 'Guaranteed!'

At that moment, the door opened as Jed Crowther and Lisa Calder entered the MIR. They both looked somewhat bedraggled with Calder in particular looking as if she would benefit from ten minutes under a hair dryer.

'Thought we might find you here,' Crowther sighed as he flopped into the chair behind one of the vacant desks. Calder decided to prop herself against the desk and started threading her fingers through her wet hair. 'Is the boss in?'

Selitto gave Crowther the eye. 'Looks like both of us are here,' he said mischievously, looking towards Grace Kendall.

'Ah, sorry Sarge, I meant is DI Hunter in?' Crowther corrected himself.

'Thought she would have been with you two,' Grace replied. 'Haven't you all been at the site in Chingley Wood?'

'No, we've been at Tideswell looking for an ILS system,' Calder chipped in. 'And we think we've found something!'

'Tell us more,' Grace insisted, her interest piqued.

Calder looked across at Crowther who seemed content to let her continue. 'Well, following on from Captain Donaldson's briefing, we decided to see if we could find anything which looked remotely like a VHF localiser bearing in mind that we don't really know what one looks like. So we started by taking the line of flight and projecting it through the mansion and then into the grounds at the back. That's when we got the idea that it could be hiding in plain sight because it really couldn't be anywhere else.'

'Have you been up there yet?' Crowther butted in, looking at Kendall and Selitto. Grace replied that she had only seen photographs of the devastation and the grounds around the house. Selitto simply shook his head.

'Well, you'll have seen pictures of the Winnebagos and the motorhomes then,' Lisa Calder continued. 'They're still all parked at the back of the building and, just walking round them, we realised that some of them were in the direct line of flight. But what we hadn't noticed before was that there was one motorhome outside the ring that the others had all parked in. In fact, it's standing quite a distance from the mansion.'

Both Sellitto and Kendall raised their eyebrows at this revelation.

'And, whilst the CSIs have all done their thing with the inside of the vehicle, no one seems to have paid much attention to what's on its roof. We've taken a look and found that there are quite a few antennae along with a satellite dish. Now, that could be to do with TV but Jed and I think that this isn't the normal sort of equipment people have on their motorhomes for the purposes of getting a TV feed. It certainly doesn't look like the equipment which is on the roofs of the other motorhomes.'

'So, what are you implying?' Grace cut in.

'We believe that this could be where the VHF localiser is located.'

Crowther had been fiddling with his phone and now looked over towards Kendall. 'Photos should be in your in-box.'

Selitto moved across the room to stand beside Grace as she downloaded the photos Crowther had sent. They studied the antennae on the roof of the motorhome although Selitto had an uneasy feeling that none of them really knew what they were looking at. What did a VHF localiser look like anyway? Did the sum total of all the antennae make up one localiser?

'Perhaps I should send these to Donaldson and then give him a call.' Kendall suggested.

'Well, before you do that, you had better let us explain what else we found,' Crowther chipped in.

'Yes,' Calder took up the commentary again. 'Donaldson told us that any ILS system, no matter how basic, would have to also have a UHF glideslope transmitter to provide vertical guidance. So, we searched the areas to the side of the mansion because Donaldson also said that a transmitting glideslope antenna would be located off to the side of the approach.'

'And you found something?' Selitto asked before realising that he was probably stating the bleeding obvious.

Crowther indicated to Kendall that there should be some more photos in her in-box.

'Eventually,' Calder continued. 'Another motorhome had been parked deep in the woods on the western side of the mansion and has probably been missed by the CSIs. There's no sign that they have been inside it and, indeed, it was locked when we got there. Anyway, there's a red and white hooped antenna inside the vehicle and a hole has been cut in the roof to allow the antenna to be contained. A metal box has been welded onto the roof to cover the protrusion.'

Selitto and Kendall stared at the photos Crowther had sent through.

'Isn't it all a bit mickey-mouse?' Selitto eventually said. 'A few bits of metal on the roof of one motorhome and what looks like an elongated traffic cone in another. It just doesn't seem to be robust enough to guide an aircraft with pinpoint accuracy to its destination.'

Crowther looked as if he had had the wind taken out of his sails, but Lisa Calder was far from finished.

'It doesn't have to be all singing, all dancing. We're not trying to land a jumbo jet on a one-and-a-half mile international airport runway. We're trying to provide a sufficient signal to guide a small plane to a reasonably large target object. I doubt the guidance system has to be too intricate just as long as it's sending out the right signals to the receiver.'

Everyone was nodding. They could see the point Calder was making, and they knew that it made some sense.

Grace Kendall was still idly scrolling through the photographs. 'Okay, let's see what Donaldson's got to say, But well done you two. If this really is a guidance system, then it would seem to prove that this was a deliberate act. By the way, did you get the registration plates for the two motorhomes?'

Calder got her phone out and started scrolling through some information. 'Yes, here they are. I'll send them to you now. Both foreign. French, I think.'

Selitto's jaw dropped.

50

Sunday 3 May

Arriving at yet another set of traffic-light-controlled road-works, and with the red light shining brightly through the rain, Sarah Hunter tapped her thumbs on the steering wheel to the beat of *Viva la Vida*, the Coldplay masterpiece. In an idle moment, she had looked into the background of the song as she was fascinated by all its historical and Christian references, and found that it was inspired by a Mexican artist by the name of Frida Kahlo. Following years of pain and suffering, she had started a huge painting in her house which basically rejoiced in the old adage '*Long Live Life*'. Sarah had admired the determination of the woman and loved the song.

Eventually arriving at the outskirts of Maidstone, Hunter executed a couple of 'back-doubles' she had learned from Carolyn Pennant who knew them from her days as a Traffic officer before she had moved to Tonbridge CID. Once she was through the security gates of the Kent Police HQ complex, she drove round to the visitors car park. It was virtually empty so she was able to park very close to the building in which the Serious Crime Directorate had their suite of offices.

Knowing that she hadn't agreed a time of arrival with Pennington, she decided to call Grace Kendall for any updates. Grace quickly gave her the news of the discoveries made by Crowther and Calder. Hunter listened, giving Grace's report her full attention.

'So why hasn't anyone seen all this equipment before?' Hunter asked. 'Surely the AAIB had a good look around or are they still thinking it was a tragic accident?'

'Difficult to say,' Kendall replied. 'We haven't really had much contact with them since they managed to get their hands on the aircraft, and I'm pretty sure that they haven't been down to Tideswell since it was taken away. Anyway, Jed and Lisa say that the motorhomes were positioned well away from the mansion and pretty much out of sight. In fact, the CSIs seem to have only found one of them. The one with the UHF transmitter was untouched when Lisa stumbled upon it.'

'So, what's the plan?' Hunter asked whilst, at the same time, feeling as if she was now wasting her time at Maidstone. This sounded like a bit of a breakthrough to her yet here she was sitting in a rain swept car park about to discuss a seemingly unrelated crime with people who had little knowledge of or, perhaps, even interest in the destruction of Tideswell Manor.

'I've got a call booked with Donaldson in about an hour,' Kendall replied. 'He's got the family round for Sunday lunch but can spare some time once he's finished his pudding. In fact, he's quite happy to talk to us as it gets him out of helping with the clearing up. I've sent him all the photos by email.'

'Okay, we need to find out where these motorhomes came from. Did their journeys actually originate in France? Have they got bona fide plates from country of origin? Did they come across the Channel recently? Anything about ownership? My guess is that they'll have rogue plates and be untraceable but you never know. And, if they are rogue, then it's likely they weren't put on until the vehicles were safely in the UK.'

Whilst yet another connection to France was interesting, Hunter didn't hold out much hope of tracing the vehicles through their registration plates. Even using engine numbers to initiate a trace was a pretty thankless task these days and, in any event, was likely to only give them an idea of where the vehicle was originally manufactured. But they had to go through the process just in case.

'By the way, how's the young girl?' Hunter suddenly thought that she hadn't had a medical update for a day or so.

'Still too traumatised to be interviewed. Apparently, the medical staff don't think she's ready to be given the news about her mother yet. In fact, her mind's so screwed up that she hasn't even asked why her mother hasn't been in to see her. From talking to the ward sister, I get the impression that a visit from us is a long way off.'

Hunter thought about this. How much of a priority was it to talk to the girl? It was probably unlikely that she would be able to tell them much more than they could ascertain by simply analysing the crime scene at Tideswell Manor. No, it was something they would have to do at some stage but it wasn't critical at the moment, particularly now that the perpetrators were likely to be amongst the dead.

Sarah was just thinking about ending the call when a vision of Baz Biondi came into her mind.

'While you're on, Grace, did we ever get any further with the possibility that Biondi had been flown to Nantes?'

'Not really,' Kendall replied. 'We're as sure as we can be that he was escorted to a private jet which had filed a flight plan to Nantes. It took off but doesn't seem to have ever landed at its destination. It's been difficult finding out exactly what went on but it seems that the pilot filed a new flight plan when he arrived in French airspace and, after that, no one seems to have a clue where the plane went. It could have landed on any of the hundreds of small airstrips they have in France and we'd be none the wiser.'

'So Biondi's disappeared,' Hunter concluded. 'My money's on no one ever seeing sight nor sound of him again. He poked the Hennenbont nest one too many times and had to be removed from the grid. These boys do not mess about when it's time for revenge.'

'Agreed,' Grace said. 'He's probably been thrown to the fish with a slab of concrete for company. The others who were partying at Tideswell when the plane struck were probably all his closest allies so in some weird way Hennenbont's done us a favour. But it could destabilise the drug market in our area which would provide us with other headaches.'

Hunter thought about this. Perhaps Grace was right. Only time would tell.

'Okay, I'm going into see SCD now,' Sarah said, suddenly realising that she had spent too much time on this call. 'Are you going to be there for the duration?'

'Looks like it so I'll just see you when you get back. Shall I try and find somewhere that does food on Sunday nights?'

'Great idea! I'll be starving by then.'

51

Sunday 3 May

The rain had eased slightly so Sarah Hunter was able to dash across to the entrance of the main building without getting too wet. Once inside, she was greeted by a young female police constable who said that she had been sent by DCI Pennington to escort her to the SCD suite. She quickly checked Hunter's ID and signed her in before leading the way to the lift and up to the second floor.

They walked along the corridor past what Hunter knew to be the main operations room and then stopped outside a door with the initials *SCD-A* emblazoned on it. The constable knocked on the door before opening it and showing Hunter into the room.

Sarah was initially taken aback by the group of police officers that had been assembled in the room. Pennington was quickly on his feet and welcoming her to SCD whilst seated around the table she recognised Jordan Wright and, of all people, Rory Easton. So that's where he had got to, she thought. There was also a woman she did not recognise and who was dressed head-to-toe in black biker leathers, and there was an older man who she similarly had never seen before.

'Good to see you, Sarah,' Pennington effused as he made his way across the room. 'Coffee and biscuits over there if you want some. Water as well. Get whatever you want and come and join us.'

Although she could have murdered a strong coffee, Hunter decided to forego the temptation. She just wanted to get stuck into whatever it was they needed to discuss with her, so she politely refused the offer and took the seat opposite Pennington. This put her next to Rory Easton.

'Have we been looking for you!' she murmured as she turned to face him, trying to keep her voice to a whisper but clearly not succeeding.

'Yes, sorry about taking one of your officers, Sarah,' Pennington intervened. 'Should really have mentioned it to you but you'll see why I didn't as we get into the briefing. Now, I presume that you don't know DC Abbie Knight. She's a key part of our surveillance team.'

Sarah nodded at biker girl who returned the nod. She had never had any interest in joining a surveillance unit and knew that it took a very particular sort of mentality to cope with the stresses of watching suspects for long periods of time. It was also a very risky occupation as one of Pennington's officers had found to his cost recently.

'And over there we have Stig Shanahan,' Pennington continued. 'He's not actually Scandinavian but has apparently always been called Stig. Anyway, he is to me what Grace Kendall is to you. Invaluable.'

Hunter nodded at Shanahan and then picked up the pen in front of her and made a note of the names, knowing that she would forget them if she didn't.

Pennington seemed keen to get on and was now pacing in front of the window.

'Right, let's cut to the chase. For your benefit, Sarah, I'll just summarise the objective of *Operation Tayberry* although I know you have received an outline briefing from Jordan in the last couple of days. Then we can move onto planning our strategy.'

Hunter was intrigued.

'For a number of months, we have been on the trail of one of the largest county lines gangs to have ever operated in Kent, and we believe that we now have a golden opportunity to dismantle this gang completely. After countless hours of surveillance, we believe that we have identified the runners, suppliers, dealers and line holders. We also know the identity of the top man and this is him.'

Pennington had retaken his seat and now pushed a photograph across the table towards Hunter who reached over and pulled it towards her.

'This is Johnnie Arcane,' Pennington continued. 'He runs a complex group of dealers across Kent with, it seems, ambitions of breaking into the south-east corner of London. One of the keys to his success seems to be that none of the dealers know each other. He rules them with a rod of iron, and we believe that he now controls a significant number of lines.'

Hunter realised that this was what Jordan Wright had been alluding to when he had visited her. Not only had SCD identified Arcane as a key player in Kent's continuing war on the county lines gangs, but they had now clearly set their sights on bringing him down along with the rest of his gang.

'We're not sure exactly how many lines he does control although we've discovered that they've all been given names which relate to the *Apocalypse* and *Zombie* genres.'

At the mention of this, Hunter remembered that the CSIs had found various snow globes with apocalyptic scenes in Rachael Buckley's bedroom. Could there be a connection here? She decided to bide her time before mentioning this.

'A couple of months ago,' Pennington continued, 'we noticed

that Arcane seemed to be in contact with one of his dealers in particular so we concentrated on following this guy.'

Another photograph was pushed across the table.

'This is Vinnie Garrett who operates the Chatham and Medway towns area. He's older than Arcane and has been around the block a few more times. He's also got a conviction for possession. From what we can gather, Arcane depends on Garrett's counsel a lot of the time so we have been looking at whether Garrett could somehow give us Arcane. That's when the team came up with the idea of getting Arcane interested in buying some Fentanyl. I think Jordan mentioned this to you.'

Hunter nodded.

Pennington looked across to Rory Easton as if inviting him to continue.

'Yeah,' Easton started, 'the idea was to offer to supply Arcane with the strong opioid painkiller, Fentanyl, on the promise that it would make him a very rich man. But, in order to get anywhere near making such a proposal to him, we needed to know how he operated. So we lifted Garrett.'

'Jeez! That was brave,' Hunter muttered, 'or foolhardy.'

'One thing in our favour is that, although he operates in the Medway towns area, Garrett actually lives deep in the countryside around Detling Hill so the chances of anyone catching us executing a dawn raid at this time of year were remote. We found plenty of gear on the premises so we've been able to charge him and keep him on remand.'

'And then you went to work on him, presumably,' Hunter surmised.

'Didn't take much to get him interested in some plea bargaining options. Once they were sorted, he started singing as if his life depended on it. Chapter and verse on how to communicate with Arcane, where he lives, when he goes out, where he tends to go, all his little foibles.'

'And then all you had to do was spring the trap!' Hunter had to agree that it was a bold stratagem although fraught with danger, particularly if Garrett hadn't been cooperative.

'Yeah, so I've been meeting with Arcane, putting the deal together, talking quantities and price, and now we're due for the delivery to be made in the next thirty-six hours.'

Pennington had been listening to Easton's summing up of the sting operation, arms resting on the table, fingers interlocked, thumbs occasionally rotating around each other. Now his hooded eyes swept round the table as if he was about to impart some terrible news.

'But now our plans have changed,' he said, looking directly at Hunter.

'Presumably not just because there is a huge risk that a sting could be interpreted as entrapment in the courts,' she wondered out loud.

'Well, that's always a risk,' Pennington blustered, 'but, no, the problem, if it is actually a problem, is that we think our man Arcane was at One Tree Hill. In which case, he was probably responsible for at least one of the deaths which would be a much more satisfactory way of taking him out of circulation.'

'Have you been liaising with Beth Dench on this one?' Hunter asked.

Jordan Wright took up from where Pennington had left off. 'Yes, she's given us Gavinder Ramdeen but no identities for the others in the taxi. Ramdeen, or Gav as he's known on the street, is an out-and-out thug and has been one of Arcane's dealers for about nine months. He's a Rastafarian without the dreadlocks and runs some of the bigger lines right on the edges of the south-east London ganglands so he's used to having to fight his corner – literally. Both he and Arcane are known to be extremely protective of their territories and we've been looking at whether this protectionism may have had something to do with the One Tree Hill incident.'

Hunter was wondering if Pennington's team had perhaps been doing rather a lot of blue sky thinking just to try to shoehorn Arcane into the frame for the shootings. Yes, okay, Gav was one of Arcane's henchmen but that didn't mean that Arcane was also there.

'And you'll remember that I mentioned a guy by the name of Charles Stone who also goes by the nicknames of Dancer and Stryker?' Wright continued.

Hunter nodded, again recalling the discussion they had had during his visit to Pembury Road.

'It looks like there's a match between the blood on the ground at One Tree Hill and the man who was left outside the Medway hospital. That man was Stone who is, or rather was, identified by Garrett as being another one of Arcane's principle dealers.'

Pennington interrupted. 'I think Beth Dench is of the view that the guy sitting behind the driver had been shot in the head at pretty much point blank range which conclusively proves that there was a second gunman.'

'And you think that's Arcane?' Hunter questioned.

'Well, there has been another development that we're now working on which should provide us with absolute proof that

Arcane was at One Tree Hill,' Pennington replied as he pushed another photograph across the table.

To start with, Hunter wasn't sure what she was looking at as the picture was very grainy. But she could just about make out a lone figure walking along a path. Was it a coastal path, she wondered. It looked like there was an expanse of water in the background and she could just make out little white crests on the tops of waves.

'Not great detail I'm afraid,' Pennington continued as he retrieved the photograph and had a look at it himself. 'But that is Arcane returning from a visit to an armourer by the name of Eric Judson. He's located on the east coast of Sheppey. Old-school type. Oily rags, hand tools, that sort of thing.'

'What? You guys just happened to be staking out the armourer and Arcane turned up?' Hunter was finding this all a little far-fetched.

'Not exactly,' Pennington retorted. 'One of the surveillance teams from Medway has been keeping an eye on Judson for a few weeks now just so that they can get to know who's visiting and how much business is going on. They took some other shots of Arcane walking on the coastal path which are much clearer but this is the shot which shows him exiting the armourer's location.'

'So, have you now arrested the armourer?' Hunter asked.

'Took him in yesterday and carried out a detailed search of the premises,' Jordan Wright explained. 'The old boy was working on what we think is one of the firearms used at One Tree Hill. Ballistics are now taking a look.'

'And there was more activity up there this morning,' Pennington continued. 'Abbie?'

Knight sprang forward in her chair and placed her elbows on the table in front of her. 'Yes. I followed the subject from his home to the Isle of Sheppey. He stopped at a couple of addresses on the way which may have been the homes of some of his street dealers. We're checking that out right now. I followed him down to the Leysdown and Shellness Beach areas of Sheppey, and I subsequently observed him trying to gain entry to the premises of the armourer.'

Pennington pushed another photograph across the table which clearly showed Arcane kicking the door of a green caravan.

'As you can see, he wasn't at all happy to find that the armourer wasn't there,' Knight continued. 'You can also see that he had a holdall with him which would seem to indicate that he had gone there to do some business.'

'And yesterday?' Pennington encouraged.

'I spent yesterday following Arcane in Chatham and Thamesmead,' Knight continued. 'In Chatham he seemed distracted but was then observed meeting a punter in a car park. Couldn't be sure whether he was dealing or not. He then had an altercation with another punter in a flat above one of those cheap pound shops where he was very obviously dealing because he dropped a couple of wraps of H in his hurry to get out of the shop. Later on, I followed him to a house in Thamesmead which we now know is owned by Charles Stone.'

Pennington butted in. 'We immediately got in touch with forensics and gave them the information Abbie had given us about how to access the property. With Stone lying in the mortuary, it seemed best to get his place searched as soon as possible.'

Hunter nodded her agreement. Pennington's team had certainly been busy.

Rory Easton now had some further thoughts about his sting.

'It's becoming clear to us that Arcane is having difficulty getting the cash together for the delivery that we're arranging and, based on what Abbie has now discovered, we're wondering if he was trying to get his hands on a bundle of extra cash by offloading some firearms which he has had stashed away somewhere.'

Hunter was beginning to get a feeling of unease. Why were they telling her all this? They clearly had Arcane in their sights and, by the sound of it, they were building up sufficient evidence which would put him at One Tree Hill quite apart from the potential for lifting him if they executed the drug sting. However, as far as she could see, Arcane had no relevance to her investigation of the Tideswell Manor incident.

So what did they want from her?

'I know you had a briefing from Beth Dench's team yesterday,' Pennington continued, 'but some new information has come in overnight. The techies have been working on the phone that was found on the body of the taxi driver, Ramdeen, and they've been trying to trace the origin of the text message.'

Hunter recalled Donny Campbell telling them that the phone had only been used once to receive a text with the word 'NOW'. She nodded at Pennington.

'What I hadn't realised at the time was that Rory had made a call to Arcane asking for an idea of when he would be ready to pick up and pay for the Fentanyl.' Pennington looked across at Easton.

'Yeah,' Rory said, taking over from Pennington, 'I was just

checking that he wasn't having second thoughts and, although he sounded a bit panicky, he was adamant that he had the cash. I didn't really think any more about the call until we were again reviewing the one-word text message.'

Pennington took over again. 'So we gave the techies Arcane's number to see if it could be a match with the phone that sent the one-word text?'

'And it was, I assume,' Hunter concluded. 'But that doesn't necessarily put Arcane at the scene of the shooting.'

'No, but it does indicate that some sort of signal was sent to the driver just before the shooting began.' Pennington looked around the table as if seeking confirmation that this was the course of action they had followed.

'So, let's look at what happened next,' Hunter suggested, more for her own benefit than for the benefit of the others. 'The word *NOW* would seem to indicate that the driver was required to carry out a pre-planned action. Was it to exit the taxi as quickly as possible to avoid the gunfire which was about to start? Or was he to turn round and start shooting the passengers? I, personally, doubt that it was either of these scenarios because he seems to have remained seated looking ahead whilst the passenger behind him took aim and blew his brains out.'

Pennington's team seemed to agree with her deductions thus far based on the limited information they had.

'So, what else could the driver do which was presumably going to help the gunmen?' Hunter wondered.

An eerie silence descended on the room as each officer tried to come up with a believable reason why the word *NOW* had been texted to the driver.

'Okay, let's leave that for the moment.' Pennington declared, looking at his watch. 'Some of us have to be elsewhere this afternoon so I'll keep this brief.'

Hunter was pleased to hear that she could soon be on her way back to Tonbridge. She had much to do there and didn't want to spend any more time with Pennington's people than was absolutely necessary.

'As you may have by now noticed, Sarah,' Pennington continued, the sound of her name bringing Hunter's thoughts back to the briefing, 'each member of my team has been closely involved in identifying and implicating Arcane in serious criminal activities. But I don't want them to be identified as being involved in his arrest and subsequent interrogation. I would like that done by an officer who, although fully conversant with his activities, is someone that Arcane will never have either heard of or seen in his life.'

If she was honest with herself, Hunter had probably guessed that this was what Pennington had been leading up to but, even so, she got a bit of a jolt when he actually confirmed what she had been expecting.

'So, let me just get this straight,' she replied. 'I'll be the arresting officer as well as leading on the interrogation, and your guys will provide all the heavy lifting when we arrest Arcane. Firearms I presume. And he'll be booked into the custody suite here. Is that how it's going to work?'

'Pretty much. With his background, we'll be going in heavy handed to pick him up – firearms, dogs, the lot. Once we've got him cuffed, and you've read him the charges, he'll be processed here at Maidstone. We'll then let him sweat for a while after which you can get started.'

'And this is planned for when?' Hunter asked.

'As soon as we've got the results from ballistics, we'll put everything together and you'll be fully briefed. We reckon the phone's the key. If we can get the phone Rory called him on, then we can link it to the phone in the taxi cab. Similarly, if we can link the gun he took to the armourer as being the same as the one that was discharged on One Tree Hill, then we can question him on that. If you like, we'll see if he can prove that he *wasn't* there.'

Pennington lapsed into silence whereupon Hunter decided that she had heard enough.

'Okay, let me know how things progress with ballistics. I presume the people in this room will be doing the briefing so just give me a bit of notice about when you want me back here.'

There was a general murmur of agreement around the table as everyone got to their feet and gathered papers up from the table. Hunter said her goodbyes and was then escorted back to Reception by the young police constable. She walked out of the building into what was turning into a sunny afternoon.

Once inside her car, she checked her phone for messages and then started the engine. Reversing out of her space, she headed for the exit, picking up speed as she went. Suddenly, she heard a series of clicks in the car.

She slammed on the brakes and stared straight ahead through the windscreen, white-knuckled hands gripping the steering wheel.

'Of course!' she murmured to herself. 'Of course!'

She instinctively knew what the *NOW* message was all about.

52
Sunday 3 May

Arriving back at Pembury Road, Sarah Hunter was annoyed with herself for forgetting that the car park was closed for maintenance today. So she drifted on down St Stephen's Street until she found a space almost at its junction with Priory Walk. There had been a heavy shower on her journey back from Maidstone but the sun was now breaking through as she made her way back towards the station.

She was still going over her meeting with the SCD team, trying to grasp the wider implications of what she was being asked to do. Without thinking, she impulsively checked for missed calls and messages on her phone even though she had already done so before getting out of the car.

So, she was a bit taken aback when she became aware of a figure bearing down on her from the direction of the police station. Taking avoiding action, she stepped closer to the edge of the pavement to allow the other person to pass.

'DI Hunter?'

The sound of the male voice jolted her into the here-and-now, and she spun round to confront its owner. She found herself looking into the narrowed eyes of a tall man wearing a dark blue rugby shirt with a thick red stripe outlined in white, black needlecord jeans and a pair of white trainers. With sunglasses perched on top of a foppish mane of nut brown hair and probably a fortnight's growth of brown facial hair, he smiled at her which accentuated the laughter lines at the corners of his eyes.

'Who wants to know?' Hunter snapped, feeling a need to assert her authority on proceedings. It wasn't often that she was recognised by people in the street and, on the rare occasions that it happened, she was always immediately on her guard. In this instance, she was relieved that she was so close to the station and she quickly assessed her options for an escape route.

'Sorry to trouble you out here in the street but it seems to be the only way I'm going to get to speak to you.'

Hunter gave the man a quizzical look.

'I'm Rocco Vance,' the man declared. 'We spoke on the phone yesterday.'

She stared at him. 'Have you taken leave of your senses, Mr Vance? Accosting me in the street like this?'

'I just thought it would be useful if we met so that we could at least put faces to names.' He smiled revealing a prominent set of gleaming white teeth.

'It looks like you have already done that in my case which would seem to put me at a disadvantage,' she told him.

Vance certainly sounded confident which also annoyed Hunter. She had clearly failed to either put him in his place or temper his enthusiasm for questioning her about her investigations.

'I've already told you that I will contact you when I have something to tell you,' she emphasised. 'I'm not going to start giving you information about an investigation which hasn't yet been subject of a thorough review by the investigating teams.'

'Yeah, I can understand that. But I'm operating in a very competitive environment. My competitors already seem to know more than I do and they're starting to corner the market on these stories.'

'Well, they can't be publishing anything worth reading because we haven't held any news conferences or spoken to anyone from the press. There has been a news blackout. I don't know where you got your information about the devastation inside Tideswell Manor but publishing such information could seriously undermine the work of the police and may result in an injunction being issued against you. Similarly, any information about One Tree Hill is also most definitely off limits for the time being.'

Vance removed the sunglasses from his head and ran his fingers through his hair, pushing an unruly strand back onto the top of his head. Clamping the sunglasses back into place, he then started to stroke his fledgling beard with the back of his hand as if seeking inspiration for a further attempt to get information out of the detective inspector.

Meanwhile, Hunter took an opportunity to study Vance. He appeared to have a strong physique and could well have been a rugby player. He had a very expressive face which was accentuated by sharp cheek bones and pronounced frown lines. His nose looked as if it had been broken which seemed to re-emphasise the connection with rugby unless someone had previously got fed up with his insolence and whacked him one.

He was certainly a handsome specimen, she thought, and, before she could stop herself, Hunter found herself offering an olive branch to Vance.

'I'm not used to being accosted in the street, Mr Vance, and I'd impress upon you not to do it again as there might be a very different outcome next time. However, there is one thing that you and your readers – or whatever they are – can help us with.'

Vance stared at her, wide-eyed.

'Do you know the name of the owner of Tideswell Manor?' Hunter asked.

'Yep. Baz Biondi last time I checked,' Vance replied.

'Do you know where he is right at this moment?'

'Nope! But probably out of the country. He's not got much time for old Blighty these days.'

'Okay, Mr Vance. Here's how you can help us.' She paused for maximum impact. 'Find him!'

Vance's jaw visibly dropped which gave Hunter a bit of a kick. She was suddenly enjoying this encounter.

'Well now, hold on! Aren't you going to give me any clues?' Vance spluttered.

'If I had any clues, do you think I would ask you for help? You claim to have all these readers or subscribers from all over the world. I would have thought that this would be an ideal project for your people to engage in. What a lot of fun having a live person to hunt down. Because we definitely want to talk to him. So, if you find him, who knows what sort of business we might be able to do with you in the future.'

Vance had recovered a bit of his composure.

'And when I find him?' he asked.

'Well, you come and tell me of course,' Hunter replied, 'but not in the street. The station would be a better venue for our next meeting.'

His face took on a rather bewildered look as if he couldn't quite believe that she was asking him to help her.

'And don't you come wasting my time unless you've got solid evidence that you know where he is,' she added. 'Just remember who's doing who a favour here.'

And then she was gone.

53

Monday 4 May

With sleep still seemingly not within touching distance, Sarah Hunter stared at the ceiling above her bed even though, in truth, she couldn't see anything of it. The shutters on her bedroom window kept out most of any moonlight there was and the thick curtains cut off any slivers of ambient light which might have penetrated the wooden slats. The sound of Grace's gentle breathing told Sarah that she was the only one awake in the house so she determined to make good use of the time in which sleep resolutely refused to come.

Sunday afternoon had been spent mainly with Grace and Selitto although Jed Crowther and Lisa Calder had dropped in to report back on the findings of Annalise Vardy's forensics team. They had then gone back over all the information they had on the crash site to make sure they weren't missing anything. Eventually, Selitto had to leave as he'd arranged to meet some friends for a meal in Sevenoaks.

Sarah and Grace had then decamped to The Vauxhall for a plate of Sunday roast just to provide sustenance, Sarah in particular having had very little to eat all day. Their conversation was rather shallow which was more a reflection of the exhaustion which was beginning to overwhelm each of them. So the sight of Sarah's little cottage and the welcome embrace of her warm duvet should have sent her straight off into the land of dreams.

But there was still so much to think about, details of her investigations to review, information to forensically examine.

There was something about the meeting at Maidstone which had felt bizarre but she couldn't put her finger on exactly what it was. It was clear that none of them wanted to question the suspect for fear of blowing their own cover. Fair enough! But why were they apparently going through with the drugs sting if they thought that they had Arcane bang to rights for the One Tree Hill killing? Or was there still some doubt about that?

Hunter recalled pointing out that, just because Arcane's phone had sent the message to the driver's phone, it didn't necessarily prove that Arcane had been there in person. She also had her own private doubts about the validity of the evidence of the gun found at the armourer's workshop on Sheppey. Although Arcane had been caught on film making two visits to the premises, it didn't prove that he had shot anyone with the firearm. He could make out that he had only been getting rid of it for a mate in which case he might be convicted as an accessory to the crime but not an out-and-out killer. He could also say that he had never seen the gun before and had simply been making a kindly social visit.

This was going to be tough!

She would have to work out her interviewing tactics carefully. Would she discuss them with Pennington first? Would he expect to dictate to her how he wanted the interview conducted? Should she have Ted Selitto with her rather than some faceless sidekick from the Serious Crime Directorate?

She turned over so that she was now facing the bedroom door and was pleased to see that there wasn't a thin line of light showing under the door. In the early days of overnighting at Sarah's house, Grace seemed to have a blind spot about turning off all the lights downstairs before going up to bed and, although she was now much more diligent, there were occasional nights when Sarah had to get up and go down to turn off an offending light.

Her mind turned to the destruction of Tideswell Manor and the disappearance of Baz Biondi. Thankfully, there had been progress on their investigation after Captain Donaldson had confirmed that the equipment photographed by Crowther and Calder was probably some sort of crude ILS system, although he was still amazed at how the aircraft had hit the manor with such pinpoint accuracy.

Donaldson had still been on his call to Kendall and Selitto when Sarah had got back from Maidstone so she had taken the opportunity to quiz him about making people disappear from the departures lounge at Gatwick Airport. Although he had professed not to know much about how airport security worked, he had told them that he believed it would be possible to move someone from the main lounge to the private lounge without too much trouble. He gave the impression that all major international airports had miles of narrow corridors which were totally unseen by the travelling public. He also felt that formalities were much more relaxed in private lounges so it was unlikely that anyone would have suspected that Biondi was being escorted out of the country against his will. Even if they had drugged him, Donaldson didn't think that the men would have been denied passage to their aircraft.

But Sarah was still wondering just where Biondi had been taken. Could Pascal Hennenbont really have organised what amounted to the kidnapping of both Biondi and Frobisher? It certainly seemed that way although they had probably been split up on arrival from Bermuda with Frobisher being taken to the cellar at Tideswell. Had Biondi also been taken there? Perhaps the plan was to put him in the snake pit as well. Or somewhere else on the premises where he would be killed by the aircraft ploughing into the building. So, did Hennenbont organise the plane crash to get rid of Biondi and some of his cronies who were also going to be there? If so, why was he suddenly whisked off to a private lounge in Gatwick Airport and then flown out of the country to northern France? Perhaps the Frenchman had wanted to kill Biondi himself. The destruction of Tideswell goes ahead as planned, Frobisher's already dead in the cellar, the crash takes out any number of minor dealers who could have been a nuisance to Hennenbont's organisation, and the big man himself gets to deal with the cherry on the cake – Biondi.

Sarah blinked in the dark. Her head was swimming with the points and counter points of her case against Hennenbont. And then her thoughts suddenly turned to the two passengers in the taxi.

'Of course!' It was more than a whisper as she castigated herself for failing to follow the signals which Beth Dench had been giving her about the connection with France. Could it be that the men were two of Hennenbont's henchmen? Had they arranged some sort of business meeting with Arcane at One Tree Hill? If so, why had they been killed?

Jordan Wright's words also came flooding back to her.

'Both Ramdeen and Arcane are known to be extremely protective of their territories and we've been looking at whether this protectionism may have had something to do with the One Tree Hill incident.'

Her eyes were drilling into the blackness of the room, unable to penetrate its all-enveloping aura. And then another thought.

Ramdeen was unarmed. He couldn't have shot anyone. But he had been complicit in bringing the two Frenchmen to One Tree Hill. He had *delivered* them. He had *delivered* them to a carefully planned ambush.

The more she thought about it, the more she convinced herself that the only purpose of the encounter was to kill the two in the taxi and that Ramdeen was the conduit to achieving this. She was also convinced that the *NOW* text was a pre-planned signal to Ramdeen to unlock the doors of the vehicle. Once the two passengers heard the clicking as the doors unlocked, they immediately realised the peril they were in. Ramdeen had to pay the price.

But was Arcane actually there? Stone couldn't have acted alone so there would have to have been another gunman. But was it Arcane? More importantly, who were the two passengersin the taxi? She needed identities.

Turning over so that she was now facing her friend and colleague, Sarah closed her eyes but still sleep wouldn't come.

54

Monday 4 May

'So, you're saying that you can definitely detect an accent in these recordings, and that this accent is not that of a native English-speaking individual?'

Grace Kendall was sitting in the Interview Suite which now had the acronym *IS One* although no one knew why it had been given a number as there wasn't enough space for another such room within the police station.

Kendall was putting the question to a rather prim young woman who sat opposite the DS with a set of headphones clamped over a bob of black hair. A pair of rimless glasses was perched on a classically shaped nose and her hazel eyes roved across the desk in front of her as she furiously concentrated on what she was listening to. Eventually she lifted one of the ear cups and clamped it to the side of her head.

'It's only a very slight distortion but I'm sure the speaker is either a natural bilinguist or he has lived outside his homeland for so long that most traces of his mother tongue have disappeared.' The woman leant over the desk and clicked the mouse to stop the recording and then sat back in her chair looking at Kendall.

'Any guesses?' Grace asked more in hope than anything else. She knew how much these so-called experts tried to protect their opinions, particularly if there was an area of doubt no matter how small. Anything that might make it difficult to get their theory accepted in court.

The woman removed the headphones altogether and laid

them on the desk in front of her. She then adjusted her position so that she now sat with a straight back, her hands clasped together in her lap. The pose reminded Grace of the teacher who had taught religious knowledge at her school. She had always struck Grace as a rather parsimonious character and, judging by the way she dressed, it seemed likely that she adopted a frugal lifestyle.

'Well, I think we can discount a Germanic or Hispanic influence,' the woman replied with an air of confidence, 'although we mustn't forget that the origins of the English language were brought to Britain by Anglo Saxon migrants from northern Germany and southern Denmark. But that was over fifteen hundred years ago and the language has evolved considerably in the intervening period.'

Kendall took a surreptitious glance at the clock on the bottom right corner of her screen. *Come on, woman, I've got a crime to solve!*

'And there is no evidence of a Scandinavian or Dutch accent or, indeed, any eastern European accents. Which really just leaves us with …'

'Good old France!' Grace exclaimed just as Sarah Hunter put her head round the door and looked towards where Kendall was sitting. Grace waved at her to join them.

'Hi Sarah, this is Faye Valentine, our linguistics expert for this case. She's a professor at the University of Kent.'

The two women shook hands and Hunter pulled another chair up to the desk. 'Making progress?' she asked.

'Probably,' Grace conceded. 'Faye is of the opinion that there may be an underlying French accent in the voice.'

'It's very feint,' Valentine cut in as if trying to defend her claim, 'but I am sure that some of the inflexions in the voice would lead us to believe that its owner was of French origin.'

'So that's another French connection,' Hunter stated, 'to go along with all the others. Which would seem to give substance to the suspicion that someone in France was not at all happy about some of the things that have been going on here. Real turf wars stuff but on a grand scale.'

Faye Valentine looked blankly at Hunter.

'Sorry Faye. Just thinking out loud about how all this is starting to fit together. But it's good to know that the pilot could have begun his journey of destruction in France.'

They had said their goodbyes to Valentine soon after her revelation about the French inflection in the recorded voice, and were now sitting together at Grace's desk in the MIR.

Grace had taken a phone call almost as soon as she had sat down so Hunter looked around the room, taking in the buzz of activity which investigations of this enormity always generated. Even though it was a public holiday outside, the civilian analysts were hard at work processing a mountain of information which had been collected from Tideswell Manor. The team had also been boosted by the arrival of a couple of DCs who had come off other cases which were winding down.

Hunter was pleased to see that DC Stuart Crosby was deep in discussion with Ted Selitto and Azzar Mishraz. She would catch up with him later as he would need to get up to speed very quickly if he was going to provide the sort of input she required at this stage in the investigation. She had also noticed a message on her phone from Carolyn Pennant who was still acting as their eyes and ears at the morgue and at the hospital where the Buckley girl was being cared for. Pennant was no doubt looking for a change of scenery which Hunter could understand but she wanted Carolyn to remain at her post for the next forty eight hours by which time the pathologists should have completed their work. She thought of calling Pennant back but then settled on sending her a text message to say that she would give her a call later on.

Looking over at Grace, she saw that the DS had a map spread across her two screens which she was studying intently. Hunter leant in to get a better view of the area covered by the map but it didn't look like anywhere that she knew. Grace had now converted it to a satellite image and zoomed in on the bottom corner of the area. Hunter now moved her chair closer to the desk and peered intently at the screen.

Kendall was rotating the cursor over an airfield which seemed to be very adjacent to the sea. The runway had the numbers fourteen and thirty-two painted in huge white numerals at either end of it and ran alongside a jagged and rock-strewn coastline. Small aircraft were parked around some buildings, one of which looked like a hangar. And then Grace zoomed in on one of the buildings and Hunter saw some words appear on the screen which really caught her interest.

Aerodrome du Grand Phare.

Where was this place? She watched as Grace zoomed out from the building and then moved the cursor slightly to the right. And there it was. A huge lighthouse on its own patch of ground about half a mile from the airfield. Grace zoomed in on the lighthouse and its outbuildings and then zoomed right out until it became clear that the structure was located on a small islet.

Hunter watched, fascinated, as thoughts started to criss-cross her mind. And then another coastline appeared at the top right corner of the screen and she was suddenly certain about what she was going to see next. Grace continued to slowly zoom out with a couple of delicate spins of the mouse wheel until the city of Nantes came into view.

There it was. The sixth largest city in France. The last known destination of Baz Biondi, international rock star and owner of what was left of Tideswell Manor. But was this really the destination of a flight which took off from Gatwick ten days previously? Hunter felt as if she was about to find out.

Kendall had quickly ended the call and was now refocusing the map on the screen to show the islet and, in particular, the airfield.

'Right! I think we might be getting somewhere,' she said breathlessly. 'You might remember that I spent time talking to an air traffic controller in France when we were trying to trace that Harrison woman. He's based at the airport at Lannion on the Brest Peninsula. Very helpful guy.'

Hunter had a vague recollection of Grace speaking to a French ATC but couldn't immediately recall the detail.

'Well, I thought I'd get on to him and see if he could shed any light on our mystery flight to Nantes. I could only give him the date and approximate time of departure from Gatwick although I also discovered that the aircraft involved was a Pilatus PC-24 with a Swiss registration number. Anyway, that was him getting back to me.'

Sarah Hunter never liked leaving loose ends so she was particularly keen to hear what had happened to that flight.

'It seems that the flight was tracked all the way to the Brest

Peninsula but then embarked on a rather circuitous route towards Nantes which took it out into the Atlantic. The next thing anyone on the ground knew was that the pilot had declared an emergency and had landed on the *Ile d'Yeu* which is this island.' Kendall pointed to the image on her screen and to the airfield on the Atlantic coastline.

'And presumably no report of anything wrong with the aircraft once it had landed?' Hunter murmured.

'No incident report or anything like that,' Grace confirmed, 'and the aircraft was gone the following day. As far as anyone knows, it's parked up on an airfield at Interlaken in Switzerland.'

'So that's it then,' Hunter sighed. 'Do we just assume that Biondi was offloaded on this island and left to his fate, presumably at the hands of Hennenbont?'

'That's pretty much how I had scored it,' Grace continued. 'Hennenbont seems to have a predilection for islands which make it more difficult for his enemies to get to him. Quite a sensible plan, really.'

Hunter was imagining what had happened next. A fast launch or rib from the Ile d'Yeu round to Bréhat followed by a bullet through the head. Or perhaps a bit of gratuitous mutilation before the bullet. And then a slab of concrete tied round his waist. Welcome to your watery grave, Mr Biondi.

'Okay, Grace, good work,' Hunter said as she moved her chair away from the desk. 'There's still a lot of supposition in all this but, from all the evidence we're collecting, and judging by what we know of the Hennenbont set up, I think it's a fair bet that Biondi's no longer with us. And that the Frenchman was responsible for the destruction of Tideswell Manor.'

55
Monday 4 May

DCI Alan Iversen sat behind his desk twirling a pen through his fingers Hunter sat opposite him trying to hide her annoyance at being unable to do this trick, all her efforts ending with the writing implement spinning out of her grasp and away to the corners of a room. God! She had tried to get the hang of it but had never mastered the art.

She was also annoyed that Iversen had cornered her in the kitchen area while she was sneaking a cup of coffee in between informal chats with members of her team. But she had dutifully followed Iversen to his office on the promise that it would only be a five minute update. He had to be in Medway by three o'clock.

'So, you're pretty sure that Tideswell's down to Hennenbont?' Iversen asked as he leaned forward, placing his elbows on the desk.

'I think so, sir,' Hunter replied. 'There are so many connections with France that everything points to someone masterminding operations from across the Channel. And we're as certain as we can be that it was Hennenbont's operation to land all that gear on the beach down near Winchelsea last year. We're also pretty certain that the assassin used to destabilise his plans was in the pay of Biondi.'

'The Frenchman must have gone to extraordinary lengths to get that woman back to the UK,' Iversen interjected. 'Arranging a pick-up in Bermuda and then getting her and Biondi back to Tideswell. Kidnapping in plain sight.'

'Meticulously planned I'd say,' Hunter continued, 'and effective. Although so much could have gone wrong.'

Iversen frowned. 'How do you mean?'

'Well, if we go back to the assault on the manor building, the aircraft could have missed the target for a start. I mean, the instrument landing system which had been installed was very crude and it seems surprising that it worked at all. And so many things could have gone wrong while transporting Biondi and Samantha Frobisher across the Atlantic. But, if it really was a meticulously planned operation, then it certainly achieved its objective. So we should probably consider that Mr Hennenbont is a very dangerous international criminal of considerable means.'

Iversen switched tack. 'How are you getting on with Pennington?'

'Well, I had a session with his team yesterday and he seems pretty sure that he can get a known drug dealer by the name of Johnnie Arcane for the One Tree Hill murders. Arcane seems to control a county lines empire which stretches over a large swathe of Kent and the fringes of south-east London. I'm hoping that his team will be able to put together a bit more of a case before we start questioning him because I don't feel that there's enough hard evidence to get a conviction – yet. Needs a bit more work.'

Iversen sat back in his chair.

'Pennington's normally nothing if not thorough,' he said, allowing his gaze to wander around the room, 'so I imagine that he thinks he'll be able to get more concrete evidence before he goes in.'

'Before *I* go in,' Hunter interrupted.

'Before *you* go in? I thought he was running this case.'

'He is but he doesn't want his team involved until he's certain that he's going to get a conviction. There's a lot going on here and the Serious Crimes Directorate seem to have spent a great deal of time working out how to get Arcane. They've even planned some sort of sting operation which may yet play out if they can't get him for One Tree Hill.'

'Yes, I think I've heard about the sting. Superintendent Eaves doesn't seem to be in favour because of the laws on entrapment but Pennington's keen to press ahead. In fact, it's already running isn't it?'

Hunter nodded. 'It is but they now think that Arcane's got some trouble finding the cash for the drugs which could scupper the whole thing so One Tree Hill becomes a very important alternative.'

'And the problem with that is what?' Iversen asked.

'At the moment, evidence seems to be heavily reliant on a text message allegedly sent by Arcane to the driver of the taxi which was a signal to spring the door locks so that the gunmen could get at the passengers. My reservation is that Arcane would not necessarily have needed to be at One Tree Hill to send the text message so a conviction for murder would be difficult unless forensics come up with something.'

'Or ballistics, presumably,' Iversen added. 'Where's your money?'

'I think he probably killed one of the men but I'm playing Devil's Advocate with Pennington's team just to make sure that they leave no stone unturned. At the moment it's not a slam dunk.'

Iversen gave her a confused stare, his brow deeply furrowed.

'A basketball term apparently,' Hunter clarified. 'Slang for an absolute certainty with a touch of drama and humiliation.'

Iversen now looked even more confused. 'Okay. Keep me up to speed on this because I'll only be getting the third degree from that bloody woman Eaves. And I don't want her to catch me with my trousers down.'

Hunter tried to stifle a laugh but it came out as more of a snort. The thought of Eaves seeing Iversen with his trousers down seemed an intriguing proposition. 'Don't worry. I'll make sure that you know just as much as she does if not more.'

'Right, better get going,' Iversen said as he abruptly rose from his chair, looking at his watch. 'The traffic should be hell at this time of day so I need plenty of time. Has Crosby arrived yet?'

Hunter confirmed Stuart's arrival but that she had not yet had a chance to catch up with him.

'Did a good job down at Canterbury by all accounts,' Iversen said as he gathered his papers and made for the door. 'Recommended for promotion to DS so we'll have to look at that.'

In the corridor, Iversen bade Hunter farewell and strode off to the stairwell, the sound of his shoes clattering on the wooden slats as he descended to the car park. Hunter stood and listened until she was sure that he had left the building.

She had a lot on her mind as she took to the stairs and descended to the next floor, feeling the stirring of a butterfly or two in the pit of her stomach as she made her way back to the MIR.

56

Monday 4 May

Sarah Hunter allowed the strains of Al Stewart's *Year of the Cat* to wash over her as she parked her car outside the building which housed the Kent & Essex Serious Crime Directorate at Kent Police HQ in Maidstone. She sat back in her seat, keenly anticipating Phil Kenzie's haunting alto sax which she found so dominating in the last instrumental section.

After Sarah had parted company with Iversen, she had returned to the MIR but had almost immediately received a call from Pennington suggesting that she get over to Maidstone pronto. She had thought of telling him that he'd have to wait as she had other matters to attend to at Tonbridge but something in the tone of his voice made her think that giving such a response might be unwise.

She now entered the building and was met by the same female police constable who had been on duty the day before. Hunter wondered if the poor woman did anything other than show people up to Pennington's suite of offices but decided not to ask in case it was deemed to be a rather frivolous or gratuitous remark.

Today, she was shown into the main SCD suite and directed towards a glass cubicle in which Pennington and Stig Shanahan were sitting, heads together as they pored over a map laid out on the table in front of them. The door was open so she just walked in as Pennington looked up.

'Ah, Sarah, have a seat. Tea and coffee over there.' He pointed loosely to a cabinet which had a couple of thermos jugs on it.

'Help yourself. I'll be with you in a sec.'

She couldn't be bothered with a hot drink which would probably be well stewed by now but she had spotted some small bottles of mineral water so she retrieved one of those before taking her seat on the other side of the table. As she couldn't really see what Pennington and Shanahan were looking at, she took out her phone and scrolled through her messages. One message caught her eye and she opened it.

My readers R on the case. Lots of sightings. I'll be in touch.

'Yeah,' she muttered to herself under her breath, 'in your dreams, Mr Vance.' Lots of sightings at any number of different locations all around the UK if not around the world, and all on the same day no doubt. Happened all the time when you got the public involved. There was another message from Carolyn Pennant asking if Hunter had received her earlier request for a call about her continuing assignment at the mortuary. She made a mental note to call Carolyn on her way back from Maidstone.

'Okay, Sarah!' Pennington's voice burst into her thoughts and she looked up to see Shanahan leaving the room. 'Sorry for the summons but things are hotting up here with the result that we've had a change of plan.'

The map had now been folded away and Pennington opened up a manilla file which had been under the map. Hunter drew her chair up to the table and rested her forearms on its edge.

'Okay, here's where we're at,' Pennington started. 'We've been working with our colleagues in Europe in an effort to see if we can identify the two bodies in the taxi and thereby come to some understanding as to why they were killed. As you may know, the UK signed a Trade and Cooperation Agreement with the EU following Brexit which governs police cooperation and the exchange of information. More specifically, this lays down provisions under which EU Member States grant access to their automated DNA analysis files, fingerprint identification systems and vehicle registration data.'

Hunter nodded. She knew about this so-called cooperation as she had had some communication with the Europol organisation following the sex trafficking case a couple of years earlier.

'Part of the agreement obliges the UK and EU member states to make all categories of data available for search and comparison to the competent law enforcement agencies of other states on a similar basis to that applying to their domestic authorities. Which, in a nutshell, means that we should be able to rely on cooperation from our colleagues across the EU in the same way as we might work together with Hantspol or Sussex Police.'

Hunter maintained eye contact with Pennington, wondering where this was leading.

'Beth Dench who, as you know, is the worker of miracles has been able to organise DNA tests for the two men who were shot dead in the taxi and, what's more, she was able to get the results in double quick time. These have now been sent off to Europol along with the fingerprints which her team took.'

Pennington started to thumb through the papers in the file. Was he looking for information received from Europol? Hunter couldn't be sure.

At last he seemed to have selected one sheet of paper for closer inspection. Hunter was getting impatient.

'Anything in there that's going to help us?' she asked, rather pointedly.

'Looks like Europol think that one of the two men in the taxi could be a certain Victor Joucas. However, they're saying it's not a particularly close DNA match and the fingerprint records seem to be corrupted. So, I'm afraid that we will once again have to rely to a certain degree on supposition, although Joucas is at least known to the French police in connection with drug dealing and money laundering.'

'Doesn't sound as if the French are particularly interested in the fact that he's turned up here dead,' Hunter mused. 'Just by saying that he was *known* to them indicates that the *Gendarmerie* weren't exactly beating a path to his door. And why would he have been here in the UK?'

'No idea,' Pennington sighed. 'We've checked with the UK Border Force people but they have no record of him arriving in the UK so he either travels on a false passport or he got here without going through an official port of entry.'

'Or he hasn't entered the UK and it's not his body in a fridge at the mortuary.' Hunter felt that her flippancy was justified in a discussion which was clearly getting them nowhere. She stared at Pennington.

'Nothing on the other guy in the taxi, I suppose?' It was more of a statement as she knew what Pennington's answer was going to be.

'Nothing through these channels of communication,' he replied, 'which could mean that the man wasn't on their radar or simply doesn't have a record in France – or, indeed, in Europe.'

'And if he's a Brit, there are no DNA or fingerprint records of him in the UK?'

Pennington shook his head.

'Not as far as we're aware. However, we've received some uncorroborated intel from one of Stig's contacts in the Met's undercover ops group. They've been shadowing a major county lines player for a few months but he now seems to have disappeared.'

'What? Disappeared as in *suddenly* disappeared after last Thursday?' Hunter asked with a note of sarcasm in her voice.

'Something like that,' Pennington confirmed. 'Anyway, the other intel that Stig picked up was that this guy travels to France quite regularly.'

Hunter raised her eyebrows. 'Must be a nice little number for the surveillance officers, swanning off to France every few weeks.'

'They're only watching him here in the UK apparently,' Pennington replied, defensively. 'Anyway, the man in question is Ajaccio Agostini. Originally from Corsica, his parents moved to the UK when he was six years old. They still live in Plumstead. Agostini runs a sophisticated, organised and incredibly violent group of county lines drug dealers and distributors in south and east London with gangs operating right to the edges of the Greater London area. Although he was known to the Met, they tend to concentrate more on taking out the distributors who are supplying the runners with the drugs. They're the line holders and cause the biggest threat. As with our own operation in Kent and Essex, disruption is the name of the game and disrupting the distribution and dealing activities is the best way of tackling the county lines problem.'

'So, has Agostini got a free pass from the Met just to go about his daily business with no risk of having his collar felt?'

Hunter had long been concerned that the powers-that-be

had become a bit selective about who they went after in some of the more sophisticated criminal activities which had become the norm these days. It sounded as if Agostini would have been a prime example of someone who was responsible for so much pain and suffering but that very little would have been achieved by taking him off the grid. Certainly not in the way that county lines operated.

'That's a rather jaundiced view, Sarah,' Pennington replied although she detected that he was trying to hide a wry smile. 'The other point to note is that Agostini doesn't seem to have spent very much of his time in the UK in the last year or so.

'So, are we to infer that he has spent a lot of his time in France?' Hunter mused.

'Well, we are going to ask Europol to put us in touch with the French police so we can find out if they have any interest in Agostini. We'll also find out if they have had any recent interest in Joucas. However, as you have pointed out, it sounds as if he is not on their radar at the moment.'

'If you ask me, it actually looks as if neither of them are on the radar at the moment,' Hunter said as she got up and wandered over to the coffee pots where she had spotted a plate of chocolate biscuits. 'In fact, did they even know each other?'

'Must have done!' Pennington exclaimed.

'So, what the hell were they doing at One Tree Hill?' Hunter asked as she re-took her seat.

They lapsed into silence, Hunter enjoying the biscuit and then licking the melted chocolate off her fingers.

'Perhaps they were on a fishing expedition,' Hunter eventually offered. 'Perhaps Agostini was assessing his options for taking over Arcane's patch. Perhaps he brought Joucas along for support. Whatever they were doing, it's clear that someone didn't approve.'

'That's what it looks like,' Pennington agreed, 'and one can only assume that Arcane wasn't prepared to even listen to anything they had to say. From the evidence gathered by the CSIs, someone – probably Arcane – just turned up and shot them. Couldn't even be bothered to have a chat.'

'Any further background on Arcane?' Hunter asked.

'Rory's done a lot of the investigation work on him. Surrounds himself with tough, uncompromising distributors who use violence and coercion to get things done. There is evidence of them carrying out acts of violence and torture on vulnerable adults who want to leave the gangs or who are suspected of keeping some of the proceeds of sale. These acts are filmed and put up on platforms on the dark web as a warning to others. We've been able to track down where one of the videos was filmed but the perpetrators had been long gone by the time we got there.'

Pennington got up to get a fresh cup of coffee.

'Anyway, Sarah, the CSI team have also paid a visit to Charles Stone's house in Thamesmead which Arcane visited on Saturday. Sounds like a typical distribution centre. Plenty of Class A gear ready to go but, strangely, very little cash. Also looks as if he had one of these torture rooms and all sorts of other delights. We've got evidence of Arcane visiting so we can use that.'

Hunter made a mental note to check this out with Beth Dench. She needed to know exactly what they had found at the Thamesmead property and why Arcane had needed to go there so soon after leaving Stone for dead outside the Medway

Maritime Hospital.

Pennington reached for the map and unfolded it to the extent that it now covered much of the table.

'Anyway, we've decided to pull Arcane now just in case he has any ideas of doing a runner. We're pretty certain that he's having to stand in for Ramdeen and Stone which he won't be enjoying and this'll be taking up most of his time. He's also still trying to find the cash to fund Rory's little deal so he'll be running around trying to get that organised. I doubt that he's going to allow the deal to slip through his fingers, and he'll be focused on the sort of earnings that Rory said he could get.'

'And when are you planning to lift him?' Hunter asked although, deep down, she thought she already knew the answer to her question.

'Around about 03.00 a.m. tomorrow morning. Okay with you?'

57

Tuesday 5 May

Sarah Hunter sensed that it was almost time to go. In the pale street lighting which seeped through the darkened windows of the unmarked police van, she could see that the DC from Pennington's team had put on his headgear and had made a hand signal to the others in the back of the van. Hunter couldn't for the life of her think what the signal meant but the uniformed officers seemed to understand as they quickly moved into position ready to disembark from the van.

Hunter glanced at the small LED clock on the vehicle's dashboard. It was now nearing 2.30 a.m. About forty-five minutes earlier, the van had ghosted along Maritime Way, past Chatham Maritime Marina and onto St Mary's Island. They were now positioned in a side street around the corner from Johnnie Arcane's apartment block. Two patrol cars had cordoned off the surrounding area.

The DC now opened the back doors of the van and the four officers jumped down to the road. Hunter, who was dressed in full riot gear, followed them as they lined up against the wall of the building. She noticed that a dog van was parked further up the street and a dog handler with a German Shepherd straining at the leash was heading their way. A smaller police van had parked beyond that.

The dog had a camera mounted on its back just behind its head so that the controller back at base in Maidstone could also see exactly what was happening immediately after entry had been effected. All the police officers including Hunter herself had body-mounted cameras which, similarly, streamed a photographic record of the encounter back to base.

The DC now stepped out into the street and craned his neck to look up to the top floor of the building. He then returned to the others and murmured that there was no sign of light in any of the windows. He had carried out the same procedure when the van had first parked up so it seemed probable that the occupant was asleep. They also knew that there was no one else at the apartment as the area had been the subject of a major surveillance operation over the last twenty-four hours.

Hunter clutched a sheaf of papers in her hand which included a warrant to arrest Arcane and one to search his property. The warrants had been obtained almost at the eleventh hour, and there had been serious concerns that the raid might have to be postponed by a couple of days – or longer. But Pennington's powers of persuasion had prevailed and they were now ready to go.

Once the group of officers had shuffled around the corner to the entrance to the apartments, one of them stepped forward to the entry mechanism and entered a code. There was a click as the main door was released and they were soon inside the building. Hunter wondered how they had managed to get a code for the door lock organised and made a mental note to ask Pennington.

Taking the stairs, they went up to the fourth floor which was the top level of the building. There were only two apartments on this floor and Pennington had discovered that one of them was unoccupied. Arcane's apartment was at the front of the building and they now stood flattened against the walls either side of the door. The DC beckoned Hunter and she moved along the corridor to stand directly outside the door. The DC nodded his head.

Hunter began rapping on the door. 'Johnnie Arcane!' she shouted. 'I am Detective Inspector Sarah Hunter of Kent Police. I have a warrant for your arrest and for the search of your property. You are required to open this door immediately.'

They all waited for what seemed like a lifetime but, in reality, was only a few seconds. She rapped on the door again, this time with more urgency, and repeated her demand that the door be opened. But there was still no response.

The DC looked at Hunter who nodded. There was only one way to gain entry here.

Bosh!

One of the uniformed officers stepped up to the door and thundered a mobile battering ram against it whilst the others prepared to storm into the apartment. The dog was pawing the floor and making little whining sounds.

Bosh!

Also known as the Big Red Key, the officer was using the ram to target the areas where the locking mechanisms on the door were likely to be in an effort to get into the apartment in the shortest possible time. The noise reverberated around the enclosed space of the corridor on the fourth floor of the block.

Bosh!

Now standing on the other side of the corridor, Hunter observed that two of the officers were carrying carbines and one of them had an X26 taser attached to the rear of his belt. As Pennington had intimated, they clearly weren't taking any chances, she thought.

Bosh!

The door finally gave way and fell into the apartment. The dog handler raced to the front of the line and let the dog off the leash. The other officers piled into the hallway, trampling over the redundant door and heading for the two main bedrooms. They had studied the layout of the apartment so knew the exact locations of all the rooms.

'Armed Police! Stay where you are! Don't move!' one of them shouted.

Sarah Hunter positioned herself just inside the apartment and watched as the organised chaos of the raid was played out in front of her. The stab-proof Kevlar vest was starting to dig into her waistband and her reinforced helmet felt as if it weighed a ton.

She heard a noise in the corridor and looked back out of the doorway to see Beth Dench and a small team of her forensics officers taking up position at the far end of the corridor. They would be ready to enter and search the apartment as soon as it had been declared safe to do so.

'In here! In here!' More shouting. Hunter could detect an urgency in the voice. The dog had been barking furiously amid the general melee which was taking place in one of the bedrooms.

'Stay where you are! Don't move! Do *not* move!'

There were more raised voices before the DC beckoned Hunter towards an open door. She passed him and entered the bedroom at the same time as the dog handler was ushering the German Shepherd out of the room.

It looked as if Arcane had been trying to get rid of some evidence in the ensuite bathroom but had been caught off guard by the dog and had sought sanctuary in the middle of his enormous king size bed. Two officers were now dragging Arcane off the bed, one of them pulling his arms behind him to slip the cuffs on. Wearing only a pair of frayed boxer shorts, Hunter was surprised by his physique. Not fat but not thin either. Muscular rather than musclebound. Tall but not particularly handsome. A number of visible scars on his body vied for space with a range of evil-looking tattoos, and were probably testament to the way he had lived his life thus far.

'Johnnie Arcane,' Hunter started, 'I am arresting you on suspicion of possession of Class A and Class B drugs with intent to supply which is classified as an offence under The Misuse of Drugs Act 1971 as amended.'

Arcane just stood there smirking.

'You do not have to say anything. But it may harm your defence if you do not mention now something which you later rely on in court. Anything you do say may be given in evidence.'

Hunter looked across the room at the man who had allegedly brought so much misery to the streets of Kent. He just smiled back at her.

'I am also arresting you for the murder of two persons unknown at One Tree Hill, Sevenoaks, on 30th April this year and for conspiracy to murder Gavinder Ramdeen at the same location and on the same date. Again, you do not have to say anything. But it may harm your defence if you do not mention now something which you later rely on in court. Anything you do say may be given in evidence.'

Pennington had decided to keep Joucas and Agostini's names off the charge sheet for the time being as they still hadn't been formally identified. In any case, he suspected that the charge was going to antagonise Arcane to the extent that it wouldn't really matter if the victims were named or not. On that supposition, he was about to be proved right.

'Hey now, just you wait a fucking minute!' Arcane shouted. 'You can't do that. That's not right!'

Hunter noticed how his face had suddenly darkened. His eyes had become narrow slits, a deep frown was etched into his forehead. Menace and hatred seeped out of every facial muscle. Dots of white saliva had formed at the corners of his mouth.

'Get him dressed,' she calmly told the arresting officers and turned to leave the room, not wanting to watch the struggle which was about to take place.

Arcane continued shouting. 'Hey! I said wait a fucking minute! Don't you lot fucking listen to anyone? Hey, come back whoever the fuck you are!'

Hunter had one foot in the hallway but hung back for a moment. She turned to face him.

'There'll be plenty of time for me to listen to what you've got to say when we're down at the station.' She left the room.

'Hey! Come back! I ain't got fuck all to do with Ramdeen.' There was a pause. 'Oi! Get your fucking hands off me!'

The sounds of protestation dimmed slightly as the door to the bedroom was slammed shut. She moved into the spacious lounge and kitchen areas of the apartment and across to where the DC was standing at one of the kitchen units taking photographs of a knife which he had laid out on the work surface.

'Not seen one of these before,' he said as Hunter approached. 'Looks like some kind of hunting knife. A fearsome weapon in anyone's language. Under the cushions on the chair over there.'

Hunter mumbled an acknowledgement. It certainly looked a very dangerous implement. Police officers had to be very careful on these raids. Weapons such as this were always secreted in places where the criminals could gain easy access.

'There's another weapon or other weapons either in the bedroom or the bathroom,' the DC continued, 'but he couldn't arm himself before the dog got him. We'll let forensics get them printed and bagged.'

Hunter had a quick look around and then walked over to the glass doors which led out to a small balcony area. She looked down on a carpet of street lights flickering across the rest of St Mary's Island after which there was a tongue of darkness which would be the River Medway. In the distance, more lights shone like a beacon from Hoo Marina. She didn't know the area well but could see that this would be a tremendous view on a sunny day.

As she walked back across the lounge, she tuned back into the stream of invective which continued to pour out of Arcane's mouth as he was manhandled out of the apartment and down to the waiting van.

The thought of spending hours in an interview room with this apology for a human being was suddenly a less than inviting prospect for DI Sarah Hunter.

58

Tuesday 5 May

The day had passed in a blur of activity. Meetings to review evidence. Meetings to discuss interview strategy. A meeting with the Assistant Chief Constable. Meetings for the sake of having meetings.

Sarah Hunter was surprisingly alert considering the amount of sleep she had had in the last forty-eight hours. After she had completed all the formalities in respect of Johnnie Arcane's arrest, she had gone home and crawled into her warm bed just as the first fingers of the dawn were caressing the base of the cloud cover on the horizon. Grace had hardly stirred as Sarah almost immediately fell into a deep and dreamless sleep.

Grace had woken her before she left the house as per the instructions that Sarah had scrawled on a slip of paper which she had placed on the kitchen table just two hours earlier. It was the last thing she had done before wearily climbing the stairs to the bedroom.

After Grace had left, she had turned over, wondering if she could snatch another half hour. But decided against it before reluctantly getting out of bed and heading for the shower. Turning the temperature control down, she had been immediately refreshed and energised by the pinpricks of icy cold water as they cascaded over her body.

After quickly towelling herself dry and dressing, she had applied a minimum amount of make-up before taking time to brush the knots out of her hair. Once downstairs, she had made herself two slices of toast and marmalade which she washed down with a mug of coffee.

On arrival at Pembury Road, Hunter had quickly got the team together in the MIR to brief them on the arrest of Arcane. She had also been able to give them information about the identities of Joucas and Agostini as well as filling them in about the probable connection with Hennenbont.

She had been pleased to see that Carolyn Pennant was seated at one of the desks. Whilst waiting in the van for the arrest team to get going, Sarah had sent Carolyn a text message to tell her that the assignment to the morgue was over and that she should return to the MIR in the morning. They had exchanged a smile across the crowded room.

Following the briefing, she had grabbed Ted Selitto and the two of them had driven over to Maidstone for a further briefing by Pennington and his acolytes. They were now listening to a presentation of the evidence gathered from Arcane's apartment. Although she would not yet have been to bed, Beth Dench looked remarkably fresh and was clearly up for the challenge of processing the evidence as quickly as possible.

'We've discovered supplies of Class A and B in various locations throughout the apartment, some of it hidden in quite ingenious places. There's also a lot of cash on the premises which he was presumably collecting so that he could get his hands on the gear that Rory was offering him.'

Easton smiled. 'Shame he won't be able to spend it now,' he quipped.

'There is, however, one significant find,' Dench continued. 'Ballistics have been fantastic on this and were quick to confirm that one of the guns removed from the armourer's premises was the one that killed the passenger sitting behind the driver. We've also found a small safe behind a false wall panel in Arcane's garage which contains guns. Using the information sent to us by Ballistics, we have been able to identify trace evidence from this gun in the safe. This would indicate that Arcane had stored it in his safe before taking it to Sheppey.'

'So it looks like Arcane killed Agostini,' Pennington summarised. 'Or at least Arcane handled the gun which killed Agostini even if he didn't fire it himself. Anything on the clothing?'

'We haven't found any clothing with the same trace evidence,' Dench replied, 'although there is one of those incinerators in the garden below the apartment which he could have used to burn his clothing. We're analysing the ashes at the moment and early signs are that a denim-based garment has been recently burned but we won't know more for a day or two.'

'Anything else from Ballistics?' Hunter asked.

'Yes,' Dench replied. 'It looks like Arcane originally took three weapons to the armourer. One was the gun that was used to shoot Agostini, and we think that one of the others was the gun used by Stone to kill Joucas. Ballistics have one of the bullets and are doing some further tests. The third weapon seems to be the one used by Agostini to kill the driver. A top-of-the-range Ruger which is probably in line with our assessment of Agostini's status. Trace on the gun matches that found on Agostini's clothes and there are prints to confirm that Agostini at least handled the weapon. There is a partial which almost certainly belongs to Arcane. As I think we've already established, Mr Joucas didn't fire his weapon.'

'And what about the driver?' Selitto asked, looking up from the copious notes he'd been making in his notebook.

'Yes,' Dench began, 'as I've just said, all the evidence points to the Ruger being the weapon which killed Ramdeen who was shot at almost point-blank range. In our view, he could have only been shot by Agostini.'

'What about phones?' Selitto probed further as he knew that mobile phones held increasingly important clues in major crimes.

'How long have you got?' Dench smiled. 'We found almost enough mobiles to start a small phone shop. They were secreted away all over Arcane's apartment. Even now, we may not have found all of them. The techies have been working flat out to make sense of what we've got. Thanks to some smart work from one of the arresting officers, we have the phone from which the *NOW* message was sent. Apparently Arcane was trying to get rid of it down the toilet when the dog attacked him and he didn't have time to flush. The quick-thinking officer scooped it out of the water and dried it on a towel. Once in the lab, they got it dried professionally and, because it was only in the water for a nano-second, they've been able to get into it.'

'So, we've got concrete evidence that Arcane's phone sent the *NOW* message?' Selitto butted in with a question.

'But that doesn't necessarily prove that he was the one who sent it,' Hunter followed up.

'There is something else we have been pondering,' Dench continued. 'The phone that received the *NOW* message doesn't show any evidence of having been kept in the phone holder in the taxi.'

Selitto looked up from his notes. 'Meaning?'

'Meaning that he may have had another phone which we have not yet found,' Dench replied.

They sat in silence.

'The driver's door was open wasn't it?' Hunter asked. Dench nodded. 'So, the only person who could have opened it was one of the gunmen. Supposing there *was* a phone in the holder, and the gunman who had opened the door was Arcane. He might have taken the phone in the holder in the belief that it was the phone to which he'd sent the *NOW* message.'

All eyes were on Hunter as she ran the sequence of events through in her head.

'Knowing that the phone would certainly incriminate him, he just had to get rid of the evidence. So, he took it without bothering to check whether it was the phone he had given to Ramdeen. It, therefore, follows that the phone we removed from Ramdeen's grasp is probably the one that Arcane gave him with the single objective of sending the *NOW* message to it.'

'Well, if that *is* the case,' Selitto interjected, 'Mr Arcane is going to get a hell of a fright when he sees that phone sitting on the table in front of him.'

59

Tuesday 5 May

Before she left to grab a few hours' sleep, Beth Dench had given them some further information about the house in Thamesmead.

'Annalise Vardy's team have been busy at the house which we know that Arcane visited. They've been concentrating on one room which is thought to be some sort of torture chamber. She described it as something akin to a padded cell. There are innumerable areas of blood spatter on the walls, on the floor and even on the ceiling. The room reeks of disinfectant and there's a lot of camera and lighting equipment lying around. Annalise reckons we should hand this area over to the Dark Web Team to see if they can get a match with any of the videos they've taken down from the net. A bit of a bonus you might say.'

'Okay, thanks for that, Beth,' Pennington concluded. 'Jordan's our liaison with that team so he'll take this over. Perhaps he can review what you've got and also take a look at the house before we get the Dark Web lot involved. Once it goes to them, we're pretty much out of it.'

Dench grunted an acknowledgment to Pennington's request before gathering up her papers and leaving the room with him in tow.

Hunter sat back in her chair. She was pleased that the evidence against Arcane was beginning to stack up. She should have plenty of scope for questioning the man once the interrogation process got under way, and his visit to the Thamesmead property gave her another angle if she needed more corroborative evidence.

Pennington soon returned having presumably seen Dench off the premises, and he held the door open for Selitto who had two mugs of coffee in his hands. He put them down on the table and took the seat next to Hunter, pushing one of the mugs in her direction as he did so. Pennington sat at the head of the table while Jordan Wright took a seat facing Hunter and Selitto.

'If that room's what we think it is, this could significantly help us in our efforts to stop these videos getting onto the web.' Pennington had clearly been buoyed by the evidence found in the Thamesmead house and looked across at Wright as if seeking confirmation that this could be a game-changer.

'Yes,' Wright agreed. 'We're trying to trace the location for the filming of the ritual torture of a young girl. Probably somewhere in north-west Kent, possibly near the border with the Met area in south London. If you're interested, I've got a short extract from a longer interview just to give you some background.'

'Okay,' Hunter agreed, 'might as well have a complete picture of what Arcane gets up to.'

'Well don't forget that this is a property belonging to Charles Stone,' Wright warned, 'and Arcane may have only visited occasionally. It is possible that he may not have had first-hand experience of what went on in the padded cell. Anyway, I'll play the tape.'

He tapped a few keys on the laptop in front of him and waited until the slightly tinny voice of a young girl could be heard.

'I was hangin' round with people who were runnin' their own lines like, know what I mean? They was makin' huge amounts of cash, you know, just mental what they was gettin' every week. And I 'ad nothink. Couldn't carry on livin' off my mum, could I? And she didn't have nothink much either.'

There was a pause, and Hunter detected sobbing and then a huge sigh.

'So, I asked this girl what she was gettin' and it was, like, six hundred quid per week. I mean, six hundred a *week*. I had to have some of that, didn't I? So, I started workin' as a courier and was takin' drugs long distances for a gang who the girl introduced me to. I was totally obsessed wiv gettin' six hundred quid each week. I just did what I was told and I'd get the money.'

There was another pause, some sniffing followed by a hoarse cough.

'Anyway, I soon realised that I didn't want to do the travellin' no more and tried to leave. You know what it's like. Travellin's boring if you're on your own. But the gang leaders didn't like that idea and beat the shit out of me. I got taken into a room with bright lights where I was beaten with fings I don't even know the names of.'

The girl's voice drifted off as she presumably recalled the horrendous treatment she had received. Hunter was finding herself quite moved listening to the girl's outpourings of grief.

'And then they strapped me into a chair and one of them pointed a gun at my head. I mean, I just shit myself. Couldn't control it. Piss and shit going everywhere as this guy spun the bullet thing. And then he pulled the trigger.'

Violent sobbing could be heard on the tape.

'I screamed but they all just laughed, didn't they. Then he

went round the back of me and put the gun to my head. I could feel the cold steel through my hair. Then I heard the thing being spun again. I was so terrified. Know what I mean? I just wanted them to get it over with. I actually wanted to die. And when he pulled the trigger I must have passed out.'

Wright turned the recording off.

'She was found on wasteland near the Thames in the Erith area. She had been very badly beaten and was barely alive. But now she's helping us with our enquiries and the Thamesmead house may well be where she was held. We also have a video of a man, probably in his thirties, being cut with a machete, burned with a blow torch and who had boiling water poured over him. These look like life-threatening injuries on the video which was uploaded earlier this year. However, we've been unable to find a record of anyone being treated for such injuries at A&E and we haven't found a body with this sort of disfigurement.'

There was silence in the room.

Selitto was shaking his head. 'This situation's only going to get worse as these gangs grow in number. They're also being bolstered by any number of criminals from other countries who are landing illegally on our beaches in Kent on a daily basis. It's like a marriage made in hell.'

Heads nodded at Selitto's summary of the situation.

Hunter looked at the clock on the wall. Time was marching on. She needed to have some preparation time before she kicked off her first session with Arcane.

60

Tuesday 5 May

As soon as he had arrived at Maidstone Police HQ, Johnnie Arcane had been taken to the Custody Suite and formally charged with possession of Class A and B drugs with intent to supply. Pennington was certain that he could make this charge stick bearing in mind the overwhelming evidence they had found in Arcane's apartment so they would proceed on this basis to start with.

Arcane had then been fingerprinted, had a DNA swab taken, been photographed and finally strip-searched which he had violently objected to. In the end, two other uniformed officers had to be summoned to restrain him whilst the search was completed. He was provided with some loose fitting clothing and ushered unceremoniously into a holding cell whilst still delivering a non-stop diatribe of verbal abuse and invective.

The plan had been to leave Arcane alone in the cell for at least twelve hours although Pennington was aware that this would eat into the time available for questioning him before they would be in a position to charge him with the more serious matter of conspiracy to murder or, indeed, murder itself. It was always a fine balancing act trying to get to the point where they had enough evidence to bring a charge before the clock ran down and they had to release the suspect. Ted Selitto had once described it as riding a unicycle whilst juggling three balls. Control and precision were key.

In the end, they had settled on starting the first session at 6.00 p.m.

Polly Wickenden had only been to Maidstone Police HQ on one previous occasion and had been trying to recall the details of that case as a Southeastern Railways train whisked her from her bijou residence in London's Pimlico to the less exuberant surroundings of Maidstone East railway station. The ensuing taxi journey to the police HQ was undertaken in complete silence. She surmised that perhaps the driver couldn't speak English or maybe he had just had a bad day. Either way, it was probably a blessing in disguise that there was no idle chat.

She had announced herself on arrival at the Custody Suite where a jolly Desk Sergeant had confirmed the details he had for her and took a note of other details which were missing from whatever file he was looking at on his computer screen. He then gave her an ID lanyard which she hung round her neck, and told her to take a seat while he contacted whoever was in charge of the case against her client, Johnnie Arcane.

Sitting rather stiffly on a hard, uncomfortable chair she again reflected on the fact that she had no previous knowledge of the man she was here to represent. Wickenden had been both surprised and rather put out when one of the Senior Partners in her firm had telephoned her and ordered her to get herself down to Maidstone *post-haste* to attend a police interview with one of their clients. It had been a working-from-home day when she liked nothing better than to slob around in loose-fitting clothes so a trip to mid-Kent meant a complete change of clothing plus a full application of make-up.

She hadn't worked for this particular Partner before and, in fact, she had not had any dealings with him at all as he had only recently joined the firm. Her visit to Maidstone had apparently been cleared with her boss but she couldn't verify this as her boss was in court all day. So she had no option but to convince herself that it would be good to get experience of another area of law, and that this assignment would give her an opportunity of doing just that.

Some information about Arcane had been emailed to her, and she had read it as the train meandered through the suburbs of London before picking up speed as it headed into the Kent countryside. However, the more she read, the more uneasy she became. This was taking her way out of her comfort zone. She stared out of the window but saw nothing, her head struggling to get a grip of the inside information her firm seemed to have on this man Arcane.

Wickenden had made her name in the Family Division of the legal system with one judge recently opining that she should come with a health warning every time she stepped into court. Of medium height, she had long auburn hair which she either pulled back and clamped with an Alice band or she wore up in a tight bun which made her look like a Victorian governess. Her ice blue eyes peered out through horn-rimmed spectacles which were far larger than she needed and only served to increase the severity of her scornful expressions when questioning unfortunate witnesses in court. Her pencil thin figure was nearly always adorned with a white high neck blouse and a navy blue two-piece suit.

Eventually, a door opened beside the reception desk and a uniformed constable crossed to where Wickenden was sitting. After checking her ID and confirming that she was, indeed, here to see Johnnie Arcane, he asked her to follow him as they went through another door leading off the reception area. After walking down a brightly lit corridor they came to a set of double doors with an array of different coloured lights above it. Obviously means something to someone, she thought.

The constable showed a plastic card to the card reader beside the doors and entered. Wickenden followed and immediately noticed the air change. It was much warmer in here and the atmosphere seemed to be redolent of sweat and toil.

She was shown into a small room which had a table and five chairs. The table was a metal construction and was bolted to the floor. The wooden chairs were arranged haphazardly around the table. A camera with red light flickering was mounted high up on the wall directly facing the door. There appeared to be no other recording equipment and, in fact, no other equipment of any sort in the room. The constable indicated that Wickenden should take a seat at the table and await the arrival of her client.

Once he had left, she had another look around the room checking for recording equipment but she couldn't see any. She had a closer look at the camera but it didn't seem to have the capacity for making a sound recording. Taking a seat so that she had her back to the camera, she retrieved her phone from her handbag. No signal.

Shit!

But what had she expected?

Putting her phone away, she pulled out her notebook and started to re-read the notes which she had been sent by email.

As she read, Wickenden became more and more concerned that she didn't have enough information to properly represent her client in the face of sustained police interrogation. She didn't feel comfortable. The butterflies were in full flight in the pit of her stomach.

She started to read the notes again but found it difficult

to concentrate as a commotion which had started some distance from where she was sitting steadily gained in intensity. Suddenly, the door flew open and two officers propelled a man into the room.

'Get your fucking hands off me,' the man raged. 'Leave me a-fucking-lone.' The officers roughly manhandled him into the chair opposite Wickenden as one of the officers looked across at the lawyer.

'Your client, ma'am. We'll be outside if you need us.'

'Fuck off!' the man shouted as the door closed.

Wickenden stared at Johnnie Arcane aghast, her face a picture of surprise and shock. Shaking her head as if to clear her vision, she quickly got a grip of herself and started to turn the pages of her notebook. Arcane stared down at the table and then let his eyes wander around the room, pausing for an instant to appraise the positioning of the camera. He looked everywhere except at Wickenden.

Silence hung in the room which only served to intensify the situation. Eventually Arcane looked at her and spoke.

'Did Goodchild send you?'

Wickenden frowned. She knew a Sam Goodchild who was one of the partners in the firm but it wasn't Sam who had sent her. Perhaps he had been working in the background and taken the call from Arcane or someone else at Maidstone and then passed it on to the Senior Partner.

'Er, no. It was Mr Latour who instructed me to come here,' she said, hoping that this wouldn't be a barrier to them getting started on the briefing.

Arcane screwed his eyes shut. 'Who the fuck's Latour?' he murmured.

Wickenden didn't want to sound as if she didn't know Latour so she chose her words carefully.

'Guy Latour is the newly appointed number two to our managing partner. He has only been with us for a couple of weeks so I don't know him very well. But he was in no doubt that I was to help you here at Maidstone.'

Arcane was suddenly agitated. 'Where the fuck's Goodchild? I wanted Goodchild to deal with these bastards! They promised I'd get Goodchild!'

'Mr Arcane! I am very sorry but it seems that Mr Goodchild was not available to make the journey to Maidstone. Which means that you now have me instead. We only have a short time to prepare for your first session of questioning and it would certainly be of far more benefit to me if we could spend the time discussing the charges against you rather than bickering about why I'm here and Mr Goodchild isn't.'

She sat back and looked at Arcane who's eyes were busily doing another circuit of the room.

'Okay! Okay! What do you want to know?'

61
Tuesday 5 May

Hunter and Selitto walked into the interview room and took the two seats nearest the door as convention dictated. Arcane and Wickenden faced them. A rather unlikely coupling was Hunter's first reaction. Selitto started the recording system, and he and Hunter introduced themselves for the tape. Polly Wickenden introduced herself and, after a pause, Arcane reluctantly identified himself. A uniformed constable stood by the door.

Hunter noticed that Wickenden looked very uncomfortable sitting next to a man she barely knew, and with whom she had just spent half-an-hour trying to understand the charges being brought against him and the response he wanted to give.

Selitto had a box containing items of evidence which he had placed on the table beside him. He also had two files and passed one of these to Hunter. There was an air of expectation in the room.

Arcane was slumped in his chair but Hunter could see that his hands were in a tight knot, the whites of his knuckles clearly visible. Meanwhile, his lawyer sat with her back ramrod straight, notebook open in front of her and her beautifully manicured right hand clutching an expensive Mont Blanc pen. The effect of her horn-rimmed glasses seemed to accentuate the size of her large blue eyes but Hunter could clearly see that they were full of fear and foreboding despite her provocative pose. She knew that she was about to make life even more difficult for Miss Wickenden.

'Mr Arcane, we'd like to start by asking you about an incident which took place at One Tree Hill, a National Trust property near Sevenoaks, on Thursday 30th April this year.'

Hunter was carefully watching Arcane as she spoke so that she could pick up the tiniest tick of recognition on his face. She certainly got more than she had bargained for when he suddenly exploded, eyes afire with pure hatred.

'What the fucking hell are you talking about?' he shouted. 'I've never even heard of the fucking place so how would I've been there?'

'Okay. Okay. Let's just agree that you've never been there. So, perhaps you can tell us what you were doing at around 10.00 p.m. on the night of 30th April.'

Wickenden perked up at this point. 'My client doesn't have to answer that as you clearly have no basis for asking such a question.'

Arcane smirked. Hunter took a different tack.

'You see, Johnnie, we think that you and others are involved in the supply of Class A and B drugs across north and west Kent, mid-Kent and along the Kent coast and Sussex borders. Another group of lads has come down from London and they're trying to muscle in on your patch. And you and your boys haven't liked it. In fact, you and your boys haven't liked it so much that you have set the London lads up and then done them over. In a nutshell, that's the allegation we're making today.'

Hunter sat back, staring at Arcane who was furiously shaking his head. Wickenden was scribbling something in her notebook.

'That's bullshit, and you know it!'

Hunter opened her file and pushed a photograph of Gavinder Ramdeen across the table. 'Do you know this man?'

'Never seen him in my life.'

'Perhaps you could actually look at the picture before answering the question, Mr Arcane.'

His head came up and his eyes shot a glance at the photograph before locking onto Hunter. 'I never fucking seen him, have I.'

'For the tape, I have shown Mr Arcane a photo of Gavinder Ramdeen,' Hunter formally announced before sliding another photograph out of the file and pushing it across the table.

'And this is what happened to your mate Ramdeen at One Tree Hill.'

Arcane glanced at the photograph which showed Ramdeen's body hanging out of the taxi. It held his gaze for a few seconds before he reverted to staring at the floor.

'No comment.'

Wickenden leant over to look at the photograph but almost immediately jerked back to her original position as if she had received an electric shock.

Selitto opened the box beside him and pulled out a plastic evidence bag which he passed to Hunter.

'For the tape, I am showing Mr Arcane Exhibit OTH/230042/56.' She pushed the evidence bag to the middle of the table.

Arcane's curiosity got the better of him and he looked at the little phone which nestled in the evidence bag in front of him. Hunter watched as the colour slowly drained from his face.

'Do you recognise this phone?' Hunter asked.

Arcane shook his head.

'For the benefit of the tape, Mr Arcane is shaking his head,' Selitto said as he handed another evidence bag to Hunter which she laid on the table beside the other bag.

'I am now showing Mr Arcane Exhibit OTH/230042/58.' She pushed the evidence bag to the middle of the table. 'Can you confirm that this is your phone, Mr Arcane?'

Arcane looked away. 'No comment.'

'Inspector, my Client clearly has no knowledge of these phones so I would ask that you desist from questioning him further in this vein.' Wickenden had come to life although Hunter's view was that she was completely out of her depth. So she just carried on as planned.

'The problem we have, Johnnie, is that there is only one number stored in the phone which was found on Mr Ramdeen's body and that is the number of the other phone which is alleged to belong to you.'

'That's crap and you know it!' Arcane spat the words at Hunter. 'You bastards could have put that number in that phone yourselves. You can put a phone number into any fucking phone you know.'

Hunter sat back and let silence fill the room.

'The problem with that remark, Johnnie, is that we could not have made your phone send a message to the other phone timed at 10.27 p.m. on Thursday 30th April. That would have had to be done by you. And what was the message you sent to your mate Ramdeen?'

'No comment!'

'You texted the word *NOW*. Why would you do that, Johnnie?'

'You're talking absolute fucking bollocks. You're in fairyland! No fucking comment!'

'You see, there's absolutely no doubt that this is your phone,' Hunter said, pointing to one of the evidence bags, 'as it has your fingerprints and probably DNA all over it. We think that you sent the *NOW* message to Ramdeen as a command to do something. Are we getting warm, Johnnie?

'Piss off!'

Wickenden sat awkwardly next to Arcane, her mouth starting to form words but never actually succeeding in saying anything. A metaphorical fish out of water.

'We also know that three phones left One Tree Hill at the same time that night. One of the phones is the one in this evidence bag which was later found at your property when you tried to flush it down the toilet. Another was a number registered to Ramdeen although this stopped transmitting soon after midnight. The third phone had been stolen and has not been found yet.'

'No comment!'

'You see, Johnnie, I've been doing a bit of thinking about the *NOW* message and I'm increasingly of the belief that you were telling Ramdeen to do something. And then it came to me. You were telling him to unlock the doors of the taxi so that you could open them and kill the occupants. Am I wrong?'

'Completely fucking deluded would be closer.'

Selitto intervened. 'The driver, Ramdeen, was the only person who could have unlocked the doors. But he couldn't have done that if he was dead so he must have done it before he was killed. And he did it on the signal from your phone.'

'That doesn't prove anything. And it certainly doesn't prove that I was anywhere near this godforsaken place. You're still talking fantasy bollocks.'

Arcane turned towards his solicitor, scowling and shrugging his shoulders.

'Inspector!' Wickenden had come to life. There was an urgency in this one word. 'Your evidence seems to be solely based on supposition. There are no hard facts and very little substantiated evidence. If you continue to accuse my client of an act or acts which are pure conjecture on your part then I will have to demand that he is released immediately.'

Hunter took this in her stride. Arcane wasn't going anywhere apart from back to his cell. She looked over at Selitto who opened the box and took out another evidence bag which he placed in the middle of the table.

'For the tape, I am showing Mr Arcane Exhibit OTH/230042/63.'

Arcane's interest was now piqued and he leaned over the table so that he could more clearly see what was in the bag. A look of fear suddenly washed over his face and he rocked back in his seat, eyes wide with loathing, veins throbbing at his temples, mouth jabbering unspoken words.

'Is this your gun, Mr Arcane?' Hunter asked matter-of-factly.

He stared at the weapon sealed in its plastic bag. After a while, he stared at Hunter.

'No comment!'

'You see, Johnnie, not only are your fingerprints on this weapon but we have admissible evidence that this was the gun which killed a gentleman by the name of Ajaccio Agostini at One Tree Hill on Thursday 30th April. We also have evidence that you tried to dispose of the weapon through a gun dealer on the Isle of Sheppey.'

Wickenden looked horrified as she involuntarily leaned in for a closer inspection of the gun.

Hunter locked eyes with Arcane once more. 'Did you

organise and take part in the attack on the taxi, Johnnie?'

'No fucking comment. You're talking out of your arse and you fucking know it. Fucking bollocks.'

Arcane was on his feet now, slamming his fist into the table. 'This is a fucking kangaroo court. You're all the fucking same. Dreamers!'

Wickenden's face had turned a delicate shade of cerise as she battled to comprehend exactly what was going on and what action would be expected of her. But she was clearly good at mediation and quickly managed to persuade Arcane to retake his seat. Having restored some kind of order to the proceedings, she then addressed Hunter.

'In view of the new allegations which you have brought this evening, I will need some time with my client to discuss these in detail and to help him to enter a reasoned response. I feel that this is only just and fair in the circumstances.'

Hunter felt that they should all take a break anyway so she got the constable to usher Arcane and Wickenden back to the meeting room they had been in before.

Selitto recorded the fact that the interview had been suspended and gave it a time check. He then turned the tape off.

Hunter slumped back in her chair while Selitto put the evidence bags back in the box and placed the photographs back in the file.

'Guilty as charged?' Hunter asked.

'Is there any other conclusion?' Selitto replied.

62

Tuesday 5 May

Polly Wickenden sat in the meeting room trying desperately to get a signal for her phone. She glared at the screen but the little bars resolutely failed to light up. They also didn't respond to a good tapping from a long manicured nail.

Arcane sat opposite, watching her with hollow eyes. He was clearly not paying the slightest bit of attention to her antics. There were far more important things on his mind.

Eventually, Wickenden gave up on the phone and opened her notebook. She glanced at the notes she had taken, realising that they had become more and more illegible as the evidence produced by the detectives had stacked up on the table in front of her. For a start, the forensic evidence seemed to put her client at the scene of the shooting, and the weapon used to kill one of the men had been handled by the man now sitting opposite her. She hadn't quite grasped all the nuances about the phones and the one message sent from one to another so she planned to now talk through the significance of this evidence with Arcane.

She cleared her throat and was just about to address her client when the door behind Arcane opened and the uniformed constable leaned into the room.

'Sorry to interrupt, ma'am, but you have someone from your office who needs to talk to you urgently. I'm to escort you back to the desk.'

Wickenden looked perplexed. She needed as much time as possible to talk to her client. What the hell was someone from the office doing here? Surely they could have messaged her with whatever information they had if it was obviously so urgent. She looked at her phone's messages – nothing there. Of course! No bloody signal, she reminded herself. Surely she couldn't just leave her client here unattended? Her face must have telegraphed this concern to the constable.

'Don't worry ma'am, we'll be keeping an eye on your client,' he said, pushing the door open further as if inviting her to follow him.

What was so damned urgent that they had to send someone all the way from London to talk to her? Or perhaps the messenger was local and working from home. In which case it made sense for him or her to just drop by with a message from on high.

Realising that she had no other option, Wickenden collected up her notebook, pen and handbag before edging her way out of the room. In the corridor, she bumped into two other uniformed constables who were approaching. As they passed her, she turned to watch as they entered the room and closed the door.

She was led along the corridor, through the double doors and back to the desk in the reception area where she had signed in earlier.

The Desk Sergeant looked up and smiled.

'Over there, Miss Wickenden,' he said, pointing to a smartly dressed man who was sitting on one of the uncomfortable chairs.

She looked across at the man but gave no sign of recognition. She frowned and turned back to the Desk Sergeant.

'Are you sure he asked for me?' she asked.

'Certainly did,' came the reply. 'His visiting card has got the details of your chambers. Same as the card you gave me when you arrived. Name of Philip Marchand.'

Who was he? She knew that she could never hope to know *everyone* in the firm, and all this working from home wasn't helping to improve her awareness of staff from different areas of law. But she had thought that they would at least send someone she knew. Oh well – perhaps he was a criminal law specialist living locally who could take over the godforsaken job of defending Arcane.

Thanking the Desk Sergeant, she turned and crossed the reception area to meet Mr Marchand.

'How long are you going to give them?' Selitto asked as he placed two mugs of coffee on the table in front of him.

They had been shown to the glass-walled meeting room in the Serious Crime Directorate suite and were awaiting the arrival of DCI Jack Pennington and his team.

He pushed a mug over to Sarah Hunter who was thumbing through one of the Maidstone freebie newspapers. Why did they call them *newspapers* when the last thing they contained was news? Another of life's little conundrums for her to think about if she ever had a quiet moment with time to excogitate.

'Looks like we could give that lawyer the rest of the night and she'd still not have got her head around the evidence,' Hunter smiled as she blew on her coffee to cool it down.

'She's not a criminal lawyer is she,' Selitto observed. 'Seems very strange to have contacts in one of the pre-eminent legal firms in Central London and then to find that you've not been sent the shit-hot bell-end you'd thought you'd get.'

'Well, she's certainly not a bell-end,' Hunter observed ruefully, 'and, on current evidence, she's not shit-hot so it'll be interesting to hear what she comes up with after her half-time pep talk with our man.'

She could see Pennington making his way across the crowded suite towards them. Nearly every desk was taken and it was already early evening. Impressive!

'Sorry to keep you,' he muttered as he entered the room and took a seat opposite the two detectives. 'Manic out there.'

Hunter, with a little help from Selitto, brought Pennington up to date on their first session with Arcane and filled him in on the misgivings they had about the lawyer who had been sent from London.

'That's the trouble you get with these large firms,' Pennington observed. 'They'll just send anyone as long as they get a fee for it. Mercenaries!'

He looked at his watch and then slipped a phone out of his shirt pocket before placing it on the table in front of him.

'Okay. What are you going to hit him with next?'

As she approached the man, Polly Wickenden became distracted by a couple of women who sat on the other side of the small reception area. One was sporting a black eye which covered most of the side of her face and she had one arm in a sling. The other woman appeared to be offering compassionate advice which was largely being ignored. There was much tearfulness, coughing and sniffling with noses being wiped on sleeves, a habit which always turned Wickenden's stomach.

Deciding that she didn't want to sit right beside the man or to have the two women in her line of sight, she left the seat next to him empty.

'Mr Marchand?' she asked as she sat down and turned to face him. She placed her notebook on the seat between them.

The man who appeared to have been watching the two women suddenly sprang to his feet and then just as quickly sat down again.

'Ah, Miss Wickenden,' he blustered, 'thank goodness they've been able to pull you out of the interview session.'

'Well, they called a break actually so I'm supposed to be in the room briefing my client. Instead, I'm sitting here talking to you so what's so bloody urgent?' She could feel her face heating up and knew that her cheeks had turned a shade of pink. But she was becoming exasperated by her lack of experience in dealing with someone like Arcane and by the fact that she was now having to waste more time talking to this man from the office.

'Well, I'm actually here to take over from you,' Marchand replied before pulling an envelope out of his jacket pocket. 'This is for you to read before we go any further.'

Maintaining eye contact with Marchand, she took the envelope and, after realising that it was not sealed, she withdrew a single sheet of the firm's headed notepaper. Her eyes immediately dropped to the name of the signatory. Once she realised it was from the same Senior Partner who had sent her on this mission in the first place, she began to read. When she had finished, she read it again to make sure that she hadn't missed anything. Then she looked up at Marchand.

'You know what's in this?'

'I do, yes. There's a car outside waiting to take you to the Refuge. It'll then take you back to London but it's vitally important that you meet up with your client in the Refuge before they are due in court tomorrow.'

Wickenden stared at the letter again before folding it up and sliding it into her handbag.

'Right, I'd better quickly brief you on our client here,' she said, opening her notebook.

She explained the case the police were making against Arcane as best she could. She briefed Marchand about the evidence of the two phones and the gun which was retrieved from a gun dealer and which was forensically linked to the killing of one of the passengers in the taxi. She gave him a description of Arcane and as much of his background as she had managed to glean during the short time she had spent with him. She had even had time to come up with some tactics she was thinking of using once the interview resumed.

Marchand made some notes on his phone and then looked at his watch.

'Time for you to be on your way,' he indicated, showing her the time.

They both got to their feet. Wickenden made sure that she had her bag and notebook with her as they crossed the floor to the entrance doors. She could see a car waiting outside as Marchand ushered her towards it before opening one of its rear doors.

Wickenden folded her body into the plush leather seat and looked back at Marchand as he waived her goodbye and closed the door. The car was already pulling away from the building by the time she realised that there was someone sitting in the seat next to her.

Polly Wickenden was powerless to stop the hand squashing a damp cloth onto her nose and mouth, and she gently collapsed onto the armrest between the two seats as the car sped away from the Kent Police HQ in Maidstone.

63
Tuesday 5 May

Marchand was escorted along the corridor leading to the interview rooms before being asked to wait. His escort then took a couple of steps forward and tapped on a plain door which was opened almost immediately. A couple of uniformed constables exited the room after which Marchand was invited to enter. The door closed behind him.

He quickly scoped the room, noting the position of the camera and assessing how much of the room it covered. He then slowly walked past Arcane and took up a position leaning against the far wall directly underneath the camera. He looked around the room again before reaching out and pulling one of the chairs towards him. There were now two chairs positioned directly underneath the camera, their backs hard up against the wall.

Arcane gave him a quizzical look, a deep frown etched into his forehead.

Still standing against the wall, Marchand introduced himself and apologised for the fact that Polly Wickenden had been called away on urgent business. She had, however, briefed him on the case before she left.

Arcane hung his head. *And still they haven't sent that fucker Goodchild*, he thought.

Pushing himself off the wall, Marchand then walked down the other side of the table before turning and retaking his position under the camera.

'Why don't you come and sit at this end of the table, Mr Arcane. I think you get more control of the room from here.'

Arcane looked around him. It had never occurred to him that any one position in a room conveyed more influence on a discussion than any other but he could give it a try. Rising from his seat, he shuffled along to the other end of the table and sat in one of the seats underneath the camera.

Marchand immediately sat on the seat beside him.

'Do you smoke, Mr Arcane?' Marchand casually asked.

Arcane nodded, idly looking at nicotine stained fingers.

'Do you smoke these, Mr Arcane?' Marchand asked as he surreptitiously extracted a packet of Gauloises from his jacket pocket.

Arcane's eyes lit up and he had to stop himself reaching out for the packet.

'No, go on, you can have them,' Marchand said as he palmed the packet into Arcane's right hand which remained hanging loosely beside him.

'Don't get much opportunity for a smoke in here,' he mumbled as he eventually snaffled the cigarettes into one of his pockets.

Marchand got up and moved his chair along the wall. He then sat back down on the side of the chair so that he was now looking straight at Arcane who had to swivel around on his chair so that he could keep his eyes on the lawyer.

'Have you ever tried those nicotine sprays, Mr Arcane?' Another casual question. They could almost have been two punters standing at the bar in a pub discussing their smoking habits.

Arcane shook his head. 'No substitute,' he declared.

'Even in here?' Marchand asked as he produced a nicotine mouth spray device from another jacket pocket.

Arcane looked across at Marchand who now pushed the spray nozzle into his mouth and pressed the button on the top of the device. He pressed it again before swallowing and then inhaling a lung full of air. After four or five seconds, he exhaled and then coughed to clear his throat.

Marchand smiled at Arcane as he slipped the device back into his pocket.

'That'll keep me going for a couple of hours before my next craving starts. Want to try some?'

Arcane stared at Marchand, his brain racing. This man was supposed to be defending him against some serious shit charges, yet here he was introducing him to the delights of nicotine sprays. What the fuck was going on?

But there was something mesmerising about the way that Marchand held his gaze.

Ragged by loss of sleep, and having had very little to eat, Arcane desperately craved one of the Gauloises this man had given him. Anything which would stop the churning in his stomach before those bastard pigs came back into the room.

'Yeah, I'll have some of that,' he declared, looking Marchand in the eye. 'Yeah, let's have a go with that.'

Marchand fumbled in his pocket and produced a device which he passed to Arcane. 'I always spray twice and try to swallow and inhale at the same time. That gives maximum value.'

Arcane plucked the device out of Marchand's hand before pointing the spray nozzle into his mouth. He carried out the instructions he had been given and then leant back in his chair before allowing the lawyer to retrieve the device from his hand.

64
Tuesday 5 May

Hunter and Selitto, in the company of Pennington and Jordan Wright, had decided on their tactics for the next interview session. Hunter's idea had been to hit Arcane with the suspicion that Charles Stone had also been at One Tree Hill and that Arcane had left his body at the Medway hospital. They would also produce Stone's weapon as well as the gun used by Agostini which they had found at the armourer's premises. As a back-up, they would show him photographic evidence of his visits to houses in the Bobbing area.

All were agreed that they would leave him to sweat for another 12 hours and then decide whether to charge him with murder or apply for an extension.

Hunter and Selitto had walked back downstairs and were now in the viewing room beside the main interview room. They looked out on to an empty arena which was readying itself for round two of this particular contest.

Selitto was despatched to bring Arcane and Wickenden back into the room but a feeling of unease suddenly gripped him as he approached the constable who was standing outside the room, looking at his watch.

'Everything okay here?' he asked warily.

'Pretty much,' came the reply. 'I've only just come on duty but apparently there's been a change of brief due to the previous one being called away.'

'So the new brief's in here?' Selitto replied with raised eyebrows.

'Not at the moment. He's just had to shoot out to his car to get some papers. Should be back any minute. That's why I was looking at my watch.'

Selitto didn't like the sound of this at all and brushed past the constable before lurching into the room.

Arcane was slumped in the chair facing Selitto, his mouth hanging open and slack, his eyes staring aimlessly at the floor. His shoulders were turned inwards and his hands hung by his sides. His face had turned a shade of cherry red. As Selitto got closer, he could detect a slight odour but just couldn't think what it reminded him of.

'For fuck's sake!' he exclaimed as he lifted one of Arcane's arms and felt for a pulse. He almost missed it but there was the merest vestiges of something there.

'Get an ambulance,' he shouted, 'or any medics who are on the premises. *NOW*!' The constable peered into the room before realising the seriousness of the situation and sprinting off in the direction of the front desk.

At the same moment, Sarah Hunter arrived at the door to the room.

'What the fuck's going on here?' she demanded as she crossed the room. Selitto was still trying to assess the strength of Arcane's pulse but was having increasing difficulty in detecting anything.

'Something about a change of brief who then had to get papers from his car,' Selitto growled. 'None of these fucking wooden tops thought of checking to see if the prisoner was still alive. This is a right fuck up!'

'Jeez!' Hunter exclaimed, scuttling back round the table so that she was now on the other side of Arcane. She squatted down to take a closer look at his face. 'What's that smell?'

'Can't place it at the moment. There are so many other odours at work here that I'm having trouble getting any of them apart from stale tobacco and a good dollop of body odour.'

Hunter normally had a good sense of smell and now concentrated on identifying the aroma that had first hit her when she approached Arcane. It didn't take long for her senses to process the evidence.

'Almonds, that's what it is. He's been fucking poisoned!'

'*Cyanide*?' Selitto exclaimed, wide-eyed.

'That's what happens isn't it? Yes, look – his skin's turning red. That's because the oxygen stays in the blood and can't get into the cells. He's suffocating because the cyanide's stopping the cells from being able to use oxygen so they just die.'

There was the distant sound of a wailing two-tone siren. Sarah could picture the ambulance weaving in and out of the early evening traffic, its crew readying themselves for action. But it's all going to be too late, she thought, as she sat back on her haunches and considered the pros and cons of doing some CPR on Arcane bearing in mind that they didn't know how the poison had been delivered.

What a complete and utter fuck up!

65

Friday 8 May

Sarah Hunter was back at Maidstone once again, this time sitting in the meeting room in which they had originally planned the arrest of Johnnie Arcane. Was it really only five days ago? It seemed like an eternity. So much water had flowed under the proverbial bridge. So many questions still unanswered. So little sleep.

She was having to dig deep into her reserves of stamina and energy.

Today, as with every day, Pennington had called a meeting to review progress over the last twenty-four hours. He was growing increasingly frustrated by their apparent inability to locate the mysterious Mr Marchand. He was also under pressure from the Chief Constable's office to explain how a suspect in custody at the Kent Police HQ had been murdered right under their noses.

Thankfully, the news of this debacle had not yet leaked out to the press which was in no little way the result of some clever manoeuvring by the Press Office led by the redoubtable Margot Westwood. She clearly knew every trick in the book when it came to outfoxing those who reported news for a living. She had simply lowered the portcullis, pulled up the drawbridge and imposed a strict news blackout. Although it was mainly the local scribblers who had smelled a story, Westwood had steadfastly swatted their enquiries away and had refused to indulge them.

Following the discovery of Arcane in the last moments of his life, the custody suite had been closed down and given over to a team of crime scene investigators who had been summoned from their base within the Maidstone HQ complex. The suite had remained closed with custodial arrests now being processed at Medway, Canterbury, Tonbridge and Ashford police stations. This had caused a huge amount of chaos and not a little ill-feeling.

The uniformed officers who had been on duty on Tuesday had been suspended along with the Desk Sergeant. A separate inquiry was taking place to establish how those officers on duty had been completely unaware of what was going on right under their noses. The key question seemed to be why no one had been monitoring the CCTV feed from the meeting room where it seemed that Marchand had administered the fatal dose of cyanide to Johnnie Arcane.

An exhaustive search of the building and the car park had drawn a blank. CCTV had quickly been consulted and showed a man getting into a car and driving away from the complex at the time it was estimated that Marchand had left the Custody Suite. The car registration had been logged at the barrier to the car park, and Pennington's team had scoured the ANPR system for the major roads and motorways around Maidstone, but had failed to identify the vehicle on any of the cameras. APBs had been issued to all ports and airports as well as the Eurostar boarding points and main railway stations but, so far, there had been no sightings of the mysterious Mr Marchand.

They had, however, found the vehicle in which Polly Wickenden had been driven away. It had been parked in a remote corner of the car park at West Malling railway station. On closer inspection, the officers from Traffic had found Miss

Wickenden trussed up in the boot of the car. She had been severely dehydrated, had a few cuts and bruises and was a bit delirious but nothing that a couple of nights in hospital wasn't going to cure.

In the meantime, Selitto had noticed that the name 'Philip Marchand' actually appeared as '*Philippe* Marchand' on his visiting card. The Desk Sergeant had simply introduced him as 'Philip' so the nuance that he might have been French had not been telegraphed to anyone at the time.

And this failure had been getting to Pennington, gnawing away at his very soul. If they had known that there was a possibility of a French connection to Marchand, would they have reacted any differently? He liked to think that someone on the desk would have asked Marchand for more proof of identity rather than just accepting a visiting card. Particularly as, by all accounts, Polly Wickenden had given the impression that she didn't know him either.

When they had contacted Wickenden's chambers, they discovered that no one had ever heard of a Philip or Philippe Marchand. And, if that wasn't enough of a surprise, DC Jordan Wright had uncovered the fact that none of the Senior Partners had instructed Wickenden to take Arcane's case and, indeed, none of them had ever heard of Johnnie Arcane. They were at a loss to explain how someone could have hacked into the organisational structure of a large London legal firm and had then managed to manipulate one of its employees in such a way.

They were satisfied that Arcane did have access to a tame legal brief from a firm which was based in London but it clearly wasn't Wickenden's chambers. So someone had managed to intercept Arcane's call to his solicitor, and had then randomly selected and instructed Wickenden to attend the interrogation as his lawyer. Once she was in position, they could then get their own agent on site to replace Wickenden and administer a fatal dose of cyanide to the unlucky Arcane. But what planning it must have taken with such fine lines between success and abject failure.

Arcane, himself, had only just lasted until the medics got to him but had been pronounced dead by the time they had loaded him into the ambulance. Dr Toby Swartzman had given the cause of death as poisoning – probably due to the inhalation of hydrogen cyanide. They were, however, still doing some tests to conclusively prove what toxin had been administered. Although the device used for delivering the deadly chemical had not been found, Swartzman had opined that it could well have been a nasal spray or some other oral spray. Whatever sort of device it was, it had delivered a hugely potent dose of one of the most toxic chemicals known to man.

The Chief Pathologist had also provided Pennington's team with another conundrum when he informed them that there was absolutely no evidence that Arcane had been involved in a struggle. In fact, he had gone as far as to say that there wasn't a mark on him. In which case, how had Marchand persuaded Arcane to take a fatal dose of cyanide without being forced to do so?

This question had also exercised Hunter's mind as she had first-hand experience of Arcane's violent temper and his preponderance for maniacal outbursts at the least provocation. How had Marchand managed to administer the poison without any reaction from Arcane? No, she reasoned, that would have been impossible. So, had Arcane administered the fatal dose himself?

Surely not! He didn't seem to be the type to take his own life just to avoid a long prison sentence. And, anyway, he hadn't even been formally charged yet. He must have still harboured thoughts of a bright young lawyer getting him off or at least a reduced sentence if he was found guilty.

No, Arcane was not a quitter.

Today's update meeting had gone much the same way as those that had gone before it. There was little new information to help them move the investigation forward, and they were still awaiting a full report from Forensics which they hoped would help to open up other lines of enquiry.

At the end of these meetings, those involved normally left the room promptly and today was no exception although Hunter and Selitto had remained in their seats, staring at each other across an empty room.

'A penny for them!' Hunter smiled. She could tell that her DS had a thought spinning around in his head.

'No, nothing really,' he sighed. 'Just thinking about how Marchand delivered the cyanide without Arcane realising that he was in mortal danger. I mean, I agree with you that the evidence from Swartzman points to the possibility that Arcane administered the poison to himself. Which sounds a crazy idea!'

Hunter looked around the room. At least it was nice to see some sunshine coming in through the window. She had felt deprived of daylight over the last few days. But her mind was still striving for a solution.

'Could you bear another session in front of the CCTV?' she asked.

Selitto grimaced. How many times had they already watched

the five minute clip? But there was little else he could think of doing so another viewing was probably as good as anything.

'Okay,' he replied, grudgingly.

Hunter left the room and soon returned with a laptop which she put on the table in front of them. She accessed the relevant file and set the tape running.

They watched as Marchand came into the room and walked towards the camera. He then disappeared from view although his head kept bobbing in and out of shot. He then pulled a chair towards him but that soon disappeared from sight.

'We're agreed that he must be standing directly under the camera with his back against the wall,' Selitto observed. 'And that he's got the two chairs beside him which we saw when we entered the room.'

'Yeah,' Hunter grunted, 'but then he must have said something because Arcane gets up and takes the seat next to where Marchand is…'

'Who then takes the other seat so that they're sitting next to each other.'

'I'm sure that something happens here,' Hunter was saying as she tried to sharpen up the images on the screen. 'See how they're turning to each other? Arcane is looking down but what at? Is Marchand giving him whatever it was that delivered the cyanide?'

'Wait!' There was a sense of urgency in Selitto's command. 'Is that where he got the Gauloises? Is Marchand slipping him the packet of cigarettes?'

Hunter had frozen the tape, her eyes roaming the screen to see what on earth her DS was talking about.

'Have you read the pathology report?' he asked.

'Skimmed it. Why?'

'Arcane had an unopened pack of Gauloises in his pocket. So, that must have been what he was looking down at. Marchand must have slipped it to him out of sight of the camera.'

'So, he's given Johnnie a packet of fags but it's still unopened in which case the cigarettes can't have delivered the poison.'

'No, that's not my point. We know that Arcane was a heavy smoker. I checked with the Custody Sergeant. Arcane was forever wanting to go outside for a smoke.'

'Was Marchand offering the cigarettes as some sort of bribe?'

'What for?' Selitto looked disdainfully at his boss. They lapsed into silence as Hunter continued to run the CCTV in slow-mo.

'There!' Hunter suddenly squawked. 'What happened there?'

She rewound the tape and they both watched frame by frame. It was obvious that Marchand had chosen this spot in the room as it offered the least exposure to the CCTV camera. He would, of course, assume that someone was watching the live feed so he had to be careful not to arouse suspicion.

'Look!' she muttered excitedly. 'What's he doing now?'

They watched as, frame by frame, Marchand's right arm came up to where his head would have been albeit that it was out of shot. The arm hovered there off camera before dropping to his side again. They both felt the frustration of not being able to see everything that was going on. They could make out the bend in his elbow but his hand and his head were out of shot. He had certainly excelled in positioning himself in the dead area under the camera.

Selitto eventually sat back in his chair, a look of frustration on his face.

'What the fuck's he doing?' he exhaled. 'Why would he give him a packet of fags in the first place?'

Hunter was staring at the screen, trying to rustle up some inspiration from somewhere.

'Is it something to do with smoking?' she asked distractedly.

Selitto had been thinking along these lines but, not having ever been a smoker, he knew little about the equipment needed apart from matches or a lighter. But he suddenly recalled what Swartzman had written in his report.

'It's an inhaler,' he blurted out. 'He's given Arcane a bloody inhaler to stop his craving for a fag!'

'No! Swartzman only said that Arcane had inhaled the cyanide,' Hunter corrected him. 'He thought that it could have been delivered as a nasal spray or an oral spray but... shit! What about one of those nicotine mouth sprays which allow nicotine to be quickly absorbed into your bloodstream through the inside lining of your mouth? Jeez! That could be what Marchand was giving Arcane. One of those little pocket spray devices. Why the fuck didn't I think of that earlier?'

Selitto scowled but made no comment.

'Come on,' she commanded, getting up from the table, 'we've got an urgent appointment with a pathologist!'

66

Sunday 10 May

The weather seemed to have abandoned its pretence of moving into summer as black clouds rolled in across the Weald bringing with them violent squally rain showers. Sunday shoppers looking for bargains in Tonbridge High Street were scurrying in all directions as the rain stotted off the pavements.

Selitto watched this pantomime from the window of the MIR and smiled as another umbrella blew inside out, its owner giving a passable impression of Mary Poppins preparing for flight. As another pulse of rain crashed against the window, he turned away and was just in time to see the door to the MIR slowly open and a bedraggled Sarah Hunter enter the room carrying handfuls of soggy paper bags.

'Bloody weather!' she exclaimed. 'That's the last time I treat you lot to breakfast. In my defence, I would say that the bacon sarnies were dry when they left the shop!'

She dropped the bags onto one of the desks before slipping out of the police-issue anorak she had found in the main office. Giving it a violent shake, those closest to her were covered in a fine mist of rainwater, but that didn't deter any of them coming forward to grab one of the sarnies. At this time of the day, slices of freshly cooked bacon slathered in tomato sauce and stuffed between two slabs of white bread was all they needed to kick start tired brains.

Hunter looked around the room as her team got stuck into the sarnies. Everyone was here including a couple of civilian support staff and a uniformed constable who had been helping out with feeding information into the HOLMES computerised records system. They probably deserved better than a rather chewy bacon sarnie but it would have to do for the time being.

'Okay, thanks for coming in today,' she began. 'I thought it would be good if we could attempt a bit of a wrap on what's been going on here over the last two crazy weeks. Shall we start with Tideswell Manor?'

She looked across at Grace who was almost hidden behind the two screens on her desk. They hadn't seen much of each other over the last week what with the long hours that Sarah had spent at Maidstone. And, when they were able to snatch some time together, Sarah had been so tired that all she wanted to do was sleep. She was also finding that the current pressure of work was affecting her relationship with Grace – she just couldn't give it the time that she wanted to. And that made her feel bad. Deep down, she felt that she was dismantling everything they had carefully built up between them. Her emotions were in turmoil and she knew that she had to get a grip on things if their relationship was to prosper.

'Okay, Grace, where are we with Tideswell?'

Kendall moved over to the white board which was headed up 'Tideswell Manor' and took them through the progress made so far. With the help of Jed Crowther, she went back to the destruction of the building and the deaths of the people trapped inside.

'The pathology reports indicated that most of the bodies pulled out of the ruins contained evidence of excessive alcohol consumption in the period of twenty-four hours prior to death,' she informed the team. 'Those who died had also supplemented the alcohol with a cocktail of drugs. Cocaine, heroin, ecstasy, amphetamines, uppers, downers. Some had such a mixture of drugs in their systems that it has proved difficult to be specific about exactly what they had taken. Quantities of drugs were also found in the vehicles parked to the rear of the manor house along with an array of weapons including guns, knives and machetes.'

Kendall went on to acknowledge that, after a great deal of detailed detective work, the pathology team had been able to identify all but the two bodies which had been burned beyond recognition. Even searching dental records had drawn a blank.

'So, we've had to conclude that this was a get-together for some of the biggest drug lords in the UK and the Netherlands. The list of names reads like a Who's Who of leading drug suppliers who would have been at the top of many a police force's wish list. But why was Biondi, of all people, involved with bringing all these people together in one place?'

This had continued to puzzle the team because there didn't seem to be a reasoned answer to the question.

'So we're left with a number of possible scenarios,' Crowther was saying. 'Either he summoned them to his mansion with the specific intention of killing them all and ridding the world of these leeches on society. A late bid for sainthood, perhaps? Or was he, in fact, one of them? And was he intent on getting rid of the competition so that he could take over their county lines gangs? Or perhaps he even had designs on cosying up to them in order to build the largest county lines drugs empire in the UK and, quite possibly, in Europe.'

The room fell silent, each detective considering these alternatives. Seeing Biondi as the villain of the piece was going to be difficult for some of them. Hunter was quick to realise this, and needed to put Crowther's hypotheses into context.

'Okay, I hear what you say,' she cut in, looking around her. 'But let's get one thing clear because, up until very recently, we have considered Biondi as nothing more than one of the richest and most successful of the Eighties rock gods. Now we're inferring that he is, in fact, one of the richest and most successful exponents of the county lines system in the UK. A modern day drugs lord in the mould of El Chapo or Pablo Escobar. Hell, we've had Pascale Hennenbont down as one of the leading drug barons in Europe but are we now saying that Biondi is his equal?'

Some of the heads were shaking. Changing long-held beliefs was difficult to deal with. Could the team rise to the challenge?

Lisa Calder was the first to embrace the new order.

'It seems possible that, by creating such a large county lines group, Biondi would have been in a position to thwart any attempt by Hennenbont to get a foothold in the UK county lines set up. We know that the Frenchman has been desperate to break into the UK drugs scene for a while now, and we know that someone has been desperate to prevent that. So perhaps the person standing between Hennenbont and the UK has been Biondi. We just haven't seen the connection until now.'

Hunter thought about this. 'So you think that Biondi organised the assassinations last year? And the incident in the helicopter?' She looked across at Selitto. 'Is that what we're thinking? That Biondi organised all that?'

This question once again silenced the room.

Grace eventually joined the discussion.

'So, are we now thinking that there has been an ongoing feud between Biondi and Hennenbont over the last few years with the Frenchman trying to get established in the lucrative UK drugs market? And that Biondi has been attempting to prevent this at all costs? Perhaps the gathering at Tideswell was specifically organised so that Biondi could get all the others on his side against the common enemy which was the French invader. But poor old Baz reckoned without knowing the strengths of the organisation that Hennenbont runs. It seems that nothing is impossible as far he is concerned.'

Jed Crowther sat on the corner of one of the desks.

'Hennenbont got wind of this gathering which Biondi had set up so he devised a plan to not only prevent it taking place but to also give himself the opportunity of taking out those who run some of the highly lucrative county lines gangs in the southern half of the UK and beyond. At the same time, he kidnapped Biondi in the belief that Baz was the only person who could lead him to Samantha Frobisher. Don't forget, it was her who single-handedly ruined Hennenbont's plans to land millions of pounds worth of drugs on the Kent and Sussex coast so he would have been beside himself to seek retribution for that.'

'His thugs must have drugged Biondi up so that he meekly did everything he was told to do,' Lisa Calder continued. 'That's how they managed to get him across the Atlantic to identify Samantha Frobisher. They then kidnapped her, probably gave her the same drug as they had given Biondi and then flew them both back to Gatwick.'

'We've looked at all that airline CCTV loads of times,' Grace continued, 'and it becomes clearer each time that Frobisher doesn't know Biondi or, if she does, she doesn't know what he looks like. There's absolutely no sign of recognition. The thugs then take her back to Tideswell and put her in the cellar with the snakes, knowing full well that she'll die when the plane hits even if the snakes don't get to her first.'

'But they obviously didn't want to leave Biondi to the same fate,' Crowther suggested, 'and that's when they whisked him out of the country, ostensibly to Nantes. We suspect that he was taken to a little island off the coast to the west of Nantes where he effectively disappears.'

'You reckon he was fed to the fish?' Hunter asked.

'Probably,' Grace confirmed. 'It's close enough to Ile de Bréhat for Hennenbont's henchmen to take him there by boat. Anyway, the big man probably wanted to say a personal goodbye to Biondi before the block of concrete was attached to his feet!'

There were sniggers around the room. Hunter smiled.

'Boss, is there another scenario we should be considering here?' Selitto was now sitting behind a desk by the window. 'We know that Biondi didn't spend much time in the UK as he was living his other life in the music industry. So, just suppose that the ever-resourceful *Monsieur* Hennenbont set up the party at Tideswell Manor without Biondi knowing anything about it? Let's face it, if Biondi was kidnapped we have no idea exactly when the kidnapping might have taken place. So, Hennenbont could have conned all those people into attending a knees-up at Tideswell before sending a plane to wipe them out. Job done! Now he can simply walk in and take over. All opposition's been accounted for.'

Silence fell across the room, each member of the team considering the feasibility of what Selitto was suggesting. Eventually Stuart Crosby cleared his throat.

'We know Hennenbont can seemingly organise the most outrageous events but could he really dupe all those that attended the Tideswell party?' he asked. 'Does he have the English-speaking resources that could persuade all these gang leaders to come to a gathering at Biondi's country residence? Surely some of them would be in regular contact with the big man and would mention the gathering thus blowing the subterfuge?'

'Not if it was billed as a surprise party for Biondi with every-one sworn to secrecy,' Selitto replied.

Some members of the team looked around the room at their colleagues. Other pairs of eyes swept the white boards look-ing for clues. The rain continued to furiously hammer on the window in staccato bursts.

Hunter eventually broke the silence.

'Okay, I like your thinking but we could be over-complicating things here. The simple way of looking at it is that Hennenbont could have organised the kidnapping of Biondi and Frobisher. The timing of this just happened to coincide with a party which Biondi was throwing at Tideswell. Hennenbont decided this was too good an opportunity to miss and one where he could wipe out almost all the opposition to him getting a bloody great size twelve foothold in the UK county lines set up. End of. Organise the plane crash. Job done.'

She wondered how that sounded. Could it really have happened like that? Looking round the room, it looked like most of the team were receptive of her simplification of the case.

'Ma'am, has anyone established a connection between the murder of Arcane and the plane crash at Tideswell?' It was Carolyn Pennant who seemed keen to link the two investigations. In her own mind, Hunter had preferred to keep them apart but she knew that, sooner or later, they would have to seriously consider that Hennenbont had been involved in the killing of Johnnie Arcane.

'Yes, good question Carolyn. Although the investigation into Arcane's death is being co-ordinated by the SCD at Maidstone, we have to keep an open mind that the two incidents might be linked. We already know that the two people killed at One Tree Hill were of French origin and have been tentatively linked to Hennenbont.'

'But if they are definately linked,' Pennant persisted, 'then surely the killing of Arcane has to also be some sort of retribution or revenge. Taking someone out right under our very noses seems just the sort of thing that Hennenbont's good at organising.'

Hunter reflected that Carolyn was, of course, right to think along those lines. The killing of Arcane was a well-organised scam of the highest order, and it certainly had all the trademarks of a Hennenbont operation. It could have only been a revenge killing – but why?

Or did she already know the answer to that question?

67

Monday 11 May

DCI Jack Pennington looked as if he had aged about ten years during the seventy two hours since Hunter was last in this room with him. His hair was all over the place despite running his fingers through it at any given opportunity. He hadn't had a shave for days and, rather than sporting designer stubble, his face looked like a furry golf course with areas of fairway interspersed with deep rough. His eyelids looked as if they could close involuntarily at any moment.

But he still seemed to be in good spirits and had greeted Hunter and Selitto enthusiastically when they entered the glass meeting room inside the SCD Suite at Maidstone Police HQ.

'I understand we've got some good news at last, Rory,' he gushed as they helped themselves to coffee and then sat down around the table where Rory Easton and Stig Shanahan were already seated.

'Yes,' Easton replied, looking over at Hunter and Selitto. 'Just to give you a bit of background. We've been in regular contact with the National Drug Intelligence Bureau since the incident last year when drugs were landed on the beaches near Winchelsea and the ensuing helicopter crash.'

Selitto winced at the memory.

'Based on the intelligence we gave the NDIB at the time, they made contact with the French authorities and, together, they set up a joint intelligence cell to monitor Hennenbont's activities. More particularly, they decided to put officers on the ground in France, and we've been exchanging intelligence and working together to build investigations into the extent of the empire he controls. Very fortunately, the UK's NDIB has also had an officer on the ground on the Ile de Bréhat so we have had access to first-hand intelligence on Hennenbont's activities.'

Easton opened the folder in front of him and passed two photographs across the table to Hunter and Selitto.

'As you know, we believe that Victor Joucas and Ajaccio Agostini were killed at One Tree Hill,' he continued. 'The guys at the morgue did a great job in getting them ready for their photoshoot so we sent the pictures to the NDIB. We've just heard back from them that the officer on the ground on the island has identified both men as having visited the Rosedo Lighthouse in recent weeks. You'll remember that this is Hennenbont's headquarters which means that there is a very definite connection between Joucas, Agostini and Hennenbont. The only question now is what the hell were they doing at One Tree Hill?'

'And we think that we might have come up with an explanation!' Pennington beamed across the table. 'Stig?'

'Yes, boss.' Shanahan turned the pages of a notebook he had placed on the table in front of him. 'One of the guys at the NDIB gave us the name of an undercover officer in the Met who turned out to have been watching Agostini for months here in the UK. As we already know, Agostini operates out of south and east London, and has recently spread his interests into large parts of Essex and Hertfordshire. His avarice seems to know no bounds as he has hungrily devoured county lines gangs and imposed himself on everyone involved in the supply and distribution of Class A in these areas. Seems that anyone who doesn't toe the line just disappears.'

'Didn't we get some intel about a raid or a stake out that the Met organised?' Pennington asked.

'Yeah. Agostini's main base seems to be a unit in one of the estates in the Silvertown area, down by the river. Apparently, the Met decided it was time to check him out because surveillance had noted two of the gang members going into the unit and not coming out again. Incredibly, the raid turned up absolutely nothing – no drugs, no bodies, no incriminating evidence. A complete mystery. So we concluded that we could be dealing with a very dangerous and hugely resourceful enemy in Mr Agostini.'

'In the same mould as Hennenbont,' Hunter observed. 'But what was he doing at One Tree Hill? A bit off his manor, surely.'

'We can only assume that he was trying to expand his operation into Kent, and probably knew of Johnnie Arcane by reputation. The potential move clearly had the approval of Hennenbont who probably sent Joucas to help Agostini with the negotiations.'

'Do we know any more about Joucas?' Selitto asked.

'Sketchy detail,' Shanahan continued. 'He seems to spend a lot of his time on Bréhat, and the guys at the NDIB have a theory that Joucas was married to one of Hennenbont's daughters. He's got five of them, apparently. Nightmare! Anyway, if that's true then it's no wonder that there was such quick retribution for killing one of his sons-in-law.'

'So, you think that Agostini was already in discussions with Arcane or was this simply a fishing trip?' Hunter wondered aloud.

'We can't say for sure,' Shanahan reasoned. 'The Met

surveillance officer doesn't think that they would've met before but who knows what communication they may have had by phone, WhatsApp, Zoom, or any other electronic media platform. However, something had clearly spooked Arcane to the extent that he wasn't prepared to take things any further. He obviously lured Agostini down to Kent, even managing to get his henchman, Ramdeen, into the cab as the driver. No doubt he made a bunch of false promises to Agostini about doing a deal and then killed him. Who knows whether he knew that Joucas would also be there.'

They all stared at the two photographs on the table. What a world these people lived in, Sarah thought to herself. Never knowing if they were going to see another dawn.

'Okay, thanks for that information.' She sat back in her chair. 'We've spent some time with the pathologists at the mortuary in Tunbridge Wells where Arcane was taken. They've been looking at ways in which the cyanide was delivered, and they think they've come up with the most likely applicator.'

Hunter reached into her jacket pocket and pulled out a small phial which she placed on the table.

'Nicotine replacement therapy uses phials just like this for spraying the suppressant into the mouth. We already know that Arcane was a heavy smoker, and he was probably finding that fag breaks were few and far between in the custody cells. The pathologists found an unopened packet of Gauloises in one of his pockets which was probably given to him by Marchand. We spent hours looking at the CCTV footage in the room and, although it's difficult to see what was going on between the two men, Marchand could have given Arcane a phial similar to this. We can't be sure what happened next but the fact that

Arcane's body displayed no signs of a struggle would suggest that he administered the fatal dose himself.'

'That's pretty much what we've been thinking all along,' Pennington commented. 'The only problem was that we couldn't find the phial.'

'No, that's because it wasn't there,' Hunter continued. 'The pathologists reckon that Marchand would have been able to get it back from Arcane. Although the poison wouldn't have acted immediately, Arcane would have started to feel unwell so Marchand could have simply plucked the phial out of Arcane's hand before making his getaway.'

'Hmm. Makes sense,' Pennington said, raising his eyebrows and nodding his agreement with the suggestions that had been put forward by the pathologists. 'Beth Dench is also interested in a print she has picked up from a document Marchand had to sign at the desk when he arrived. No match on the UK database so she's fed it into the Prüm system which, as you know, is the EU's network of police databases. Hopefully, that might give us a better idea of who Mr Marchand really is and how we might get our hands on him.'

'Did the surveillance guys on Bréhat recognize him?' Selitto asked.

'We didn't get a very good shot of him from the CCTV, I'm afraid but we circulated it anyway. Came back negative.' There was a touch of frustration in Pennington's voice although he was trying to maintain a positive outlook.

After some further discussion about the surveillance operation on the Ile de Bréhat, the meeting broke up. Selitto went off with Rory Easton to look at some of the evidence of extreme violence they had discovered in the Thamesmead house. Shanahan had gone back to his desk which left Pennington and Hunter staring at each other across the table.

'Thanks for your help with all this, Sarah. It's been good to have you on the team.' Hunter detected a tone of sincerity in Pennington's voice which she appreciated. Even though he was acutely aware that there had been a complete cock up in the custody suite, he was still keen to absolve her from any blame in the whole sorry affair.

'We're going to have to arrange a press briefing in the next few days,' he continued. 'The Chief's got wind of the cat being out of the bag and he wants to get our side of the story into the papers first. Margot's arranging all that and the Chief's going to front it himself to give the announcement a bit more gravitas. It'll no doubt hit the nationals but, hopefully, we won't have to have an infernal public inquiry as seems to be the norm with most events these days. Of course, the internal investigation will have to run its course but Superintendent Eaves is pretty sure that it won't throw up anything we don't already know. I mean, how many different ways can you spell fuck-up?'

Hunter smiled. She knew the frustration that all this internal navel gazing caused just to achieve a few more ticked boxes.

'Anyway, we should arrange to have dinner again soon,' he continued, 'and perhaps spend some quality time talking about non-police matters.' He smiled at her. 'Suggest some dates when you get reunited with your calendar.'

Hunter could think of worse ways of spending an evening and promised to get back to Pennington later in the week. In the meantime, she collected her papers and stepped out into the main office which was still buzzing with activity. She hoicked her phone out of her jeans pocket and noticed an unread text message. She thumbed the screen.

Big news re yr man. Meet me G&D Tudeley tonight@7

Hunter looked back at Pennington still sitting in the glass meeting room reading through another sheaf of papers, lost in thought.

Although she felt exhausted and had been looking forward to having an evening at home with Grace, there was a frisson of excitement at the thought of meeting up with Vance again. She wouldn't mind another look at him in a less confrontational environment than their first meeting in the street. Even his slightly lopsided face with the crooked nose had its attraction. She also remembered his laughter lines. She could do with a laugh to break the monotony of this investigation.

But she had promised Grace an evening back at the cottage. Grace deserved some of her time after all she'd had to put up with recently. She couldn't let her dear friend down. Yet...

She could just tell Grace that something had come up at Maidstone. She'd have to stay a bit later than planned but should be back around nine. But...

Supposing she started to enjoy Vance's company and wanted more? She didn't want to feel that she had to commit to a time for getting home. God...

This was going to be difficult!

68
Monday 11 May

Sarah Hunter sat in the car, her thumbs drumming out a rather staccato paradiddle offbeat on the steering wheel. There was still plenty of daylight left in the sky, and she could see people sitting out in the garden of the George & Dragon making the most of the warmer weather.

She kept telling herself that she shouldn't be here. Scolding herself for even thinking that Vance was going to be able to help her.

This was sheer folly.

Madness!

Her hand reached out to start the car but faltered just as the tip of her finger brushed the ignition button. She yanked her arm back as if she had received an electric shock.

She had spent the last two hours interrogating herself, one simple question going round and round in her head.

Why had she agreed to meet this chancer?

She had castigated herself for letting Grace down, and she was furious with herself for blatantly lying to one of the very few people in the world she really cared about.

And for what?

Vance wouldn't be able to tell her anything about Biondi that she didn't already know. So, what was the point of humouring him by coming here?

But...

There was a part of her that wanted to know more about this man. The man who had had the brass neck to accost her in the street. For some inexplicable reason, she felt drawn to him even though she knew that he was trying to inveigle his way into her psyche.

But why?

Perhaps *News Notebook* was no more than a huge ego trip for Vance, something that he thought would give him more credibility than he was worth.

Was he trying to seduce her with the promise of information which he didn't have? Or was he simply trying to seduce her, full-stop?

A shiver pulsed down her spine at the mere thought of that. She was in a mess.

And then the knock on the window.

There was a good crowd in the pub for a Monday night so they opted to sit outside at a table under an awning which stretched out from the rear of the building. Vance didn't seem to require a position which offered any degree of privacy, and they had ordered their drinks from the bar as they made their way through the pub to the garden.

Hunter had taken a couple of long draughts of her Guinness in an effort to settle the butterflies in her stomach, and the dark liquid was soon halfway down the glass, its creamy head slowly inching its way to oblivion. Vance had been more circumspect in dealing with a bottle of low alcohol cider which he delicately sipped rather than glugged.

The conversation was just that – conversational. Nothing too tricky. Nothing about Sarah's investigations. They covered the weather, the state of the roads in the area, the volume of traffic, the proposed changes to the Council's bin collection days, more about the weather – all the important stuff which formed the backbone of so many pub conversations.

Sarah fiddled with the glass of Guinness, trying not to drink it too quickly. She pushed it around the surface of the table in front of her whilst trying to contribute intelligently to the banal topics of conversation. In her head, she was still mentally flagellating herself for even daring to think that this meeting would be a good idea.

Eventually she snapped.

'Your text message indicated that you had some information for me. Perhaps we could talk about that because it really is about the only reason I'm here and not where I should be – down at the station trying to solve a monstrous crime.'

For a second, Vance seemed wrong-footed by her abrupt intervention but he quickly recovered and produced a tablet from his jacket pocket which he laid on the table.

'Remember I told you I'd get my readers to search for Baz Biondi? Well, I actually got quite a good response.' He looked pleased with himself which annoyed Sarah.

'Yeah,' she sneered, 'from cranks up and down the country who sit in their bedrooms all day with nothing better to do than watch porn and invent sightings of people they've never heard of.'

Sarah could guess what was coming next.

'Of course you're right,' Vance agreed. 'Within the space of a couple of hours, Baz had been spotted in a Morrisons in Skegness and at a petrol station near Falmouth in Cornwall. He was in Madeira and on the island of Malta on the same day that he was at various other locations in Europe.'

'I'm also glad that your readers are so knowledgeable about

what Mr Biondi looks like these days,' Sarah replied, her response dripping with sarcasm. She knew that Biondi had a particular aversion to being photographed although the team did have some pictures of him which Grace had retrieved and which were taken at a recent function in Tonbridge.

'Well, yes … you're right to be sceptical and I, for one, probably wouldn't recognise him if he walked through that door right now.'

Sarah knew that there was no chance of that happening, but said nothing.

'But there is one sighting that I thought would interest you.' Vance tapped the screen of the tablet and then gave it another couple of taps. 'As I said, I might not recognize him in the flesh but I have seen some photos of him taken in the last few years.'

Sarah sat shaking her head. Impossible!

He slid the device across the table towards Sarah.

She looked down at the picture filling the screen of the tablet, the scene gradually swimming into focus in front of her eyes. Her heart started to pound in her chest as the realisation of what she was looking at suddenly washed over her.

'Where did you get this?' she growled, trying to maintain a level of balance in her voice.

'It was sent in by one of my readers,' Vance replied. 'Said it was taken at the *Bar de la Piscine* in Arcachon Bay. On Saturday. Had to look the place up myself. South-west France, on the Atlantic coast. Nice looking spot.'

In the background, Sarah could see a sandy bay stretching away into the distance with the sea lapping at the shoreline. The sun shone down from a clear blue sky.

But the focus of the picture was a table in the foreground

with two men and a woman sitting around it. The men were wearing colourful beach shirts and dark shorts; the woman was wearing a bikini underneath a transparent white button-front kimono. Glasses of beer and empty beer bottles adorned the tabletop, and there were plates of half-eaten food. A packet of Gitanes cigarettes lay unattended on the table.

One of the men had a mass of curly greying hair spewing out of the back of a dark NYC cap, wisps of the hair being agitated by the sea breeze. He wore dark sunglasses, and tattoos adorned each arm although it was difficult to make out what they depicted in the bright sunlight. He was sitting back in his chair and smoking an enormous cigar. Two hospital crutches rested on an empty chair next to him.

Sarah stared at the photograph, alarm bells starting to jangle in her head as she took in the curly grey hair and the tattoos.

A swarthy well-built man. Grace's voice was ringing in her ears. *Curly hair pulled together in a ponytail.*

She switched her attention to the crutches as Annalisa Vardy's voice now interrupted Grace. *It looks like he may have broken one of his ankles.* Vardy's voice hammered into Sarah's brain. *Someone was shuffling along, possibly dragging one of their feet.*

'Oh my God!' she whispered under her breath.

Was this the pilot?

The brim of the woman's enormous floppy sunhat had been pulled back to reveal a pretty face with huge silver rings hanging from each ear. She was laughing and pointing at the man with the enormous cigar. Sarah didn't think that she had seen the woman before. The lady-friend of Mr Curly Hair perhaps?

But it was the other man who now held Sarah's attention in a vice-like grip.

Her unblinking eyes bored into the image on the screen of the tablet. She was finding it difficult to breathe. It was as if the air was being sucked out of her lungs. Her peripheral vision had disappeared. She only had eyes for the third person sitting at the table at the *Bar de la Piscine*.

He adopted a relaxed pose, elbows resting on the arms of the chair, clearly savouring the ambience of the lunchtime session at a sandy beach café on the Atlantic coast.

But he was very definitely staring into the lens of the camera in such a way that Sarah knew that he only had eyes for her. His smile was irritatingly smug, as if he was mocking her.

Sarah blinked and shook her head in disbelief. An involuntary groan slipped out through clenched teeth.

Suave, sophisticated, and unquestionably enjoying himself, Baz Biondi was clearly signalling to Sarah Hunter that her train was on the wrong track.

Acknowledgements

As a relatively unknown author, I am excited that the *Hunter & Selitto* crime thrillers are now reaching a wider audience through word of mouth, through contacts made on Instagram and through their availability from local Kent libraries. I have also been invited to talk about my books at local events, and I am enthused by the willingness of book bloggers to read and comment on my books.

Hunter & Selitto's third outing is once again set in the beautiful county of Kent which provides the backdrop for a tale of mystery and intrigue. The complexity of the subject matter is such that I have had to undertake an enormous amount of research to make sure that the story is as realistic as possible. Although locations such as Bewl Water and One Tree Hill near Sevenoaks are well-known local areas, I may have had to make tiny changes to their layout in order to facilitate my storytelling. As usual, all errors and inaccuracies are entirely of my own making.

In writing this book, I have been kept on my toes by my sister, Lindsay Crawford Jones, who continues to offer insightful advice about plot lines. She also suggested a minor tweak to the final chapter which made the ending even more powerful. And I have been so grateful to my old mate Michael Moody aka Puggers who helped with the editing of the final manuscript. Really, really helpful.

As always, I have been well supported by my super-enthusiastic publisher, James Essinger and The Conrad Press. James is the hardest-working man I have ever come across, and his zest for helping authors to get stories into print knows no bounds.

The life of an author can be a lonely existence so thank you to my closest family and to my close friends who all share an unfailing interest in how my writing is progressing. Your support is invaluable and helps to drive me on during the hours of creativity. And the most thanks go to my darling wife, Barbara, for her unfailing patience and support, and for her help in weeding out those silly little mistakes that are sometimes overlooked in the final editing process.

Finally, a big thank-you to you, the reader, and to everyone who has read the first two books, and who has commented so positively. I know the subject matter in my books is not to everyone's taste but there is a big bad world out there and I am simply weaving reality into fiction in order to provide exciting page-turning crime thrillers which are, hopefully, difficult to put down!

Robin Nye, May 2023

Instagram: robin_nye_

Email: robinnye88@gmail.com